GUARDIAN'S LEGACY

Book Three of "The Last Princess of Latara"

DARREN SIMON

DIVERTIR
PUBLISHING
Salem, NH

Guardian's Legacy

Darren Simon

Copyright © 2022 Darren Simon

Cover design by Kenneth Tupper

Published by
Divertir Publishing LLC
PO Box 232
North Salem, NH 03073
http://www.divertirpublishing.com/

ISBN-13: 978-1-938888-32-8
ISBN-10: 1-938888-32-4

Library of Congress Control Number: 2022951909

Printed in the United States of America

Dedication

This book is dedicated to my loving wife and two sons whose support and kind words give me the strength to continue down the sometimes challenging, but always fun, path of being writer. I also dedicate this book to my late father, whose own ability as a storyteller continues to inspire me.

TABLE OF CONTENTS

Chapter 1

A Time Long Past
The Kingdom of Latara

PRINCESS THEODORA, EYES stinging from her hot tears, rode in silence atop her wind horse. She sat tall in the saddle, chin lifted high, but her heavy royal garb, buttoned tight around her neck, made breathing difficult. With each shallow breath, she fought the urge to rip away the purple cloak that enveloped her and ride away to the blue fields stretching beyond the Kingdom of Latara's gates.

But that wouldn't be proper during the funeral procession for her mother, Queen Tesarra, beloved Lady of the Castle and High Counselor of the Ten Unified Kingdoms.

The sun rose in the early emerald sky, its beams casting a pale light over Latara. Tens of thousands lined the cobblestone streets. Conjurers and non-magics alike held each other. Their cries echoed across the land. Their chants reached a deafening roar.

Theodora gritted her teeth. If only she could cover her ears. What right did these fools have to shed tears over her mother? All they did was take from her, looking to her to keep them safe during the tough times when wars brought suffering. They were the reason Theodora and her older sister, Assara, were raised by nannies and teachers. Tesarra had no time to be a mother.

Theodora threw a quick glance at her sister. Assara rode stoically atop her own wind horse, her face hidden by a purple cloak. Theodora shook her head. She'd begged her sister for a private ceremony, but Assara had refused. Her words repeated over and over in Theodora's mind.

Mother is not ours alone to mourn, sister. She belongs more to her people than to us. They deserve a chance to mourn her passing even more than we. That is how mother would want it.

Theodora squeezed the reins until her knuckles turned white. How could Assara know what their mother would want? Just because she was the oldest—or because, according to tradition, she would be queen? She was probably happy their mother was dead. Now Assara could take up the mantle as Queen of Latara.

She released a cold breath of air. *Don't give in to the anger. Not now. It's not right.* Yet hate filled her veins with fire, as if she was burning from the inside

1

out. Her cheeks flushed with heat. Beads of sweat dotted her brow. Her thoughts spun out of control, like a vengeful whirlwind screaming louder than her own internal voice. *Just focus on Mother and nothing else.* More tears slid down her eyes, like hot wax dripping from a lighted candle. She wiped the tears away with the back of her gloved hand and eyed her mother's casket just ahead.

Ornate and golden, it hovered above the street, kept aloft by the power of the elder conjurers who walked behind. They held their hands outstretched, palms up, in a sign of reverence and to maintain their invisible hold on the casket. A team of wind horses, covered in their own purple cloaks, slowly pulled the queen's final vessel through the kingdom. A rainbow of flowers circled Queen Tesarra, swirling in the air as if rustled by a gentle breeze, but the sky was calm. Magic caused their floral dance.

Theodora bit her lower lip to keep it from quivering. At least their mother looked at rest now.

She had suffered over the past year, and in her final weeks both breathing and eating had become nearly impossible. Theodora bit down harder on her lip, exalting in the piercing sting of torn flesh until she tasted the warm salt of her own blood. It had been too much for her to watch her mother fade painfully into the afterlife.

From childhood, she had always admired how her mother was such a commanding leader and her mother's role on the Council. Her mother never showed weakness, even as death loomed. A whimper slid uncontrollably from Theodora's lips. Her chest heaved. The screaming whirlwind in her mind cried louder.

"Sister, mind yourself," Assara whispered. "The daughters of the Queen must show strength."

Shut up, sister! Theodora's body trembled. She quieted herself, as her sister ordered, but the flames of rage inside licked mercilessly at her skin, causing her to squirm in the saddle.

Before day's end, her sister would be declared queen. Rolling her eyes, Theodora cursed under her breath. Because of some stupid ancient tradition, Assara was to lead their people and assume their mother's place on the Council.

Tradition didn't make it right.

Theodora rubbed her forehead. *Look at Assara. So proper, so noble, so weak. She is not fit to lead. I should be queen, and Assara knows it.*

She gazed back at the kings and queens of the Unified Kingdoms riding in formation. Their generals marched behind them with swords held high. Purple ribbons flowed from their swords' hilts to honor the Queen's family colors. *Bastards!* Theodora fought the urge to spit at the royals. They were hypocrites, all of them. Showing reverence to her mother as if they really cared. Each believed they should lead and, given the chance, they would have stabbed her mother in the heart. Nevertheless, Queen Tesarra managed to keep a fragile peace while demanding their respect. Her death would lead to chaos. There would be a power struggle within the Council, and Assara lacked the strength to hold their mother's high place.

Theodora grimaced and turned her head forward. A show of force was the only answer. She allowed herself a slight smile at that thought.

The funeral procession continued its way to the Queen's final resting place. The sorrowful cries from the gathered crowds grew louder.

Fiery lines spread across the whites of Theodora's eyes, like cracks spreading along ice. She blinked repeatedly, but the searing worsened until her vision turned blood red, like always happened when her emotions got the best of her. *Not now! Not again!* She shook her head, but her eyes blazed hotter. *Control it!* She squeezed her eyelids shut and screamed in silence until the fire within subsided. Theodora slowly opened her eyes. The crimson shadow disbursed, and her vision returned to normal.

She took a few breaths to quiet her racing heart. Later, when she could escape to the solitude of the forest, she could unleash her anger, but not now.

Theodora and her sister led the procession up a hill covered by blue grass to the towering golden gates that led into the Garden of Tera-Ma. There, endless groves of trees with thick trunks and cascading leaves arching high above marked the burial sites of a thousand generations of Latarans.

Passing under the trees, the leaves chanted their own mourning song in honor of the Queen—a chorus of a million tiny voices that sang as one. Even the various species of flying beasts and land creatures lent their voices in song for the queen whose work had tried to unite all the beings that called this world, Janasara, home.

A swoosh in the skies above stole Theodora's attention. Glancing up, her jaw flew open at the site of the largest of the winged beasts—a dragon. Could it really be? She forced herself not to point toward the skies. The dragons were no enemy of the Unified Kingdoms, but they largely kept to themselves in a far-off land. Yet, a dragon soared overhead.

"Sister, the dragons have come to honor Mother," Assara uttered, her red lips parted in a wide smile, long brown hair flowing over her shoulders. "That is how loved she was."

Theodora kept her eyes on the winged beast, marveling at its ocean blue coloring, long powerful neck, and a wingspan that could hide the sun.

Soon everyone noticed. A collective gasp rang out from those who gathered inside the garden at the presence of such a massive and beautiful creature. Some fled while others stood in place shivering. Parents grabbed their children and held them against their bodies.

The dragon, too large to land in the garden, circled over the treetops. The beast seemed to take no interest in the fear it caused.

Forcing her gaze straight ahead, Theodora and her sister continued to lead the procession deeper into the garden to its highest point where the Great Tree, the largest of all the hardwoods and softwoods in the garden, stood. It rose nearly as high as the Castle of Latara itself. That was the resting place of every Lataran queen from the earliest recorded days of the kingdom.

A nearby tree, slightly smaller in size, stood as the burial place of the kings. Their father, King Lasenak, had been laid to rest there when she and Assara were children. He died in a war against the barbarian tribes in the North. Theodora barely remembered him and didn't miss him. She certainly never thought of him, and if she did, her heart didn't skip a beat. Nor did it ache with loss, like she now felt for her mother.

A sense of emptiness left her numb.

The funeral for Queen Tesarra continued until sunset. As was tradition, her body was placed under the Great Tree face down in a bed of large brown leaves and drying flower petals, all fallen naturally to the ground as part of their own life cycle. More leaves and petals were placed over her before the ground was magically sealed with earth and wild grass.

Theodora struggled with such an unceremonious burial, but such was the way of her people. On the journey to the afterlife, one should face the Mother World that nurtures life and should in all haste have their flesh, blood, and bone become one with Her.

She shuddered as magic sealed the earth over her mother.

"I will not leave this world as my mother did," she whispered so no one could hear. "These traditions will not hold sway over me."

Assara hushed her. "Refrain sister. You will be First Princess and rule at my side. Behave like it."

Theodora nodded. Her eyes burned again. The whirlwind inside of her started to spin out of control.

§ § §

Theodora stormed into the throne room, a chamber in the shape of a half circle lighted by a brilliant crystal hovering below the arched ceiling. The funeral for her mother ended hours ago, but the pain in her heart pressed against her chest like a weight she couldn't lift. The midnight hour grew near when, in a quiet ceremony, Assara would be crowned Queen. A kingdom-wide celebration would follow in a month's time after a *proper* mourning period for Queen Tesarra. Theodora scoffed. Assara could never be the leader their mother was.

4

It should be me. She gripped the handle of the sword at her side tightly. With her free hand, she shoved her long blond ponytail off her shoulder. Her dry undecorated lips parted in a sneer. Her blue eyes still burned, but was it from sorrow or rage?

She stood in the chamber in silence surrounded by tapestries on the walls with emblems from all the lines of queens through the generations. The largest was Queen Tesarra's—purple with the emblem of two golden ropes spiraling together. Words stitched in glowing threads read 'Mona Ta-Pena, Mona Ta-Pena Loissaa, Mona Ta-Pena Loissaa Noema.' *Peace Intertwines Those Who Wish It.* Her mother had lived by those words.

They meant little to Theodora.

She crossed to marble steps in the center of the chamber leading up to the queen's throne. Queen Tesarra had rarely sat in the chair carved from silver with a backrest in the shape of a tree and armrests like sturdy branches. Theodora thought about ascending the steps but instead turned to the observation deck overlooking the kingdom.

Light from the three moons, the Three Queens of the Night, spilled into the chamber. Theodora stepped heavily into the pale illumination's embrace, stopping at the railing to peer over the darkened land.

Chanting still echoed across the kingdom as Tesarra's people mourned her passing. Soon they would chant Assara's name. *Fools.*

"Sister, I've been searching for you."

Theodora froze. Both hands tightened on the railing. Her pulse quickened, rushing blood to her head, bathing her face in heat.

She slowly turned to her older sister. "It seems you have found me, sister."

Assara strolled into the moonlight, her body hidden beneath a raven black robe. A hood covered her head, hiding her brown hair and chiseled features—but not her piercing eyes, two dark orbs surrounded by a sea of unyielding white.

Theodora rolled her eyes and approached her sister.

"Still our people cry for Mother." Assara joined Theodora on the deck. "They mourn for her, but they also fear what will happen now that the queen they loved so dearly has departed from them."

"It now falls upon you to settle their fears." Theodora folded her arms across her chest.

"I'll try." Assara faced Theodora and removed her hood. Shadows circled her eyes and wrinkles spread across her forehead. At 25, Assara was only five years older, but the lines etched into her face aged her beyond their five-year difference. Her long auburn hair sat stiffly in an up-due in preparation for the crown she'd wear. Her sun-licked bronzed skin had faded to an ashen gray, and her cheeks hung low. Weakness ebbed into her expression.

"I'm glad I have you to help me watch over our people and the Guardian Michala to help protect them." Assara placed her long, narrow hands on Theodora's shoulders.

Theodora backed away from her sister. Assara's touch burned her skin even through her cloak's thick cloth. She loved her sister. She really did. So why did the sight of Assara ignite a fire burning her from the inside out? "You'll marry Michala soon?"

Assara lowered her hands to her side. She eyed her sister in silence for an uncomfortable heartbeat before responding. "Yes, when it's proper, but not now." For the first time in days, Assara smiled, but it quickly disappeared.

"He will make a good king." Could Assara hear the slight mocking tone in her voice? Michala was a Guardian, part of a bloodline of conjurers whose powers made them the protectors of Latara and the Unified Kingdoms. But Michala was young and could barely summon his magic. What good was he then? Theodora gritted her teeth. Assara put far too much faith in him, and her love for him blinded her to the truth. A battle was coming, and only a show of force would protect their Crown.

"I'm glad to hear you say that sister." Assara inched closer to her. "I have felt some distance from you since my relationship with Michala began. I had thought you did not approve of him."

"He's a Guardian. Who better to stand at your side as you become queen?" Theodora retreated from the deck to the throne. "Soon, this chamber will be filled with those who will see you crowned. Latara will be yours to lead."

"Yes. I wish it could wait, but I know it must happen at midnight." Assara followed her sister to the base of the throne. She clasped her fingers together at her chest as if in prayer. "It's at least a comfort to have you with me. I know together and with Michala's guidance, we will serve our people and all the Unified Kingdoms well."

Theodora cleared her throat. Now was the time. Maybe she could get through to her sister and make her understand that only through a show of power could she govern not only Latara but the Council of the Unified Kingdoms. "You know there are those on the Council who will question your authority."

"I know." Assara raised an eyebrow.

Theodora raised her chin and began to pace. "They'll say you're too young, and they'll try to wrestle control from you."

"Likely."

"There may even be threats of war." Theodora stopped in front of her sister. Maybe, she finally understood. Each breath came quickly. Her heart beat faster.

"Your point, sister?" The wrinkles in Assara's brow deepened.

Theodora climbed the throne. "You know my point. We have talked of it before. You must strengthen our army and dismiss the Council of the Unified Kingdoms. They are smaller kingdoms with feeble rulers. They could not stand against our forces. You could rule over all of them and assign your generals to serve as governors. I could lead the generals. This is the only way to prevent the infighting among the kingdoms that will soon occur. You know I'm right."

Assara ascended the throne. Her voice grew louder. "Sister, I know you mean well. In your own way, you want to keep the peace, but I will not break from Mother's form of government. I will not rule by force. It is not our way."

"But—"

"Remember who is queen and keep to your place, Theodora. Besides, there is a weakness in your argument. If we took arms against the other kingdoms, they would unite against us and have a large enough army to defeat us."

Theodora's body shook. She grabbed her sister by the shoulders. "Assara, you know that's not true. They'll turn on each other rather than band against Latara. You'll see. As soon as you take your seat on the Council, the truth of my words will sting." *Why can't she understand I'm right? How can she be such a fool?* "The Council will break up regardless of your actions. Chaos will reign unless you move first to dismiss the Council, claim the authority to rule over all the Unified Kingdoms, and then stamp out the opposition through a show of force."

"No!" Assara broke away from Theodora's grip. "Do you hear yourself, Theodora? You sound like an agent of the dark arts right now. You want us to return to the old ways. I will not have it."

"Then you are a fool." Theodora grabbed her sister by the arm.

"Sister, release me."

"No!" An explosion of thoughts flashed through her mind. Scorching heat spread through her limbs. *Why won't she listen? I must make her understand.* A red, pulsating glow rose from Theodora's fingertips.

"Theodora, what are you doing?" Assara screamed. "You're hurting me. Theodora. It burns."

"You must listen to me!" Theodora's eyes shifted from her sister's frightened eyes to her glowing fingers. Scorching heat flowed from her hand. It was as if she could control the fire raging inside her and use it as a weapon. But her sister wasn't the enemy. *I must stop, but not until she heeds me.*

Assara cried out, "Sister!" Lifting her free hand, she fired a blast of green energy from her palm that slammed into Theodora's chest.

Theodora flew off the marble steps onto the throne room's stone floor. She landed on her back with a thud. A yelp escaped her mouth. Smoke rose from her chest. Gasping, she struggled to move air in and out of her lungs. It was as if someone had just pummeled her with a mace. Her chest felt scorched, and the odor of charred cloth filled the chamber.

Assara was quickly by her side. "Theodora, I'm so sorry. What have I done? Please forgive me."

She placed a hand on Theodora's chest, and a different kind of energy flowed from Assara's palm. The soon-to-be-queen was using her healing powers. A soothing white glow spread across Theodora's chest.

Theodora pushed Assara's hand away and stood painfully. "Get away from me." Her eyes simmered. If she wanted, she could blast her sister with magic that was more than a match for weak Assara.

Theodora closed her eyes. She would not kill her sister today. "I should have been queen, Assara. I know what needs to be done. You'll see. They'll all see that I was right. The kingdoms will fall."

With that Theodora ran from the throne room.

She would leave Latara and never return until she had the power to usher in a new world order.

CHAPTER 2

In the Present
The Dungeon of Castle Latara

G UARDIAN, YOU MUST *not die. There is more to be done."*
Charlee stirred. The words tickled her ears, but darkness surrounded her. It was better that way. In the cocoon of unconsciousness, her parents watched over her. Cryton, the old man she had come to look upon as a grandfather and mentor, still lived and smiled as he prepared a pizza in his hole-in-the-wall restaurant. Her best friend, Sandra, laughed inside the cafeteria at Myron Applebee Junior High. Life was as it should be. Everyone was safe.

"Guardian, you must rise. You cannot succumb to the comfort of death."

Leave me alone. A white mist enveloped those comfortable memories. The images morphed. Cryton lay dead on a battlefield, and a clone of Sandra dressed in black armor stood over him, bloody sword in hand, lips parted in a sneer.

"Granddaughter of Assara, I demand you open your eyes."

Let me sleep. The medallion hovered within the fog, on one side the etching of a burning tree, on the other side the scrawling of a withered, scarred face—her face. *No!* She remembered the battle with Theodora for the medallion inside the Kingdom of Latara's throne room. She had used its dark magic against the sorceress, but each time Charlee touched the medallion's power, it twisted her.

Charlee stunned Theodora with a blast from the medallion. The witch crumbled to the floor like a rag doll. One more bolt from the medallion would stop the sorceress forever.

It wasn't to be.

Before she could strike one last time, Charlee lost the medallion to Theodora. The sorceress quickly recovered her strength and pierced Charlee with a crimson ray that sucked out her guardian powers. Her insides ripped and snapped. Every bit of magic was torn from her body. Now, it was her turn to drop to the floor, her arms and legs like jelly. She lay there defeated until darkness took her.

The sorceress' final words echoed through the murky fog around Charlee. "I thought you might like to look into the gateway and see your world for the last time. I thought you might like to bid me farewell as I step into your world and begin my quest to claim it as my own—or to destroy it."

How long ago had it all happened? Time no longer had meaning. No matter. She had to stop Theodora from hurting the ones she loved.

"*Guardian.*"

"What?" Charlee mumbled.

The mist around her drifted away. Her mind became conscious. She blinked her eyes and sniffed the air. It stunk like rotten eggs. Drops of water splashed around her. Steel clinked together.

"Where am I?" Her eyes opened. A fuzzy blur greeted her. She didn't expect an answer but got one.

"*In the dungeon of Castle Latara.*"

Oh, yes. Charlee lifted her head from her chest. *I'm in a dungeon chained to a wall.* Theodora left her here to slowly die, and the sorceress' daughter, Assara—a clone of her friend Sandra named after Charlee's grandmother—was all too happy to let that happen.

"Who's there?" Charlee's throat burned. Her voice cracked. She licked her lips with a dry tongue. Her head dropped, but she fought to lift it again.

"*You must stay alive. You cannot sleep now.*"

Charlee blinked and her vision cleared. She was alone in the dungeon's stale darkness. Her gut ached with emptiness from hunger—or maybe it was from a despair as heavy as the steel chains that tethered her to the cold, hard stone wall. "Who...are you?"

"*Does the young Guardian not recognize my voice?*"

"You sound like...Theodora." Her words formed as a raspy whisper. Hate ignited an imaginary flame deep in her chest. Her pulse quickened. She couldn't just lay here waiting to die. She had to stop Theodora. "But you can't be. She stole my...powers. Left me...to die."

"*I am Theodora.*" There was remorse in the voice. "*I am the true Theodora. The one you found imprisoned in ice when you jumped through one of your gateways. Do you remember?*"

"I don't...know. Don't...care." Charlee scanned the darkness, but she was alone. "I just want you...dead."

"*You will have your chance.*" Just above Charlee a light appeared. It started as a glowing bubble and then expanded. Light exploded through the tiny chamber. Charlee squeezed her eyes shut, but the brilliance seared through her eyelids.

"It burns," she cried.

"*I am sorry, Guardian. Open your eyes and look now.*"

Charlee blinked rapidly until the pain eased. The blinding light dimmed to a warm yellow glow. Still, shadows danced in front of her. She blinked again and shook her head until focus returned.

"Theodora," Charlee mouthed. Blood surged to her head. Her body trembled.

Like a ghost, a younger version of the sorceress floated in the corner. Flowing golden hair encircled the apparition's face and gathered around her shoulders.

A long white dress, tied off at the waist with a silvery belt, hugged her body. Thin fingers interlocked at her chest. Theodora's head tilted to the side. The right side of her mouth lifted in a slight smile. Concern replaced hate in the sorceress' eyes.

"Do you remember me?" Theodora crossed to within a few feet of Charlee. Her form solidified but still gave off a warm light. Her words became more real — no longer spoken as if from some ethereal plane.

Charlee shook her head. Her mind was slipping. This couldn't be real. But what if it was? If only she could stand and fight. If only she could kill this witch. "Stay away...from...family. I'll...kill...you."

"It is not me who threatens your family, at least not the real me. It is a monstrous creation." Theodora reached for her with a slender arm. Charlee twisted her head away. "My mistakes have brought this on you, your family, and your world. I intend to right the wrongs I have caused, but I need you to free me."

"Get out...of...my head." Charlee tried to spit at the young form of Theodora but couldn't gather saliva. She wrestled against her chains. The rough steel around her wrists tore skin. She fought despite the radiating pain and warmth of her own blood dripping onto her fingers.

"You must survive, Guardian, and find me again." Theodora backed away. Her body pulsated like a heartbeat. "You must free me. Only together can we stop the Theodora you have come to know."

"More lies." Charlee thrashed against her chains. She would do anything to break them, to find a way to reach Theodora, but her limbs lacked the strength.

"You know I am right." Young Theodora spoke sternly. "You have felt the power of the medallion and know its darkness. You have looked into its ugly core, and so somewhere in your mind, the truth is locked away and hidden. The truth is embedded in your thoughts."

"Free me...then." Charlee's hands formed fists. Doing so hurt.

Theodora shook her head. "In my dormant state, I have no power to free you. Do not lose heart, for even now there are friends who come to rescue you."

Charlee's heart beat faster. "How do you...know...this?"

"I have seen them."

"Them?" *The Changeling — if he lived? The Dragon King? Who?*

A locking mechanism on the door clicked. Ghostly Theodora disappeared, and the light faded. The cold emptiness of the chamber again surrounded her, but the flame in her chest still burned. The heavy dungeon door swung open. Two Horengs dressed in black armor stepped inside, each grasping a crackling torch. A dancing orange light spread through the chamber, and the Horengs' wolf-like shadows bounced off the walls. Their yellow eyes shown through their helmets, and snarls rose from their snouts, curved upward and bearing long fangs. The Horengs parted as the clone of Charlee's best friend strolled into the chamber.

11

"Free...me!" Charlee mouthed, her words barely above a whisper.

"Silence." Assara slapped her across the cheek. Her head vibrated. Inside her mouth, she tasted the salty warmth of her own blood. Assara glared through loose strands of hair over her dark eyes. "It seems there are those who have come to rescue you, so for their effort I will kill you in front of them as a message that even the great Guardian will fall to my mother."

"Assara, no." Charlee spit blood from her mouth. How could she make the clone of her best friend understand Theodora was using her? "Think...for...y-ourself. You're...not...your mother."

Assara turned to her Horeng escorts. "Unchain her and bring her to the throne room." She then lumbered from the dungeon.

Charlee closed her eyes. *Can't let her hurt my protector...or anyone else. Must break free. But how, damnit!*

CHAPTER 3

The Changeling's Charge

THE DRAGON NOORRENNN lay dead, his broken body left for other creatures to feed on. Twisted bones tore through flesh. His tongue hung limply from a crushed jaw. Jagged teeth, drenched in the beast's own blood, ripped apart its snout. Thick crimson liquid pooled from its underside, like hot lava pouring down the side of a volcano. His charred remains cast a foul odor over the land. There was nothing worse than the stench of a dragon carcass.

The Changeling rested not far from the dragon. Beaten and battered, his form had dissipated to its basic essence—a glob of yellow energy, and his glow faded. He bested Theodora's dragon, but he would soon join the winged monster in death.

It was believed throughout Janasara that the mythical Changelings were immortal. He knew that wasn't true. His kind had a beginning and an end, and death was as real for them as any creature in this world.

Grunting in silence, he stretched his amoeba form to take a shape—any shape—but his body lacked strength to reform. He lay in the dirt like a puddle of water slowly dissolving into the dust. Soon, he would simply pop out of existence, becoming one with Janasara's life force.

No! He couldn't die—not yet.

The ruins of the Kingdom of Latara stood in the distance. Inside the kingdom's great castle, his charge—the young Guardian—was imprisoned. He watched over Charlee since her birth on that world called Earth. He swore to protect her from evil and any danger. He hadn't—not well enough.

Charlee had changed so much in such a short period. She had gone from a scared girl to a warrior as fierce as her grandfather, Michala. She had become a true leader. The beings of Janasara and the people of Earth still needed her.

I must reach her.

The Changeling focused one more time. His oozing limbs morphed into a winged unicorn but quickly distorted into a misshapen being, then liquefied again. Shapeless, he seeped over the ground. An icy chill flowed through him, and his glow dimmed even more. He became increasingly transparent. It would be so easy to give in to death.

No!

Summoning what little strength he had left, his glow pulsated brighter. He envisioned one of his Earthly forms. The one Charlee liked best—the bike! His globular form strained. *Stretch! Do it for the Guardian!* His body listened. Two tires formed, then a white frame, chrome-like handlebars, and a banana seat with a backrest. *Yes! Hold the form!* At first, he dared not move out of fear he would liquefy once again. This time the shift held. His energy burned brighter.

He would not die this day.

The Changeling willed one more transformation. A set of long, flowing, white wings spread from the frame. He stretched them to their full length. The air caressed the feathers, lifting the wings higher.

He turned toward the Kingdom of Latara, and with a thrust of his wings raced into the sky to save her.

CHAPTER 4

The Dragon Lord

DEEP INSIDE THE Dragon Lord's mountain, his son Kraannaannn paced his father's chamber. His spiked tail pounded repeatedly against the stone floor, rattling the cavern. Rocks and dust fell from above, crashing around him. The boulder-sized red crystal suspended magically from the ceiling swung back and forth. Beams of sunlight piercing through the fissures in the mountainside bounced off the jewel and danced across jagged walls.

"Do you see it, Father?" Kraannaannn spit fire. "Do you see the vision of the Guardian, chained, powerless, and suffering? She is alone and will not survive—and it's because she vowed to save me."

Kraannaannn clutched the fresh scar across his chest. His heart beat stronger now that the section long ago cut out by the traitor Noorrennn had been reattached thanks to the Guardian. She risked everything to return the missing piece of his heart and save his life.

Each steady beat vibrated against his touch. His blood pumped faster through his veins than ever before, and he breathed deeper. More flames rose from his snout. His lips curled up, revealing his long fangs. Noorrennn had taken nearly everything from him, and for what—to serve the witch, Theodora?

Tears formed in Kraannaannn's green eyes. His purple scales rippled along his back. His tail walloped the ground.

Noorrennn ripped out a section of his heart and killed his mother when she tried to stop him. Rather than seek vengeance and protect the world from Theodora, his once proud father, the Dragon Lord, had allowed her to rise to power. *Because of me! Because she swore that if he tried to prevent her conquests, she would plunge a knife through the portion of my heart she possessed and kill me. So, this is all my fault.*

Kraannaannn roared. His father had not responded to his question. "Father, do you see her?"

"Yes, my son, I do." The Dragon Lord's muscles bristled. His yellow fangs ground together. He swung his massive tail around and placed it on his son's shoulder. "Calm your anger. We will go to her. She will be saved, just as she saved you. I make that promise to you. I have stood by long enough."

"When, Father, when will we go?" Kraannaannn pushed his father's tail away. He rose on his hind legs as high as he could, but he still was much shorter than his father.

"I have but one duty to perform first." The Dragon Lord retreated from his son. His green scales became black as the dead of night. "Gather our warriors. I trust you will have no trouble as they already look to you as the future leader of our kind."

"What shall I tell them?" Kraannaannn's eyes widened, and his pulse quickened.

"That we prepare for war."

CHAPTER 5

The Alliances of Old Rise Again

PENAIYA WALKED AMONG her people, the remnants of the Kingdom of Latara, offering reassuring smiles and pats on shoulders. The emerald skies of day had long since given way to the darkened skies of twilight, but the three moons—the Queens of the Night—shed a golden light over their island refuge.

Her head was heavy as the events of the last few hours weighed on her. The young Guardian had kept her promise and delivered them to the Realm of the Dragons. She had magically transported many Latarans instantaneously through a portal. Penaiya had been among them.

She had been the first to step into the blue light generated by the Guardian. It had been like stepping through a doorway filled with blinding energy that stung the eyes. She shielded them with her fingers. When she removed her hands, she stood on the shores of an island at the base of a great mountain with a crest carved into dragon wings.

Others followed until more than half of her people huddled together as close to her as possible. Then the portal's blue light vanished. Many hadn't made it through. They were stuck back across the sea on a narrow patch of land between mountains and a shore where Empress Theodora's Horeng army surrounded them.

Those gathered around her wailed for lost friends and family members. She assured them another portal would soon open and more people would arrive, but the blue light did not return. Penaiya had wept then for her people, for the young Guardian, and for her daughter who lost faith and joined Theodora—and likely died by dragon fire.

She couldn't despair long. She couldn't let her people see her in a moment of weakness, so she had done what all leaders must—hid her emotions. Wiping her eyes, she forced a smile, wrapped her disheveled hair into a ponytail, and did her best to comfort everyone else.

Then came the shouts among her people.

"Look to the skies!" some shouted.

"Dragons!" others cried.

Penaiya arched her neck toward the Three Queens, which hovered high to the west. The dragons were visible against the brilliant moons, their wings

17

glimmering in the night's twinkling embrace. There must have been dozens, and they raced toward the island and toward her people.

Screams rose among them. The massive creatures had stayed away when the Ten Unified Kingdoms needed them most. They hid in their realm as Theodora conquered the kingdoms and killed so many.

Penaiya gritted her teeth. She hadn't wanted to come here. She wanted nothing to do with the beasts, but the Guardian thought it best. So, what now? Had the dragons come to feed on them? Would their flames extinguish what remained of the people of Latara? Had the Guardian led them to death?

Then the unexpected occurred.

One by one, the dragons landed on the shore, and from their backs slid all those who had not escaped in the portal. Ten, twenty, forty—the numbers of Latarans grew as each dragon gently touched land. Cheers and praise for the dragons echoed across the shoreline. Penaiya had stared in silence. A single tear fell from her cheek.

That had been hours ago.

The dragons had flown away as quickly as they arrived, soaring east toward other groupings of islands. None delivered the Guardian. What had become of her? The young warrior Aryean, whose feelings for the Guardian had left him in despair when she wasn't delivered to the island, had said she still lived when the dragons rescued them. He told of how he watched a dragon grasp her in its talons and fly her away, believing they'd be reunited, but it wasn't to be. Had she died, sacrificing herself? She was so young, so brave, and she'd given everything to save people in a world that wasn't her own.

As the deeper hours of night unfolded, a chill covered the island.

More than once from the mountain, a terrifying roar shook the island. Fear and uncertainty replaced the joy of being reunited with loved ones. She put her people to work, sending them into a nearby forest to gather wood for fires and to find food.

Some fires already blazed along the shore, crackling wildly. The flames offered warmth from the night's chill. Exotic fruits found in forest trees were being rationed in small portions. Though far from enough to keep away the pains of hunger, it was something.

Penaiya walked up to one fire pit encircled by twenty of her people. "May I join you?" They quickly made space for her. "How about a song?" Penaiya knelt in the sand.

Before anyone answered, she started to hum an old Lataran lullaby mothers and fathers would sing to their children—a comforting tune that everyone would know. Soon other voices joined from the other fires. The humming turned to words, and their song became louder than the waves crashing on the shore, until...

A mighty wind slammed into her people, knocking many down and extinguishing most of the blazes.

The island trembled, and Penaiya tumbled into the sand. She didn't need to gaze up to know a dragon was close. But would the beast be friend or foe? Her people were defenseless. If the creature attacked, she could do nothing to save them. Needle pricks of panic spread between her shoulder blades. Spitting sand from her mouth, she slowly stood.

Gasps and whimpers from her people affirmed her fears. A very large dragon had landed. The Latarans gathered behind her, huddling close together. Many pointed, whispering the word *dragon* over and over. The dragons had saved them, but why? Were the beasts going to feed on them? No, that didn't make sense. They would have struck hours ago if they hungered.

Penaiya straightened her hair.

The winged beast towered above her a stone's throw away. Even under the cover of darkness, there was no mistaking the Dragon Lord. She'd never seen him but heard tales of his majesty—a titan even among his own kind. The stories didn't do him justice. Penaiya fought the urge to run. A spiked head rested atop a long muscular neck. Eyes as orange as the sun glared at her. She forced herself not to look away. Wings tucked against him, covering his body like a silk royal robe. Moonlight reflected off an armor of green scales atop his back. Sword-length fangs protruded from his snout.

Penaiya crossed her arms to keep from shaking. "You are the Dragon Lord?"

The dragon nodded a massive head. Black smoke rose from cavernous nostrils. "I am Sheorrriaaaan." His words were spoken in Lengoron, so Penaiya would understand. With unexpected grace, he lowered his head to her until just a few feet away. Penaiya held her ground, but a bead of cold sweat dropped from her brow. "You have come to the Realm of the Dragons."

"I am Penaiya." Lifting her chin, she stepped closer to the dragon's snout. "You speak our language well."

The Dragon Lord tilted his head. "Dragons are very adept at learning languages. You lead these people?"

"I do…for now, until the rightful Queen of Latara returns. I thank you for providing us a safe shore from the Horeng."

"Do not thank me, Lady Penaiya," the Dragon Lord retorted. "Though it be distasteful and cowardly, I would have let you die at the hands of the Horeng. You are here now because of my son, who showed greater courage than I ever could. And the only reason I let you remain here now is because of the bravery of your Guardian."

"Where is she?" Penaiya blurted. "She lives?"

The Dragon Lord lifted his head and nodded. His scales clinked with each movement. His eyes blinked once. "She does for now, but she is locked away in Theodora's dungeon and grows weaker with each passing moment. I fear she will not survive long without help."

Penaiya cleared her throat. "What concern is the Guardian to the dragons? Your kind turned their backs once on the greatest of the Guardians and on the people within the Unified Kingdoms. Your silence enabled Theodora—"

A roar from the Dragon Lord pierced the night. Penaiya did not flinch.

"The past is the past...I had my reasons." The Dragon Lord inched closer to Penaiya. The heat of his breath surrounded her. Her eyes watered from the stench of hot sulfur. "Your young Guardian and my son have reminded me what true courage is. She is in danger because she acted to save my son. It is time for me to return the favor."

"What are you saying?" Penaiya moved around the dragon's snout and stared into his right eye.

"Tonight, the dragons bring war to the House of Theodora, a war that is long overdue." The Dragon Lord bared his fangs. "Your people have been through much this day, but I come here to ask if you might stand with the dragons the way we should have stood with you long ago."

Penaiya's heart leaped. She wanted to cry out *yes*, but she could not speak for her people. She stepped back and turned to them. They were hungry, exhausted, lost, and afraid. There were too few to be of much value in a war against an enemy tens of thousands strong.

She addressed them. "Have you heard the words of the Dragon Lord?"

"Yes," many shouted.

Penaiya sighed. "What say you?"

Silence greeted her at first until Aryean, his face covered in his own dried blood, unsheathed his sword and raised it over his head.

"For the Guardian." His voice cracked as he spoke, and a tear slid down his cheek. Penaiya nodded to him. There was no denying their connection.

Another warrior, a young woman, stood up. "For the Guardian."

Another voice rang out, "For Latara."

"For all the Unified Kingdoms," Penaiya reminded them.

Cheers followed.

Penaiya turned back to the Dragon Lord. "You have your answer."

"Good." The Dragon Lord's lips curled up in a grin. "We shall fight as one. Come and let us prepare. There shall be food for your people, and armor, bows, and blades. When in the end we stand victorious, history will tell of how the Unified Kingdoms and the Realm of Dragons fought together as in days long since passed and bridged the way to a new time of peace in all Janasara."

CHAPTER 6

On Earth

CHARLEE'S MOM STARED at her husband. Their eyes shifted from each other back to their youngest daughter, Charlee's two-year-old sister, Megan. The little one sat in her highchair, giggling, a bubble gum-sized blue ball of light dancing between the palms of her hands. It radiated a glow that illuminated Megan's porcelain skin despite the gloom of a foggy San Francisco morning.

Charlee's mom, Tira Smelton, placed a hand over her own mouth, muffling a gasp. Was it possible? Had Megan manifested a gateway, just like her big sister?

Tira's husband, Joseph Smelton, adjusted the wire-framed glasses on his bearded face. He bent down to his youngest daughter. "What do you have there, baby girl?"

Megan giggled some more. Her blond hair danced across her face. She smiled ear to ear, her crystal blue eyes locked on the tiny energy ball floating between her hands. "Charlee...home."

Tira Smelton nodded to her daughter. She had no idea what Megan meant by that. How could a two-year-old fathom just how profound her words were? That little ball hovering playfully between her tiny fingers could be a way across the dimensional divide that kept them from reaching Charlee.

Her husband stroked Megan's hair. "You don't think she knows the way to Janasara, do you?"

Tira blinked her tired eyes and shook her head. "How could she? She's so young. But look at her, Joseph, she's generating a gateway. There's no way she should have that kind of power—not at her age."

Joseph wrapped his arms around his daughter and lifted her from the chair. He held her close to his chest. "Maybe it shouldn't be possible, but she's doing it."

Minutes ago, Tira and her husband were lost. Their eldest daughter, Charlee, had used her Guardian powers to open a gateway to Janasara for herself, her old mentor, Cryton, and a Changeling sworn to protect her. Her husband tried to stop her, but he'd failed. Charlee was stubborn, *just like me.*

Charlee crossed the dimensional divide to stop Theodora without Tira or her husband. She felt responsible for the people of Janasara suffering after trapping Theodora back in that world to keep her from conquering Earth.

Charlee had paid a terrible price, and her parents had to get to her. Megan might provide them that chance.

Joseph rocked his daughter in his arms. "Somehow, she's creating a gateway. There's got to be some way to reach Charlee now."

Tira shook her head. Frown lines, mostly hidden by her brown hair, formed along her forehead. "Joseph, it's just a bit of magic. It's not a true gateway. She's not strong enough yet. Besides, even if it was a gateway, she can't control it. She wouldn't know how to reach Janasara. A Guardian must be able to visualize their destination."

"We have to try!" Joseph's chin quivered under his beard. "There must be a way. Can't you use your magic to amplify Megan's?"

She clasped her hands and held them under her chin. Was there a way? No, her husband just didn't understand magic. How could a man from Earth? For all his support, for all the love he showed her, despite her being a transplant from another world, another dimension, he could never truly understand. "It doesn't work that way. I'm not a Guardian. And even if I could do something, how do we know it wouldn't hurt Megan?"

"Because your magic could never harm our daughter." Joseph Smelton placed his hand gently on his wife's shoulder.

Tira swung back to her husband. Her husband was right. They had to try, and there simply was no other way. Megan was offering them a gift, one Tira had to accept. "I don't know if it's possible, but I'll try to feed some of my magic to Megan, and if she's able to manifest a gateway large enough to transport me, I'll try to guide her thoughts to Janasara. But, if I sense she's in distress even the slightest, I'll stop it."

Joseph grasped his wife's hand. "You're not going there alone. If our little girl here succeeds, we're all going. I won't have our family separated again—ever!"

Chapter 7

The Break of Day

CHARLEE'S FEET DRAGGED limply across the stone floor of a dimly lit hallway. A stench filled the air. It could be the stink of the two Horeng henchmen who roughly held her by the arms—or maybe it was her. She probably didn't smell like a flower after being chained to a dungeon wall, but it didn't matter. Assara, the confused clone of her best friend, Sandra, would kill her soon anyway.

As they neared the massive arched doorway to the throne room, the double doors opened on their own. Beyond was the chamber where Charlee had battled Theodora only to lose the medallion, the one weapon that could destroy the witch. Charlee shuddered. The agony of the moment Theodora used the medallion to steal her magic was still fresh. Her body was still hollow, as if her soul had been ripped away.

"Leave us," a voice commanded.

The two beasts threw Charlee farther into the room. She slammed against the floor and rolled onto her side. A yelp slid from her lips. She lay there like a worm unable to do little else but slide her legs closer to her chest. Pain radiated from stiff muscles, weakened by confinement in heavy chains.

"You have arrived just in time."

Charlee took a deep breath. She had to stand and face the clone. If she were going to die, it wouldn't happen while lying on a floor like some frightened child. With a loud grunt, she lifted herself, but her wobbly arms failed.

Assara's gleeful laugh filled the chamber. "Oh, how weak the Guardian has become. What joy to watch you struggle. If only there were time, I could delight in your weakness all day."

"Shut up!" Charlee uttered through parched lips, her words not much more than a gritty whisper. Pounding the floor with a fist, she tried again. Shaky arms underneath her, she pushed against the floor. *Come...on, damn...you!* Gasping out shallow breaths through clenched teeth, she painfully climbed to her knees.

Assara's laughter stopped.

Every muscle screamed and pain sensors flashed like tiny explosions throughout her body. Charlee reached her feet but quickly caved, slumping again to her knees. Okay, if this was the best she could do, so be it.

Chest heaving from the effort, she gazed ahead. The throne, a chair made entirely of the bones of Theodora's conquered enemies, stood before her. Leg bones held up the chair, arm bones served as armrests, and skulls lined the base for the seat. A collage of bones, skulls, rib cages, hands, and feet covered the back of the chair and rose high in an arching display of death.

Assara sat, legs crossed, at the throne.

"If you want...to kill me, just get it...over with," Charlee mumbled. "I'm tired of this...tired of you."

Assara frowned. Dampened by sweat, her brown wispy hair clung to the hard edges of her face. "You will die as a new day begins, but not just yet. I thought you might like to see the show that is about to begin."

Charlee forced a deep breath. "What do...you...mean?" A million thoughts raced through her mind. This monster had taken so much from her already. But there were so many others she could hurt.

"Come, let me show you." Theodora's clone creation, dressed in the same black armor she wore when they first battled on a mountaintop, climbed down marble steps to Charlee. Clamping a gloved hand around Charlee's neck, she forced her to stand.

"You do wreak, don't you," Assara teased. "Too bad you'll not have time to bathe before you die."

"Yeah, too...bad." Charlee lacked strength to struggle against Assara's grip. If only she had a little magic hidden away, untouched by Theodora's medallion. But there was nothing left but a void in her gut.

The clone dragged her across the throne room to the balcony overlooking the Kingdom of Latara. A raven black sky covered the land, but a hint of light shown in the east as daybreak neared.

"What do you see?" Assara's brown eyes focused on the dark horizon toward jagged mountain peaks, shadowy and desolate, that marked the kingdom's southern border. A confident defiance laced Assara's voice, but the tiniest of cracks in her words revealed something else. Was it fear?

The ruins of Latara stretched beneath the castle. The fires of Theodora's factories burned through the night, coughing up columns of glowing black smoke. A low moan echoed from within those evil constructs, maybe from the machinery or maybe from those who once lived peacefully in the kingdom but now slaved under wretched conditions. Charlee bit her lip. She had failed them.

"Stop this...Assara." Charlee straightened and pushed away from Theodora's daughter. She would have collapsed but caught herself on the railing. Quivering arms barely held her up. "It's not too late...to change."

Assara grabbed Charlee by the hair and yanked her close. Her hot breath brushed against Charlee's ear. "You have not answered my question, Guardian.

24

What do you see?" Charlee swatted at Assara's hand to try to free herself, but the clone forced Charlee to her knees.

"Answer!" Assara shouted. Her voice bounced off the chamber walls.

Charlee pulled herself up and glanced over the kingdom. Dread sucked all the blood from her head. Blinking uncontrollably, she peered over the railing and followed a trail of uprooted trees and gutted, abandoned homes to Latara's protective outer walls. Beyond the walls, like an endless ocean barely visible through a morning mist, thousands of the Horeng army had gathered. They stood as an impenetrable barrier to the kingdom—but why?

"You see them, don't you?" Assara wrapped an arm around Charlee's neck.

"Yes."

"A rescue attempt, Guardian."

"What?" Charlee grabbed Assara's arm.

"It seems you have inspired that cowardice Dragon Lord to rise up against Mother's armies." Assara's voice vibrated with anticipation of a war.

Bleak clouds crowned the sentinel ranges off to the east, but golden streams singed the peaks. The early sun fought against the dark shroud over the land to announce its presence. A few beams barely cracked through the gloom—enough to glint against something big atop the closest peak. Charlee strained for a better look. The dawn of a new day revealed the outlines of a dragon's wings.

"The Dragon Lord." Charlee couldn't contain her excitement—or her fear. Her knuckles turned white as her hands tightened around the railing. Her knees shook underneath her torn animal-hide pants—the same ones Cryton had gifted to her.

As if he could hear her muffled words from such great distance, the great dragon roared, and fire rose from his snout to greet the morning.

"Yes, he has come for you." Assara rubbed her chin and glared at Charlee. Her lower lip quivered slightly. "It seems you saved his only son."

Charlee's eyes shifted from the Dragon Lord to Assara. The clone feared the dragon despite her best efforts to hide her fear, but her face remained hard even as she stared into the vengeful hate of a dragon. What did Assara have planned? What trap would she unleash on the Dragon Lord? Charlee had to warn him. She had to make him stay away.

"Does it bring you joy to see the beast?" Assara's lips parted in a twisted grin. "Do you think you'll be saved now?"

Charlee shook her head. There was a mysterious power in Assara's words. It made Charlee shudder. The clone was too confident. "Assara, why am I here? You could have left me in the dungeon."

"Yes, I could have, but that wouldn't be as much fun." Assara gripped the sword at her side. Amusement now stirred in the playful tone of her voice. Her eyes bulged. "I thought you would like to see just how prepared Mother is for an attack by the dragons. When they are defeated, they will see me drive a sword through their Guardian. I thought this moment deserved a public death."

"Wait, let me talk to the Dragon Lord. I'll send him away." Each word burned, but she had to stop Assara. Her, pain, thirst, hunger, and fear no longer mattered. She couldn't let the Dragon Lord be hurt.

Charlee took a wobbly step toward Assara, but the clone whipped out her sword and pointed the blade at Charlee's neck. "Stay back. You will die in time. Try to enjoy what's to come."

"No!"

"Yes!" Assara kept the blade tip close to Charlee's chest. "You brought this on yourself by hurting Mother. You never should have tried to take what was hers."

"I didn't take anything." Charlee gripped the steel with one hand. Assara tugged it free, slicing across Charlee's palm. She cringed but didn't cry out. Blood oozed down her wrist. "Theodora used me to reach my world, and she tried to hurt a lot of people, including my best friend." Charlee squeezed her hand, more blood dripping between her fingers. She gasped against the sting but kept talking. "Assara, she used me like she's using you now. Think about it. Why'd she leave you here? Why didn't she take her only daughter with her? She doesn't care what happens to you. She got what she wants, and she left you behind."

Assara studied the crimson liquid coating her blade. A quiet rage turned her bronze skin red. "Stop it!" she finally shouted. "You're trying to twist me against Mother, but she warned me of your tricks."

Charlee lumbered to Assara. "You know I'm right."

The back of Assara's gloved hand slammed into Charlee's cheek. Her head jerked backward, rattling her brain as if shocked by a sudden burst of electricity. Her vision blurred. She fell to the ground, clutching her face.

Spitting blood from her mouth, Charlee clutched her head until the spinning stopped. "Hitting me just proves you know I'm right." Slowly rising, she tried to ignore the radiating ache spreading from one side of her face to the other.

Assara raised her sword as if to bring it crashing down toward Charlee, but the roar of the Dragon Lord stopped her.

"The war with the dragons begins." The clone swung back to the balcony.

Charlee glanced beyond Assara. Streaks of emerald stretched like tentacles across the sky, pushing away the remains of the night. An orange sun peaked from behind the mountains.

The Dragon Lord launched into the sky with one mighty thrust of his wings. *I must make him stop!* Charlee wrung her hands and closed her eyes. Those with magic abilities could speak telepathically. Maybe he could still sense her, hear her thoughts, even if she had lost her powers. The dragons were creatures of the purest magic. None was stronger than the Dragon Lord.

Hear me, damn it! Please, hear me! Sheorrriaaaan! she shouted with her mind, *Stay away from here. You're flying into a trap. You can't help me. Just turn back.*

§ § §

The Dragon Lord heard the Guardian's warning. He snorted, shook his massive head, and soared faster toward the castle.

Thousands of the Empresses' Horeng army stretched across the desolate plain outside the kingdom's walls. They might be wolves, but to the Dragon Lord they were prey he'd slaughter in one fiery breath. Nevertheless, he was no fool. The Horeng were a diversion from whatever weapon she planned to unleash.

Theodora no longer had her own dragon. The Changeling had seen to that. The burned corpse of the traitorous Noorrennn lay rotting in a nearby field.

The witch had something else planned. His orange eyes shimmered. He bared his fangs. Fire rose up his throat. The green scales on his back clamped down tightly against his body in anticipation. Too many years had passed since he'd felt the exhilaration of battle. He'd take the bait.

"Guardian, if you can hear my words, have no fear. I know danger lies ahead. Do not underestimate the cunning of the dragons. Rest assured, you will be saved, and order will be restored."

His jaws parted. A stream of fire poured out.

§ § §

Rest assured, you will be saved, and order will be restored.

The Dragon Lord's words flashed through Charlee's mind as clear as if she stood beside the great beast. He heard her plea but hadn't listened. She couldn't stop him. This war was about to begin, and she couldn't do anything to prevent it.

Charlee pounded the railing. *Turn back! Please!* She got no response. Just the Dragon Lord's resolute thoughts overshadowing the numbing sense of fear radiating throughout her body. She peered over the side of the castle to the courtyard hundreds of feet below. A fall that would kill her. Yes! If she were dead, he'd have to turn back.

She started to climb, but a Horeng claw grasped her shoulder.

"You don't get to die that easily." Assara flashed a smile. Her eyes gleamed with amusement. All signs of fear vanished from her smooth face. Charlee's eyes shifted from the clone to the Dragon Lord.

27

Sheorrriaaaan dove at the Horeng, his wings whipping against the air with a thunderous crack, like gale forces slamming into a tall ship's sails. The dark army's archers launched an attack on the great beast. Their arrowheads whizzed through the air, swarming toward the dragon's underbelly.

A blast of fire from the Dragon Lord's snout proved enough of a defense. From Charlee's vantage point, not a single arrow found its target. She tried to shake free from the Horeng gripping her shoulder. A deep guttural growl rose from the guard. He dug his claws into her skin, cutting through flesh. She cried out, dropping to one knee but quickly stood. She had to keep her eyes on the battle—had to figure out Assara's trap before it was too late.

More fire shot from the Dragon Lord's snout, ravaging lines of Theodora's army. The Horeng howled wildly and broke their formations to flee the great dragon. The crackle of orange flames charring their bodies echoed throughout the land. Black smoke climbed from the fallen wolves, many rolling in the fields until the sizzle of their burning flesh silenced their cries. Others pounded against the outer walls until the dragon's breath engulfed them in a fiery dance of death.

Assara laughed.

"What's so funny?" Charlee pulled herself along the railing toward Assara. Her stomach clenched as if she'd been punched. Assara's cackle was too much like Theodora's—evil, twisted, and confident even as her army fell. "Your Horeng won't last long against the Dragon Lord."

"No matter." Assara retreated from the balcony, her eyes fixed on Charlee and her mouth curved up in a sneer. She back stepped to the center of the chamber, and then gracefully climbed onto the throne.

"Mother knew that someday the dragons would rise against her, so she used her magic and the power of the medallion to prepare a surprise." Assara pressed down on the right armrest, and the throne began to rotate toward the balcony.

Charlee placed trembling hands to her mouth. What deadly force was Assara about to unleash on the Dragon Lord? *Sheorrriaaaan, stop now! Get to safety!*

Two controllers, like old video game joysticks, rose from the skulls at the end of both armrests. A crystalline object the size of a bathroom mirror, translucent with a white glow, slid from an opening in the floor and hovered in front of Assara.

"Come and see," Assara beckoned with a wave of her hand.

The Horeng gripped Charlee's shoulders and squeezed as if to crush her bones. Air painfully rushed from her lungs. She gasped, but pain didn't matter. Her focus locked on Assara. The clone wore a stone expression, but her eyes were alight with joy. *Damn her! Have...to...stop...her!*

Snarling, the Horeng lifted Charlee until her feet dangled inches above the floor, then stomped to the throne. The wolfen beast dropped her against the cold marble steps beneath Assara.

Charlee's legs collapsed. She caught herself with her arms and slowly lifted her face toward the crystal hovering before the throne. The gem was like a TV screen, and it was playing an image of the battle scene outside the castle. The Dragon Lord continued his assault on the Horeng army, burning the creatures alive. The flames crackled and danced. The Horeng and the Valley burned, leaving a blackened scar along the hillsides.

"What is this, Assara? Tell me!" Charlee's words limped from her throat.

"Mother calls it the dragon killer." Assara raised her chin and glared down at Charlee. "Watch how it works."

"No!" Charlee's limbs trembled. Hate gave her strength. *Have…to…save… Dragon…Lord!* She started to crawl up the steps, but Horeng guards grabbed her around the torso and dragged her away. She screamed, fighting wildly to escape. Her fingernails scraped against the floor. "Assara, don't…do this!"

The clone ignored her pleas.

"I see you, dragon scum." Clutching the joysticks in her gloved hands, Assara unleashed hell on the Dragon Lord.

CHAPTER 8

Hell Unleashed

A N EXPLOSION FROM somewhere deep in the belly of Castle Latara shook the throne room. The floor beneath Charlee shuddered in protest. A gush of hot air blasted through cracks in walls. What was happening? The two Horeng guards holding her lost their balance and released their grip. She awkwardly reached her feet and lumbered to the balcony just in time to see a red beam the size of a spotlight fire from a tower overhead.

The death ray angled toward Sheorrriaaaan.

Charlee's jaw dropped, and her heart all but stopped. She couldn't draw a breath but forced out a scream to warm the Dragon Lord. But it was too late. He never had a chance to maneuver out of the way. He probably never saw the beam until it was on him.

The ray cut a gash through his armored chest, tore through his body, and ripped a hole in his back as the red energy zipped beyond his body higher into the sky. His green blood and flesh sprayed into the sky. The Dragon Lord roared in pain and plummeted toward the earth.

"No!" Charlee's eyes fixed on Sheorrriaaaan.

The Dragon Lord's wings flailed uselessly. Smoke rose from his wound, creating a black smoldering trail. His body slammed into the ground with a rattling thud. Charlee cringed, looking away. As the dust and dirt settled around the great dragon, she peered back to see if he moved — if there were any signs of life.

Nothing. The Dragon Lord was still.

She spun to Assara. "What have you done?"

Laughter drifted from the throne. "What I must to defend Mother's rule."

Charlee shook a fist at the clone. "You're going to die for what you've done."

"Maybe." Assara casually leaned back against the throne. "But I'll make sure you die first."

"Then come and kill me." Charlee stepped toward Assara, but two Horeng guards were on her, wrapping their claws around her arms. She wrestled, thrashing her body in every direction, but they wouldn't let go.

"Do not release her again." Assara started to climb from the throne.

The sky beyond the balcony exploded in a swirl of oranges, reds, and yellows. The castle trembled and swayed back and forth. This time it wasn't the weapon.

*What the…*Charlee glanced up. Dragons soared overhead, spitting a barrage of flames at the laser tower. Blocks of stone crumbled to the ground, and an entire section gave way. The tower collapsed in a thunderous rumble.

Theodora's dragon killer was destroyed before it could kill anyone else. Charlee's mind locked on one thought. The Dragon Lord sacrificed himself to expose whatever weapon Assara had to stop the dragons. Once the weapon fired, the dragons pinpointed their attack. Now there was nothing to stop them.

Spurred by the dragons, a new strength coursed through her muscles. Adrenaline took over. She broke free from the Horeng and stood on legs that no longer shook. "You're done, Assara."

"Hardly." Theodora's daughter still spoke with an air of confidence. Cheeks flushed, eyes resolute, she raised her sword. "You think Mother would so easily fall to those foul beasts. Watch again." Assara turned her sword over so that the handle pointed up, revealing a crimson gem in the base.

What now! Charlee rushed at the clone. "Assara, what are you doing?"

"Stupid, Guardian. Mother turned the entire castle into a weapon. Watch the dragons die as Mother's power is unleashed." Assara's voice was cold and exact. She pressed the gem.

Red beams sliced wildly across the gray morning sky. The dragons did their best to race away, but one by one they were caught in the deadly blitz. Their green blood splashed against the clouds. One dragon was hit in the neck, its head nearly severed. Another's wings were sliced off. A third lost a leg. They hurtled to the ground, slamming into the earth. The crash of their bodies striking the land was too much for Charlee. She covered her ears, but it did little to block out the dragons' pained cries as the Horeng jumped on them, delivering death blows with their heavy axes and massive swords.

Charlee gazed away from the carnage. All this death was because of her. Why couldn't the Dragon Lord listen to her? Why didn't he just stay away? Why hadn't she killed Theodora with the medallion when she had the chance? She unleashed her own blood-curdling cry. It was met by more of Assara's laughter.

"I told you from the start you were weak, Guardian," The clone flipped her sword in the air and caught it so that the blade pointed at Charlee's chest. "Now, as you have witnessed the defeat of the dragons, let those beasts that remain watch their Guardian die."

"Damn, you!" Charlee sprang at Assara.

The two Horeng guards grabbed her. They dug their claws into her shoulders and slammed her against the floor. She twisted and squirmed, but this time her unexpected burst of strength failed her. With their hind legs, they stepped on her back, mashing her against the icy stone. She struggled for a breath. *Get up…Guardian. Do…something. Can't end…this way!*

32

Assara skipped gleefully to the edge of the balcony. Her gaze shifted from the death below to Charlee. "Bring her to me."

The Horeng dragged Charlee back to the clone, forcefully lifting her as if they meant to tear her arms from her sockets. With a deep breath, she swallowed a scream.

Death filled the Valley below. Fires raged, lifting columns of choking black smoke to the somber heavens. A handful of dragons lay dead, their heads roughly sliced from their bodies by the few Horeng not decimated by the flames. Their deaths were on her. She'd never forgive herself. Then again, she'd join them soon in the eternal realm, if there was such a place.

Charlee shook her head. "What have you done, Assara?"

The clone slid within inches of Charlee, a grin twisting her lips. "Made Mother proud."

"You fool!" Charlee's cheeks burned red hot. Though her throat ached, she spoke as if delivering her last words. "You don't matter anymore than the Horeng to Theodora. She doesn't care. She abandoned you here. You—"

"Shut your mouth." Assara's eyes grew wide and savage. She raised a gloved hand to strike Charlee.

A bird's gentle song stopped her.

CHAPTER 9

Hope Arrives

A GLOWING WHITE dove flew into the throne room from the balcony and circled overhead. Charlee dropped to her knees. It was just like the winged creature that watched over her all her life. The dove's high-pitched song filled the chamber. Dare she hope? Could it be the Changeling? Her body tingled as if she'd been jolted with electricity.

The little dove fluttered above Assara, then attacked. Wings spread wide, the slender bird screeched, pecking at the clone's cheeks and pulling her hair.

It is the Changeling! Charlee climbed to her feet.

Assara cursed. "What trickery is this?" Theodora's daughter, lips pursed, swatted at the dove first with her free hand and then with the sword. The tiny creature easily evaded each strike.

This was Charlee's chance. *Move...now!* She launched herself at the clone.

"Enough," Assara screamed. She pointed the tip of her blade at Charlee's chest, stopping the Guardian. A backhand from the clone smashed into the dove. The winged one careened into a wall, slamming into it, then dropped to the floor.

"Damn you!" Charlee pushed Assara's blade away with limbs strengthened by rage. "You'll pay for that!"

Assara lifted her sword high. "Death comes for you—"

The dove sang out, launching itself into the air. The bird raced to Charlee's side, transforming as it flew. Its body creaked and hummed like a live wire. The Changeling morphed into a glob of yellow glowing energy, then into the form Charlee knew best—the white-framed bike—the one she had tried to ditch in an alley back home before she understood their destinies were linked.

"Bike!" Charlee blurted. Her protector was here to give her a fighting chance. Warmth spread across her cheeks. She wasn't alone anymore.

Assara gripped her sword with two hands. Her mouth set in a grim line. "What form of being is this? No matter. I'll kill the both of you."

"I...don't...think...so." Charlee reached for the bike's handlebars. If she could touch the Changeling, its energy would flow through her and give her strength. Maybe her magic would return. She reached for her protector.

Assara grasped her arm. "You will not be saved!" The clone yanked her away from the Changeling.

35

Charlee tried to jerk free, but Theodora's daughter was too strong. Assara dragged her across the throne room, sword pressed against her neck. The blade sliced into her skin. She cringed and stopped struggling. Droplets of blood fell from her neck onto the stone floor. Each splash echoed in her ears.

The Changeling rolled toward them.

"Any closer and she dies." Assara yanked Charlee's head back and dug the blade deeper, tearing though more skin. Charlee screamed. More blood oozed from her flesh. A fiery pain radiated from her throat. Once across the chamber, Assara released her grip on Charlee. The Guardian slumped to her knees, wheezing, grasping her neck.

"Now see how alone you are, Guardian." Assara twisted her sword's handle. A shimmering green barrier rose from the floor, separating the throne room in two, with the Changeling on one side and she and Charlee on the other. "No one can save you. It is just you and me."

The Changeling rushed at the barrier, crashing against it repeatedly, but it couldn't breach the glowing wall.

Assara snorted, strolling toward the barrier, sword resting on her shoulder. "You arrived just in time, strange creature. You can watch your Guardian die for her crimes against Mother."

"Not…today…Assara." An infusion of adrenaline shook Charlee's body. Hands coated in her own blood, she planted them against the floor and climbed to her feet. With what little strength remained in her limbs, she threw herself at Assara, tackling her to the ground. Assara's sword flew from her hand, clanging against the stone. A shriek escaped the clone's lips.

Charlee's legs thrashed wildly against the floor as she locked her arms around Assara. Fury heated her chest. She rolled over and over, grappling to hang on to the clone, but her limbs quickly weakened. Each breath could barely rise from a crusted throat. Assara easily broke away and stumbled to her sword.

"Fool." Assara gripped the blade and swung around, aiming it at Charlee's heart. The clone's chest heaved. "I grow tired of you. Time for this to end. Time for everyone to see their Guardian die."

Assara, cheeks flushed and scratched from the dove's attack, grasped Charlee by the wrist and tugged her to the balcony. The Changeling reformed into a unicorn, kicking the green barrier with its hind legs. The barrier would not cave.

"Bike!" Charlee reached a shaky hand toward her protector. Assara laughed, dragging her along the cold, hard floor. The unicorn neighed furiously, his glowing yellow eyes bulging. He rammed the barrier one more time but still couldn't break through.

Once on the balcony, the clone hefted Charlee to her feet as easy as lifting a doll. The clone shoved the tip of her blade against the small of the Guardian's back with just enough force to prick Charlee's flesh. An icy chill radiated from where the razor-sharp point pierced her skin. Her legs wanted to crumble, but if she fell the blade would cut deeper. *Don't fall. Don't give up.*

"Does it hurt, Guardian?"

Charlee forced a smile. "You can never hurt me."

Assara twisted the blade against Charlee's back, ripping more skin. Charlee suppressed a cry. Shock waves of pain raced through her body. Assara leaned in closer. "Now it is time for you to d—"

Two Horeng burst into the throne room and bolted the chamber door behind them. One of them spoke, its voice a guttural mix of barks and growls. Charlee somehow understood the language. "General, army of Latara broke through castle. Dragons more attack. We not hold out longer much. We dying. Too many. What we do?"

Assara lowered the blade. "What army of Latara? I saw only the dragons in the Valley, and they were destroyed by the castle's defenses. The rest fled like cowards."

The wolf gasped. Its brown fur bristled, fangs showing through a black helmet. "No. More dragons come. Bring Latara people on backs. They kill us."

Charlee blinked through the pain. Again, a flame of hope sparked inside. She turned toward Assara.

The clone's chin quivered, and she lowered her head. When she gazed up again, her bronze skin turned ashen gray, but a sneer returned. "Recall a couple of our legions to the castle. That should be enough to stop a weak group of Latara warriors."

"They reach throne room before we stop them," the second Horeng soldier warned in a high-pitched howl. The beast wore no mask. A black patch covered one eye. Its chest rose and fell rapidly underneath dark armor.

Assara whipped Charlee around to face her. The clone's hot breath brushed against her cheeks. "Excellent. This chamber can withstand any assault, and when they arrive, they will find their Guardian dead. That should be enough to break their spirit."

"And what be of the dragons?" the first Horeng asked. The wolf's pointy ears, sticking out from its helmet, twitched. "They kill us with dirty fire breath."

Charlee gazed over the balcony. Assara did the same. The dragons gathered again and were tearing through the Horeng. One dragon, smaller in stature than the others, led the way. *The Dragon Lord's son!* She dug her fingers into the balcony. Her cheeks trembled, and her eyes widened.

"They will die like their brethren as the magic of this castle cuts them down one by one." Assara pointed to the one-eyed Horeng. "You, sit at the throne and fire on the dragons with all of this castle's power."

"Assara, you can't win." Charlee grabbed her arm. "Stop this."

"I will quiet you once and for all," Assara lifted her sword.

Charlee reached for the clone's sword hand. Assara threw a swift kick to her chest, knocking Charlee backward. Air rushed from her lungs, and her back and head struck the stone floor. She tried to force air in and out as the back of her skull rattled. Her head spinning, she would have been sick if her stomach had food or drink.

She blinked away dizziness enough to speak through weak breaths. "You think…killing me…will stop this…war. It…won't."

Assara stood over her, the tip of her sword quivering. Assara's brown eyebrows scrunched together. The sneer was gone from her lips. "That may be true, but you will not be around to see it." Assara pressed a boot down on Charlee's chest. "Die, Guard—"

Pained howls and yelps came from outside the throne room doors. Steel crashed against steel. The doors shook and creaked. Were bodies smashing against them in a desperate battle?

Assara's focus shifted to the doors.

"Hold positions…hold your—" a Horeng barked from outside the throne room. Its words ended in a grunt and a gurgle—then, silence.

A drop of sweat fell from the clone's forehead. The Horeng inside the chamber looked to her for a command. They stood frozen, their yellow eyes shifting from her to the door. Their fur bristled and noses twitched. Vicious growls slid from their snouts. The beasts lifted battle-axes to their chests.

Assara pointed her sword at the Horeng. "Fortify the—"

Something heavy crashed against the doors. They shuddered but held. A second crash followed, and then a third. The doors cracked and splintered.

"They're coming, Assara," Charlee whispered.

Assara shook a fist at her. "Do you think I am not prepared? Mother has foreseen such a challenge to her rule." Reaching for the handle of her sword, Assara twisted it. A new wall of green energy rose from the floor in front of the doors.

Outside, a fourth thud against the doors buckled them. With a crunch, they splintered into jagged pieces. Lataran warriors, led by Penaiya, wielding a bloodied sword, poured through the doorway. Charlee gasped. Penaiya, the true leader of the Latarans, lived and had come to save her.

But the barrier separated them.

Penaiya, her long hair flowing wildly over her shoulders, struck the glowing wall with her sword. "Remove this barrier at once. You are defeated, seed of Theodora."

Assara laughed. "Hardly. Watch and see how your Guardian dies because of your actions this day."

"Child, you have lost." Penaiya sheathed the sword. Her words softened. "Throw down your weapon and release her. This need not go any further."

Charlee slid along the floor away from Assara, who inched the blade closer to Charlee's heart. "Look how your Guardian slithers away like the snake she is. She will pay for all your crimes against Mother." Gripping the sword with both hands, she raised it high. "Now, this ends."

CHAPTER 10

The Queen

T HE UNICORN DELIVERED one more kick of its hind legs against the barrier separating him from Charlee. Cracks formed like a spider web, then spread to the green wall blocking Penaiya and the Lataran warriors as if the barriers were connected by Theodora's magic. The sound of shattering glass echoed through the chamber.

Assara's sword hand shook. "Die, Guardian!" She swung her blade at Charlee's head.

"Not…today." Charlee brought her arms up, her hands grabbing Assara's. She grunted, tapping into her last bit of strength to save her own life. Her arm's shook and muscles burned. Assara pressed with all her body weight, driving the blade closer to Charlee's face.

"It's still just you and me, Guardian." Assara said through gritted teeth. "You can't last. You will lose."

Charlee bit her lip. She had to dig deeper and find the strength, but the sword inched closer and closer.

Crash. Swish. Thud. Assara screamed, an arrow piercing her shoulder. Her sword dropped from her hands as she rolled on her side, twisting in pain.

Charlee slowly turned her head toward the barrier, which blinked out of existence. There stood Penaiya, a massive bow in her hand. Charlee allowed herself a weak smile. Slowly, painfully, she lifted herself from the floor. Her body trembled, and she could only manage shallow breaths through her dried, cracked lips, but she stood. Her head was heavy, her shoulders rounded and legs ready to crumble, but she limped toward her rescuers. They'd given her a chance to stop Theodora, and one more chance was all she needed.

Penaiya lowered her weapon and raced toward Charlee. The Changeling did the same.

"Not yet, Guardian!" Assara gasped. Charlee turned back to the clone. Assara reached her feet and wildly swung her sword as if to cut Charlee in half.

A blue beam cut through the chamber, striking Assara in the chest. She flew back, slamming against the throne. A moan escaped her lips as smoke rose from her chest plate.

What the? Charlee glanced around. Where had that magical attack come from? Penaiya stared back through the chamber's open doors. So did the unicorn. So did every other Lataran.

A figure hidden underneath a black robe and hood crossed through the doorway. Silence spread through the chamber. The mysterious being seemed to float more than walk, drifting toward Charlee. Everyone backed away, save for Penaiya and the unicorn, who stood in the being's path.

Charlee didn't dare blink or give in to the sleep that beckoned to her. She had to see who this being was and know who wielded the magic that produced a blue beam. She'd only seen that magical color once before, and it was from…

"Show yourself, stranger." Penaiya pointed her sword at the dark figure. "You will not harm the Guardian."

"I am not here to hurt her." The stranger removed the hood. "I'm here—"

"Mom!" Charlee shouted. Tears she couldn't control slid from her eyes. Could it be? But how? Charlee stood tall and squared her shoulders. The sight of her mother filled her with new strength.

"Yes, baby." Charlee's mom smiled in the same comforting way she always did. Her blue eyes had the same loving sparkle. Her sandy blond hair framed her soft cheeks before unfurling over her shoulders.

Penaiya didn't lower her sword. She shook her head but didn't utter a word.

The unicorn didn't budge, either. He sniffed the air, the white feathers of his wings bristling and his ears twitching. He leaned his unicorn head forward and sniffed the stranger again. His tail rapidly swished back and forth. He allowed his head to rest on the woman's shoulder.

Any doubt Charlee had about whether this was real or not vanished. The Changeling knew Tira Smelton as well as anyone. He'd been sent to Earth to watch over her from the time she was baby.

Charlee stumbled forward. "Mom!"

Penaiya lowered her sword and stepped out of the way. Tira Smelton lunged forward, catching her daughter in her arms.

"I'm here, Charlee." She held her daughter tighter than she ever had before. The warmth of her mom's embrace surrounded Charlee, soothing her. Her body tingled. It was her mom's magic touch already starting to heal her.

"How, Mom?" Charlee rested her head on her mom's chest and listened to the comforting rhythm of her heart.

"Your sister, Charlee." Tira ran her fingers through her daughter's hair. "She's just like you."

From afar came another voice—a man's voice—her father's. "Hey, don't forget about us."

Charlee lifted her head. "Dad?" Her heart thudded wildly. Joseph Smelton walked through the chamber's doorway, Megan giggling in his arms. His same wire-framed glasses clung to his face. His slightly graying beard was long, as if it hadn't been trimmed for weeks. Megan's blond locks were longer, too. Her usually chubby face was thinner, as if her baby face appearance had begun the transformation into a little girl.

"Thank God, you're alive." Joseph crossed to his eldest daughter, joining in a hug that included the entire family. "I'm never letting you out of my sight again, little girl."

"I'm sorry, Dad." Charlee fought the urge to sob. She glanced from her mom to her dad. His eyes were red with tears. "I blew it. I let Theodora win. She's got my powers, and the medallion. I thought she was going to kill—"

"Stop, Charlee." Her dad gently touched her cheek. "You're a hero, Guardian. You saved us all. We'll stop Theodora. I promise you—together. But right now, we're reunited again, and that's all that matters." He kissed her forehead. She marveled at how he looked like a Lataran warrior in brown animal skin pants and a drawstring shirt that hugged his thin, lanky frame. It was so different from the tweed jacket he wore as a history professor back home.

"Such a touching moment." Assara crawled toward her sword. "But it doesn't change the fact that the Guardian dies today. You all will die. You'll see. Mother knows all. She will return and destroy you."

"No, child," Charlee's mom broke from the embrace with her daughter and strolled toward the clone.

Charlee, supported by her father's strong arms, shook her head. "Stay away from her, Mom."

Her mom didn't listen. She stopped by Assara's side. Assara tried to grab her sword, but Charlee's mom kicked it away.

"Mother, return to me now and show these treasonous pigs your power," Assara screamed. "Strike them down. Or give me the strength to strike them down to glorify you."

"Child, the being you think is your mother will not return to you." Charlee's mom spoke in the Lengoron language. "She's left you alone. This fight is over. There's no need for more blood to be shed."

Assara, the arrow still embedded in her shoulder, grimaced. "Who are you? What magic has brought you here?"

"My mother," Charlee answered. "She is the rightful Queen of Latara."

Charlee's mom extended a hand to Assara. "Stand down, child, and let me speak with you of peace."

Assara shook her head. "You dare call me a child. I am my mother's greatest general. I rule this world. I do not need my mother to return. I will kill you all."

"Young one, look around you." Charlee's mom pointed throughout the chamber to the Lataran warriors, to the Changeling, and to the dead Horeng.

"A cunning warrior recognizes when they are defeated, so that they might fight another day. I beg of you to stand down. No more harm will come to you. None of this is your fault. You have been misled by Theodora, just like so many before you." Tira Smelton spoke to Assara like a mother talking to her daughter. "If you allow me, I can help you to see the truth."

Charlee frowned. What was her mom saying? How could she treat Assara like a victim? "Mom—" Charlee began to ask.

Tira Smelton stopped her daughter. "Everyone deserves a chance at redemption, especially if they had the kind of start I fear this child has had."

"I do not need redemption. I need to kill you all." Assara scrambled to her feet. Charlee's mom raised her hands. An unseen magical force swept Assara's legs out from underneath her, and she crashed to the floor.

Charlee glared at her mom. "Kill her."

Her mom frowned in a motherly way. A few wrinkles shown on either side of her mouth. "No, we will try to save this poor creature."

"She killed…Cryton." Charlee's hands tightened into fists. She tried to break from her dad's embrace, but he held her tight. Her mom stood in silence. Her eyes reddened and her body trembled. Charlee cursed herself for blurting out Cryton's death. The old man had raised her mother. He was the closest thing to a father for her on Earth.

More tears slid down her mom's cheek. "We will do no harm to her; otherwise, we are as bad as Theodora. We will consider this child's fate later. Right now, sleep, child." She waved her hands over Assara's face. The clone's eyes immediately closed. She didn't move but air still passed through her lungs. Her chest gently rose and fell.

Turning back to her daughter, Tira scooped her back into her arms. "Oh, my poor daughter. I'm so sorry, so very sorry. I thought they'd killed you. I thought I'd never see you again."

Charlee's father and Megan once again joined in the hug. All cried without uttering another word until Megan giggled. Then they separated, though her mom still held her in a warming magical embrace. The tingling sensation coursed through Charlee's body. Blood rushed to her head, pushing away the desire for sleep. Her weary, broken body pulsated with new energy.

Her mom lifted a pouch from her robe. A knowing smile crossed her face. Her eyes were bright. "Charlee, drink a little of this. Just a few sips will help."

She placed the pouch to Charlee's mouth and tilted it until a cool liquid slid past Charlee's dried, cracked lips. A sweet fluid awakened her senses. She tasted orange, raspberry, apple, and watermelon all at the same time. *So…good. More… please…more.* With a strengthened arm, she tried to snatch the pouch away from her mother. She wanted to gulp it all.

Her mom shook her head. "No, just a little at a time. You haven't drunk anything in a while. Too much at once could do you damage. Besides, this is a special elixir. It will help with your healing, but you cannot have too much."

Charlee licked her lips. She grabbed her mom with one arm and motioned for her dad and Megan to again join in a hug.

"Tell me how?" Charlee rocked in her parents' arms. "How could Megan create a gateway? How could she find me?"

Her mom touched Megan's nose, and the little one squirmed. "Charlee, it shouldn't be possible for one so young to display the power of a Guardian, especially a child that is half human, like you. She must be very powerful." Tira's eyes shifted between her daughters. She drew a long breath.

"Somehow, she created the tiniest gateway," her mom continued, "and I used my magic to strengthen hers, to see if together we could generate a gateway that we could travel through."

She paused, taking both Megan's hand and Charlee's in her own. "I then mind-melded with her to show her the pathway to Janasara. I wasn't sure if you'd still be here, but we had to try. I can't believe it, but it worked, Charlee. Her gateway got us to the edge of the Kingdom. Once we arrived, I felt you right away. I knew where you were, and that you were in pain. We saw the battle, but I didn't think we'd reach you in time. Then, a young dragon found us. He brought us here, Charlee."

Charlee thought of the Dragon Lord's son. It had been him her mom was describing. She just knew it.

Her mom peered at Penaiya. "But your friends here...they'd already saved you. I am so grateful."

Charlee's mind raced. They'd all risked so much to save her. She stared at her sister. "Megan, you're my hero. Thank you."

Her mom slowly stood. She faced the Changeling and Penaiya. "I am Tira, daughter of Queen Assara. I was sent away long ago to save my life, and I am sorry I have not been here to stop your suffering. But now, I ask for your forgiveness, and I ask for a chance to meet our people, though I know I have no right."

CHAPTER 11

Long Live the Dragon Lord

SITTING ATOP THE Changeling, which maintained his winged unicorn form, Charlee rode through the gates of Latara to the smoldering battlefield. Her mother sat just behind her on the unicorn's back, an arm wrapped around her daughter to keep Charlee steady. Though stronger, she was too weak to ride on her own. Yet, she had to get to the Dragon Lord. *Please be alive. Please.*

The stench of death and burning flesh made her eyes water. Thousands of Horeng lay dead beyond the kingdom's gates, their bodies ravaged by dragon fire. Choking black smoke rose into the air, turning day into night. A somber darkness spread over the land. But high above, an emerald sun tried to slice through the blackness. Cracks formed in the gloom, allowing a few rays of sunlight to dot the landscape, like beacons of hope.

Trudging over the dead Horeng, Charlee fought off the sickness that rose from her stomach to her throat. Her head pounded. Her mom tried to convince her to remain in the castle, which stood strong despite the fallen tower, but she had to see the Dragon Lord. If alive, she had to try to save him. If dead…he couldn't be dead, he just couldn't.

The unicorn stopped, and Charlee peered ahead. There, beyond the corpses of the Horeng, lay the Dragon Lord. He didn't move. His son, Kraannaannn, stood over him, head lowered to his father's. An icy chill spread across her back.

Her mom tightened her grip around Charlee. She leaned in close, her lips near Charlee's cheek. "I sense he still lives, but—"

"We must hurry." She nudged the unicorn forward. Her dad and Megan, atop a wind horse, galloped behind them. Penaiya also joined them.

Reaching the Dragon Lord, Charlee gasped. She placed her hands to her mouth to keep from crying out. The great Dragon Lord, Sheorrriaaaan, lay broken along the ground, turned on his side, his shredded wings splayed out on either side of him. Smoke rose from a gaping hole in his chest. His blood spilled onto the valley floor, covering the weeds, dirt, and rocks in a thick green coating. His glowing eyes were closed. A handful of other dragons also lay in the fields—their lives sacrificed for hers.

Charlee turned to her mom, burying her head into her mom's chest. "This is all my fault. I did this."

"No, Charlee. Theodora did this. Remember that." Her mom held her close. "Go to him."

The unicorn lowered itself so Charlee could slide off. Her mom climbed down first, then, arms around Charlee's waste, helped her to the ground. Charlee gazed into her mom's blue eyes.

Her mom nodded. "It's okay."

But it wasn't okay. How could she ever repay the dragons or the Lataran warriors who died storming the castle? She would never be able to—except to never stop fighting Theodora until the witch was dead.

With heavy legs, she approached the massive dragon. His son raised his head to look upon her with green eyes, reddened by tears. More dragons landed just beyond them, watching her closely. Still others soared over head.

Kraannaannn bowed to her. Steam flowed from his snout, brushing against her cheek. "My father still lives, but he is weak. I fear his time grows short, but he had to know you were well. He wanted to speak with both of us before his time ends."

Charlee nodded and approached the Dragon Lord. "I'm here, Sheorrriaaaan, It's Charlee."

The Dragon Lord coughed, and a small flame escaped his snout. "Is that the Guardian's voice I hear?" His words were faint. Charlee drew closer. She reached out to touch him but withdrew her hand.

"It's me." She fought back tears. "You saved me, Sheorrriaaaan. I'm alive thanks to you. I'm just so sorry."

The Dragon Lord opened his eyes. The fire in them had dimmed. "This is not a sad occasion, young Guardian. This is a joyous time. Lataran and Dragon stood together today to forge a new beginning, and now we have two young leaders to guide a new generation to a time of peace." Sheorrriaaaan coughed and blood dripped from his snout. Still, he smiled and turned his head toward his son.

"Father, you cannot leave me." Kraannaannn crashed his tail against the ground. "This world needs you. There is more you must do."

"No, my son, my time passes as it should. You and the Guardian are this world's greatest hope. I know you both shall lead well."

Charlee shook her head. "Theodora is still out there…somewhere. She's still dangerous. We need you."

"You will find a way," the Dragon Lord answered. "Have faith in each other and those around you. Look to each other and to those who stand by you. I shall watch from afar with pride. Today my heart is full. Thank you."

Sheorrriaaaan gasped, then drew one long breath. His eyes grayed, then closed. In that moment his life ended.

Kraannaannn roared, and the other dragons joined him.

Charlee lowered her head, and the tears flowed uncontrollably. Her mother placed an arm around her shoulders. Her father patted her head. She owed the Dragon Lord so much. Her fists tightened. She would make sure Theodora paid. Somehow, she'd make her pay to honor the Dragon Lord, her teacher, Cryton, and all those who died along this journey.

When the dragon roars ended, Penaiya was the first to speak. She approached the son of the Dragon Lord. The young, winged beast withdrew, raising his long, graceful neck. His emerald eyes blinked like a scared child. His green scales rose and fell up and down his back.

"Your father was very brave, and today the people of Latara and all the Unified Kingdoms are in his debt and yours." Penaiya, her faced bloodied and clothes torn, with eyes as resolute as always, stopped just beneath the dragon. "I think I speak for all of us when I say we would very much like to forge a new beginning with the dragons in honor of your father and the others who sacrificed their lives today. And we will start by helping you to care for your dead."

Kraannaannn stood in silence, his gaze shifting between his father and the leader of the Latarans. With a sigh, he pushed out his chest. "Thank you for your kind words, but we dragons must tend to our dead in our own way." He paused, his eyes blinking rapidly. Then he spoke again. "I, too, look forward to a new time, but first I must rid this hate that fills my heart by stopping Empress Theodora before anyone else suffers from her evil. Where has the cowardice witch fled?"

"To Earth." Charlee leaned against her mom.

Charlee's mom's eyes widened. "Earth? When?"

"I don't know for sure," Charlee turned to her mom. "She used my powers to open a gateway. I was still in the dungeon. It could have been yesterday. It could have been days ago. I was scared she was going to come after you. She said she'd kill you."

Her mom and dad exchanged glances. Her dad spoke. "No, Charlee. We never saw her. But, if she went to Earth, we've got to get back there."

"Yes, we must move to save your world." Kraannaannn lowered to Charlee until his massive jaw was inches from her face.

She shook her head. "You need time to grieve. We'll handle—"

Kraannaannn slammed his tail into the earth. The ground shook, and Charlee nearly stumbled to her knees. "I will have my revenge, Guardian! I will fight until Theodora is no more. And it will be my honor to fight for your world as you have fought for ours."

Charlee swallowed back tears and nodded. "I understand."

Lifting his head skyward, Kraannaannn barked an order at his fellow dragons. They swooped down and gently lifted the Dragon Lord's body. With a massive thrust of their wings, they carried Sheorrriaaaan into the sky toward the mountains. Other dragons carried away the remaining dead.

Charlee watched the Dragon Lord slip from sight. She wished there was time to mourn. She had something to tell everyone that no one would believe, especially Kraannaannn, who now would have to learn to become the next Dragon Lord.

He and everyone would need to know the truth. There were two versions of Theodora—the evil Empress and the phantom who spoke so gently to her—the one imprisoned in some nowhere realm trapped in a forever sleep. How could she tell them? It was crazy. *But I must.* That other Theodora could be the key to killing the Empress.

§ § §

The battle had ended.

Standing on the throne room deck, Charlee gazed toward a smoky red horizon, the work of the dragons who mercilessly pursued what remained of the Horeng legions, decimating them in fire for the death of the Dragon Lord. The Horeng had fled the valley once they learned their young general had been captured and their Empress hadn't returned to lead them. Charlee's mom suggested leaving them in peace to try to rethink their lives. The Dragon Lord's son refused. He wanted revenge and ordered the dragons to consume the beast army in flames.

Charlee agreed. A slight smile crossed her lips. With one hand, she stroked her rose smelling hair, clean for the first time since…she couldn't remember when she last bathed before this day. To steady her legs, still far from full strength, she held onto the railing with her other hand hidden beneath the two-sizes too big satin white robe given to her by Penaiya.

She studied the mountains to the east burned under the scorching blaze left in the dragons' wake. Her smile faded. Is this what Cryton would want? He was a warrior who killed when necessary, but he didn't believe in slaughtering for the sake of revenge.

She closed her eyes. "I miss you, Cryton. I'm sorry I couldn't save you. I let that stupid clone kill you when it was me who should have died."

His smiling face flashed before her. Little crinkles formed on either side of his bright eyes. His white mustache curled up. He winked at her. *Remember, you are the Guardian. You still have so much life to live. So much to give. Do not grieve for me.* It was his voice echoing across her thoughts. Or was it her own thoughts? She stood tall and reached out to him. Opening her eyes, she was alone on the deck.

Her shoulders sunk. She leaned against the railing to keep from crumbling to the floor. "I will stop Theodora," she uttered. "I promise you, Cryton."

"What are you doing here?" Her mom approached from behind and placed an arm around her. "I thought I told you to stay in bed. Let my healing spell do its work."

Charlee let her body sink into her mom's arms. "I miss him so much. I'm sorry I—"

Her mom held her tight. "Charlee, you must stop blaming yourself for Cryton's death. He did what he thought he had to do. What he thought was right, just like you did."

Charlee pushed away from the embrace. Her mom's head tilted to one side, her long hair covering half of her face. A dark shadow surrounded the one visible eye. The lines around her mouth seemed deeper. "Mom, I should have listened to you. I should have never come. He'd still—"

Her mom's chin quivered as her chest convulsed under the dark, flowing robe. "If anyone is to blame, it's me. This was my fight. I should have faced Theodora long ago rather than hiding." She grabbed Charlee again and tugged her in close. "But we're together again, and we will fight together as a family when the time is right. First, you need to get back to bed. You have a lot more healing to do."

Charlee peered over the railing at the Kingdom of Latara and its people, saddened from burying their dead but already hard at work to reclaim their long-lost home. Strands of sunlight pierced the cloudy skies, tearing at the despair that still hung over the land. An emptiness spread through her stomach, not for lack of food, but the loss of so many lives, especially the loss of the Dragon Lord. It was like a weight pressing hard against her shoulders.

She pointed with a shaky finger at the people of Latara. "If they aren't going to rest, I can't either."

Her mom shook her head. "Charlee, I—"

"May I be so bold as to join you both?" Penaiya's voice came from the doorway into the chamber. Without waiting for a response, she strolled in, hands clasped in front of her. An unadorned blue gown clung loosely to her body from her neck down to the floor.

She stopped in front of Charlee's mom. "I never thought I would have the chance to see the daughter of my Queen, and yet here you stand before me." She placed her hands against Charlee's mom's cheeks. "I see her face—her strength, and her power—when I look in yours. This is a joyous day."

Penaiya then turned to Charlee, placing one hand on her shoulder. "When I look into your face, child, I see generations of your family—both Queens and Guardians. I would be proud to have you both take on the mantle of leading our people to a new beginning as mother and daughter—Queen and Princess…Queen and Guardian."

Charlee's mom lifted her hand to Penaiya's. "I wish I had a memory of my mother. Perhaps, you could teach me about her. There's so much I want to know, but Penaiya, you are the true leader of our—"

"Mom…Penaiya, you're talking like the war's over. It's not." Charlee struck the railing with a fist. "Theodora must be stopped. She could be back home right now doing horrible things."

Her mom shook her head. "I understand that, but you must finish healing."

"Agreed." Penaiya wiped her tears.

Charlee wrapped her arms around her body to fight off a chill rising from deep inside her gut. They had not broken Theodora's dark hold over the kingdom, despite the sun's best effort to cut through the darkness. Like a plague, her magical grip sickened the land. Would the grass and trees ever return? Would their people ever really recover? Would the Unified Kingdoms ever stand again?

Before the healing could begin, she'd have to do what she'd failed to do twice— kill Theodora and throw the source of her power, the medallion that granted her immortality, back into the swirling fire from which it had come.

She ran her fingers through her hair to shake out the last drops of water that remained after she bathed. She hadn't wanted to stop for a bath. No time for one, but her mom insisted—she said it would help. Maybe it had, but her head spun, making her dizzy. Thoughts of Theodora crashed like waves through her mind. Two versions of the sorceress, the evil Empress and the concerned phantom, fought for control of her thoughts.

She rubbed her temples. *Uh, would the real Theodora please step forward.* She had to know the truth, and that meant finding a way back to that nowhere land where the young Theodora lie encased in ice. First, she'd have to find a way to reclaim her Guardian powers, then convince the others to let her go.

"Mom, tell me again about Megan." She bit her lip to control her racing thoughts. *Try not to look desperate.*

Her mom sighed, taking Charlee's hands in her own. "Then will you rest?"

"Yes." That was a lie and probably a waste of time. Her mom was inside her head. Her gentle thoughts caressed Charlee, like fingers stroking her hair and urging her to be calm. Back home, Charlee hated this and saw it as an invasion. Right now, it was like a comforting blanket warming her on a cold winter morning.

If her mom knew she was lying, she showed no outer sign. Her faced remained soft—not rigid, like when she was angry. No frown crossed her lips, and her eyes showed no frustration—just hope Charlee would listen.

Releasing Charlee's hands, her mom leaned against the railing. "It turns out your sister has your ability. I don't know how she did it. I don't even know if it was an accident. But, when your father and I were at our lowest, with no way to reach you, your sister giggled, and a blue marble of energy formed in her hands."

Charlee, weary from standing so long, nearly dropped to the ground but caught herself on the railing. Both her mom and Penaiya reached for her, but Charlee waved them off. "I'm okay. I just can't believe it. I'm not the last Guardian. Well, I'm not a Guardian at all anymore without my power." She squeezed the railing until her knuckles turned white. "Mom, I must get my powers back. Maybe, Megan—"

"I know what you're thinking." Her mom placed her hands on Charlee's shoulder. She leaned in close until their eyes were only inches apart. "You want to see if Megan can somehow restart your powers like jump starting a car."

"Right!" Charlee grabbed her mom's arms.

Her mom shook her head. Lines crossed her forehead. "I don't know if such a thing is possible or even safe for either of you. What I do know is that Megan seems to have a capacity to absorb magic. That's how I was able to amplify her powers. But, to drain her magic...that scares me."

Charlee turned away. "It scares me, too, but we must stop Theodora, and I don't see any other way. Now Megan's in danger. Theodora will come after her just like she did with me. I can't let her do that. I must stop her." Charlee's body tensed. "And we don't have any more time. We must get back to Earth. Sandra... everyone...who knows what that witch has done to them."

Her mom grabbed Charlee by the shoulder and swung her around. "You're right. I know you're right. It's just that I have you back and right here, right now, you and Megan are safe, and I want to keep it that way. I almost lost you, Charlee. I can't face that again."

Charlee hugged her. "Mom, this isn't over. None of us will ever be safe so long as Theodora lives. I must get my powers back. I promise I won't let Megan be hurt. I'll stop if I see her having a hard time." Did she mean that or was she being selfish, driven by a desire for revenge and a desire to hold the medallion again? No! She had to stop Theodora, and the only way was to get her powers back. Besides, it seemed even at such a young age, Megan had strong magic. Maybe she was the last true Guardian.

Her mom nodded. For the first time, her cheeks looked drawn and her eyes tired. "Let's get your powers back."

Penaiya cleared her throat and offered a slight smile. "Charlee, you are wrong about one thing."

"What?" Charlee asked.

Penaiya leaned in closer. "You are a Guardian, the strongest Guardian, with or without magic."

Charlee shook her head. If only Penaiya's words were true. Another thought flashed through her mind. Images of a young, handsome warrior she'd fought alongside when trying to lead the Latarans to the Realm of the Dragons. He hadn't been there in the throne room when she was saved. Did that mean...a sudden wave of panic made her heart flutter.

"Penaiya, where is Aryean?" Charlee asked. "He's not..."

Penaiya's graying eyebrows cinched together. "He lives, Guardian, but he was badly injured in the assault on the castle. He—"

"I must see him!" Charlee grasped the older woman's shoulder.

"I'm not sure—"

"Please!" Her heart pounded wildly for the young man. For the moment Earth could wait. She had to see him.

CHAPTER 12

Take the Battle to Earth

CHARLEE LEANED OVER and gently raked her fingers through Aryean's dark, curly hair. A tingling spread from her hand through her body, like a jolt of electricity. She lifted her hand away. Her eyes burned with fresh tears. Aryean, the young warrior who fought by her side during every battle since she arrived in this world, didn't stir.

He lay unconscious in bed, his head and half his face covered by bandages. Dried blood blotted the wrap around his forehead. His bare chest, muscular and strong, rhythmically rose and fell with each breath. Sunlight spilled in through a window but stopped short of the bed as if to not disturb his rest.

Penaiya crossed the room to his bed. Her head tilted slightly, and she placed a hand over his heart. A smile crossed her lips. "Good steady beat. He's a strong young man."

Charlee kept her eyes on the warrior. "Will he be all right?"

Penaiya's smile faded. She lowered her eyes. "Time will tell. He's strong and wants to live, if not for himself, then…"

Charlee gazed at Penaiya. Why hadn't she finished that thought? She decided not to ask. "What happened to him? How could he be hurt by anything?"

"He's a powerful warrior, but he's just a man." Penaiya dipped a rag in a bowl of water and placed it over his forehead. "He led the storming of the castle and fought bravely to reach you, Guardian. But when another injured warrior was about to fall under the axe of a Horeng, Aryean threw himself in the way. The blade caught him in the forehead…the face. Guardian, he lost an eye. He has been unconscious ever since."

Lowering to her knees, Charlee swept up Aryean's rough hand in her own and held it to her forehead. "He'll be okay! He must be!"

Penaiya nodded. "I sought out your mother's healing powers to help. She has been watching over him. He has a good chance, but his wound is deep. It will take time."

Charlee squeezed his hand. "Mom's powers will save him. I just know —"

Aryean's inhaled deeply. His remaining eye fluttered, then opened. He stared blankly for a moment, blinked, then focused on her. Charlee's heart did somersaults. She kissed his hand. Even Penaiya's mouth dropped open.

He smiled weakly. "Guardian. Sorry...not...there...for...you."

She touched his cheek. Warmth radiated through her body. "You were there. You saved me."

A tear slid down Aryean's cheek. "Never...leave...you...again. Fight... for...you." His eye dimmed, then closed.

"Aryean...Aryean!" She threw her arms around him.

Penaiya placed her fingers against his neck. "Guardian, take ease. He has just fallen back into unconsciousness. He needs time to heal. But the power of his emotions awoke him...only for you."

Slowly rising from his side, Charlee carefully lowered Aryean's arm to the bed. "Penaiya, please take care of him. When he wakes up, tell him...tell him I'm grateful for everything he's done to stand by my side ever since I arrived in this world. Tell him thank you for believing in me. And tell him I hope to see him again."

"It shall be done, Guardian." Penaiya bowed to her.

Bending down, Charlee kissed his forehead then slowly retreated from his chamber. Would she ever see him again? The thought thickened her throat, making it hard to breathe. She walked heavily through the bleak hallway of the castle littered with chunks of stone from walls damaged by the assault to free her. She shivered against the chill of the castle—or maybe it was because of the swirling emotions poking at her like tiny needles. Whatever the reason, she tensed her muscles and focused her thoughts. She had to speak with her parents and tell them about the apparition of Theodora. How could they believe two versions of the sorceress existed? She wasn't sure she even believed it.

§ § §

She stood before her mom, dad, Penaiya, Kraannaannn, and the Changeling in Castle Latara's courtyard. The sprawling grounds were the only space large enough to fit a dragon inside the castle's walls. The day's last light started to fade. A cool breeze swept her flowing purple robe, revealing the gray tunic she wore underneath and the sword at her side. She closed her eyes and lifted her head to capture the brisk air against her face. It reminded her of the chilly morning air that drifted on shore from the Bay back home.

Her stomach ached. She'd spew if she gave in to the sensation rising in her throat, but she couldn't. She asked for this gathering. For two days since the battle, she'd held off telling them her secret, but she couldn't anymore.

Her mom, still wrapped in a black robe, spoke first. "Charlee, you are so pale. You still need your rest."

"Mom, there's no more time." Charlee's eyes shot open. After two days of healing magic, her voice surged from her mouth, strong and clear. "Theodora's out there. She took my powers with the medallion and opened a gateway to Earth. Who knows what she's doing there? Who knows who she's hurting? We must stop her."

An image of her best friend invaded her thoughts. Her voice quivered. Theodora had taken Sandra once before and used her DNA to create the clone, Assara. What would the witch do to her now? Charlee had to get back to Earth, but first...

She took a long breath. "There's something I must tell all of you. It's hard because you'll think I've lost it."

"What is it, Charlee?" her dad shifted his wire-rimmed glasses up higher on his long, thin nose. "You can tell us anything."

Her glance shifted to each standing in the courtyard. Penaiya, stoic as ever, interlaced her fingers under her chin. Her mom gently rocked Megan in her arms. Kraannaannn tilted his spiked head to one side and lowered closer to her. How would they take what she had to say? Could they believe her?

"I...I'm not sure the sorceress we're fighting is really Theodora at all." She paused for a reaction. Silence greeted her, so she continued. "I think the real Theodora may be frozen in time, you know, kind of like suspended animation."

Her little sister Megan, tucked in their mom's arms, sneezed. The others glanced back and forth at each other. The Dragon Lord's son snorted. White smoke poured from his nose, dousing her in a warm mist.

"I know how it must sound, but the Theodora who has caused so much pain to all of us may be a clone." She started to pace. "Somehow, the dark medallion magically created her, just like Assara is a clone of my friend, Sandra. I don't know how or why, but you've seen Assara. You know she's an exact copy of Sandra, so it's possible—right?"

Penaiya raised a graying eyebrow. "Guardian, your words are strange. I have never seen or heard of magic being used in such a way. Even if it was possible, how have you come to this knowledge?"

Charlee stopped pacing in front of Penaiya. "Theodora told me."

"Honey, what do you mean?" her mom asked.

"Before I lost my powers, I accidentally opened a portal to, I don't know, some strange dimension—that's the only way I can describe it. I found her trapped in a block of ice. I thought she was dead, but then her eyes opened for just a moment. At least, I think they opened—I'm not so sure."

Penaiya shook her head but did not speak.

"There's more." Charlee inched closer to Penaiya. "When I was in the dungeon, a young version of Theodora came to me, like a ghost or a vision or something. She comforted me and tried to give me hope. Twice I saw her, and on the second time she told me I needed to free her and together we could destroy the medallion and stop the fake Theodora."

Kraannaannn huffed and reared his head back. "Guardian, I cannot speak to what you think you saw while in a portal, but could your experience in the dungeon be nothing more than an illusion? Or worse. Theodora is a trickster. She could be twisting your mind."

"I don't think so." Charlee approached the dragon, matching his intense stare. "It was real. I'm not crazy. You must believe me."

"I do believe you." Her mom joined her by the dragon with Megan pressed tightly to her chest.

"You cannot—" Penaiya started to say, but Charlee's mom raised a hand to silence her.

"Charlee, I believe you saw something, but I agree with Kraannaannn." Her mom rubbed Megan's back. "Theodora is playing with your mind for some evil purpose. You, more than anyone else here, knows what it is to have her in your thoughts, and how she can try to confuse and manipulate."

"I know, Mom, but this is different."

"How can you be so sure?" Her father gripped the handle of the sword at his side. His thinning hair danced in the breeze.

"That's the thing, Dad." Charlee turned toward him. "I'm not sure of anything. It's just a feeling I have that this isn't Theodora just messing with my head. I know what that feels like, and this is…different."

"Guardian, what are you proposing?" Kraannaannn again lowered his head until his snout was just a few feet away from her and her mom. Megan, still in her mom's arms, showed no fear of the beast. She reached out to touch his snout.

"I have to try to find her and free her." Charlee lowered her gaze to the black boots she wore. She knew what the response would be, but her body still clenched.

"No." Her dad raised his voice.

"It's too dangerous," Kraannaannn roared.

"This is foolishness," Penaiya scoffed.

"No, she's right." Charlee's mom placed a hand on Charlee's shoulder.

"But—" Charlee's dad began.

"She deserves a chance to investigate her belief," her mom interrupted. "She has earned that right and our faith in her."

"The Guardian has lost her abilities," Kraannaannn reminded everyone. "How would such a journey even be possible?"

"Yes," Penaiya folded her arms. "Would you risk your other daughter who right now appears to be the only one with the power to open a gateway?"

Charlee patted Megan on the head. "You're right, Penaiya. I'm not willing to risk her life. I wish she didn't have this power, because now no matter what she's in danger. That witch Theodora will come for her now, just like she did with me. That's why I must do this—it may be the only way to stop her. But maybe there's a way I can borrow some of Megan's magic with the help of the Changeling."

She approached the Changeling, still in the form of a unicorn, who, like always, remained silent but vigilant. "What do you say? Can you do this? Can you tap into my sister's power and transfer some of it to me?"

The Changeling responded by nudging her gently with his snout.

Charlee smiled. "I'll take that as a yes."

She whirled back toward her mom. "Are you okay with this?"

"I guess I have to be." Her mom kissed Megan's head. The little girl nestled her head against her shoulder. "But if this is possible and you make this journey, you are not going alone."

Charlee patted the unicorn's neck. "I know. The Changeling will be with me."

"Not just the unicorn." Her mom's face tightened. "I'm not going to let you out of my sight ever again."

§ § §

Charlee held her sister close to her chest. Megan played with a strand of Charlee's hair, a wide smile on her face. Her crystal blue eyes, the same color as Theodora's, burned bright, like tiny beacons inside the shadowy throne room. She quietly hummed some melody, probably a tune from a cartoon she watched.

The time had come to attempt a transfer of Megan's Guardian abilities to Charlee. At her age, could Megan understand the great power she had? Charlee kissed her sister on the cheek, and Megan wiped her face. This little girl, who seemed so oblivious to the danger around her, would someday be a Guardian and maybe even Queen. It was Megan who somehow opened a gateway so that their parents could cross over to this world. Even though still so young, she had been able to tap into her abilities and save them all. How was it possible? How strong would she become? *Stronger than me. She will make a great Queen, better than I ever could.* Charlee kissed her sister on the cheek again, and for a second time Megan wiped the kiss away.

Charlee crossed to the Changeling, now transformed into the shape she liked best—the old white bike—balancing on two wheels by the balcony. "You're sure this won't hurt her?"

The magical being didn't answer. Instead, it emitted a pulsating glow. Its body popped, like kernels in a microwave. The bike frame folded in on itself. Charlee backed away. The Changeling was morphing again, but into what? With a blast of blinding light, the bike disappeared, and in its place, floating before her, was a golden amoeba the size of a beanbag chair. Her protector's natural form.

Nearly translucent, radiating a soft glimmer within its globular form, the Changeling hovered close to her and her sister.

Charlee studied her protector. She'd seen the Changeling in its natural state only once before—when injured by fire spewed by Theodora's evil dragon. She took a deep breath. "So, this is really you? Well, I'll take this as your answer to my question. This isn't going to harm Megan."

The Changeling's body vibrated. His glow brightened.

Standing on the marble steps to the throne, her parents huddled together in an embrace. Penaiya stood near them, her fingers interlocked under her chin. Charlee nodded to her parents. Her mother smiled briefly, but her expression quickly shifted to a frown while her dad offered a wink.

Charlee squeezed her sister gently. Megan's heart thudded softly. Such a contrast to Charlee's pounding beat. Was she doing the right thing, or did she just miss her magic? *No, I must do this to save everyone.* But there was more to it. She couldn't shake an ache in the pit of her stomach—an emptiness inside that couldn't be filled. She wanted her powers back, needed them back. And then there was her desire for the medallion. *Wait…what?* Like an itch she could never scratch, part of her longed to have it back, the part willing to risk Megan's life right now. *No! That's not it. This is the only way.* She took a deep breath and tried to quiet her thoughts.

"Let's do this." She reached for the Changeling with one hand. The other grasped her sister.

Chanting rose from the throne. Charlee's gaze shifted to her mom who offered a healing incantation. Was it for Charlee, her sister, or both?

The glowing creature extended a tentacle toward her, engulfing her hand. A slimy goo spread along her arm. Then a tingling sensation snaked through her body. A second tentacle from the Changeling attached to Megan's arm. The young one immediately fussed, trying to free herself. She screamed and cried.

Charlee fought the urge to pull her away and stop this, but she had to trust in her protector. He wasn't capable of harming anyone in her family. If this transfer of power endangered her sister, the Changeling would stop.

A circle of shimmering light pulsated from the glowing amoeba. The illuminance crested just over her head and splashed down on top of her and Megan. Charlee closed her eyes and shielded Megan with her chest. Her body shook violently. A painful shock wave of energy burned her insides.

She screamed, or was it Megan? *I must stop this!* Except…her arms strengthened as her legs hardened. The numbing emptiness in her gut gave way to flaming embers coursing through her veins. Her body no longer felt like a rag doll held up by strings. It was working. But Megan…

Light spilling in through her closed eyelids faded, and Charlee blinked. The

Changeling released them and hovered a few feet away. Megan's face, normally rosy, looked pale. *Oh no, did I take too much of her magic? Please, Megan, be*—before she finished that thought, the color returned to Megan's cheeks, and her little sister smiled.

"Are you both all right?" Charlee's father swooped in, placing his hands on both of their heads. His brow wrinkled, and his chest rose and fell rapidly as his hands trembled, rattling Charlee's forehead.

"I think so." Charlee gazed at Megan. Though her little sister's eyes were red and puffy, the young one giggled and reached for her older sister's nose. She seemed okay.

"Did it work?" Penaiya asked.

Charlee didn't answer at first. *Could it have worked?* She handed Megan to her dad and backed away from them. Stretching her body, she stood taller. Studying her hands, she opened and closed her fingers. Tiny sparks of energy danced across her fingertips, tingling her skin—just for a moment before they disappeared. *What the hell was that?* Little tremors rushed through her body and then ceased. She wrapped her arms around her waist. For the first time since Theodora used the medallion to rip away her magic, her skin no longer simply clung to an empty vessel. *I feel…whole.*

Her mom slowly approached, her hands outstretched and eyes wide. "Charlee?"

"I…feel…better." Charlee retreated farther from the others, motioning her mom to stop. "But let's see."

Taking a deep breath, she placed her hands in front of her as if pushing against a door. Feet braced against the floor and stomach tightened, she strained to open a portal. A grunt escaped her lips. Charlee pushed harder. Her arms shook, her legs quivered, and sweat dripped from her forehead. *Come on, make it happen. You must.* Her head started to throb as her eyes squeezed shut. *Just a little blue bubble—that's all I want to see.*

"Charlee," her mom gasped. "Look."

Her eyes opened. In front of her was a glimmering blue gateway the size of a door. Stormy clouds swirled inside the portal, like a vortex. Faint voices cried out to her from inside the maelstrom. *Help us. Save us. Why have you not come?* Charlee backed away until she reached the edge of the balcony.

"Charlee, what is it?" her dad asked.

She remained silent, but the voices continued. *Why have you abandoned us?*

"Baby, snap out of it." Her dad placed his hands on her face. "Look at me, Charlee. You're safe from whatever's in there. Close the portal."

Charlee stared into her dad's eyes. Fear clawed at her like a crazed animal. "They need me. They're calling to me. I must go to them."

"Who, baby?" Her dad leaned in closer.

She peered back at the portal, mouth wide open, cheeks trembling. "Everyone on Earth."

CHAPTER 13

The Lost Princess

AN INVISIBLE ROPE wrapped around Charlee's waste, tugging her toward the swirling blue maelstrom. She inched closer to the opening. Images played before her, like a movie. People, hands outstretched, eyes rolled back into their heads, wandered aimlessly along some city street. They lumbered like zombies, some moaning, others crying. They slid past abandoned cars with broken windshields, glass shattered over the pavement. Blood and oil mixed together at their feet.

One woman, face bloodied, walking with a child in her arms, stopped. Her vacant gaze focused on Charlee as if she could see her through the portal. The woman's mouth dropped open. Her head, hair matted to one side of her face, tilted. "Guardian, you did this. You didn't save us. You left us alone. Why?"

Charlee gave into the unseen force pulling at her. "I'm sorry. I'm coming now. I promise. I'll save you."

She reached for the portal. *I must get to them.* She wouldn't leave Earth to suffer. *Must. Go. Now.* She lunged for the portal.

Arms wrapped around her, pulling her back. Voices called to her, garbled as if she were under water.

"Charlee, close the portal!" someone shouted.

"What are you doing?" another cried.

The arms grasping Charlee wrenched her away from the glowing doorway. She thrashed her arms and legs. *Let me go! I have to save them all!*

Whoever held her lifted her from the ground, then carried her to a far wall. "Let me go!" Charlee reached for the portal.

"No, Charlee!" Her dad pressed her against the wall, sliding his hands to her shoulders. He shook his head. Why couldn't he understand she had to get to Earth?

He reached for her face with both hands. His palms pressed lightly against her cheeks. "Charlee, close the portal...now!" His words cut through the confusion.

"No. I have to go." She tried to gaze beyond him. His grip tightened.

"Focus on me, Charlee." He pressed his forehead against hers. "Focus on my words. We will go home, but together when we are ready. Not this way. Not Theodora's way. Think like the warrior you are."

She locked eyes with her dad, but Cryton's kind face flashed through her mind. The old man had said almost the exact same thing to her. It seemed so long ago now. But he was right then, and her dad was right now. She had to break from whatever magical force compelled her to enter the portal. Closing her eyes, she envisioned the portal shrinking to a marble, then popping out of existence. Her dazed thoughts cleared, and she slowly opened her eyes.

Her father pulled her close in a heavy embrace. "You did it, Charlee. It's going to be all right."

Taking a deep breath, she gently nudged him back. "No, it's not. Theodora's destroying our world. I saw it."

Her mom, face gaunt and colorless, placed Megan in Penaiya's arms and crossed to her. "Charlee, it was a trap."

Charlee's head throbbed. She rubbed her temples with both hands, her lips parted in a painful grimace. "I saw people in pain."

Her mom drew near and kissed her forehead. The warmth of her lips should have been comforting, but it wasn't. "It was Theodora. She was making you see things that weren't there."

"No, it's real, Mom." Charlee blinked her eyes. The images of zombie-like men and women wandering the streets lingered. "Everyone's in danger. And what about Sandra? I can't let her be hurt again."

"You'll go to her in time." Her mom raised an eyebrow. Her cheeks tightened.

"Mom—"

"Charlee Smelton, have faith in us." Her dad placed an arm around her shoulder. "We will not leave Earth to Theodora."

Charlee shifted her gaze between her mom and dad. Dropping to her knees, she buried her face in her hands and couldn't stop the tears from falling. How could she stop so much suffering?

"I know how you feel, Charlee." Her mom lowered to her and lifted her chin with a single finger. "Believe me. I know the constant pain of feeling like you are failing the ones you care for. When the time is right, we'll return to Earth, and if Theodora is there, we'll stop her. But right now, you need to follow through with your plans to uncover the truth of what we're facing. If you're right and my real aunt Theodora is out there somewhere in need of rescue, we need to find her and save her. She may be the key to breaking the medallion's dark magic and bringing peace to Janasara and Earth."

"Look," Charlee's dad beckoned. "Look at Megan."

Her little sister held her hands out as if she offered a piece of candy or a toy to Charlee. A glowing blue marble danced in her palms.

Charlee wiped her tears. Her sister still had her Guardian powers. The Changeling's mysterious powers had returned Charlee's abilities without harming her sister. Maybe the Smelton sisters together could stand against the medallion and the evil sorceress who wielded it. Or maybe the truth was Megan's abilities now placed her in greater danger than anyone else.

Charlee's hands tightened into fists. She wouldn't let Theodora hurt Megan ever. *I'm going to kill that witch.*

Her mom was right, though. First, secrets had to be unlocked. That meant opening another portal and finding the real Theodora.

§ § §

The gateway stood before her, like the entrance to a swirling blue tunnel that led to some unseen abyss. Her body trembled slightly as sweat dripped from her brow. Her muscles ached from the effort of willing the portal open, but the emptiness inside was gone. Her heart beat stronger, and her lungs breathed deeper. It was as if her soul had returned, but that was a scary thought—as if she could no longer be Charlee without her powers. What did that say about her? Who was she becoming? She forced such thoughts away. Now was not the time. She concentrated on the portal, her mom to her right an arm's length away and the Changeling, still in the form of a unicorn, to her left.

An hour passed since her first attempt at opening a gateway with her renewed abilities. The voices she heard still filled her thoughts. She buried the sadness deep within her gut, a soft chronic pain she'd live with for now.

Would this gateway lead to the nowhere land where she had found the sleeping Theodora before? She gulped a load of saliva. *I hope.*

Charlee moistened her dry lips. She rubbed her fingers against sweaty palms. Moments before she opened the gateway, an image of that magical plain, which seemed to exist between worlds, pricked at her mind, like tiny pinholes. Soon, a clear picture eclipsed all other thoughts. A sprawling desert landscape with sand dunes the size of giant waves underneath a purple sky. Planets swarmed like paintings across an endless canvas so close she could touch them. Her adrenaline spiked, leaving her breathless. She locked on the image. If her Guardian powers worked right, that should be enough of a road map to get them there safely.

But who planted the image? It had to be the trapped Theodora. Who else? *She's reaching out to me, guiding me to her. I can feel it!*

Charlee reached for her mom. "Are you ready?'

Her mom nodded and gripped Charlee's hand. Together with the Changeling, they strolled into the glowing blue portal...and the voices returned.

Help us, Guardian. Why have you not come for us? We're suffering.

The hair on the back of her neck stiffened. She tilted her head side to side. "Get out of my mind, witch."

Theodora's shrill laughter replaced the voices.

Charlee glanced at her mom's hand in her own. The fingers stretched unnaturally, becoming thin and wrinkled. Charlee's gaze bounced to her mom's face. Gone was her long, blond hair, replaced by a wild mane of white locks flapping around her face. Her eyes glowed red, and a sinister smile spread high on gray, wrinkled cheeks. *Theodora!*

"I know what you're doing, Guardian." The Empress squeezed her hand and winked. "I've been watching you the whole time. I know your every move. Come to me if you dare. But don't wait too long, or everyone in this magicless world of yours will die. I only wish I hadn't arrived too late to kill your parents first, but I will soon right that error. My delay to your insignificant planet was worth it. I have discovered another world — ripe with magic — that I will consume, and I will drain what little resources Earth has to achieve that end. I will soon be a God, untouchable by the likes of you or anyone else. But, by all means, try to stop me. I will crush you, but not before I destroy all that you care about."

Charlee ripped her hand away and cupped her eyes. "It's not real. Get out of my head, witch!"

"Do you think your little discovery will make a difference?" Theodora spoke slowly as if each word was a dagger aimed at Charlee' heart. "You cannot kill a God."

Charlee squared her shoulders. "I've got my powers back, Theodora, and I'm coming for you. We stopped your daughter, destroyed your army, and took back Janasara."

"Child, do you think I have not foreseen all of this?" Theodora clapped her hands together in an exaggerated motion. Her lips twisted in an ugly grin. "I have so many more worlds to conquer."

"Theodora!" Charlee screamed, but the witch disappeared. Her mom once again stood beside her inside the portal along with the Changeling.

Charlee clenched her teeth, forcing away any thought of the evil Theodora. At that moment, they all emerged from the portal, the glowing tunnel slowly closing and popping out of existence behind them.

They arrived in the nowhere land — at least it looked like the same magical landscape she remembered when she last found the young Theodora trapped in a block of ice. Charlee's eyes widened. A sense of light-headedness made her stumble against the unicorn. She clung to the beast's neck as she peered in each direction.

A deep purple haze hung over the land. Flowing white sand stretched to the horizon where it seemed to touch a field of planets, some just peeking above the horizon and others climbing higher into the heavens.

Her mom stood still, her body rigid and her mouth slack. "What is this place?"

Charlee shook her head. "I don't know, but this is where I found her. I'm sure of it."

Crossing to Charlee, her mom placed a hand on her shoulder. "Charlee, are you all right? You look...shaken."

"Mom, Theodora came to me while we were inside the gateway."

Her mom frowned. "Which Theodora?"

"The one we're fighting." Charlee swept strands of hair from her face. "She said she's watching us. She knows we're going after the real Theodora, and she doesn't care. She knows we beat her army and...her daughter...and she said she'd foreseen it all. She's waiting for us to return to Earth to kills us. Mom, with that medallion, she's unstoppable."

Her mom embraced her. "I'm so sorry I let Theodora get into your head when it should have been me she was challenging. But the fact is that you and she have a connection, and she is not letting go. Right now, she's just trying to warp your mind and stop you. She knows you can defeat her, and she's scared. I don't know what we'll find when we return home, but whatever it is, together we'll fix it and stop her by destroying that medallion."

"Mom—"

"Come on, Guardian, lead the way." Her mom spoke in a steady, low-pitched voice. Hands formed fists at her waist. "I am ready to follow you anywhere."

Charlee nodded and offered a watery smile that quickly faded. Kneeling, she touched the sand. The silky grains ran through her fingers, like she remembered—fluid, yet not wet. She scanned their surroundings. Nothing but sand spread in every direction. An eerie silence filled this land. Even the air remained still. How would they find a young frozen Theodora buried underneath all this white barren emptiness?

Charlee threw up her hands. "All right, Theodora, I'm here, like you told me. Now help me find you, otherwise I'll go find a way to stop that other Theodora on my own."

More silence greeted her.

She turned to her mom and shrugged. Then, a low rumble broke the silence. It grew louder, like an approaching storm. *What the hell?* Charlee wrapped her arms around the unicorn's neck. What was happening?

Mounds of sand slid away and separated as if massive unseen hands dug a trench, creating a trail for her to follow. The trembling stopped. Rumbling gave way to a soft moan, then nothing. The land quieted.

Charlee gazed at her companions. "I think a path has been set for us to follow. I'd say we see where it leads."

Her mom placed her robe's dark hood over her head. "Yes, but we should proceed with caution and be prepared to turn back if anything goes wrong."

Charlee nodded, but her mom was only half right. There was no turning back...not when they were so close.

CHAPTER 14

The Woman in the Ice

MORE SAND GAVE way, carving a trail that bent and curved, hiding corners where anything evil could attack. Still, Charlee had to follow—had to see this through to the end. She glanced back. Her mom and the Changeling followed close behind. Those were two of the most powerful beings she knew. If this were a trap, at least they'd have a fighting chance with their combined magic.

With tiny steps, she maneuvered along the path, her pulse picking up with each step. The trail curved one more time, then stopped. Charlee crouched and peeked around the bend. A block of ice, still half buried, protruded from a wall of sand that marked the trail's end. Someone lay inside. A chill spread up her back, but she tried to ignore it. Standing, slightly hunched, she crept toward the discovery.

She reached the ice and bent down on one knee a sword blade's distance away. Her mom and the Changeling soon reached her side.

"It's her," Charlee whispered. "It's Theodora."

The ice divulged the face of a young woman. Charlee inched closer to the frozen prison. The woman inside had long golden hair surrounding pale cheeks and a long thin neck, just like the first time Charlee saw Theodora in a dream. She had seen the sorceress floating in a stream with the same flowing golden locks and pale skin. The Theodora in her dreams had been a trick—a magic creation of the dark medallion. This imprisoned young woman had to be the real Theodora. A flicker of hope burned inside her chest.

"How can you be sure?" Charlee's mom furrowed her eyebrows.

"I just am." Charlee studied her mom. What must be going through her mind? She was facing her aunt, the woman who killed her mother...or not...if this was a different Theodora.

"But how do we free her?" Her mom removed her dark hood. She slid finger-nails over the ice. "How do we bring her back from whatever spell she's under. I don't know if my magic is strong enough to revive her."

"We can do it." Charlee placed a hand over her mom's. "We have to try."

The unicorn nudged Charlee's back. She turned to her protector. "What is it?" His black eyes focused on her, and he nudged her a second time. His neck muscles twitched, and his tail stood at attention. A snort rose from his nostrils.

What was the Changeling trying to tell her? She reached back and stroked his snout. "What—"

A wave of energy invaded her body, like a lightning bolt surging through her limbs. Her veins protruded through her skin. Muscles weary from opening the gateway vibrated with new strength. A hum rose from her expanding chest. She flexed her arms and opened and closed her fists. Every muscle in her body tightened. She breathed deeply. Adrenaline sparked hyper alertness. Not only did her own heart echo in her ears, so did her mom's. Maybe she could punch through the ice.

Charlee squeezed her fists.

"What are you doing?" Her mom took a step back. Could she sense Charlee's newfound power?

"This." She raised her closed hands high and smashed them down against the ice, like hammers. The collision rattled her body. A stinging shock wave rose from her wrists, spreading through her arms into her shoulders, neck, and head. The ice did not budge.

"You can't break this block of—"

Charlee struck the ice a second, third, and fourth time. Shards of ice broke off—small pieces at first, then larger chunks. Blood dripped from the ice. She peered at her fists. Her own blood dripped from her shredded skin.

"Charlee, your hands." Her mom reached for her.

"I'm okay, Mom." The words barely reached a whisper. Her lungs burned from the effort, but she offered her mom a crisp nod.

A crack sounded from somewhere deep inside the block. The ice splintered into a maze of cracked lines, like a glass door struck by a rock. Breathless, Charlee smiled at her mom and continued her assault, driving her bloody fists into the ice.

Her hands and arms ached, but she couldn't stop.

Her energy surge fading, muscles turning to mush, she raised a fist over her head for one final blow. Grunting, she drove her hand into the block, and the ice gave way with a crunch. From the maze of cracks, a larger rift formed from the top of the ice block to the bottom, and it split in two with a thunderous explosion that echoed across the land.

The young woman inside was freed. Her rigid body slid from the ice. Charlee caught her before she fell into the sand, but Charlee's legs failed her. Together, they slumped to the ground. Charlee inhaled, holding her breath deep in her throat. Her tired muscles tensed. She glared at the young woman's blue face. Black circles surrounded closed eyes. Her lips were permanently parted in a silent scream.

"She's so cold, and I can't tell if she's breathing." Charlee tugged the young woman onto her lap. Some of Charlee's blood dripped onto the frozen woman's white dress, staining the sleeves.

Her mom knelt and touched the woman's forehead and chest. "She lives, barely, but she remains under a spell. I can't break it on my own. It will take the three of us—you, me, and the Changeling—to combine our powers if we are to have any hope, but even then, I'm not sure."

"I'll do anything, Mom. Just tell me what to do." Charlee's hands throbbed, but the skin had already started to repair itself. The blood disappeared. It must be that the Changeling's energy still coursed through her, helping her heal.

Charlee brushed strands of damp hair away from the young woman's sunken cheeks. She had Theodora's face. What had happened to her? How did she end up like this? They had to find a way to revive her. If she truly was Theodora, she could hold the secret to stop the sorceress who now went by her name.

"I will use my healing powers to try to awaken her." Charlee's mom placed her palms together as if in prayer. She slowly inhaled and exhaled. "But I will need to channel your power and the Changeling's, so touch him with one hand and take hold of mine with the other. No matter what happens, do not let go. This is going to hurt."

Charlee slowly nodded. A slight lump formed in her throat. She reached for her mom's hand, but her mom recoiled.

"What is it, Mom?"

"I don't know." Her mom closed her eyes and released a long breath. "I feel like I'm looking into the face of evil. This is the face of the woman who killed my parents and forced them to send me away from the world of my birth. At the same time, I'm looking into the face of a part of my family. I just don't know if we're doing the right thing."

Charlee grasped her hand. "We must do this."

Her mom blinked, and her normally bright eyes dulled. A sheen of sweat formed across her upper lip. "I know, but if anything should go wrong, or if she awakens and turns on us, I want you to open a gateway and get yourself out of here as fast as you can. I will make sure you have a chance to escape. Promise me you'll do as I say."

"I will." Charlee's body tensed. *Yeah right. No way would I abandon you.*

A grimace crossed her mom's face. She hesitated before speaking. Squeezing her eyebrows together, she shifted her gaze from Charlee to the limp body of Theodora. "Okay, then…here we go. Don't let go of me or the Changeling."

Her mom placed the palm of her free hand upon the unconscious Theodora's chest, then started to hum a tune, softly at first. Charlee tilted her head. What was the melody? It was dark and heavy—not gentle, like a mother's song to a daughter. It was more like a battle hymn by soldiers marching to war.

The humming grew louder, and her mom's body shook. Charlee's hand, still grasping her mom's, burned, like someone held a candle underneath her palm.

71

She fought the urge to pull away. A white glow formed around their joined hands. Charlee turned to the Changeling. The unicorn's massive body twitched. He lifted and lowered his head, snorting. A thick white mucus slid between his lips.

Her own skin heated, not just over her hands, but the nape of her neck and her brow, like her blood was boiling, and she was cooking from the inside out. *Mom, it hurts*, she wanted to say, but she bit her lip and muffled a cry.

Her mom screamed and arched her head back. A blinding flash, as bright as the midafternoon sun, exploded from her hand atop Theodora.

Charlee squeezed her eyelids shut, but her pupils sizzled. She whirled her head away but kept her grip on the bike and her mom. Squinting through the pain, she glanced back uneasily. The light cocooned them all in a white shell, blocking a view of the world outside.

A heartbeat later the light faded away. Charlee shook her head to clear her blurry vision. Her mind wildly spun. What happened?

"Mom!" Charlee called out.

She got no response, but her mom's hand slipped from hers. Charlee released her grip on the Changeling. Rubbing her eyes, she turned toward her mom. *No!* Her mom lay slumped over Theodora. Neither moved. Charlee grabbed her mom by the shoulders.

"Mom…mom!" Charlee laid her mom's head in her lap. "Mom, are you all right? Come on, you must be all right. Please be—"

"I'm…okay." Her mom slowly opened her eyes. "I haven't had that much power flow through me before. Don't think I want to do that again." She lifted herself into a cross-legged sitting position. "Anything…from our…patient?"

"No," Charlee answered.

Theodora hadn't stirred. Her eyes remained closed, surrounded by dark circles, her skin pale and sickly but no longer blue.

Charlee's mom knelt close and placed her head against Theodora's chest. "I don't hear a heartbeat. I'm sorry. My magic just isn't strong enough to break—"

Theodora exhaled a long breath and grabbed Charlee's mom by the arm. "Your magic is quite strong, daughter of my sister." She spoke barely above a whisper, her words, spoken in the Lengoron language, broken between deep breaths.

Charlee leaped to her feet, her palms aimed at Theodora ready to unleash a magical attack. Was any of this real?

Theodora's eyes blinked and opened a crack. She peered toward the purple sky. A pinkish color spread across her cheeks. The black circles around her eyes vanished. She opened her eyes wider. They were crystal blue, like Megan's. Her chapped lips softened and parted in a weak smile. "Charlee!" she uttered. Theodora extended a long, slender arm toward her.

Charlee retreated a step. A moment of doubt clouded her emotions. Had she made a mistake reviving this woman? Hearing a voice that matched the evil Theodora's broke the certainty she had just moments ago. The Theodora she knew was a manipulator and always one step ahead. "Who are you?"

"You know who I am." Theodora tried to rise on her elbows but dropped back into the stand.

"Answer my daughter's question." Charlee's mom stood over Theodora, face rigid except for a slight quiver of her lips. What emotions was she holding back?

Theodora forced herself into a sitting position. Her body moved stiffly, each limb cracking. She pushed away thick strands of golden hair from her eyes. The gray vanished with each breath she took. She smiled weakly at Charlee's mom. "Oh my, you look so much like your mother. I see my sister in your face, and I can feel her strength flowing through you."

Her mom crossed her arms. "One more time, answer the question."

The woman licked her full lips. "I know how hard this is for you to believe, but I am Theodora." She eyed Charlee's mom. "I am your aunt." She then glanced at Charlee, blinking eyelashes as golden as her hair. "And your great aunt. It was me who came to you in the dungeon. It was me who guided you to this place, and you came. I knew you would. You freed me, and I thank you. I will forever be in your debt."

Charlee remained speechless. Her thoughts scrambled until her head ached. They had come on this journey to find her, and now they had. How could she trust her own eyes? Hate wrapped around her body, squeezing her until it was hard to breathe. But she wanted to believe, wanted to hope.

She inched closer to this young Theodora. "Why should we believe you?"

Theodora filled her chest with air. She twisted her long, thin neck as to shake off her long sleep. "Because you have no choice." She uttered her words slowly, heavily, and lowered her eyes.

Charlee's mom raised an eyebrow. "Oh, we have a choice. We could leave you to rot here. If you really are Theodora, you have much to answer for. So much blood is on your hands."

Theodora slowly, painfully stood. Her legs crumbled once, and she stumbled to one knee. Sighing, she again climbed to her feet, this time squaring her shoulders and thrusting out her chest. Her white gown, still damp, clung to her curves. She trembled at first, then found her balance. Her blond locks slid down over her shoulders to nearly the small of her back. Her blue eyes glistened.

Charlee's fists tightened. She crossed to the Changeling, standing rigidly next to the unicorn. Her mom did the same.

Theodora raked a shaky hand through her hair. "You are right. I do have blood on my hands, but not for the reasons you think. I am so sorry for everything that has transpired. I wish I could change it all. Go back in time and just hug my sister. Be there for her marriage to her love. See you grow up, daughter of my sister. Bring peace back to our beloved Latara."

"Enough. Tell us what's really going on." Charlee pounded a fist against her open palm. She studied the young woman's face for a slight upturn in her lips. A subtle roll of her eyes. A twitch of her nose. Anything that might reveal her lies, but there was nothing. This Theodora stared flatly, eyes unflinching. Her shoulders curved over her chest. Her voice cracked.

Theodora clasped her hands together. Her chin quivered as she addressed Charlee's mom. "I know how hard this is, but I am who I appear to be. I am Theodora, daughter of Queen Tesarra and Princess to the Kingdom of Latara, sister to your mother, and the one who is to blame for unleashing evil on the world."

She started toward Charlee but stopped. "You, young one, have the bravery of your grandfather, the Guardian Michala. You have faced trials no child should have to, and you have done so with a true warrior spirit. I will forever be in your gratitude for this day, and I pledge that I will stand by your side from this day forward."

Charlee shared a glance with her mom who scratched her chin and pressed her lips into a fine line. Her mom's face remained a stone with no sign of emotion.

"You still haven't told us anything we need to know." Her mom placed herself in between Charlee and the young Theodora. "We need—"

Charlee placed a hand on her mom's shoulders and stepped forward. "You helped me, too. You kind of kept me going when I was in the dungeon. How did you do that?"

"Yes, while my body was imprisoned, I had just enough magic in me to transport my spirit to you." A pensive smile crossed Theodora's face. "But you would have survived even without me. You are much stronger than you know, and soon you will realize your full abilities. I can help."

Shuffling her feet, Charlee inched closer to the woman who claimed to be her great aunt. She sensed no dark magic in this Theodora. But what did that mean? Could she tell the difference between the dark arts and good magic? Even if she could, Theodora could easily mask her evil. "Thank you for—"

"Okay, enough." Her mom grasped Charlee's arm and tugged her back. "I don't know if you're really my aunt or not, or whether this is some kind of trap, but I'm far from ready to simply welcome you back into the family. Like I said before, you have a great deal to explain, Aunt Theodora."

"You are wise to be cautious." Theodora slumped into the sand and folded her hands in her lap. She stared at the ground. "I will begin my tale, but I make one request."

"What is it?" Charlee's mom knelt closer.

"That when I am finished, you will allow me to join you in your crusade to stop that foul creation who calls herself Theodora and to throw the dark medallion back into the fires that gave spawn to it."

Charlee's mom placed her palms close together. Blue energy sparked between her hands. "That depends on whether I believe you—and right now, I'm not sure I do."

CHAPTER 15

Theodora's Tale

THEODORA SAT CROSS-legged in the sand. She motioned for Charlee and her mom to join her, but Charlee, like her mom, remained standing, as if they were judges ready to pronounce sentence. Maybe this was the real Theodora, and maybe she could be trusted, but right now trust didn't come easy. This could just as easily be the witch who left her in that filthy dungeon. Charlee shuddered at that memory.

She rubbed her temples. What should she do? Trust this Theodora or abandon her in this nowhere dimension, where day and night blended together and planets hovered like models strung from some unseen ceiling—so close it seemed she could reach out and pluck them into her hand as easy as tugging loose an apple from a tree?

Her head spun. They'd come here to free this Theodora. They came hoping she could help them stop the Theodora who called herself an Empress, even a God, and threatened Earth. But her brain ached wrestling with what to do.

At the very least, they'd hear this Theodora out.

The young woman placed her hands in her lap and lowered her eyes. Her soft skin turned ashen. Her blond hair clung lifelessly to her face. She sighed deeply and then spoke. "I remember every detail as if it just happened. Well, in a way for me it all just did happen."

She lifted her head. Tear-soaked eyes stared past them toward the purple sky. She inhaled one more time, filling her chest, and spoke again—her words slow and heavy, her voice somber.

"After my mother died, my sister was next in line to be queen as the oldest daughter. I was to be first princess, but I always had different ideas about how the new queen should rule. She wanted to follow our mother's ways. I wanted a harsher more disciplined system of government. I was certain the other kings and queens of the Unified Kingdoms would challenge my sister's rule, and there was only one way to stop it...through a show of force. But she disagreed."

Theodora paused, her hands balled into fists, and her voice cracked as she started again. "The night of her coronation we argued, and Assara used her magic against me. She was so sorry, but I couldn't forgive her. I was angry. Maybe I just couldn't cope with the loss of our mother, or maybe I was greedy and wanted

77

the crown for myself…I don't know. I left my sister and the Kingdom of Latara, vowing never to return."

§ § §

I rode off on a wind horse that night. For days I journeyed without end. The more distance between me and my sister the better. I passed through the valley, and to avoid the other Unified Kingdoms, I turned south to circle around the Monera mountain ranges that overlook Latara. Beyond the mountains lie the badlands where the barbarians once lived before the great wars. As children, Mother taught us to never venture to those lands. They were marked by death and dark magic.

I no longer cared.

I rode for days, maybe a week without stopping, without thought of the strain on my wind horse or food and drink. We reached the badlands on a gray morning as thunder clouds hung high, offering an explosive welcome followed by cracks of lightning that split the sky. My wind horse slowed to a lumbering crawl. White phlegm dripped from his snout. He snorted and huffed wildly. If I pushed him much more, he'd die.

My head dropped against my chest. My legs ached from the strain of holding myself up in the saddle. My shoulders sagged. Hunger and thirst weakened my body. My arms and legs were like loose string. What a fool I was to leave Latara with nothing but the clothes on my back and a sword at my side. I had not brought one morsel of food or pouch of water.

Thunder boomed overhead. My wind horse unleashed a painful cry, ripped his head back, and fell to the ground. I managed to roll away before he squashed my legs. When I gazed upon him, blood mixed with foam around his gaping mouth. His chest heaved. He tried once to lift his head but dropped back into the dirt. A moan slid from his throat.

I patted the damp fur along his neck. "Come on, you'll be okay. Just rest for a moment. I'll find us food…drink." My own parched throat made it difficult to talk. I stroked his mane. "You're going to be okay."

But that was a lie. His eyes dimmed. Death was coming for him, but not just yet. He fought against it, trying one more time to rise. More blood and mucus flowed from his mouth and nostrils.

I slowly stood, grasping the handle of my sword. I unsheathed it and raised it over my head. The blade was heavier than I remembered. My hands shook. I hesitated for just a moment, avoiding his eyes, which glared at me. Was he pleading for death or to live? How could I know? "Goodbye, my friend."

I drove my blade into his belly. He shuddered and his body tensed. I forced the blade deeper. He exhaled one more time. His eyes widened, then closed forever. One last breath slid from his throat, and then he was still.

Dropping my sword, I slumped to my knees and cupped my hands to my eyes. I cried over his body for I don't know how long. Did I cry for my dumb steed? Did I cry for myself? I don't know. Without water, my death would come soon. I had left the only home I had ever known so that I might die in a foreign wasteland alone and forgotten.

I wasn't ready to die, at least not like this.

When my tears stopped, I gazed at my surroundings. Nothing but dirt and rock surrounded me in every direction, save for the mountains behind me. A few dried washes hinted at the water that once flowed, but none remained. With what little strength remained in me, I grasped my sword and thrust the blade into the ground over and over. There had to be groundwater. If I dug deep enough, I'd find it and save my life, but I found nothing — just dry rock and sand. My hands throbbed from the effort. My racing heart slowed to a limp. I dropped onto my back, gasping, licking dry lips with a sandpaper tongue.

The thunder clouds, black and bruised, teased me with the hope of rain, but none came. Lightning strikes ignited the skies in a fiery blaze. A hot wind blew across the sands, kicking up dust in a wild dance.

Then the scavengers came.

First came their low, guttural growls echoing around me. I raised up on my elbows, craning my neck in every direction. My jaw clenched and eyes widened.

Terrible creatures, unlike anything I'd ever seen, emerged from holes in the ground — four legged beasts the size of small wolves with long snouts. They were earless and eyeless with massive nostrils flaring as they sniffed the air. I plucked my sword from the ground and stood on tense legs, ready to run but frozen at the same time.

These monsters gnashed razor sharp teeth. Two long fangs protruded on either side of their snouts. If they had any flesh, it was hidden under a green exoskeleton. A long tongue, almost the length of an arm, shot out from their snouts as if licking the air — like they could taste the cold sweat dripping from my brow.

I hefted my sword above my head. The blade shook uncontrollably, the hilt loose in my damp palms.

At least twenty emerged from the ground at first. They circled the hole, then unleashed a high-pitched cry. I flinched and started to back away. More emerged, maybe dozens, from the hole, like an ant colony on the hunt for food. Backs arched, snouts held high, they stalked me. My body trembled. I had no other thought but to save myself. But how? I peered over my shoulder for anywhere I could hide — a boulder, a cave...anything.

An outcropping of isolated jagged hills dotted the rugged terrain behind me. My only chance was to turn and run, but I wouldn't make it. They'd be on me long before I could make the climb.

One of the beasts raised its head to the sky, spit out its tongue and screamed. The others did the same. I covered my ears but couldn't block out their shrieks. Dizziness overcame me, and numbing fear spread through my veins. Death would soon be upon me.

They charged.

The ground shook under their thunderous stampede. They clamored over each other in their frantic race to tear me to pieces. I broke through the crushing weight of fear that tethered me to the ground…and I ran.

"Use your magic." A fatherly voice breached my mind. I stumbled to the ground.

"You have power you can't imagine." The voice eclipsed all other thoughts.

A beast cried out behind me. I clamored to my feet and blindly swung my sword just in time to cut through the unprotected neck of the monster. Thick green blood splattered from the gash. The creature screamed, then dropped to the sand.

The others were almost upon me. I ripped my blade free and raced toward the hills. The voice returned. "Your steel cannot save you. Only magic."

"Shut up!" The hills were so far away, and the beasts were so close the snapping of their jaws attacked my ears. I didn't dare look back.

Then I stumbled once more.

I fell to the ground…or rather, I fell through the ground, crashing through the rocky surface into an unseen hole. I bounced off rocks, slamming my back against rough edges. My shoulder struck another rock and I yelped. Pain radiated with each blow. Then, I slid on my stomach, arms outstretched, down a sandy embankment for what seemed an eternity. Dirt flew into my mouth, choking me. Rocks scraped my skin, like tiny blades cutting my flesh.

When I finally stopped, darkness surrounded me. I coughed and spewed up dust. Foul air made breathing a struggle. I lay there, legs curled up to my stomach, fighting for each breath, sobbing and whimpering.

"Arise, young one, and light your way." The voice reached out to me from the void.

"Who's there?" I peered in every direction, but blackness cocooned me like a box. I couldn't see beyond a foot or two in any direction.

"You are a conjurer, are you not?" This time tension laced the voice. "Draw upon your powers as you have been taught to since you were a child."

Reflexively, I wrapped my arms around my stomach. How could this disembodied voice know anything about me? I extended my hands along the cold stone floor, feeling for my sword handle but found nothing. A tingling sensation spread through my limbs, tiny pinpricks warning me to flee.

"We await you, young one. Why do you hesitate?"

I slowly stood and backed away. "You never answered my question. Who are you?"

"We are the way."

"What does that mean?" I dragged my hands through the air as if to protect my personal space from an unseen attacker. Despite the chill surrounding me in the darkness, sweat dripped from my forehead.

"It means we are here to guide you." The voice echoed louder, piercing my brain as if burrowing through my skull.

I stopped and tensed my body. "Enough with the riddles."

The voice was right. It was time I stopped being afraid and engaged my magic.

Closing my eyes, I quieted my thoughts and uttered an incantation, one taught to me long ago by my mother. My arms vibrated gently. The veins just beneath my skin glowed, a fiery glimmer rising from my flesh. Holding my hands in front of me, a soft white light emanated from my palms, illuminating my surroundings.

"Good," the voice uttered.

"Shut up." I pushed my hands in front of me. "I've had enough of this. I'm getting out of here. Do you hear me?"

The voice did not answer.

I tightened my wrists. My veins radiated heat, and my arms convulsed. Like a sharpened blade, the light from my wrists stabbed into the void.

My mouth fell open and I shuddered. Skeletal remains spilled from the walls. Skulls peeked out from crevices. Broken limbs hung limply. The stale odor of bodies long since decomposed and souls forgotten made my nose wrinkle. I turned to flee, but death surrounded me. My belly fluttered. A wave of nausea crept up my throat. The white light from my palms caused shadows to dance around me. My thoughts jumbled. I closed my eyes and forced myself to think. These had to be the remains of barbarian bloodlines.

"Do not be afraid. Come to us." The voice spoke gently to me.

Broken skulls covered the path ahead. Skinless arms seemed to reach at me from narrowing walls. I backed away from all that death. I didn't dare desecrate the burial chambers of our vanquished enemies.

Above me came the hisses and cries of the scavenging beasts, but they didn't follow me into this abyss. Maybe they didn't know I'd fallen. Maybe they did and were too frightened to enter.

"Come, child." The words swirled around me.

"Show yourself." I stretched out my palms as far as my arms would allow, but the light revealed no one. The darkness beyond my magic's reach was like an impenetrable barrier.

"In due time. Have no fear, child. You are safe. You have traveled a great distance to reach us. It is not much farther now. Complete your journey."

"I don't understand."

"All will be revealed very soon. Come, young one."

Though the voice spoke comforting words, my thoughts warned me to stay away. The hairs on the back of my neck stiffened. Evil lay ahead, and yet for reasons I cannot explain a force compelled me forward through the passage.

"Yes, rise above your fear," the voice without a body uttered.

I walked stiffly with heavy steps. My hands led the way, palms glowing to light the way. The chamber grew icy the farther I walked. A mist rose from my mouth and my nose with each breath.

"My child, you don't know how long we've waited to greet you." The words hung before me as the passage grew tighter and the walls closed in. I bent my shoulders to keep from bumping against the rocky ceiling.

Unseen forces pressed against my chest, making each breath a struggle. Static in the air made the hairs on my arm stand. A soft hum reached my ears. A sense of unease swirled around me, squeezing my brow. I recognized it all as signs of magic laced with evil.

"I sense dark magic." I stuttered my words.

The voice responded with a hint of irritation. "The concept of light and dark magic is the manifest of weak minds that cannot see the full power of unrestrained magic as it was meant to be practiced — as it was once practiced by the ancient conjurers who ruled the realms and the heavens above."

My knees locked, and my shoulder blades cinched together. A tremor ran through me. In our history lessons, we were taught of ancient times when cruel magic conjurers used their abilities to conquer and rule — not only this world, but they sought to use their power as a bridge to other worlds. The Guardians waged a war against them, and the kingdoms united to stop the spread of evil. A generation of war followed. In the end, the Guardians, joined by the armies of the Unified Kingdoms, the dragons, and those conjurers who used their power for good, defeated the dark conjurers.

The voice urging me on spoke the words of that ancient, twisted sect. I knew this, yet for some reason my legs started moving again along the path as if controlled by some other source. Or was it me? Had the voice reached that part of me that was already filled with hate.

The farther I walked, the smaller the tunnel became, until only a tight crawl space remained. I lowered to my hands and knees, clumsily stumbling over skulls and other skeletal remains. The air thickened. I could only manage shallow breaths.

Up ahead an orange light, like a beacon, cut through the gloom. It was warm, inviting, a stark contrast from the bleakness surrounding me. I should have turned around and fled from whomever awaited me. I didn't.

I inched forward.

From behind me came a rumbling, like the ground had become angry. The rocky surface shook, and dust and dirt spilled around me. I peered over my shoulder. An explosion ripped through the passageway. The ceiling behind me collapsed.

The voice returned. "Hurry, child."

The passage roared in fury. I scampered toward the light pouring into the passageway through a hole just large enough for me to slide through. Now on me belly, I pushed away the remains of the dead and dragged myself through the hole. The ceiling on the other side caved, slamming the entryway shut behind me. I rolled up in a ball and gasped. Dust coated my throat. I coughed and wheezed, fighting for air.

"Rise, child," the voice urged, like a caring parent.

My chest heaving, I wretched up dirt and mucus. When it passed, I wiped my mouth clean and rubbed my burning throat. With a deep inhale, I forced myself onto my knees. Before me rose the source of light impaling the darkness. A vortex of dancing flames spun in the center of a cavern at least as large as the throne room at Castle Latara. The fire spread along the ground, like roots, and climbed to the ceiling where it arched as if the top layer of a tree.

I shielded my eyes at first, but quickly removed my hands. Warmth and a soothing glow spread from the tree of fire.

"Do not be afraid," the voice declared. "We mean you no harm. We have caused you to be here, so that we might be introduced and learn from each other. First you must drink and replenish your health."

My mouth fell open. The voice came from the fiery creation before me. What magic was this? Who or what hid within the flames?

"Do not fear. Partake in what we provide to you." The fire tree slid away, revealing a sparkling pool of water and a loaf of bread atop a boulder.

My legs tensed as if instinctively preparing to leap into the water. I licked my cracked lips, but I didn't budge. "You haven't revealed yourself to me." My raspy voice was little more than a whisper. "Why do you remain hidden inside the fire? I hear only one voice. Why do you refer to we?"

The orange flames shifted colors. Yellow, then red, replaced the orange. "We stand before you as we are."

"Fire?" I asked.

"Please eat and drink, and then we will share more."

My eyes shifted from the fire to the water and food. Finally, I gave in to my thirst and ran to the water. I drank just a sip at first. The water was sweet and chilled. I plunged my head in without thought. As the dust cleared from my throat, I threw myself at the bread, devouring it quickly.

"Good," the voice proclaimed. "You must be healthy for what lies ahead."

"Enough." I lifted myself on steadier legs. "You speak in riddles. Now tell me who or what you are and what you want with me or release me."

"My child, you are not our prisoner." The fire tree dimmed a bit, except at its center where it blazed as bright as the sun. "Gaze upon us," the voice commanded.

Like a scared child, I heeded the command. I peered into the light. From the blazing tree strolled the burning form of a man. A beard of wild flames crackled from his chin down to his chest. His face burned brightest. A fiery mask hid his eyes, nose, and mouth.

I stepped back and reached for my sword handle. Stupid. I'd lost my blade. I lifted my hands in front of me, palms facing the burning stranger. I summoned magic, stuttering through an incantation. Green energy pulsed between my fingers.

"We mean you no harm, child." He walked with a steady stride, a flaming staff in one hand and a red-hot sword in the other. He stopped an arm's length away from me and lowered the sizzling blade to his side. He tilted his head as if studying me.

I cleared my throat. "I would ask again, sir, who are you?"

"The more proper question would be, who were we when we had a physical form. As you see, we are spirit now," he answered.

"Okay, who were you in life?" I kept my glowing palms aimed at him.

"You can call us Serior. We are the collective mind of the Council of the Brotherhood who sought to bring unity to a world corrupted by the simple minds of the non-magics. Do you know of us?"

My mouth slackened and my stomach hardened. It couldn't be true. I had to be dreaming. This had to be some nightmare. The terrible stories mother had told me. I stretched out my fingers and stiffened my neck. "I've heard of the Brotherhood. You wanted to enslave those without magic abilities and steal the abilities of those conjurers outside the Brotherhood. You massacred men, women, and children. Tens of thousands, more, until the Guardians, the dragons, and Unified Kingdoms stopped you."

Serior blazed red hot. I turned my head away from his heat. "Lies told to children. Your mind has been warped by a flawed understanding of history. We sought peace. The Guardian's chose war, and in their barbaric use of steel and their reliance on the self-serving dragons, so many lives were sacrificed. They destroyed the Brotherhood and robbed the world of the good that could have come from our guidance. But our time has come again, and that is why we summoned you here."

I raised an eyebrow. "You didn't summon me. I chose to leave Latara and to travel to the badlands. You had nothing to do with it. It was by chance that I fell through a hole that led me here."

"You know that is not the case, child." Serior's flames dimmed. His voice softened. "Your entire life has led you to this point and to us. You have incredible untapped magic and the vision to forge a new Brotherhood. I have seen this in you."

"Shut your mouth." My hands tightened into fists. My cheeks burned.

"We speak the truth." Serior bowed to me. "When the Brotherhood foresaw their end, we chose one to become a vessel for our collective spirits. Our brother Serior was chosen for that honor. We joined with him. Together, we vowed to protect the secrets of the Brotherhood until one should arise who could reclaim our glorious vision. That is you, child. Think about your past. You've always felt different from your poor mother, whose soul joins with the earth in which she rests, and from your sister. You have always sought a different path, have you not?"

My hands dropped to my side. I sucked in a quick breath of air and started to cough. How could he know I had a sister or about my mother, about her death? My hands pulsed again with green energy. I raised them to Serior. "How dare you speak of my mother."

Serior bowed again. "I meant no disrespect. I only wish you to understand we have watched you…and chosen you. We have seen you grow, and your energy become strong… stronger than any other conjurer in the known realms. You just don't know it yet."

I covered my ears. "You speak lies."

He shook his burning head. "No, you have the power to lead us back to glory. We can help you realize your true potential and your life's true purpose. Together, we will guide our world and so many others to an unparalleled time of peace."

My legs weakened. A light-headed daze nearly toppled me, but I remained on my feet. "Why should I believe you?"

He inched closer to me. "Because you know, deep inside, I speak the truth. You know you long for the kind of ultimate power we offer." He paused for a moment. His chest rose as if he took a long breath. "We have a gift for you that will help you along your journey toward this noble venture." Serior waved his staff, fanning the flames that engulfed him.

A crimson shade bled throughout the fire tree. A raven black object formed inside. The rounded object emerged from the flames, then hovered next to Serior. My eyes were drawn to the object—a dark medallion that seemed to swallow light, like a portal to emptiness.

"Do you know what this is?" Serior asked.

I slowly shook my head, but that was a lie. I'd heard stories about a medallion forged by evil with so much magic it could grant immortality to the one who wielded it, but its existence had always been a myth, a fearful legend.

"My brothers, before the time of our passing, summoned all of our power to conjure this medallion." Serior caressed the object. "Once we had created it, we infused our life force into the medallion so that one day, when the time was right, the one who would guide a new age of the Brotherhood would take hold of it and use its power to carry our message of hope or conquer those who would defy the Brotherhood."

I leaned toward the medallion. The hair on my arms and neck rose. My breath quickened. "I can't be the one you speak of."

"Oh, but you are the one, because the medallion has chosen you." Serior waved his staff and the medallion floated to me. "Gaze upon it and tell me what you see."

The medallion circled me. I followed it, studied it. One side had the etching of the fire tree. The other side…I gasped and shrank away. My face was etched in the medallion, but how could that be?

"It's not possible," I mumbled.

"You see it, don't you?"

I blinked rapidly. "I don't believe it."

Serior tilted his fiery head. "Why do you doubt your own senses? You know our words are true. You only need to hold the medallion and take the first step toward your destiny. We and the medallion will teach you, and when it is time, you will go out unto the world and deliver our message of hope."

I fought my desire to possess the medallion. I reached for it but recoiled more than once. Sweat dripped from my palms. My nerves tingled. I soon gave in, snatching it from the air and holding it against my chest, like cradling a child.

A wave of energy rushed through me. A brilliant flash exploded before my eyes, but without pain. I peered into the light. The faces of long dead conjurers, the Brotherhood, spilled into my thoughts. Their voices filled my head. I dropped to one knee but still clutched the medallion. The voices slowly faded, but their thoughts eclipsed my own. Their wisdom became mine. Their magic became my magic. I felt power vibrating through me, and I craved more.

"Already, you bond with the medallion." Serior now stood next to me. He placed a fiery hand on my shoulder. It didn't burn. "Now we must begin your training. We will teach you to control the power you now possess."

"Yes, teach me." I stood and held the medallion in front of me with both hands, marveling at its dark beauty.

"When you are ready, you will harness the power of the medallion to crush all who stand against you and the Brotherhood. You will unite the world under one rule—our rule. When you have done so, you will then spread our power across the heavens and across time as this medallion will grant you endless life to serve the Brotherhood, my child."

"Yes." I nodded to Serior. "Let's begin."

§ § §

Theodora gazed up as if momentarily leaving behind the past and acknowledging the present. A tear slid down her cheek. "I cannot tell you for sure how long I remained under ground with Serior, whether days, months, a year, or more. During that time, I didn't eat, I didn't drink, and I didn't sleep. I no longer cared about day or night. I never desired to see the morning sun or the moons. I required none of that to sustain me. The medallion was my sustenance, and Serior's teaching was all I lived for. I was losing myself until one day came when I questioned my teacher." Her eyes then lost focus as she returned to that long-ago time. Her story continued.

§ § §

"Child, you have learned so much." Serior's praise meant so much. "Our time together is almost complete. Very soon, you must leave this place. You must return to the world and bring about a new age under the good word of the Brotherhood. You are the Brotherhood. You will be Empress Theodora. Worlds will stand with you or fall before you. With the medallion by your side, none shall be able to defy you."

"The Brotherhood shall live through me." I smiled wide.

"You have but one test to prove yourself ready." Serior burned brighter than I had ever seen.

"A test?"

"Yes, my child." He stood before me and drew his sword. "You must end your sister's rule over Latara and break the Unified Kingdoms. In your absence, she has grown strong and has united with a Guardian in marriage. Soon, they will have a child. You must kill your sister and the Guardian."

I stepped back. I was ready to crush anyone who would defy the Brotherhood or my absolute right to rule, but kill my sister? She deserved to die for casting me away, right? But she hadn't cast me away. I had run away because we fought. No, she feared me, so she sent me away. That's not true. My mind swirled with confusion. What was the truth?

Serior's flames crackled louder. "I see weakness in you, child."

"No, it's just—"

"Perhaps you are not ready for the task ahead." He spoke like an angry father.

I lowered to one knee and bowed my head. "I am, but why do I have to kill my sister? I will happily kill the Guardian, but do not ask me to kill my sister. Let me drive her away. Shouldn't that be enough? The Unified Kingdoms will fall without her."

Serior stood silently. "I will consider your words." He turned his back on me and disappeared into the fire tree.

I knelt like a child, as I would when I had disappointed my mother. I tightened my grip on the medallion. I vowed then that if anyone should try to take the medallion from me, even Serior, I would make them suffer. If the Brotherhood thought me weak, I'd show them just how much I had learned and how powerful I had become.

But I lingered in my thoughts too long.

"Child."

I turned toward Serior just in time to see his flaming staff crash down toward me. The staff struck the side of my head. Something cracked. Searing pain radiated through my brain. Then came darkness.

When I revived, I was no longer the pupil and Serior my teacher. His magic suspended me so that my feet couldn't touch the floor, and my arms and hands were tied tightly to my body by unseen rope.

The medallion hovered in front of me, rotating slowly. I groggily watched it through hazy eyes. Though my head ached and my belly roiled with nausea, that didn't matter. I had to have it back. It belonged to me. I wrestled against my invisible restraints but couldn't budge.

"Serior, what is this? I demand you release me!"

"The Brotherhood has decided," The fire that engulfed him dimmed to a soft orange.

"Decided what?"

"That a mistake has been made."

"What does that mean?" I squeezed my hands. My body trembled.

"You, or should I say this form of you, is not the one to usher in our new age. We thought we had excised all that is weak in you, but we failed. As long as you care for those beings out there, starting with your sister, you will lack the strength to do what must be done. We cannot have that."

"Serior, I am to be empress," I cried. "You dare speak to me this way. I will make you pay for your actions."

"You should rejoice, child, for the Brotherhood still believes that a leader lies buried

within you, and they have decided to extract it from you. In that sense, you will be empress while the rest of you — should you survive the process — will be imprisoned for eternity."

"Serior, you can't do this. Please."

"You speak now as a scared child. Tsk, tsk...you see how weak you truly are. I look forward to addressing your inner self — to meeting the Theodora who is quite deserving to be empress. Shall we begin?"

"No — "

A crimson beam fired from the medallion, striking me in the chest. My insides boiled while my skin popped and bled. My bones cracked and my body convulsed. It was as if the medallion tore out my very soul.

I screamed and pleaded for mercy. None was offered.

As the beam sucked away my life, a shadowy figure took shape beside me. All I wanted at that moment was to shut my eyes and never feel anything again, but despite my agony I focused on the creature forming next to me. To my bewilderment, the beast beside me was me. The Brotherhood had used the medallion to recreate me.

The last thing I beheld was my twin staring at me with the evilest grin I had ever seen — one I will never forget.

§ § §

Theodora's tale ended. The young woman long imprisoned in ice lowered her head. More tears fell from her cheeks.

"I guess I survived the extraction process, because I wound up imprisoned here in this magical plain of existence trapped forever in ice, not dead, but not living either." Theodora rested her head in her hands.

Thoughts of her own face, scarred and aged, emblazoned on one side of the medallion, and the unyielding desire to possess the dark object flooded Charlee's mind. The agony of having her powers ripped from her body by the medallion's magic pained her like a wound that would never fully heal.

Her mom maintained a steely appearance. "Why didn't they just kill you?"

"So that I might watch their Theodora kill everyone I ever loved and harm the people I should have protected while I lay in a frozen prison unable to help or even communicate. Through some twisted magic that forced me to see the world through the fake Theodora's eyes, I watched my sister die, all because of my anger and greed."

Theodora paused and took a deep breath. "But the Brotherhood, their Theodora, and the medallion didn't count on the strength of your daughter." Theodora slowly stood. Her eyes widened. "They may have foreseen that a young Guardian would arise, but they didn't know the depth of her power."

She tried to place a hand on Charlee's shoulder, but Charlee retreated out of reach. Theodora bowed. "Young Guardian, you are stronger than you know. So strong that, through your magic, I was able to open a conduit to your mind and finally make myself heard. Now that you have freed me, the time has come for me to have my vengeance on the Brotherhood."

Charlee scratched her chin. She opened her mouth, but no words came out. The situation was suddenly much worse. The enemy wasn't just a mad empress. It was a crazy clone and an entire brotherhood of evil, dead conjurers whose spirits lived in the medallion. She shook her head. *What the hell?*

Then again, how could she trust *this* Theodora? Her entire story could be a lie. This could still be one big trap, but something deep inside told her it wasn't. This Theodora deserved a chance to right the wrongs that she caused, but she would be watched closely.

Charlee closed the distance between her and Theodora. "Join us, then, and have your vengeance. But if you cross us, there will be nowhere you can hide to escape me or *my* vengeance."

CHAPTER 16

Back to Latara

CHARLEE LEANED AGAINST the unicorn inside the portal. Blue clouds swirled around them. Electrical currents flashed like lightning bolts, and the winds cried. Her brain vibrated within her skull, but she was gaining back her strength. Controlling the gateway took considerably less effort. Her attention focused on her mom who stood close, an arm wrapped around Theodora's waist…probably as much out of distrust as to keep her standing on wobbly legs.

Theodora's head rested against her chest with her shoulders rounded, like someone filled with regret and prepared for whatever punishment awaited her. Charlee's eyes shifted between the two women. If only she could read minds. What was Theodora truly thinking? Could her mom get into Theodora's head, just like she did with Charlee?

Like a doorway opening, the gateway flashed brilliantly, then swooshed out of existence, delivering them in the courtyard of Castle Latara. As had been agreed upon, Penaiya and Kraannaannn were there waiting. Charlee's dad was there as well with Megan in his arms. The young Dragon Lord unleashed an ear-piercing roar, raising his head and displaying his razor-sharp fangs.

Penaiya unsheathed her sword and lunged at Theodora, grabbing her by the neck and raising her sword overhead. Her cheeks burned red as her lips quivered. "Witch, you will pay for stealing my daughter from me."

Charlee's heart sank. Penaiya's daughter had been twisted to serve the evil Theodora before she was consumed by the fire breath from the dragons as they attacked the witch's forces on the beach, saving the Latarans. Penaiya's pain must be great, but it was a different Theodora that manipulated and destroyed her daughter. Charlee grabbed Penaiya's wrist. "What are you doing? You knew—"

"Yes, I knew what you were thinking." Penaiya's eyes bulged. "But it doesn't matter. She must die!"

Charlee's mom, still supporting Theodora, spoke calmly. "You have to stand down."

Kraannaannn slammed his tail against the ground. Charlee struggled to keep her balance in front of him. How could she stop a dragon hell-bent on revenge? She raised her hands. "This is not the evil Theodora! You can't kill her! She can help us!"

The dragon lowered his head until inches from Charlee. His hot breath surrounded her. "How can you of all people defend her?"

"I'm telling you this isn't the same Theodora." Charlee reached out and touched Kraannaannn's snout. The dragon snorted and backed away.

Penaiya kept her grip on Theodora's neck. The young version of the evil Empress did nothing to fight back. She coughed and wheezed but made no motion to break free.

"She has you under a spell." Penaiya's face and neck turned red.

"No." Charlee's mom shook her head. "I've seen into her mind. This is not the same person who has caused so much suffering to our people."

Charlee gazed at her mom. She could read Theodora's mind. That was a comfort, unless the young woman had the power to hide her true intentions somewhere so deep in her thoughts that not even Charlee's mom could see the truth. She swallowed that thought so as not to reveal her doubts to the others.

"We've heard her story." Charlee placed a hand on Penaiya's shoulder. "The Brotherhood used her magic against her. They created an evil clone and then entombed this Theodora, the real Theodora. She's come to fight at our side. I think she deserves a chance."

Penaiya's hand dropped to her side. A noticeable shiver rose through her body. "Did you say the Brotherhood?"

"Yes, Penaiya." Theodora rubbed her throat. Her face turned ashen gray. "I know you understand what that means, for you were taught the same stories as me and my sister. You know what they once did in ancient times. They have risen again, and it is because of me and my mistakes, but I am not the same Theodora who killed my sister, destroyed so many other lives, and took our home. I am not the one who took your daughter from you, though I feel as responsible as if I were."

Kraannaannn inched his head toward this Theodora, baring his fangs. A heavy growl rose from deep within his throat.

Charlee stood in front of him, but Theodora brushed her away. The young woman offered a curt nod. She stood solidly in place. "It's okay, Guardian."

Taking a slight step back, Charlee turned back to the dragon. The new Dragon Lord reached Theodora. His green scales bristled, clicking as they stood upon his back. His eyes narrowed as his nostrils flared. He sniffed, then raised his head high above and snorted. He rapidly shook his snout, then lowered his head again. "This being's scent is both similar and different. She has the stench of the witch, but there is a subtle change I do not recognize, as if our paths have never crossed."

"You see." Charlee released a lungful of air and relaxed her shoulders.

"It means nothing." Kraannaannn shook his massive head. "The witch is powerful. She could alter her scent."

Charlee's mom stepped in front of Theodora with her arms crossed, her face rigid. "We have to give her a chance."

Theodora stepped around her. She bowed to the dragon and Penaiya. "I plead with you to hear my story. If after, you decide I am not to be trusted, I will accept whatever you decide to do with me, even if you decide I should die. I believe death is my fate no matter what you decide. I just hope to seek my vengeance before my life ends."

Penaiya and Kraannaannn glanced at each other, then Penaiya spoke. "We will hear your story, witch."

Charlee crossed to her mom and the Changeling. Her dad joined them, gently cradling Megan. Charlee hugged her dad and sister in silence. She said nothing more to defend Theodora. The young woman had said she wanted to stand before them to answer for the crimes of her twin—the Theodora clone generated by the medallion.

Theodora stood in the center of the courtyard as if on trial. A soft breeze blew her golden hair around her face. Her white dress, stained yellow and tattered, clung to her body, revealing a bone-thin frame. Though she trembled, Theodora stood tall and straight as she retold the events of her life just as she had when Charlee and her mom freed her from the ice. Her voice cracked at times, and she paused for long breaths, but she never wavered from her story. She believed it even if the others didn't. New tears streaked her cheeks as she finished her tale.

Kraannaannn lashed out first. "Your tears mean nothing to me, trickster." He lowered his neck until his snout was just a few feet from her. He gnashed his jaw. "Your tears will not bring back my father."

"I understand your hate, and I am sorry for the death of your father and the other dragons that fought at his side, but I have not lied to you this day." Theodora didn't retreat from the dragon. "I don't deserve it, but I ask you to give me a chance to help you stop the sorceress who goes by my name."

Penaiya, a hand wrapped around her sword handle, circled Theodora. "Even if I believed your story, *Princess* Theodora, can you possibly fathom what your greed has brought upon your people, all because you desired your sister's crown?"

"From my frozen prison, I watched it all unfold, and I was unable to stop it. I do know the pain I have caused, and I can never make it right. I am not asking that you accept me back among our people, but rather that you grant me the opportunity to sacrifice what remains of my life to stop that Theodora and return the medallion to the fires that forged it. That will be the only way to destroy it."

"You ask too much," Penaiya turned her back on Theodora. "I will not stand beside you—ever. I have lost everything because of you. My home, my daughter…"

Charlee stepped toward Penaiya. How could she make their people's aging leader understand? "Please—"

"No, Guardian." Penaiya glared at her and pointed the tip of her blade at Theodora. The tip shook. "I have followed you so far, but not this time. You should not have brought her here. If she was imprisoned, you should have left her there to rot away. We do not need her help."

Charlee searched for the right words. What could she possibly say that would make the difference to two who had lost the ones they loved to the Empress?

Charlee squeezed her hands, then loosened them. "Penaiya, you've trusted me so far, and our people are safe now—at least for the time being." She tried to mask the doubt in her voice. "I'm asking you to trust me one more time."

"Why, Guardian?" Kraannaannn asked. "Why are you so convinced this woman is a friend and not a demon? Have you not been misled by the sorceress before? How can you put so much faith in her now?"

She lifted her chin to the dragon. "Don't you think I'm scared about this, too? I'm asking you to trust her when I'm not all that sure she can be trusted. Can't you see how hard this is for me?"

"Why then?" Penaiya's nostrils flared just like the dragons.

"Because something inside tells me we have no choice but to trust her." Charlee approached Theodora and stopped just inches away. "I can't explain it, but I know the only way we can stop the sorceress is through this Theodora's help. Believe me, if she turns on us, I will be the first to take her out."

Theodora crossed to Penaiya. The elder Lataran aimed the tip of her sword at the young woman's heart. Theodora didn't stop until the blade cut a hole through her dress and the tip pierced her skin. Blood dripped onto the white gown. Charlee stared wide-eyed. Theodora never flinched. "I will do whatever I can to stop her, to stop the Brotherhood, and bring peace. You do not need trust me, but you need to use me. Once we have the medallion, I am the only one who can guide you to the fire tree that holds the spirits of the Brotherhood. I still feel a connection to them, and we will need that to open a gateway to them."

Penaiya pulled her blade away. Her eyes locked on the blood dripping from the blade. "It makes no sense to return the medallion to those who created it."

"It is the only way to destroy it." Theodora balled her hands into fists. She didn't even bother to dab the slight wound on her chest. Her face was rigid, showing no signs of pain. "I don't claim to understand it, but I had a chance to look into the mind of my teacher, Serior. I saw that if the medallion were placed back into the heart of the fire tree, you would extinguish the flame and forever vanquish what remains of the Brotherhood's power."

Charlee's mom raised an eyebrow. "Why do we need you to guide us back to the fire tree? You've told us it lies under the badlands beyond the mountains. We can find it with or without you and throw the medallion into the fire ourselves."

Theodora sighed. "I wish it were that easy. I learned something else by gazing into Serior's mind. The fire tree is only in one place from sunrise to sunset. To those standing inside the cavern that encloses the fire tree, the shift is imperceptible, nevertheless the change does come. Before, the shift was limited to our world. I fear now that the medallion, and my twisted double, has the Guardian's ability to open gateways, that the fire tree can shift between worlds and dimensions."

"Perfect." Charlee's dad rumbled.

"I can get you there—I swear it." Theodora raised her voice. "Even now I can feel the Brotherhood buried deep within my thoughts. Once we have the medallion, my mind can lock on the fire tree. Please…please let me do this in the name of my mother and my sister."

"You dare—" Penaiya began.

"Enough," Charlee shouted. "There's no more time to argue about this. Who knows what's happening on Earth right now? We must cross over and stop that Theodora, get the medallion, and find that damn fire tree. I'm going, and this Theodora is going with me. If no one else will stand with me…fine."

The unicorn neighed, raising his head and stomping his hooves.

Charlee smiled at her protector. "Well, I figured you'd go, too."

"Your father and I have already discussed it," Charlee's mom strolled to her. "I will journey with you. He has, somewhat reluctantly, agreed to remain here to watch over Megan and to help our people rebuild."

"Uh, I agreed on one condition," her dad corrected. "I'll give you forty-eight hours to contact me. If I have not heard from you by then, I'll have Megan open a gateway, and we'll come join the fight."

Charlee nodded at her dad. He knew the truth—the only way Megan opened a gateway large enough the first time was with their mom's help. No, he and Megan would be stuck in this world for the time being. He was willing to stay back to protect Megan, even if he wanted his own vengeance against the evil Theodora.

"I'll join you, Guardian." Kraannaannn fluttered his wings. "I have a taste for sorceress blood."

Charlee shook her head. "Uh, Kraannaannn, I'm not sure a dragon would go over so well back home. And if we have any chance to surprise Theodora, I'm not sure having a massive dragon along is the best way to go. Don't get me wrong, I want you there. More than anything. But—"

Kraannaannn reared his head back. "I'm going, Guardian. There is a power dragons have among non-magics. We can disguise our presence and appear invisible. It does not work on those with magic abilities. Theodora will know of me, but she'll probably sense you anyway. The humans will not see me if I do not wish them to. Guardian, I will be joining you on this journey. Do not challenge a dragon."

Smiling, she patted his neck. "Thank you, my friend."

Penaiya frowned. "I will go, too."

"I think it would be better for our people if you remained here, Penaiya," Charlee's mom suggested. "They need you to be with them now more than ever."

"On the contrary, you are Queen." Penaiya extended a hand to her. "You should be with our people. They will be comforted to have their true Queen lead them toward a new beginning."

They embraced, then Charlee's mom spoke. "You are the only leader they know. Please, stay with them. If I return, we can determine the future then. For now, be the leader they deserve. My husband will help all he can."

"Yes, my Queen." Penaiya started to bow.

Charlee's mom stopped her. "You do not bow to anyone."

A silence fell over the courtyard, interrupted by Theodora. "I have one more suggestion. The young girl who goes by the name Assara and believes herself to be the daughter of my double should join us. She may be a magically-generated creature herself and quite confused, but her journey is not yet ended. I would like a chance to speak with her."

§ § §

A torch in one hand, key in the other, Charlee stood in front of Assara's dungeon cell. Young Theodora was just behind her. A damp chill cocooned her. The crackling flames pushed away the darkness, but the gloom pressed against her chest. She hesitated before entering. On the other side of the heavy wooden door was the clone of her best friend, Sandra. How could she face her? Feelings of hate, regret, and sadness swirled like a cyclone across her thoughts.

Charlee had condemned Assara to the same isolation she'd gone through so deep beneath the castle. Charlee inhaled deeply. She would never shake what it felt like to be left to rot in this dungeon. Sure, Assara was given food and water, but her waist had been chained against the wall. She was just too dangerous.

Was it a mistake to lock her in such a foul place? Maybe, but what about all the death she'd caused? She had to pay for the lives she'd taken even if her mind had been warped by the evil Theodora.

Assara had a choice, and she chose the wrong path.

Charlee squared her shoulders. She glanced back once at Theodora, who nodded back to her. Charlee then slid the key into the lock and turned until the mechanism click-clacked. Releasing a sigh, she slowly opened the door, which creaked loudly.

Light spilled into the dungeon. Assara blinked but did not look away. Though pale, her hair matted against her face, she lifted her chin and pushed out her chest. Next to her sat the food and water bowls, kicked over. Nothing had been eaten.

Assara glared at Charlee with fire in her eyes until young Theodora stepped around Charlee and crossed through the doorway. Assara's eyes widened, and her mouth dropped open. She reached for the woman she thought was her mother.

"Mother, you have come for me," she blurted, wrestling against the chains around her waist. "I have called to you, but you did not answer. I feared you forgot your daughter, but you have returned to me. I am so sorry I failed you."

"You have failed no one, Assara," Theodora answered. "You fought bravely on behalf of your mother."

Charlee's face grew hot. What was Theodora saying? She started to speak, but Theodora motioned for her to remain silent.

Assara stopped thrashing about. Her eyes reddened, or maybe that was just the reflection from the torch's flame. "Thank you, Mother, but I beg for your forgiveness."

"Young one—" Theodora started to say.

"Mother," Assara interrupted, "your face is different. You look much younger. What has happened to you?"

Charlee cringed. *Here we go.* This little reunion was about to get ugly.

Theodora leaned toward Assara. "Young one, that is because I am not your mother. I am Theodora, but I am not the one who brought you into this world. In fact, Assara, this will be difficult for you to hear, but the woman you call mother, the one who left you here, is nothing more than a creation of magic. She is not real, but I am."

Assara wedged up against the wall. Her lips tightened. "Guardian, you would twist my mind by bringing this impostor before me. I wish you were dead. I should have moved with greater haste to kill you."

Charlee knelt to one knee. "I hadn't thought about it, but you had so many chances to kill me, and you didn't. You hesitated. Why? Maybe you do have a little of my friend's blood inside of you. Maybe you couldn't kill me."

"Hand me a sword and let's find out." Assara kicked her legs against the ground.

"Assara, I am no impostor." Theodora sat down, crossing her legs, hands in her lap. "I am Theodora, the real Theodora. It is your mother who isn't real. She has no love for you. She will not come for you. She has no capacity to care for you or anyone else. She only knows to conquer those who stand in her way because that is how she has been programmed by the spirits that created her."

"Lies." Assara spit at Theodora. "She will come for me, and she will make you suffer for imprisoning me."

Charlee's eyes shifted from Assara to Theodora. How would the young woman frozen by Assara's mother react—with anger?

Theodora simply wiped the spittle from her cheek. Her voice was gentle.

"A moment ago, I told you that you fought bravely for your mother. I meant it, but it doesn't mean you fought for the right cause. You have been manipulated just as I was. I have a story to share with you."

"I have no interest in your words." Assara turned her head away.

"Nevertheless, you will listen." Theodora slid up against the wall next to Assara. She then began her story, sharing the details of how she had found the fire tree and was told by Serior that she was to usher in a new age of rule by the Brotherhood aided by the power of the medallion. She told of how, when she showed weakness, the medallion had been taken from her and used to generate a cloned Theodora, one without compassion filled with only one thought—to rule worlds by force.

When she finished the story, Theodora explained how Assara, too, had been cloned from a girl named Sandra from Earth who had been held hostage by the Brotherhood's Theodora.

"You, Assara, were created for one purpose—to break the Guardian's spirit and kill her. Not because the Guardian is evil, as your mother taught you, but because the Guardian tried to stop your mother from carrying out the Brotherhood's dark mission."

Charlee held her breath.

Assara turned her head toward Theodora. Her eyebrows furrowed. The muscles in her neck quivered. "I will not bend to your lies."

Charlee rolled her eyes. "It's all true, Assara. Has your mom come back for you? No. She's left you here. She doesn't care about this world anymore. She wants mine and probably others since she stole my powers."

Theodora stood and dusted herself off. "Young one, whether you believe my story or not makes no difference. Soon you will know the truth."

"And how is that?" Assara uttered.

Theodora raised an eyebrow. "Because you're coming with us to Earth."

CHAPTER 17

The Homecoming

EVERY MUSCLE IN Charlee's body screamed in agony inside the gateway. Blood dripped from her nose, and a salty taste slid onto her lips. More blood oozed from her ears, the warm liquid spreading down the sides of her face. Her head pounded as if an explosion had detonated in the back of her skull. She extended her quivering arms, but a force pushed back, like a heavy weight she just couldn't bear.

Though contact with her sister had replenished some of her Guardian abilities, her powers had not fully returned. Opening a gateway for four people and a Changeling—not a problem. Opening a gateway large enough for a dragon when you're already weak was a stupid and painful idea.

She dropped to one knee against the weight of the gateway, and a grunt escaped her lips. The blue energy field surrounding them dimmed. If she didn't hold it open long enough, who knows where they might end up. They'd be lost, and she might not have enough magic to open another portal.

You have to hold on. She tried standing, but her legs wobbled.

"Guardian, I should not have come," Kraannaannn shouted. "I'm too big. It's killing you."

"I'm fine…just a little longer." Charlee wiped away blood pooling around her mouth. "We're almost there."

A familiar laugh echoed in her mind. *"Does it hurt, Guardian? Why do you cause yourself to suffer so? Stop this reckless quest against me. You cannot win. Why don't you just accept your defeat, and instead of challenging me, join me. There is still time for us to forge a relationship where you serve at my side. I can forgive all that has transpired."*

Shut up, Theodora. Get out of my head. Charlee forced herself to stand. *We're going to stop you and destroy that medallion.*

The sorceress laughed harder. *"Tsk, tsk, Guardian, always so rude. All right, as you wish. Come to me and die."*

Charlee grabbed her head. *I said, get out of my—*

The blue gateway slammed shut behind them. It had reached its terminus, but where had they emerged? Charlee's legs failed her. She fell backward. Two sets of hands grabbed her before she struck the ground. They softly laid her onto a bed of cool damp grass. Her mom and the young Theodora knelt on either side of her, both holding her hands gently.

"You did it, baby." Her mom tore off a piece of black robe and cleaned the blood from Charlee's face. "You got us home."

Charlee's head spun. She fought against nausea swirling in her stomach. "But where are we?"

"In the park not far from our house," her mom answered. "We're back in San Francisco."

The sky over her mom's shoulder was dark but clear. Nighttime had already fallen over the city. Stars dotted the skyline, and a few gray puffy clouds floated overhead. A soft breeze rattled leaves in nearby trees. The sweet scent of recently mowed grass hung heavy.

An eerie silence hovered over the park.

"Help me stand up." Charlee rose on her elbows.

Her mom shook her head. "Take your time—"

"There's no time." She grabbed her mom by the shoulders and slowly stood.

Charlee gazed beyond the park toward the Bay. If Theodora had attacked, no signs of a battle lingered. The lights of the city shined as usual, casting a familiar yellow glow into the night and across the water. Where was the destruction? Where were the people Theodora had transformed into her monstrous army? Where were the fires and the screaming sirens?

The city seemed at peace.

"Something is very wrong here." Charlee swung around to look at each member of her group.

"We should not let down our guard," the young Theodora offered. "This calm could belay an unseen danger."

"Maybe your world has accepted Mother as the rightful ruler." Assara stood with her arms tied behind her back. A second rope entwined her waist, the other end wrapped around the Changeling's unicorn neck. "See, mother doesn't bring war. She brings peace. You are the ones causing bloodshed."

Kraannaannn lowered his massive head toward Charlee. "Stand ready. Someone approaches from among the trees. It is a rather small life form…a child."

Charlee cringed. What was that child going to think of a dragon in the middle of the park? The screams of terror would bring trouble. "Uh, Kraannaannn, maybe you should do that invisible thing."

The dragon snorted. "Do not fear. No one will see me unless I allow it."

Her mom scratched her chin. "I think our bigger concern should be why a child would be out alone at night. Something doesn't feel—"

A crunch of a dried leaf on the ground revealed movement from the line of trees. Kraannaannn was right. Something, or someone, approached.

"I could just devour the little being." Kraannaannn's grin widened. "I am a bit hungry."

Charlee frowned. "I know you're joking."

Another crunch of a leaf revealed someone hid among the trees. Charlee gripped the handle of the sword at her side but did not unsheathe the weapon. She inched toward the trees, motioning for the others to wait.

"Whoever is there come on out," she urged. "It's okay. We're friends. We're not going to hurt you."

A face peered from behind a tree. Charlee stepped closer. It was a boy's face, surrounded by a mop of red hair with chubby cheeks and deep-set light blue eyes clearly visible despite the night shadows reaching out from the trees.

"That's right." Charlee knelt. "Come on out. You're safe with us."

The boy eased away from the tree but quickly retreated, hugging the tree trunk. "I'm scared," he mumbled in a high-pitched voice.

"It's okay." Charlee slid even closer. She forced herself to smile despite the chill between her shoulder blades. "What are you doing out here by yourself after dark? Shouldn't you be at home? Are you lost? Don't be afraid. We can help."

The boy pushed away from the tree. He wiped his nose with a sleeve of his red sweatshirt, tucked his hands into his pant pockets, and slowly crept toward Charlee. "You really won't hurt me?"

"I promise." She studied the boy. He stood several inches shorter than her. His arms and legs were thin despite a slightly rounded stomach, kind of like her. Freckles dotted his cheeks.

"Who are you?" he asked softly.

"I'm Charlee. I live here in San Francisco, like you." She peered over the boy's shoulder toward the trees. No one else was visible. "What's your name?"

"Jeremy." He wiped his nose for a second time.

"Cool name. Jeremy. Isn't it kind of late for you to be in the park by yourself?"

"I don't know."

"Where are your parents?"

"I...I don't know."

Charlee's blood turned to ice inside her veins as the hair on the back of her neck stiffened. He didn't know where his parents were? She turned toward the others. Something was terribly wrong.

Her mom walked up to Jeremy and lowered to one knee. "Jeremy, how old are you?"

"I don't know." Jeremy stuck a finger into his nose. He stared at them without blinking. Charlee stood and backed away.

Her mom offered a comforting smile. "Jeremy, is there anyone else around — maybe hiding in the park somewhere?"

"Maybe yes…maybe no." Jeremy tilted his head to the side. He smiled ear to ear. "That's for me to know and you to find out."

Charlee reached for the handle of her sword. "Kraannaannn, do you sense anything or anyone?"

Kraannaannn scanned the park. "None are in the park, Guardian, but I sense a large group not far away."

Charlee knelt again toward the boy. "Hey, Jeremy—"

"What do you want, Guardian?" A change came over Jeremy's voice. The soft pitch became deep and crusty. He glared at her without blinking, the smile fixed to his face.

"What did you call me?" Charlee backed away from him.

Jeremy's expression shifted. His lips curled into a frown. His head tilted to the opposite side. His voice was once again a child's. "I called you…Guardian." He began to jump and dance around, singing the name over and over. "You're the Guardian. La, la, la…Guardian. La, la, la…Guardian. Death to the Guardian. La, la, la…Die, Guardian."

"Jeremy, what are you saying?" Charlee's lifted her sword.

Jeremy froze in front of her. Blood dripped from his eyes, nose, and ear. "I said, die, Guardian." His words gurgled as more blood spilled between his lips.

"Jeremy!" Charlee extended her free hand to him.

"No!" The boy reached behind his back and pulled what looked like a handgun from his pocket. The gun shook in his little hands. Bloody tears slid down his cheeks. "Mommy and daddy said I have to kill the Guardian for the Empress. They said I can't come home until I kill you."

Charlee's face numbed. She hadn't come home to be killed by a kid under a Theodora spell, but she couldn't harm him. "Jeremy, listen—"

A flash of green energy whizzed by her, striking the gun, ripping it from his hands. Jeremy cried out and dropped to his knees. Charlee swung around. An emerald glow encircled young Theodora's hands.

"No, he's just a boy! It's not his fault!" Charlee rushed to Jeremy's side.

Shrieking, he clutched his hands. "You hurt me. The Guardian hurt me. The Guardian is evil, like Mommy and Daddy told me." His cheeks covered in his own blood, he climbed to his feet and ran away. "Help me, the Guardian is here. The Guardian is bad. Mommy and Daddy, Empress, the Guardian is evil."

In the distance shouts could be heard. "In the park," a female voice declared.

"The evil one…she's come, just like Empress Theodora said," a man yelled.

"She must be stopped," another man screamed. From the streets outside the park came the thunderous sound of a mob's footsteps.

Assara laughed. "That boy is right. You are evil. You see, Guardian, even your own people know the truth. They have joined with Mother."

"Shut up." Charlee's thoughts raced. What had Theodora done to everyone? How many people were infected by her?

Her mom crossed to her and placed a hand on Charlee's shoulder. "Clearly, Theodora is using some kind of mind control."

Watching Jeremy slip away, Charlee turned to her mom. "We'll have to figure out a way to help...everyone, but right now there's a bunch of very confused people coming after us. We best get out of here, fast."

"I could easily remove the danger." Steam rose from Kraannaannn's snout.

Charlee shook her head. "Kraannaannn—"

In the distance came Jeremy's voice. "The Guardian is there. She hurt me. She's very bad." The trees on the outskirts of the park shook. Voices, maybe hundreds, maybe more, mingled together in a chorus of fear and anger.

"Death to the Guardian."

"She'll destroy our world."

"We must protect Empress Theodora."

Charlee turned to the others. "Everyone, climb onto Kraannaannn's back."

The young dragon lowered his body. "The Guardian's right. We must take to the skies and find safe haven."

As everyone did as she directed, Charlee climbed onto the unicorn. She then removed the rope that attached her protector to Assara and handed it to her mom. "Take Assara with you. I'll fly with the Changeling and lead them away from you. Hurry. Kraannaannn, get them out of here."

"No, Charlee, we can't separate," her mom protested.

"It's me they're after, Mom."

A crowd burst through the trees. Some held bats and knives. A few grasped handguns. Still others brandished assault rifles. Blood began to drip from their eyes, noses, and mouths the moment they saw her—just like Jeremy. What had Theodora done to them?

"Go!" Charlee screamed.

"Kill them." A man dressed in camouflage aimed his rifle at her.

Kraannaannn roared. "Humans, face a dragon!" He spit fire into the purple sky. The man with the assault rifle fell back, and the weapon dropped from his hands. Everyone else screamed, retreating into the trees.

They could see Kraannaannn!

Charlee exhaled. She wasn't sure if that was wise, but he probably saved her life...again. She peered back at him. "Go! Now! Get out of here!"

The dragon, with everyone on his back, spread his wings and leaped into the sky. Charlee and the Changeling did the same, launching high over the crowd, hovering above them as they massed in the park's center. The crowd swelled as more people filled the park, like waves rolling on shore.

All bled.

"I can't believe what I'm seeing." Charlee gripped the unicorn's mane. "What has Theodora—?"

A gunshot rang out from below. The round zipped past the unicorn. Charlee mashed her body against the unicorn. "They're firing at us!" More gunfire erupted in bursts, rounds zipping past them.

"Get us out of here!" Charlee screamed.

The Changeling shot like a rocket into the night. Higher and higher he climbed above the park. Charlee peered down and gasped. Like a scene from some zombie movie, people wandered the streets. They shook their fists at her, chanting for her death in some sick chorus that echoed through the city.

"We've got to find somewhere to hide." She gritted her teeth. How could she have let this happen? All those poor people were under some type of mind control, but where was the sorceress? Why had she not appeared with the medallion to face Charlee herself? She had the medallion and unimaginable power. She must know they'd crossed over. "We've got to figure this out. We must find a way to help all these people."

The Changeling swerved away from the park and cut a line toward the Bay. Yes, maybe they could hide among the docked ferries. She needed time to gather her thoughts.

Before they got very far, a blinding light targeted them from below. The Changeling ducked away, but another light zeroed in on them, and then a third and fourth. Spotlights blazed from the city, sweeping the night skies for her and the unicorn.

"This is crazy!" Charlee bit her lip. "How much of the city has Theodora infected with her magic. Does everyone want to kill—"

A new light ensnared them—this one from the sky. A helicopter flew at them from the west. "Look out!"

The Changeling arched its wings to soar away only to find another helicopter barreling toward them from the east. A third and fourth charged from the north and south. She and the unicorn were surrounded. Charlee tensed her muscles and breathed through gritted teeth. What was she supposed to do? She couldn't fight back and hurt anyone.

The helicopters hovered around them. Their spinning rotors unleashed a deafening cry. A voice spoke through a loudspeaker. "This is the San Francisco Police Department. We have orders from Empress Theodora to take you into custody. Comply and you will not be harmed. If you do not, we will open fire. It's your choice, Guardian."

Every muscle in her body stiffened. She leaned closed to the Changeling's ear. "Move it...now!"

As always, the Changeling silently responded. Throwing its wings back, it dove toward the street. The helicopters gave chase, nimbly tipping toward the street, their engines screaming from the effort.

The unicorn eased out of the dive between two skyscrapers just above a crowded city street where squad cars, their sirens blaring, joined in the chase. More shots rang out. Rounds whizzed by close—too close!

She pressed her body against the Changeling. *Is everyone under Theodora's control?* Even if everyone wanted to kill her, she still had to find a way to help them and break the spell. She just had to. She was done letting Theodora get the best of her.

The unicorn slid around one corner, then another, slipping between the giant buildings. All four helicopters matched each maneuver.

"Let's see how high they can go!" Charlee leaned forward, her head even with the unicorn's. They arched skyward, climbing so fast her feet lost their grip. Legs flailing behind her, Charlee wrapped her arms around the beast's neck. A quick glance back revealed the helicopters had fallen behind.

"We're losing them!" Charlee released a lungful of air. Her legs reclaimed their position on either side of the unicorn. "Keep climbing!"

An array of stars glowed bright as the city lights faded far below. Calm filled the night sky this high up. Even the whine of the helicopters spinning blades grew faint. Charlee shivered against the cold. A silvery mist escaped her mouth and nose. Her lungs started to burn, and her chest grew heavy.

"Let's level out and find a place to hide. Regroup. Find the others." She spoke softly, her words broken between shallow breaths. "I hope they're all right." How could they not be? They had a dragon.

Channeling magic, the Changeling wrapped her in a protective yellow air bubble. Her body quickly warmed, and her breathing slowed. She was safe for the moment.

"Thank—"

A thunderous rumble cut through the high-altitude silence. Light surrounded them…again.

What now?

"This is Brigade Unit One of the San Francisco Army Reserve, and this Black Hawk gunship has its cannons trained on you," a man's voice explained matter-of-factly over a loudspeaker. A massive, armored beast of a helicopter hovered before them a stone's throw away. "Surrender, Guardian, or we will be forced to fire on you."

Charlee's mouth dropped open. *Think, Charlee. Don't lose it.* She placed her lips against the unicorn's ear. "I'm going to try to speak to them. Can you make my voice loud enough for them to hear?"

The Changeling nodded.

"Please listen to me." Her words boomed louder than the roar of the helicopter's spinning rotor blades. "I'm not your enemy. You're under mind control. You must believe me. I can stop all of this."

"Comply with my orders or die." The voice became gruff.

"I can't surrender to you. If I do, the person whose done this to you will win. You must believe me." Charlee's hands balled into fists. She shook her head.

"One more chance." The man slowed his words.

Charlee pounded a fist into her open palm. "Then you'll have to shoot me because I'm not going to give up."

"You leave us no choice. Fire…"

The unicorn spun away. Big guns exploded to life, spewing rounds at her and the Changeling. Charlee covered her head, but no bullet struck her or the Changeling. Instead, the bullets ricocheted off something big, as if each round slammed into steel.

She slowly lifted her head.

The dragon hovered between her and the helicopter, his natural armor more than a match for the gunship. Kraannaannn unleashed a roar and spit fire toward the stars. In response, the helicopter turned and fled.

"Are you all right?" the dragon asked.

"Thanks to you and the Changeling."

The young Dragon Lord kept his eyes on the fleeing helicopter. "May I chase down that craft and devour the occupants?"

"No, we're going to save them, not eat them."

"Then come with me." Kraannaannn's voice hardened. Maybe he was disappointed he couldn't feed. "The others are waiting for us. We have found something that might suggest not everyone is against you."

CHAPTER 18

Can It Really Be?

CHARLEE AND THE Changeling followed Kraannaannn across the city to the rolling hillsides of Golden Gate National Park. What could the dragon have to show her? Her mind tingled, even as the weight of what she was up against pressed against her temples, like a vise slowly crushing her. She had to stop Theodora, or whomever this witch was, without harming an entire city, or worse, the whole world, ready to kill her under some spell.

Kraannaannn fluttered his wings ahead of them and landed on a lush green cliff. Not far away, the Golden Gate Bridge—ablaze in an orange glow beneath the darkening skies—stretched across the Bay. The others emerged from thick shrubs growing throughout the park.

Charlee and the Changeling landed softly next to the dragon. Before Charlee could climb off the unicorn, her mom wrapped her in a tight embrace.

"What were you thinking?" Her mom gently grasped Charlee's cheeks.

"What do you mean?" Charlee lifted her mom's hands away.

"Never do that again." Her mom pulled her close again. Her heart beat so heavy Charlee could feel it through their embrace. "We are in this together, and we stay together no matter what. I told you I'm not letting you out of my sight again, and I meant it."

"Mom."

Her mom shook her head. Deep lines formed under her eyes. "No, you listen. You may be a Guardian, but I'm still your mother, and as risky as this little adventure is, my job is to do everything I can to protect you, and that means you always stay by my side."

From behind them came laughter—Assara's laughter. "So touching. Really. It will be even more touching when you die together."

Kraannaannn lowered his massive head down to Assara. "You would be wise to watch your tongue, girl."

Assara sneered. "I don't fear you, dragon. Soon you'll be dead, too, like your father. None of you have very long to live."

The young Theodora, who held the rope attached to Assara's waist, wrapped an arm around the clone's neck and forced her to her knees. "Child, how foolish are you to challenge a dragon, especially a hungry one who would take great joy at ripping away your flesh and dining on your bones. Very soon, when the truth comes crashing down, you will be glad for the company you now keep, for your life will depend on them."

Assara glared at Charlee but did not speak again.

Charlee again grasped her mom's hands. "Sorry, Mom, I'll try to do what you tell me, but I can't promise. I must stop Theodora—or whatever that crazy witch is."

"We all have to stop her." Her mom raised an eyebrow.

Charlee swallowed her next words. *No, this is all my fault. It has to be me. Can't you see that? I let her escape twice now. None of you should even be here. I should have come alone. You're all in danger because of me.* The silence of that moment spread across the hillside, interrupted by the crashing of the sea against rocks at the cliff's base.

"Guardian," Kraannaannn finally chimed in. "I told you I had something to show you...something that might give you hope. Look to the bridge." The dragon pointed toward the Golden Gate Bridge.

Something hung from pylons above the bridge, but it was too far away to see it clearly. She embraced the Changeling's neck, allowing her protector's energy to enhance her strength. Her whole body pulsated, and weariness slipped away.

She scanned the bridge again, this time with her vision magically improved. A banner hung loosely from the bridge. Someone had painted a simple message in red letters. Her mouth dropped open, and she couldn't hold back a gasp.

The banner read, *The Guardian is a Friend.*

§ § §

"We do have friends." Charlee's mom joined her by the cliff's edge and placed an arm around her shoulder. "Theodora hasn't turned everyone against us."

"Yeah, but who are they, and are they safe?" Charlee bit the inside of her cheek and slid away from her mom. She paced back and forth, eyes locked on the banner, then froze. A warmth spread through her. Could it be her best friend Sandra? Could she be unaffected by the spell, or had she fallen prey to Theodora?

Charlee rubbed the back of her neck. She had to find her friend and save her if she was in danger. But right now, there was another question to resolve. "The bigger question is where is the witch and why hasn't she come after me herself?"

"Because she fears you. More importantly, the Brotherhood fears you." The young Theodora brushed her blond hair away from her face. "They know if you're here you have your powers back. And they know they can't control you. The medallion can't control you."

"Mother fears no one," Assara glared at Charlee with a rigid face. "Guardian, she'll kill everyone in your family and make you watch before she ends your miserable life."

Charlee clenched her fists. "I've had enough of you and your mouth."

Assara smiled wide. "Then silence me, Guardian. You know you want to."

"You'd like me to do that, huh?" Charlee crossed to her, stopping just an arm's length away. A boiling heat spread through her veins, but, taking a deep breath, she let the anger fade and stepped back. "No, I won't. I'm not like you or your *mother.*"

She retreated toward the cliff's edge and studied the banner strung from the Golden Gate. Crossing her arms, Charlee turned to her mom. "There must be a way to figure out where the witch is. If she won't come to us, we're going to have to go to her."

"That's exactly what she wants." Kraannaannn crashed his tail against the ground. It struck with a thud. "She is setting a trap for you."

"Let her." Charlee threw up her arms. "I don't care anymore. I just want to face her and end this already."

"We have to outthink that fake Theodora." Her mom gently brushed her fingers over a yellow flower. "If she's setting a trap, we have to use it against her."

Charlee scoffed, "None of you know her like I do. She's been in my head. She's still there. She's watching me even now. I can feel her presence. There's no way to trick her. We just play her game until someone dies...hopefully her."

"The Guardian is right." The young Theodora's face hardened. "Force is how we defeat her, defeat the Brotherhood, and destroy the medallion in the fires from which it was created."

Kraannaannn snorted. His scales clicked as they rose up his back. "It comes as no surprise to me that you would want us to deliver the medallion back to such fires, Theodora. How can we trust anything you say? I still question bringing you on this quest. For all we know, you desire all the power for yourself to carry out your own conquests."

"She's telling the truth." Charlee spoke through clenched teeth. They didn't have time for this bickering.

"Charlee, maybe Kraannaannn's right." Her mom spoke softly as her eyebrows drew closer together. She tapped her steepled fingers together. "I'm not sure I trust this Theodora either. I don't see how you can be so sure."

"Because of Cryton, Mom...he told me the same thing." Charlee's gaze shifted from her mom to the dragon, then to the young Theodora. "That the only way to destroy the medallion was to throw it back into the fire. He believed that, and I must believe it, too. I'm asking you to have faith not in Theodora, but in me."

"You know I do. You're my—"

A crack rang out.

Her mom convulsed. She crumbled to her knees, eyes and mouth wide open as if in shock. "Charlee," she uttered, falling onto her stomach. Blood seeped from underneath her dark robe just below her right shoulder blade.

"Mom!" Charlee's body hollowed out. Her ears pounded with the sound of the gunshot. Time seemed to slow.

Another crack echoed through the park. A round struck the ground at Charlee's feet, kicking up dirt and grass. Before another shot could find a target, the unicorn leaped over Charlee and her mom, spreading his wings to hide them. Kraannaannn roared and stretched his body over Charlee and her mom, shielding them from danger. More shots rang out, ricocheting off the dragon's armor.

His mouth glowed orange. He aimed his snout toward an outcropping of trees. "Let me light the trees on fire and burn our attacker to ashes."

"No." Charlee knelt at her mom's side and slowly rolled her onto her back. Her mom's eyes blinked as short shallow breaths escaped her mouth. She smiled weakly and lifted a hand to Charlee's face.

"Mom, you're going to be okay. Please be okay." Her mom nodded but didn't speak.

More shots ripped through the night.

"Guardian, we—" Kraannaannn began.

"Allow me," Theodora interrupted. She stepped away from Kraannaannn and stretched out her hands toward the trees. She uttered an incantation. Her eyes burned red, and a yellow energy encircled her hands. "Enough."

Bolts of lightning exploded from her palms. The fiery burst smashed into the trees, splintering the trunks and slicing branches into pieces. Cracked wood littered the grass. Silence followed and the gunshots stopped.

Young Theodora took a deep breath and lowered her hands.

"Did you kill them?" Charlee stared through the black smoke rising from the mangled trees.

"I doubt it," she answered. "I just scared them off. But if I did kill, right now that is not our main concern."

"Charlee," her mom whispered. Her face grew pale. She coughed and gasped for a breath. "Don't worry…"

"Don't try to talk, Mom." Charlee's vision blurred from hot tears beneath her eyelids. Her fingers were coated in her mom's warm blood.

Theodora joined Charlee standing at her mom's side. "I can help her. Will you let me?"

Charlee nodded. "Yes, please…hurry! She's losing a lot of blood."

"Oh, this is just so sad." Assara, who stood off to the side, smirked. She inched away but couldn't get far. The dragon stood on the end of the rope, the other end still knotted around her waist. Her hands remained tied behind her back.

"Shut up," Charlee hissed. "Just shut your—" Another helicopter approached from the sea, charging toward the cliff.

"Shall I dispatch that noisy flying machine?" Kraannaannn's tail twitched. His spiked ears stood at attention.

"No...wait." Charlee's gaze focused on Theodora. "Keep her safe."

Theodora leaned in closer to Charlee's mom. "I will."

Gently placing her mom's head on Theodora's lap, Charlee rose to her feet and faced the thundering flying machine. The helicopter reached the cliff and circled overhead. Dirt kicked up all around them. Charlee shielded her eyes and turned back toward her mom. The Changeling shielded her with his wings. Kraannaannn raised his head to the craft, ready to blow it out of the sky with one spit of his fire breath.

"Don't do anything." Charlee placed a hand on the dragon's hind leg.

The whining propellers drowned out her voice. Her body tensed, waiting for shots to ring out, but none came. No one spoke from the helicopter, demanding she surrender. *Strange.*

The craft circled one more time and landed on a flat stretch about half a football field away. Charlee rubbed dust from her eyes. Glancing back at the dragon, she moved toward the helicopter. Her fingers sparked with energy.

"Guardian, stay back," Kraannaannn urged.

"Not this time," she answered.

A shadowy figure, tall, face shielded by a flight helmet, climbed from the helicopter and slowly walked toward her. Charlee's hands squeezed into fists. A white glow spread from her fingertips, illuminating the night around her. The individual, dressed in jeans and a jacket with the words *San Francisco Police Department* on the front pocket, stopped maybe twenty feet away.

Charlee turned her body sideways. The best way to dodge any bullets. "Have you come to kill me?"

"So, Guardian, above everything else, now you're going to unleash a dragon on my city," a man's voice responded.

Charlee's mouth shot open. It couldn't be, could it? The man removed his helmet and crossed the rest of the distance to her. Charlee couldn't help but cry. "Mr. Flores!"

CHAPTER 19

We Are Not Alone

CHARLEE COLLAPSED INTO Mr. Flores's arms. The father of her best friend and the city's deputy police chief held her tightly to his chest. His hand stroked her hair. Then, he gently gripped her shoulders and ended the embrace. He smiled through quivering lips as his normally hard eyes softened. Dark circles surrounded them.

No blood dripped from his eyes, ears, nose, and mouth.

"Welcome home, kid." His deep voice was tinged with pain. Why? Was Sandra okay? "Is that really a dragon you've brought to my city?" He gazed past her at the beast.

She ignored the question. "Is it really you?"

"It's me, kid." He released her but kept a hand on her shoulder. His gaze drifted back and forth between her and Kraannaannn. "Your witch has sure created quite the mess here in your absence, young lady."

Charlee studied his face. A scrubby, graying beard covered his narrow cheeks in patches. Still, he looked like she remembered. He recognized her, and not as some destructive evil force come to harm everyone. Had he not been brainwashed like everyone else? Maybe he was. Maybe he was setting her up, but there was still no blood—like everyone else whose mind had been corrupted by Theodora's magic.

She'd still have to watch him carefully, but so many questions swirled through her mind. "Mr. Flores, Sandra?"

"She's okay." He held his hands up as if to thank a higher power. "Most of my family is safe, for now." He paused and lowered his head. "My oldest though... she fell under the spell."

Charlee blinked away tears. "I'm so sorry. I'm sorry I let all this happen, but I'll make it right. I'll save her and everyone else. Mr. Flores, can I see Sandra?"

"Yes, I'll take you to her. In fact, the sooner we're on our way the better. You're going to be spotted here."

"We already were." Charlee gazed over her shoulder to her mom. "My mom's hurt. She's been shot."

"How is she? I have a medical kit in the helicopter." He pointed to the aircraft. "We can't take her to a hospital. It's too dangerous. Nothing here makes sense."

113

Charlee turned back toward the others. "I think there is someone with me who can help her. It's better that we stay together anyway."

"Do you still have that magic bike?" Mr. Flores placed an arm around her shoulder.

"Yes, but there's someone else." Charlee stepped out of the way, so he could see the woman crouched by her mom.

Mr. Flores' eyes bulged. "It's her...the witch!" He lifted a gun from his pocket and aimed it at the young Theodora.

Charlee placed her hand over the gun. "No!"

"What are you doing?" Mr. Flores glared at her. "I have to stop her!"

"No, that's not the woman you know as Theodora." Charlee tightened her grip on the weapon. "This is a friend."

He shook his head. His cheeks turned blood red. "She's tricked you."

"Please, trust me. I can explain it all, but not right now." She motioned for him to lower the weapon. He slowly did. "I have someone else to show you, first. This may be even harder for you to understand." She pointed to Assara, who stood quietly by the dragon. "Mr. Flores, this is Assara. She is the daughter of the woman who is responsible for everything that has happened here."

Mr. Flores gasped. He tucked the gun back into his pocket. His eyes shifted from Charlee to the girl who resembled his daughter. He stumbled toward her, his mouth agape.

"How...how is this possible?" He stopped an arm's length away. "What has the witch done?"

"Like I said, I have a lot to tell you." Charlee wrapped her hands around his arm.

"Does she know who I am?" His voice cracked.

Assara stared at him but didn't speak. Even if she had, it wouldn't have mattered. Unlike the dragon and young Theodora whose magic abilities allowed them to understand English, Assara still only spoke Lengoron.

"She doesn't know you, and she doesn't speak English." Charlee stepped in front of him. "I'm sorry about all of this, Mr. Flores. I really am, and I'm going to stop Theodora, but I must know how bad things are."

He sighed, his focus still on Assara. "Things are very bad. I'll explain, but let me get you somewhere safe."

Kraannaannn lowered his head and sniffed Mr. Flores. Sandra's dad retreated a few steps, his hand clutching the handle of his gun. "Guardian, how do you know we can trust this human." Kraannaannn, speaking English, bared his fangs. "He could be a slave to Theodora. If we go with him, he could lead us into a trap."

Mr. Flores shook his head as his lips pursed. "A dragon that speaks English. Not something you see every day." He stepped closer to the beast, his hand still clutching the gun. "Listen, you overgrown lizard, I'm under no spell. And if you want to survive the night, you'll come with me."

Charlee placed a hand on Kraannaannn's snout. "We can trust him. We have to trust him."

The dragon huffed and licked his sharp teeth. He inched his head closer to Mr. Flores. "If you lie, you'll be my first kill."

Sandra's dad scratched his chin. He eyed Charlee. "When this is over, you and I will have to have a talk about setting some boundaries. First off, no more witches or monsters—and definitely no dragons in my city."

§ § §

They flew under cover of an early morning murky sky as black as the dungeon where Charlee had been left to die. She soared on the unicorn's back with Mr. Flores seated behind her. He'd abandoned the helicopter. Kraannaannn declared the noisy machine too dangerous. Better to fly in silence. The dragon was once again invisible to any non-magics.

The young Dragon Lord cradled Charlee's mom inside his talons. Mr. Flores protested, saying she'd be better off inside the helicopter, but Kraannaannn insisted he be the one to carry her, and it was best not to argue with a dragon. Assara and the young Theodora perched atop his spiked back.

Charlee' eye fixed on her mom, barely visible within the dragon's protective grip. Her eyebrows drew together. She couldn't hear her mom's thoughts any longer. Ever since they'd found each other again, her mom maintained a mental lock as if she grasped Charlee with her mind and wouldn't let go. She was always there, but not now. *Please be okay, Mom.*

A flicker of a response, weak and pained, flashed through her mind. *Do. Not. Worry. Stay. Focused.* Her mom's words were little more than a whisper, but it was enough.

Just stay with me, Mom.

Charlee tightened her grip on the unicorn's mane. They flew fast and at a high altitude to avoid being spotted by any craft still searching for them.

At Mr. Flores's direction, they flew across the Bay toward Oakland. Searchlights illuminated the night sky beneath them. Those under Theodora's spell searched for her with one apparent goal—to kill her.

She tensed her muscles and leaned back toward Mr. Flores. "Where are you taking us?" She raised her voice over the rush of air that wildly blew her hair.

"Away from the city," he answered.

She nodded and turned forward again. The unicorn passed the Bay and reached land. The lights of Oakland blazed, but no searchlights scanned for them yet. So

115

far so good, but could Mr. Flores really be trusted? On the cliffs she convinced the others to follow him, but what if Theodora controlled him? The witch knew him. She'd faced him in the fight at Alcatraz before Charlee tricked her back to Janasara. *This could be a mistake. No, if Theodora has Mr. Flores under some mind control, I'd know…wouldn't I? There would be blood. Yes, I'd know. Either way, we must be careful.*

She lowered herself to the unicorn's ears and whispered, "Keep a watch out for signs of trouble." Her protector nodded.

They raced beyond Oakland. The shimmering lights of the city slipped away. Only a few pockets of glowing yellow and orange covered the dim landscape. That meant farmland. Mr. Flores was taking them out to the agricultural areas, like where she grew up before her dad moved the family to San Francisco.

"Turn south!" Mr. Flores squeezed her shoulders.

Charlee tugged the unicorn's mane to the left. The Changeling banked to the south. Kraannaannn followed her lead.

"Not much farther." Mr. Flores shouted against the wind.

Nodding, Charlee smiled tightly. Not much farther to what? Until they were safe? Until he delivered them to the evil Theodora? She closed her eyes, inhaled deeply, and drew energy from the Changeling. An electrical current raced through her body. Her limbs vibrated and her muscles pulsated. Opening her eyes, she scanned the horizon with sharpened vision.

The night sky brightened as if the sun pierced the darkness. She peered in every direction but saw no helicopters, no drones, and no aircraft of any kind approaching. She also saw no sign of the Empress. Still, the hairs on her neck stiffened. They flew the rest of the way in silence until Mr. Flores pointed toward the ground.

Below lay a patchwork of land stitched together, like the mixed fabrics on her mom's '60s cut-out jeans. Pockets of light signaled the small towns and isolated farms which bumped up against rolling hillsides that stretched into the night.

"There," he shouted. "My family's farm is down there."

Charlee lifted an eyebrow. "You have a farm?"

"It belonged to my father," he answered. "I could never bring myself to sell it when he died. When all hell broke out, I needed to get my family out of the city, and this seemed like a good choice."

Charlee leaned into the Changeling's unicorn ear. "You heard him. Time to descend. Keep your eyes open for danger." The Changeling hesitated. "It's okay." She patted the unicorn's head. In silence, the Changeling responded. Tipping his right wing and raising the left, her protector dove toward the vast fields.

"The gathering of lights down there is the city of Lodi. Stay away from there," Mr. Flores suggested. "You see that one light by itself up against that hillside? That's our family farm. Fly there."

Charlee drew in a long breath and held it for a heartbeat before exhaling. She patted the unicorn's neck. "You heard him." She peered over at Kraannaannn, who circled above them, watching. She sealed her eyelids tightly. Could Kraannaannn hear her thoughts the way his father could? She tried. *Kraannaannn, I think we can trust him, but don't land until I give the okay. Keep my mom safe."*

The dragon answered. *You be safe, Guardian. If he proves a foe, he'll burn.*

She glared at the dragon. No way would she let him harm Mr. Flores or anyone under Theodora's spell. But how would she stop a dragon? *Just please take care of my mom no matter what.*

I will protect her life with my own, Guardian. The dragon flew higher into the night, vanishing into the protective cover of the dark.

Charlee, the Changeling, and Mr. Flores reached the ground quickly. The Changeling's unicorn hooves touched down on a dirt road with fields of tall alfalfa stretching on either side. If anyone or anything hid among the thick crops, not even her enhanced vision revealed them.

Mr. Flores climbed from the unicorn and took a few steps up the road, which led to a farmhouse dimly lit by a single porch light. Charlee didn't follow.

He turned back to her and grinned softly. "I know you're not sure whether you can trust me. I get it after what you've been through. But you need me. You need my help. I'm not under her spell. And there's others, too, who are hiding scattered about. I know because I've brought them food and water. I've told them about you and that you'd be coming back. We're the ones who strung that sign across the bridge."

Sliding from the unicorn, she cautiously stepped toward him. "You did that? Thank you, but how were you not infected? How were the others not infected?"

He ran fingers through his hair. "I can't really explain it. I brought my wife and Sandra here before your Empress had a chance to use that medallion of hers to control minds. When she first showed up back in the city, I feared she'd come looking for Sandra, so I got my family here and hid them in the basement. It was the best thing I could have done. It protected us from whatever spell she cast. I just wish I could have gotten my oldest daughter, Karla, but she was away from home at university. There was no time. I guess there were others in the city who also happened to be in basements at the right time, and that was enough to block the spell."

Charlee's heart pounded heavy in her chest. "Are they all safe?"

"For now," he uttered.

Her mind quickly focused on her best friend. "Are you saying Sandra is here? She's safe?"

He nodded and motioned toward the house. "See for yourself."

Charlee started slowly to the house but quickly shifted to a fast-paced strut.

A sense of lightness spread across her chest. Adrenaline made her body tingle. Halfway toward the house, a screen door opened and two people emerged on the porch—Sandra and her mom!

Charlee gasped and tears formed. Rocking back and forth on her feet, she lunged forward into a sprint toward the house. Sandra leaped from the porch, stumbling over the dirt path, then charged toward Charlee.

They skidded to a stop an arm's length away and stood in silence. Sandra hadn't changed a bit. Her long brown hair, done up in a ponytail, flowed like a tail down her back. Her eyes still had that determined expression—a mix of anger and concern. Her smile offered the same warmth as when Sandra had first approached Charlee in the school cafeteria.

Sandra was the first to speak. "You're too skinny."

Charlee wiped away a tear. "Yeah, it turns out the best way to lose a few pounds is to be locked away in a dungeon."

With a chuckle, Sandra stared at the ground before looking back up. She kept her hands tucked in the back pockets of her jeans. "Are you okay?"

"I think so...you?"

"Yeah, but I'm worried about my sister, and I've...you know...missed you. You never said goodbye."

Now Charlee glanced toward the ground. "I know. I'm sorry. I wanted to. I even flew by your window on the Changeling."

"I saw."

Charlee felt her chin quiver. "Sandra, are we still friends? Uh, I really need us to still be—"

Sandra threw her arms around Charlee. "Don't ever leave like that again. You're my best friend, and friends stick together always. Your fight is my fight."

They held the embrace until Mr. Flores cleared his throat. "Okay, enough of this sappy crap. We've got a crazy woman out there with an all-powerful weapon to stop. If you girls can bring an end to your moment, there is much for us to discuss, including what you plan to do with a dragon and that clone."

Sandra cocked her head. "Dragon? Clone?"

"I'm sorry." Charlee tried to bore a hole in the ground with her toe.

Mr. Flores placed his arms around both girls and walked them toward his wife. He then joined her, grasping her shoulders. "There is something...rather someone...Charlee has brought with her, and I'm not sure how you both are going to take it." His gazed flitted between his wife and his daughter. "I'm still not sure how to deal with it, but we're going to have to."

"What is it, Peter?" Mrs. Flores gripped his arms.

A gust of wind from above washed over them, kicking up dust. Kraannaannn circled once over the house, then hovered just above the ground, opening his hind claws. Charlee's mom softly rolled onto the road as the dragon landed next to her. Charlee ran over to her, lifting her head.

Her mom blinked and smiled. "I'm better."

Sandra, her mouth wide, cautiously moved toward Kraannaannn. "Charlee, you have a dragon?"

"I belong to no one," Kraannaannn lowered his head and spoke English.

"He's a friend." Charlee still held her mom as she spoke. She frowned at the dragon. "I thought you were going to wait for my signal."

Kraannaannn's ears pricked up. "I could hear your conversation, and I sensed no danger." He sniffed the air and shook his head. "I do not like the smell of humans, but I do not sense evil in their intent."

Young Theodora climbed from the dragon's back with Assara, still held by a rope, at her side. The two stepped from the shadows into the orange glow shed by the house's porch light. Assara's eyes were covered by a cloth strip—the dragon's idea in case the Empress established a mental lock with the girl she called her daughter.

"It's her!" Sandra cried. "The witch!" She scooped up a baseball-sized rock from the ground.

Charlee placed a hand on Sandra's arm. "Not exactly."

CHAPTER 20

Sisters of a Sort

SANDRA'S EYES BLAZED with the wildness of hate not even the darkness could hide. Her teeth ground together with a gnashing sound as fearsome as Kraannaannn's. She squeezed the rock in her hand until her knuckles whitened. Her body tensed, limbs trembling. It was all Charlee could do to hold her back.

"It's Theodora...it's her!" Sandra broke free of Charlee's grip and again raised the rock.

"Sands, no." Mr. Flores spoke softly but with the firmness of a father whose words were not to be challenged.

Sandra turned to him. The rock remained gripped high over her head. "What are you saying?"

He gently grasped her hand until she loosened her hold on the jagged weapon. She then threw her arms around him, dropping the rock into the dirt. Mr. Flores lowered to one knee, brushing Sandra's brown hair from her eyes. "I'm saying listen to your friend. None of this is going to be easy for you...for any of us."

Sandra's chin quivered. She nodded to her dad, then stepped around him to Charlee. Her face flushed and hands formed into fists while her eyes were rigid and unblinking. "Tell me...everything."

"There's so much to say, but we don't have a lot of time." Charlee tried to hold Sandra's gaze, but the intensity of her stare became too much. Charlee lowered her head as if her best friend forced her to. "So, here's the short version. The Theodora you know, the one who...took you...is not real. She's a clone created by the medallion, which I guess contains the souls of an evil brotherhood of magic conjurers who a long time ago tried to use their power to conquer Janasara. When they were defeated, they put all their power into the medallion, which tried to seduce the real Theodora over to, you know, the dark side. When she refused, they imprisoned her in ice and made a clone of her. This young woman here is the real Theodora, and she's here to help."

Theodora stepped forward and bowed. "I'm sorry for the pain you have faced because of me."

Sandra shook her head. "Shut up! I don't want to hear from you."

"I understand." Theodora stood tightly in front of Sandra. She opened her mouth as if to speak more, but instead drifted back.

Charlee took hold of Sandra's hands. "There's someone else I need you to meet, and it's going to be difficult."

She motioned to Theodora, who back stepped to the dragon. Next to the dragon stood Assara, solemn and unmoving, her eyes still blindfolded. Theodora took hold of Assara's arm and tugged her forward into the soft glow of the porch light. With her free hand, Theodora slid off the blindfold, exposing Assara's face to everyone.

"Oh my God!" Sandra's mom cried. Mr. Flores embraced his wife.

Sandra glared in silence. Assara did the same. Neither spoke nor even seemed to breathe. They both took a step closer to each other, studying their mirror image.

Charlee slid between them. "Sandra, all I can tell you is that when that evil version of Theodora kidnapped you, she got some of your DNA and used it to, uh, create a clone of you. She named her Assara, after my grandmother, and called her a daughter. I'm sorry. I didn't want to bring her, but maybe it's for the best, so she understands the truth."

"What is this witchcraft?" Assara, speaking Lengoron, spit at Sandra's feet. She writhed her body to break free of the young Theodora's hold but gave up when Theodora tightened her grip. She breathed heavy. Her gaze zeroed in on Charlee. "You speak of the truth, but this is all part of some trickery."

For the first time, Charlee thought about extending the clone a comforting hand, but that thought quickly faded. "You need to get real, Assara. No one is trying to deceive you but your freaking mom. This person standing in front of you is my best friend Sandra, whose blood runs through your veins."

Sandra turned her back on the clone. She ran both hands through her hair. "I can't deal with this right now. This is crazy, Charlee. Stupid crazy."

Closing the distance to her friend, Charlee placed a hand on her shoulder. "I know. It's hard to believe, but it happened. I'm sorry I couldn't stop it. I should have done more to make sure you were safe."

Spinning around, Sandra nudged her hand away. "You can't blame yourself, but what the hell is she? Is she me? Is she like my twin?"

"I don't have the answers right now." Charlee felt a sharp pain in her chest. How could she put her best friend through this? How could she help her come to terms with it?

"Is she like me at all?" Sandra peered over Charlee's shoulder at her clone.

"Not...really." Charlee placed an arm around Sandra's shoulder. "She's really twisted, Sandra, and she's done some bad things to serve Theodora. She killed Cryton. She killed a lot of good dragons, including this one's father, the Dragon Lord. You see, she's nothing like you. She doesn't have your heart."

"Maybe she just needs our help to find her true heart." Sandra's mom came up behind them.

"No." Charlee shook her head. Mrs. Flores ignored Charlee. She inched toward Assara, extending a hand to her cheek. Assara twisted away.

"I see so much pain and confusion in your eyes." Mrs. Flores smiled at the clone. Her voice was tender, like a mother speaking to her daughter instead of a freakish monster or a killer. To Mrs. Flores, the clone was just a misguided part of her family.

Mr. Flores crossed to his wife. "Baby, she's not—"

His wife quieted him with an icy stare. "I don't care. She needs us. We can't abandon this child, no matter what she's done or how she came to be. Look at her. I see your eyes and my nose. She's part of us."

Assara curled her lips in a twisted grin. "Death, you all...suffer. Mother... kill...she will." She spoke in a broken English. Charlee's eyes bulged. How was that possible?

Sandra raised her fist. "Shut your mouth."

Mrs. Flores held out her hands to both her daughter and the clone. "There has been too much violence. The only way we will all survive is to rely on love. And if there is one thing I know about my family...love conquers all. This child is under the shadows of confusion. We'll show her the way."

Assara again tried to shake free. "You...will...suffer." She broke out in crazed laughter.

The young Theodora tugged hard on Assara's arm, holding her in place. In Lengoron, she uttered, "Sooner or later you're going to realize you are among the only friends you have. I just hope it's a lesson you don't learn too late."

Mr. Flores held his wife. "Okay, baby, we'll do whatever we can for her."

Sandra threw up her hands. "Has everyone gone crazy?"

Charlee half smiled. "A little bit. All I know is for the last time I must face evil Theodora to destroy her and the medallion."

"We will, together." Sandra placed her forehead against Charlee's. "This time we do it together."

§§§

Charlee peered through a wooden shutter at the fields just beyond the farmhouse. In the dead of night, still a couple of hours before sunrise, a white mist settled over the tall alfalfa, like a blanket hiding whatever evil might be slithering their way. An eerie quiet settled over the countryside, save for the chirping of crickets singing to the darkness. Or were they spies for the sorceress, beckoning her to the farm?

She shivered. Was the mist closing in on the farm or was it her imagination. If Kraannaannn weren't already camped outside, keeping watch over the grounds, she'd be out there. But right now, she had to determine their next move. She turned back to the others in the living room.

Sandra sat holding her mom's hands at the dining table. Instead of looking at her daughter, Mrs. Flores stared at Assara, who sat on the floor, one wrist handcuffed to the base of the refrigerator. Assara, legs crossed, kept her head bowed. She hadn't uttered a sound for hours. Young Theodora rested on a couch, her head against a pillow, eyes closed. Exhaustion had overtaken her after using her magic to heal Charlee's mom, who slept in a bed upstairs. The bullet wound had vanished, but she'd be too weak to move for days, Theodora said. Charlee sighed. At least her mom would be okay.

Mr. Flores sipped a cup of coffee on the other end of the couch. Each time he lifted the cup to his mouth, he threw a side glance at Theodora.

Kraannaannn, on guard outside the house, kept his head lowered to an open window on the right side of the living room. One emerald eye was the only part of his body visible. Upstairs, the Changeling, transformed into a dove, perched on a windowsill, holding vigil over Charlee's mom.

Charlee, suppressing a yawn, turned her attention to Mr. Flores. She joined him on the couch. "Tell me again how it all went down. How quickly did the witch take control?" He'd told the story once, but she had to hear it again. She had to understand if she was to defeat the sorceress.

Mr. Flores took a drink, then cleared his throat. He lowered the cup to a wooden table, then rubbed his stubbly face. "She appeared on a Sunday, hovering over the city like some dark angel. To make her presence known, she fired on downtown buildings, shattering glass and tearing through steel. That got the attention of the police, of course, but more importantly the media. News helicopters swarmed, giving her the coverage she wanted. She told the city she had come to rule and said very soon everyone would bow to her and willingly accept her as their Empress."

Rising from the couch, he began to slowly pace. "I have to be honest, I feared for Sandra, so my first instinct was to get her to safety. It wasn't easy; the streets were filled with terrified people gathering their belongings to get out of San Francisco. I'm not proud of running, but my family was my first responsibility. We managed our way through the traffic jams and reached Lompoc just in time." He stopped in front of Charlee. His hands tightened into fists. "But I failed my older daughter. I pleaded with her to come home. She refused, saying she'd stay with her friends at school. I told her I'd come for her once Sandra was hidden, but I was too damn late. I couldn't reach her." He gazed at his wife with pained eyes. "I'm sorry. I'm so sorry. Theodora unleashed that medallion on everyone so quickly. Damn her to hell."

His voiced cracked, but he continued. "I hid Sandra and my wife in the basement here. Then I saw it on the news." His gaze shifted to young Theodora. His chin quivered as he pointed a shaky finger at her. Theodora, now awake, held his gaze, her lips pursed together. "Your twisted doppelganger held the medallion high over the city, and red energy poured from it, spreading like some damned virus, engulfing everything. Schools. Parks. Freeways. Downtown. It spread over the Bay to Oakland and as far as I could see."

Assara lifted her head, and her eyes brightened. "No defeat Mother. Too powerful." Her English was getting better.

Charlee studied the clone. The girl must have magic to be learning English so quickly. Or was it Theodora somehow in her head? Charlee didn't respond to her. She turned back to Mr. Flores. "What happened next?"

Mr. Flores flopped down onto the couch. He took another sip of coffee. "After that, everyone was changed. They started chanting 'Empress Theodora' and bowed down in the streets to her." He slammed the cup on the table. It shattered into tiny bits. What was left of the coffee splashed onto the floor. Charlee jumped. Sandra did, too. Assara grinned ear to ear. Mr. Flores stared at the shards. "Just like that, without so much as a protest or a whimper, we became a conquered people."

"But you weren't affected?" Young Theodora raised an eyebrow. She too spoke English, stronger than Assara. Charlee reasoned it was possible in the same way she just knew the Lengoron language without having been taught. Magic was powerful.

Mr. Flores scowled at the young Theodora and delayed his answer.

Charlee repeated the question. "You all weren't affected?"

"I guess the basement was deep enough below ground to protect us," he said, releasing a breath of air. "Once everyone was under her spell, I left my family here and returned to the city, partly to avoid suspicion. You see, the Police Department, like everyone else, now serves Theodora. I also wanted to find my oldest. I did, and she was also affected. My God, I left her there at the school. What kind of a father…"

"I'm so sorry." Charlee leaped to her feet. Now it was her turn to pace. The wooden floor creaked under her footsteps. "I'll stop Theodora and make sure everyone in your family is safe. I promise. But do you know why everyone wants to kill me? And why does everything seem normal, like nothing has changed, other than everyone hating me."

"Once she had control of the media, she had them display your photograph, and she declared you public enemy number one." Mr. Flores slowly started to lift the broken pieces of his cup from the floor. "Everyone now believes she is a good and loving Empress. More than that, she is even called a goddess, and you are the dark lord out to harm her and everyone else."

125

He sighed. "As for everything being normal, things are far from it. Charlee, she hasn't just taken San Francisco. She controls the world. She unleashed that medallion on country after country. No one had time to put up a fight. Now, the White House has become her castle, and from there she is gathering all the world's military powers for something big. I don't know what, but something…big. And she has put the world to work making more weapons. There is no more school or work, just assembly lines to build her weapons. Oh sure, essential services are still going. The water still flows. The power is still on. Stores are still open. People have food, but only because those services keep people alive to serve her. I mean, even the President has become her court fool, and he smiles as he sings for her. I've seen it on the news. We're all her fools for whatever she has planned."

Mr. Flores squeezed the porcelain shards in his palm until his own blood dripped onto the floor. He never flinched. "I guess the one good thing is that, under her world order, there is this strange peace across the globe. But what could she possibly have planned with those weapons? Do you have any damn idea?"

Charlee buried her face in her hands. She fought the urge to scream. "She's going to strip Earth of its resources to get what she really wants."

Kraannaannn, still peering through the window, blinked his eye. "The Guardian is correct. She wants to conquer worlds, and while the medallion's mind control powers may be enough to conquer the minds of simple humans, it might not be enough for more evolved life forms. She is building an army to send across a portal to other worlds as a show of force. She doesn't care; she'll sacrifice every last one of your kind for her power lust."

Assara lifted her chin and shifted back to Lengoron. "The people of this world should be honored to sacrifice their meaningless lives for Mother."

"What did she say?" Mr. Flores rubbed his hands together. His blood spread from one palm to the other.

"Nothing worth repeating." Charlee shook her head.

"Don't ignore me." Assara shouted.

Mrs. Flores started toward the kitchen. "Maybe I should try to get her something else to eat. She's so thin."

"Mom—"

"I have to try." Mrs. Flores wiped tears from her eyes.

Charlee studied Sandra's mom. Her hands trembled slightly. She frantically searched through the cupboards. "We must have something she'll eat."

Mr. Flores joined his wife, wrapping an arm around her. "Baby, I know what you're going through."

She pushed his arm away. "Do you? Then explain it to me. All I know is I've lost one daughter, and now you show up here with a child who looks like she belongs to me, but she'd rather kill me. What am I feeling, Peter? Tell—"

Assara wrapped her legs around Mrs. Flores's ankles and with one swift motion knocked her to the ground. The clone then grabbed her hair, yanking her head back. "Free me or die." The language—English—for all to understand.

"No!" Charlee sprang toward Assara, but a green beam of energy struck the clone first, slamming her body against the refrigerator. She crumbled against the floor, her body slightly twitching.

Mr. Flores grasped his wife, lifting her away from the clone.

Charlee turned to young Theodora. Smoke rose from her hands. She shook her head, like a disapproving mother, and spoke in Lengoron "There's a lot of anger in that one. Perhaps I was naïve to bring her…to think she could change."

"Did you kill her?" Charlee inched toward Assara.

"No, she'll survive." Theodora rubbed her hands together, then clasped them together under her chin. "But perhaps death would be better for one so lost."

Mrs. Flores pushed away from her husband, then lowered down to Assara, cradling her in her arms. She scowled at Theodora. "What have you done? She's my…" Sandra's mom stopped herself. Tears formed. She still held the clone to her chest, brushing hair from the unconscious girl's face.

Mr. Flores reached for his wife. "She's not our daughter."

"I know." Mrs. Flores finally released Assara, gently lowering her head to the floor. "But look at her."

From behind came a thud. Charlee swung around. Sandra held a reddened fist close to her face. A small hand-sized crack had formed on the wall next to her.

"You okay?" Charlee crossed to her, but before reaching Sandra, her friend ran from the farmhouse, slamming the door behind her. Mr. Flores started after her, but Charlee grabbed his arm. "Let me," she offered.

He sighed. "Go."

Charlee flung open the door. Sandra was already well ahead, dashing away from the house along the dirt path. She'd already reached beyond the orange glow of the porch light. The mist began to surround her, hiding all but her legs.

"Sandra, wait!" Charlee charged after her, but Sandra disappeared into the night. Charlee rushed through the white cotton-like barrier. Pivoting on her feet, she swung in all direction, but the mist boxed her in on all sides.

Kraannaannn joined her. "Do not fear. Your friend is there." With a flap of his massive wings, he drove away the drifting haze, revealing a tractor parked beside a field not far ahead. Sandra sat in the tractor seat, head lowered to her chest.

Charlee nodded to the dragon, then strolled to Sandra, kicking a rock along the walkway until she reached her friend.

"Remember that day we first met when we went to M's Diner after school, ate burgers, and played video games?" Sandra spoke without looking up at Charlee.

"Yeah, that was so much fun." Charlee leaned against the tractor.

Sandra slid from the tractor. She raked her fingers through her long brown hair. "You didn't' know it, but I was so happy that day. I finally had a friend. I ran home to tell my parents. I was that excited."

"Really…I was the excited one." Charlee smiled. Visions of that day danced through her thoughts. "You were tough and cool. You didn't need anyone, but you chose to be nice to me."

Sandra chuckled and bumped Charlee's shoulder with her own. "You always think I'm so tough."

"You are."

"I'm not." Sandra gazed toward the eastern horizon, still bathed in the misty shadows of night. "It's a front. I'm as scared as everyone else, all the time, but when we became friends, I felt braver, but…"

Charlee kicked at the dirt. "But you never should have come up to me that day in the cafeteria. Knowing me has screwed up your life. I know it. I brought that witch into your life. I've caused you so much pain."

Sandra rounded her shoulders and lowered her head again. Her face twitched, something Charlee had never seen her friend do. "Not so much me, but my parents. You saw my mom. She's freaked out, man. I mean, she's losing her mind. You know my parents can't even tell my sister where we are because she's one of Theodora's zombies now. She sounds like my sister and acts like my sister, but she's under the witch's spell. My parents have talked to her a few times. She keeps asking them to come join her in offering prayers to Goddess Theodora. Yeah, she calls her a goddess. And now this clone of me is here, and I see it in Mom's eyes. She's real broken up about it—doesn't know what to think. I guess I don't either. I thought I was okay with it, but seeing her just brings back what that witch did to me."

Charlee grasped Sandra's hand. An emptiness as bad as she felt in the dungeon made her legs rubbery. "I'm sorry for everything. I wish things could go back to the way they were. I wish this was all some nightmare. It's not, and I have to stop her before she hurts you, your family, or anyone else ever again."

Sandra tugged her hands away. Her face twitched again with a slight movement in her cheek and a quick quiver of her upper lip. "I know, and I want to help, but now that I see what's happening to my mom, I have to help her first."

"You should, and I should just get out of here." Charlee backed away. "I guess take that freak clone and that…Theodora…and hit the road, so you can help your mom."

"Maybe you should." Sandra's cheek twitched one more time.

"Are you okay?" Charlee reached for her friend but recoiled her hand.

Sandra shook her head. "I don't know anymore. I just think it would be best if you weren't here."

Charlee wrapped her arms around her stomach. Her guts ached as if she'd been slugged. She swallowed hard and forced out a lungful of air. Her face grew flushed. Sandra was right, but hearing it hurt worse than when the medallion ripped her powers away.

"I'll leave at daybreak." Charlee retreated, nearly tripping over a rock.

"I'm sorry." Sandra threw her arms around her.

Charlee pushed her away. "No, it's me who's sorry."

CHAPTER 21

The Witch Beckons

DAYBREAK WAS STILL more than an hour away.

Exhausted, everyone slept inside the farmhouse. Even Assara, still recovering from young Theodora's magical attack, slept on the floor, her body curled into a ball. Outside, Kraannaannn had closed his eyes and rested his head on his front legs. The Changeling remained alert at his post by Charlee's mom.

Charlee stood in the doorway of the master bedroom, where her mom lay. Thanks to Theodora, the bullet wound in her back had healed. Now, she needed sleep to regain her strength before she faced that crazed cloned version of Theodora, but Charlee couldn't endanger her mom or anyone else any more than she already had. She would leave her mom here at the farmhouse with the Flores family.

Right before sunup, she'd try to open a portal to the nation's capital to face the evil Theodora together with the real Theodora, the dragon, the Changeling... and Assara. *We must get away from Sandra and her family. They need a break from all of this. I just wish there was some way I could go back in time and undo all the bad I've caused.* But there wasn't. Her powers could open gateways, not time portals.

She blew her mom a kiss, turned away from the master bedroom, and tiptoed back toward the family room where young Theodora slept. The time had come to wake her and the others and quietly slip away. Her mom would be mad, and likely try to come after her. With a little luck, before that, she could steal the medallion and stop...no kill...the witch.

Charlee bent down to tap young Theodora's shoulder, but a glowing green mist slithering underneath the front door into the house startled her. The mist rose from the floor and danced, like a snake eyeing its prey.

Charlee's body clenched. "Damn," she whispered.

She crept toward the door. The wooden floor creaked, but no one stirred. Before Charlee reached the doorknob, the mist slid away.

The hairs on Charlee's arm stood at attention. *It's her. She's come for me. Now everyone's in danger.* Charlee grasped the knob. With a twist, she slowly cracked the door just enough to reveal a sky shaded in ocean blues. Night had finally started to give way to morning. She pushed the door all the way. The green mist floated just above the dirt walkway at the base of the steps.

Charlee crossed her arms. "I know it's you, Theodora." Eyes focused on the mist, she inched down the steps. "Show yourself. Face me alone. I'm the one you want, no one else."

No response came from the mist. The formless green smoke retreated along the path, then turned left into an alfalfa field. The uncut crop was almost as tall as Charlee. Scratching her chin, hesitating just a heartbeat, she followed. The mist led her deep within the field, far from the farmhouse.

"Answer me, Theodora." Charlee trudged past the rows of alfalfa.

The mist stopped in a clearing and hovered in front of her. It swirled, like a vortex, before it vanished, leaving Charlee alone, walled in by the tall alfalfa and shrouded in the final hour of darkness.

"I am so touched that your hate for me has kept you alive." Theodora's voice circled over her. "I would have been saddened if you died in the dungeon."

"Yeah right." Charlee swiveled in all directions, but Theodora remained hidden. "Show yourself."

The glowing mist reappeared, like a flash of light from a camera. Charlee shielded her eyes and glanced away. When she looked back, a ghostly image of Theodora hovered before her, hair flowing wildly around her face, cheeks thin and wrinkled. A white robe draped over her body, hiding her legs. Her arms, underneath the robe's long sleeves, crossed over her chest.

"I have to say, Guardian, I am impressed you freed the shell from which I was born." Theodora smiled broadly.

"You mean the real Theodora." Charlee stepped toward the floating sorceress. "So, you know you're not the real Theodora. You know you're something else... something that came out of that medallion."

"Perhaps, but I have all the strengths and none of the weaknesses that prevented that child from having the true vision to realize the dreams of the Brotherhood. I didn't just replace her. I improved her, and she will never reclaim her name. Like you, she will die very soon. All those who follow you will die soon."

Charlee lifted her hands. An orange glow rose from her fingertips. "Even your daughter?"

"She failed me." Theodora gazed toward the farmhouse. "She allowed the dragons and those Lataran scum to defeat my armies. I have no use for those who fail me. She will die like the others, and when I feel like it, I will return to Janasara and have my revenge. When I am finished, Janasara will cease to exist."

"You would destroy your own world?" Charlee's hands vibrated as her body tingled. If this were really Theodora and not just a ghostly vision of her, she'd blast the witch back to the fires from which the medallion was born.

"I have no more use for it."

"Why are you here, Theodora?" Just to be sure, Charlee swung a glowing hand through the apparition, like passing through air. "You know I'm coming for you. You can't hide behind the White House. It doesn't matter how many people you send to kill me. I'll find a way to get to you, I'll take back the medallion, and everyone will return to normal. It's just a matter of time." Would the sorceress believe her air of confidence?

Theodora laughed. "I do await you, Guardian, really, I do. You are right. We are destined to face each other once again, and I look forward to it. I have reached out to your mind to offer you a warning and a chance to save your friends, your mother, your father...and your sister."

Charlee retreated from Theodora. *Had she said, sister?* An icy chill washed over her even as her face burned.

The sorceress floated closer. "That's right, Guardian, your sister. You thought she'd be safe in Janasara, but you left her defenseless with that weak human man you call your father. I have them both."

"No!" She swung at Theodora, but her fist again found no flesh. "I don't believe it. You're lying, witch."

"Ahh, I see you need proof." Theodora waved her hand, and an image formed in Charlee's thoughts, like a movie playing in her head. Her sister, blindfolded and held aloft by unseen forces, floated in the center of what looked like the Oval Office inside the White House. The Presidential Seal covered the floor beneath her. The U.S. flag, burned and torn, lay on the floor nearby. Her sister's head drooped against her chest. Her arms hung limp at her sides. She breathed deeply, as if asleep.

"What have you done to her?" Charlee's fists tightened.

"There is more, young one." Theodora waved her hand and another image filled Charlee's mind. The front steps of the White House came into view. Blood pooled on one of the steps.

Charlee studied the image closer. A giant man walked through the front doors of the White House. It was Tribon, Theodora's henchman, who pretended to be Charlee's mentor while all the while he served Theodora. After all this time, after being burned alive by the dragons, he still lived, or whatever this was he called an existence. He was more zombie than anything else. His burns had mostly healed, but scars still covered his face. The red hair that once circled his face, like a lion's mane, was gone. Cracks covered his bald head, but it was still him. Black metal gloves reached up to his elbows. Wait, they weren't gloves at all. Theodora had fashioned artificial limbs for him. That's right, Charlee had ripped off his arms in a portal.

Tribon held a chain, and he yanked on it. A smaller man limped from behind Tribon, his face bloodied and his arms bound. Blood dripped from a wound in his side. Charlee dropped to her knees, her mouth agape and body frozen. It was her father. His rounded glasses, the lenses shattered, hung loosely from one ear.

133

"Dad!" Charlee screamed. He didn't respond or even look at her. "Dad, can you hear me?"

"He cannot hear you, child." Theodora's voice mocked her. "This is merely a picture I have allowed you to see, so you can understand the danger your family now faces because of your actions."

"Let them go." She stood, her fists squeezed so tightly her nails dug into her skin. Theodora would die for this.

"I would be happy to." Theodora's voice inched closer to her. "I have but one request, and if you meet it, they will be freed."

"What?"

"You come alone."

"Gladly."

Theodora whispered in Charlee's ear. "If you bring the others, or if they come to your rescue, your father and your sister will die." Her hot breath brushed against Charlee's skin. If the sorceress was only there in ghostly form, how was that possible?

Charlee swung around, expecting to face the witch, but she wasn't there. At least not in any physical form. "They'll come anyway. How can I stop them? How can I stop a dragon?"

"Send them away." Theodora's voice hovered overhead. "Open a gateway."

Charlee shrunk away. How could she face the sorceress alone? She still lacked strength. Theodora knew it.

She wouldn't play by the witch's rules, not anymore. She crossed her arms and quieted her thoughts. "If you want to face me alone, you have the medallion. You have my power. Why don't you open a gateway and send them away? Better yet, since you're so powerful, why don't you send me away like you did the real Theodora to some nowhere land and lock me in a slab of ice? No, even better, why don't you just kill me now and be done with it. Command everyone around here to come after me, or you come here for real and use the medallion against me."

Theodora reappeared, her ghostly form materializing on the path just a few feet away. Her eyes turned a fire red and then shifted back to icy blue. "The medallion and the Brotherhood do not wish you dead yet, young Guardian. You have impressed the Brotherhood; otherwise, I would reach across this distance and end your miserable little life. And these feeble humans whose minds I have so easily controlled are no match for you. I have always known that, but it's been fun to see you run for your life rather than harm them."

Theodora faded. A grimace crossed her face. "I have spoken. It is now your choice. Send the others away and come to me alone or your father and sister die. I will expect you by the day's end. If the sun crosses the sky, and you are not before me, they will meet a violent and oh so tragic end. The choice is yours."

134

The sorceress vanished. Charlee staggered a few steps as if a terrible weight became too much to bear. Her knees crumbled, and she dropped back into the dirt. She slammed her fists into the earth. Her body trembled. She screamed silently and felt the warmth of her tears.

She had no choice but to obey the witch.

§ § §

Charlee emerged from the alfalfa field and lumbered to the farmhouse. The chirp of crickets followed her, interrupting the country silence. She tiptoed along the dirt path past Kraannaannn, whose massive head rested on a leg, his eyes closed, his nostrils flaring with each rhythmic breath.

She stopped at the front steps. A sigh slid from her lips. How could she send them away? How could she send her mom away…the Changeling, Kraannaannn? *I must do it.* Did she even have enough magic to open a gateway large enough for the dragon and the farmhouse? Pointing her fingertips straight ahead, Charlee focused her mind on the world of Janasara.

"This is a mistake, Guardian."

Charlee froze. The burnt breath of a dragon washed over her. She turned toward Kraannaannn whose long neck curled up, lifting his head high above her. His eyes blazed, like fire.

"You don't understand," she whispered.

"I do, Guardian" The dragon lowered his head to within a few feet of her face. He spoke barely above a whisper. "I heard your entire conversation with the sorceress."

Charlee blinked. "How? I thought that was all in my head."

"You don't know the extent of a dragon's magic." Kraannaannn spread his lips in what could have been a smile, but it appeared more like an intimidating snarl. "Right now, I have a mind lock on you. What you see, I see."

Charlee pursed her lips. So not only her mom, but also the dragon crept inside her thoughts—an invasion for sure. Her neck muscles tightened. "Then you know she has my sister and my dad, and she's going to kill them."

The dragon's ears twitched. He inched his head closer to her. "You don't know that."

"Yes, I do."

"If it is true, only together we can save them." The muscles in Kraannaannn's neck rippled. "We must stay together."

Charlee lowered her head. "I can't risk it."

From behind came the fluttering of wings. She swung around just as a white dove, the Changeling, landed on her shoulder.

"I guess you heard the conversation, too. Is everyone in my head?" She reached for the bird, which jumped on to her arm and faced her. The Changeling nodded in response. "Then you know what I have to do to save them...to save everyone."

"Guardian, you'll die." Kraannaannn's tail rose behind him. "She's too strong, and you do not have all your magic. What happens then? Your sister, your dad, and everyone else dies? No good can come from this."

"I have to try. If I fail, then you must keep Janasara safe. You'll find a way. You're a dragon. You're the Dragon Lord now."

Kraannaannn blinked and raised his head slightly.

"I'm sorry, Kraannaannn, I shouldn't have said it like that." Charlee touched the dragon's front leg. "You haven't even had a chance to think about your da—"

"You're right, Guardian. I am the Dragon Lord. So, heed my words when I say you need me by your side. You need your Changeling by your side. You need us both."

Charlee gazed at them both. The Dragon Lord was right, but that didn't matter. "I don't have a choice."

"There's always a choice." Kraannaannn shook his massive head.

"Please, you have to go." She crossed her arms.

Kraannaannn huffed. His gaze seemed to focus on the Changeling. The scales covering his body bristled, clicking as he slowly lifted his massive frame. "All right, Guardian. Your mother will never forgive me for letting you go off on your own, but you have made your decision. May my father watch over you and protect you."

The Changeling, still in dove form, flew from her and landed on the dragon's shoulder. They stared at each other in silence, then returned their focus to her.

"Thank you for understanding." Her face numbed and her shoulders slumped. This wasn't what she wanted. She didn't want to go off alone. "Please tell my mom and the others it had to be this way. Tell Mr. Flores I'll try to keep his other daughter safe. Tell Sandra I'm sorry for everything. Let them all know if I stop Theodora, I'll return to Janasara, and together we'll find the burning tree and destroy the medallion, ending this forever."

"If you fail?" Kraannaannn asked.

She bit down on her thumbnail before answering. "I won't. I can't."

Lifting her arms, she closed her eyes and envisioned the Kingdom of Latara. A picture formed in her head of the castle, the scarred land and the ruins left in the wake of Theodora's rule. She reached out with her hands. A warm energy coursed through her palms. A hum rose from her chest. Her body shook. A wind stirred around her, kicking up dirt.

She opened her eyes. A glowing blue portal hovered before her, slowly growing. Her head felt as if a vise crushed it. A warm salty liquid dripped from her nose down over her lips. Each beat of her heart thundered in her ears like a deafening rock concert, vibrating against her skull. With limited powers could she create a large enough portal? Could she keep it open? *Stop…questioning…yourself!*

Just beyond the portal, the Changeling morphed into his true self—a formless mass of yellow energy. Dim at first, he radiated brighter, sparkling like the afternoon sun's image over the rolling waters of San Francisco Bay.

An invisible wave of energy slammed against Charlee, nearly knocking her over. Her muscles tightened. Her arms no longer shook. The ache in her head disappeared. *It's the Changeling. He's giving me his power.* Charlee extended her arms farther. The portal extended above the trees and spread out wide enough to embrace the farmhouse.

Like pushing against a door, she willed the portal to slide toward the house, toward Kraannaannn and the Changeling.

"Goodbye, Guardian." Kraannaannn bowed his head.

"Goodbye," she uttered.

With a grunt, wind whipping her hair in every direction, Charlee gave the portal one last shove. It spread over the house, the dragon, and the Changeling. They all disappeared into the blue radiance. Her muscles on fire, chest heaving, Charlee dropped her arms and fell to her knees.

The portal vanished. Silence surrounded her, except for the sway of alfalfa in the dying wind, her own labored breathing, and the echo of her racing heart.

She stared at the empty lot that just moments ago had been the farmhouse where her mom was in bed recovering from the gunshot wound, where Sandra and her family had hidden from a world now under Theodora's spell, and where the young Theodora kept watch over Assara. If only there had been some other way. She didn't want to send them to Janasara. She needed them by her side.

Charlee crawled toward Kraannaannn's claw print in the dirt next to the house and brushed her fingers over the indentation in the ground. Warmth rose from his print as if he remained close.

Worst of all…once again she had separated from the Changeling, her protector. *It's good that he's back in Janasara. He can help them fight Theodora if I blow it.* Charlee sighed. But without him and his vast supply of pure energy, what chance did she have?

Over her shoulder, the sun made its first appearance, bathing the sky in the early day's pale light. From behind her came the roar of approaching propellers. Once again, the tall alfalfa bristled as a rush of wind caused the fields to sway wildly. Charlee shielded her eyes from the dust that swirled around her. Standing, she peeked around her fingers at the heavily armored helicopter that landed on the roadway in front of her. A massive gun mounted on the front targeted her.

"Well, I guess Theodora has sent an escort for me," Charlee mumbled over the helicopter's roar.

Four soldiers in camouflaged military uniforms and armed with assault rifles—at least that's what they looked like—approached. The soldiers stopped about ten steps away, the barrels of their weapons aimed at her. One soldier, a rather large man with a chiseled face, marched away from the others until he reached an arm's distance from her.

"Empress Theodora has sent us to collect you, Guardian. We have orders to fire on you if you refuse or if you struggle. Do you understand?" He spoke like a soldier addressing an enemy—professional and controlled. Tears of blood slid along his cheeks and from his nose. *Did he want to kill her? Did he really think she was evil?* Even a trained soldier couldn't fight against Theodora's spell.

Charlee shook her head. "Sorry, military dudes, I have my own way to get there, and it'll be much quicker." A gateway was the fastest way to save her dad and Megan. She closed her eyes and stared to envision Washington, D.C.

"The Empress thought you might say that." The words came from the same soldier. "She insists that you come with us if you want your family to live."

Charlee opened her eyes. Rifles and handguns quivered in the soldiers' hands. She could stop the soldiers and easily escape into a portal, but she had to take Theodora's threat seriously. She had to play the witch's game for now. But, when the time was right, Theodora would pay. *I'm going to make her suffer. Somehow... someway, she'll pay.*

She bowed her head. "I understand. I won't fight. Take me to her."

The soldier grabbed her gruffly by the arm and led her to the helicopter. The others followed, their weapons still pointed at her. All bled.

"Get ready, Theodora," Charlee whispered under her breath, her fists clenched. "I'm coming for you."

CHAPTER 22

Public Enemy Number One

THE MILITARY LINED both sides of Pennsylvania Avenue. Transports, tanks, and heavily armed soldiers secured the roadway to the White House. It was all for her. Charlee, her wrists and ankles shackled, stared through the passenger window of the black van she'd been placed in immediately after arriving at the Ronald Reagan Washington National Airport. Behind the soldiers, crowds lined the sidewalks, shouting, raising their fists, and pointing at the van. Some waved signs.

Long Live Empress Theodora.

Death to the Guardian.

Every one of them had bloody tears and snot. Some bled from the mouth and ears. Did they feel pain? Were they in agony? If she succeeded in breaking the spell, would they be okay?

Inside the van, tall, quiet men and women in black suits and sunglasses sat on either side of her, handguns holstered inside their jackets. Wires dangled from their ears. Blood dripped from their faces onto their collars.

It had been nearly a full day since the military whisked her away from the farm fields in Northern California. She had been flown to a military base near San Francisco. She heard the helicopter pilot refer to Travis Air Force Base. There, more soldiers shuffled her into one of those large military cargo planes where armed guards handcuffed her hands and feet and strapped her into a chair in the plane's cargo hold.

No one had spoken to her, except for one guard who had been nice enough to let her use a bathroom aboard the plane. He said nine words to her—*try anything and your father and sister will die.*

When she landed in Washington, D.C., an entire military envoy and a gathering of black vehicles greeted her. At gunpoint, she shuffled her chained feet as best she could to walk from the plane to the secret service vehicles where the men and women in black suits directed her into the rear door of a van with dark tinted windows. Magic still coursed through her veins. She could feel its power with each heartbeat. She could break her bonds and escape, but there was no escape, not really—not when her dad and Megan were in danger. She flexed her muscles and whipped strands of hair from her face.

The White House loomed up ahead. Theodora said Charlee had to arrive by day's end. Overhead, the sun still shined on the nation's capital, but not for much longer. Still, she'd made it as per Theodora's order. Hopefully, the witch hadn't done anything else to harm her family. If she had…

Charlee forced that thought away. Her hands and forearms tightened. The steel handcuffs that bound her wrists cut into her skin. She winced and relaxed her limbs. Already drops of her blood coated the steel where it had ripped into the skin.

"Do these have to be so tight?" she asked her escorts.

"Quiet," the man on her right ordered. He was older than the others with graying hair, but he sat tall with biceps that bulged underneath his jacket. Sunglasses covered his eyes. Blood dripped beyond the black lenses.

She breathed in and released it. "Do you know who you're serving?"

No one in the van responded.

Charlee tried again. "You're serving a witch who has you under mind control. Think back. Aren't you supposed to be serving the President of the United States? Aren't you supposed to be protecting him? Don't you see you're under a spell? You don't know what you're doing."

"I said…quiet," the man with gray hair barked. "I know my duty. I serve the Empress. Very soon she will deal with you."

"Come on." Charlee tried to grab his arm, but he shoved her away. "You're a secret service agent who's supposed to protect the President. Try and remember."

The man removed his sunglasses. His bloodied hazel eyes bulged. "I've had enough of your mouth, girl." He raised his hand to strike her.

"No." Theodora's disembodied voice echoed through the van. "Do not lay a hand on her. Do as you were instructed. Bring her to me."

The aging agent lowered his hand and returned his sunglasses. They continued the rest of the journey in silence.

They passed the Lincoln Monument. She had seen it once before while on vacation with her parents and had never forgotten what it was like to be so close to the huge marble statue. Only now, Theodora had replaced the statue of Lincoln with her own image.

"I can't believe it." She turned back to the gray-haired secret service man. "You let her deface the Lincoln Monument. Don't you even remember President Lincoln? He's like only one of the greatest presidents ever. You must remember."

The man didn't respond and didn't even glance at the monument. Charlee thrust her chin up. Her lips curled into a smirk. "Man, you guys are on the wrong side, but I know you can't help it. Sure would be nice though if I could find some way to break the—"

They reached the White House, and the van came to a stop at an entry gate that led onto the grounds. Armed soldiers and more men and women in black stood just outside a guard station in front of the gate. There must have been about fifty in all, and each held some type of gun aimed at the van.

After a few moments, the entry gate slid open, and the van pulled forward onto a concrete path that led them past a fountain to the northern façade of the White House where columns encircled the front entrance.

"Out," the graying secret service man ordered when the van stopped.

The door swung open. Two agents grabbed her by the arms and pulled her from the vehicle. Another gathering of soldiers surrounded her. Red dots appeared over her chest. The laser sights on the soldiers' rifles zeroed in on her heart.

"Clear a path, gentleman." The words came from beyond the soldiers who lowered their weapons and stepped aside. "That's better."

Charlee recognized the President's voice. She'd listened to him give speeches when her mom and dad watched the news. He slipped between the soldiers and walked up to her, stopping just a few feet away. Dressed casually, he wore torn blue slacks and a white button-down shirt with the collar undone. Half of his shirt was untucked.

He slowly shook his head side to side, like a disappointed parent. His graying hair, normally perfectly cut without a strand out of place, looked jumbled, as if he'd just woken up. His blue eyes, which seemed so kind on TV, now glared at her with hate. Bloody tears slid down the corners of each eye. More blood stained the sides of his mouth.

He studied her in silence as a twisted smile formed. "So, you're the one causing all this mischief." The President rubbed his chin. "You're just a child."

Charlee tried to shuffle toward the President, but she stumbled over her shackled feet. Two secret service members grabbed her before she hit the ground and held her by the shoulders.

"Mr. President, you're under a spell. Everyone is. You're the President of the United States. You're like the top world leader. You must fight this."

The President ignored her. "I don't think these shackles are necessary any longer. Remove them from her hands and feet."

"Please, Mr. President, fight this," Charlee begged.

"Kid, I wouldn't want to be you." The President stepped in close as two secret servicemen removed the chains and handcuffs from around her ankles and wrists. "Empress Theodora is not happy with you. If it were up to me, I'd have these soldiers shoot you now. That would probably be more humane, but the Empress wants a word with you before she kills you in her own special way."

"Mr. President, I'm not the enemy."

"This way, my dear." The President motioned for Charlee to move toward the front steps of the White House.

141

The secret service members who still held her by the shoulders released Charlee. She lowered her head and walked ahead of the President, rubbing her wrists where the skin had torn from the cuffs. Soldiers who blocked the path retreated just enough for her to squeeze by them.

Charlee glanced over her shoulder at the President who followed close behind. "Sir, I'm going to fix this."

"Guardian, you're going to die today." His smile contorted into a wild grin.

She stopped at the base of the stone steps that led up to the White House's main entrance. Just like her vision in the alfalfa field, drops of drying blood spread along the steps. Whose blood? Her dad's? Had Theodora hurt anyone else? The witch would pay. Somehow, Theodora would fall.

Charlee climbed the first step.

"Well, Guardian, our paths cross again." The voice belonged to Tribon.

He stood at the top of the steps, his legs covered by black armor. He was bare chested, revealing the burns suffered when the dragons engulfed him in flames during their battle on the shores of the sea on Janasara. Charred skin also covered his head and face. His once long red beard only grew in blotches over his scars. Black iron arms and hands replaced his real limbs, severed when Charlee closed a portal on him.

"Ah, what do you think of them?" Tribon smiled broadly as he opened and closed his fake hands. "Theodora had them made special for me. They're quite functional. I never had the chance to repay you for what you took from me."

"What I took from you?" Charlee climbed two more steps. Her teeth ground together as her breath turned flaming hot with rage. "You did it to yourself, coward. You're nothing but a walking zombie. You don't even have a heart. You're a shell. One of these days I'm going to find a way to make sure that when you die you stay dead."

Tribon's smile disappeared. He drew his sword and pointed the blade at Charlee. "Come closer, Guardian."

"Where are my dad and sister?" Charlee eyed the tip of Tribon's sword. More blood coated the blade.

"You'll see them—"

"Everyone, you're making a mistake!" A soldier broke ranks and charged up the stone steps. "She's right, you're under some spell. We're American soldiers. We don't follow an Empress." The soldier aimed his assault weapon at Tribon. "I'm going to put a stop to this."

The crackle of gunfire rang in Charlee's ears. She dropped to her knees and covered her head. Then came the sound of a weapon falling against the stone steps and an agonized cry. Charlee lifted her head. The soldier lay wounded on the steps, blood spilling from several wounds in his back, legs, and shoulders.

She crawled to him. His blue eyes blinked. They did not bleed like those under Theodora's spell. He coughed as blood spilled from the side of this mouth. He grinned painfully at her. "We're not all against you." He breathed deeply between each word and spoke just above a whisper. "I'm sorry I couldn't stop this."

"No, I'm sorry." Charlee placed a hand on his arm. Who was this soldier? How was it possible he hadn't fallen under the spell? And why risk his life for her—someone he'd never met. With each weakening breath his life slipped away, and his eyes dimmed. She gripped his arm tighter. He didn't deserve this.

Tribon wheezed out a laugh. "He still lives? Good—bring the traitor to me."

Two other soldiers pushed Charlee away and gruffly lifted him, dragging him to Tribon at the top of the steps. The soldier cried out as his body convulsed.

Tribon sheathed his sword and grasped the handle of one of his knives. "What is your name, boy?"

The soldier split blood into Tribon's face. "You're not going to get away with this. We're stronger than you think. We're not your slaves."

Charlee raised her hands. The magic coursing through her limbs heated her flesh. She had the power in her palms. One energy pulse, and she could stop Tribon, but then what would happen to Megan and her dad? *Screw, Tribon!*

Green rays exploded from her palms and smashed into Tribon's chest. He flew backward, dropping the soldier. His heavy body slammed against the stone steps. Smoke rose from his wound as he gasped for a breath. Charlee raced to the soldier, reaching him just in time to hear him wheeze out a final breath. His lifeless eyes stared back at her. She gently lowered his head, then glared at Tribon.

"Does it hurt, you bastard?" She raised her hands again. One more blow might kill the stupid traitor, but soldiers grabbed her from behind, forcing her to her knees.

Tribon coughed and slowly stood. His eyes widened as his lips shook. "You'll pay for that, you little—"

"Bring her to me...now!" Theodora's voice boomed over Tribon's. "I will deal with her, not you."

Tribon's eyes shifted as if searching for Theodora. She was nowhere to be seen. "But, my Empress, allow me—"

"Do as you're told, servant."

Tribon's eyes still raged, but his shoulders slumped. "Yes, my Empress." He motioned to the soldiers holding her. "Bring her forward."

Charlee took a long breath. She would need some extra power if she was to fight Theodora, and there was only way to do it—use her magic to consume the life energy from the soldiers. It wasn't right to take their life force without their consent; it was like stealing. It was an invasion of their very being, and it wasn't right to endanger them. This was a power she never used. She depended solely on borrowing power from the Changeling, but he wasn't here now. *I must do this. But only this once.*

She closed her eyes and reached out with her magic, like tentacles, to the soldiers holding her. She extended her reach beyond them to the other soldiers standing close by with their guns aimed at her.

Their energy flowed through her veins. Her pulse quickened as her lungs breathed deeper and her muscles stretched. Her senses heightened. She could hear not only her own heartbeat, but the heartbeats of every soldier surrounding her. Their breaths echoed in her ears as their adrenaline became hers. How far could she take this? How much energy could she consume? How powerful could she become? *No, you could hurt them. You've taken enough.*

She released her magical embrace of the soldiers, who must have been momentarily affected by her magic. They did not immediately respond to Tribon's orders.

He marched closer to them, hands balled into fists. "I said bring her forward." This time the soldiers did as they were ordered. They shoved her up the steps. She put up no struggle.

Tribon stopped them before they could pass. He grabbed Charlee's shoulder. "You and everyone you love are going to die today."

Charlee spit in his face. "I've heard that before, but you never seem to succeed. So just suck it, you piece of trash. I promise you, before this is over, you'll be dead and forgotten."

Tribon tightened his grip on her shoulder until it felt like he'd crush her bones. She winced but fought the urge to cry out. She'd not give him the satisfaction. Tribon released her, then back stepped to the fallen soldier. "Hey, Guardian, here's your little savior. Let's have some fun with him." Tribon unsheathed his sword. With one jab, he pierced the soldier's lifeless body, lifted him from the steps, and hurled him into a crowd of his fellow soldiers. "See how we throw out the trash? That's all these humans are to her. She will use this entire world and discard what remains, like trash."

Charlee gritted her teeth. "We'll see."

Tribon lifted his sword. "Watch as these slaves serve her." He lifted his word. "All hail Empress Theodora."

The soldiers, the secret servicemen, and even the President all shouted out in unison, "Long live the Empress."

Charlee lowered her head. It was better to act like she'd been weakened. "You heard what that soldier said. There are others, and they'll rise against you. Just wait. They'll find a way to break the spell."

Another voice responded. "Oh, I think not, Guardian."

The evil Theodora stood at the front doors leading into the White House.

A long flowing white gown covered her bony frame. Its long train extended behind her. A single golden tassel tied around her waist revealed just how thin she'd become in her aged form. Her graying hair surrounded her narrow cheeks and slid over her shoulders. Theodora cradled something in her arms.

Charlee crossed the distance to the sorceress, then slowed to uncertain steps until she realized the witch held Megan. Charlee stopped and covered her mouth with both hands as the blood drained from her face and her legs wobbled. The witch caressed Megan's cheeks.

"Give her to me!" Charlee ripped free of the soldiers' hands. When they tried to grab her again, she magically nudged them back with a wave of her hand.

Theodora chuckled. "Good, put these meaningless beings in their proper place—at your feet." Her cackling ceased. She teased Megan's blond hair in her fingers. "I would be glad to return this child to you, but I don't think she wants to. Come and see."

Charlee inched her way toward the sorceress and her sister. Megan turned her head to Charlee and started to cry. Bloody tears slid down her cheeks. More blood dripped from her nose. She buried her head into Theodora's arms. "Bad person," Megan uttered. "I'm scared."

Theodora gently bounced Megan in her arms. "Child, there's nothing to fear. You're safe with me. I'll always protect you."

"What have you done?" Charlee again sparked her magic to life. Sparks of energy danced across her fingers.

"A little mind manipulation, maybe." Theodora winked.

"If she's hurt, I'll make you suffer, witch!" Charlee's hands started to glow. Her skin vibrated.

"Tsk...tsk. Careful now, Guardian." Theodora retreated, burying Megan in her chest. "We wouldn't want this precious creature to be hurt, would we?"

Charlee lowered her hands. The glow dimmed and vanished. Sweat dripped from her brow. "Look, I'm here now. Let me send her somewhere safe."

Theodora shook her head and frowned. "In time, young one. First walk with me. Now that we have been reunited, there is much for us to discuss."

Theodora turned from Charlee and strolled with Megan toward the massive doorway into the White House. The doors leading inside were burned, cracked, and barely hung from their hinges.

Charlee followed. Tribon's heavy footsteps fell not far behind. She didn't bother looking back at him. Her gaze remained locked on Theodora's nearly skeletal form. "I came alone, Theodora, so where's my dad. Let him and Megan go. You have me. I'm the one you want. Leave them out of it."

Theodora stopped, then glared back at her. "I know you've come alone. I watched through your eyes as you sent your friends and your mother away.

If I thought otherwise, you and I would not be having this conversation now, and your sister and your father would be dead."

"So, let them go." A tingling spread through Charlee's body. Her mind raced, searching for a way to steal Megan away from the witch.

Theodora turned again and continued her stroll. Her high heels clanked against the floor with each step. "As I said, in time."

From the front doorway, they passed into a cavernous hall. Portraits of each President covered the walls, but their faces had magically been replaced with Theodora's. Vases and sculptures lay shattered into pieces across the floor, and burn marks scorched the ceiling.

"Do you like how I have redecorated my new castle?" Theodora swung around, admiring the destruction.

"I wouldn't get too comfortable." Charlee studied Megan, who kept her eyes hidden in Theodora's dress.

"You still think you can defeat me...how delightfully determined you are." Theodora led Charlee from the main hall to a colonnade, the pathway to the west building of the White House—the famed West Wing. That's where the President had his Oval Office. She remembered that from the family vacation years ago. "I have the medallion. I have your abilities—you have nothing, and now your friends are gone."

Charlee rubbed her bloodied, scratched wrists. Theodora had said the Brotherhood were impressed by Charlee. That was why she was here and why Theodora hadn't killed her. The Brotherhood were going to try to twist her mind. She'd have to fight them, but was she strong enough? Even now, she felt a longing inside, tugging her toward the medallion, which was close. She couldn't see it, but she felt the icy chill of its presence.

"When do you plan to bring me before this Brotherhood?" Charlee asked.

"I would not be in such a rush, for they will usher in your end." Theodora raised an eyebrow. The casual smile on her face slipped away, replaced by grim down turned lips.

From the colonnade, they entered a doorway into the west building. After another short walk along a heavily damaged hallway, where carpet had been ripped away and tapestry on the walls burned, they reached the Oval Office. Charlee glanced at the floor. The Presidential Seal, the familiar Eagle, had been scorched away, leaving a charred circle.

"Where's my dad, Theodora? Before anything else, I need to know he's all right." Charlee inched farther into the chamber.

Theodora walked around the President's oak desk and sat in his chair, Megan still in her arms. "He most certainly is not all right, but he does live. Here, see for yourself, and enjoy this momentary family reunion, for it won't last."

146

With a wave of her skeletal hand, a back door to the office opened, and a large rectangular table top on its side floated into the room, revealing nothing—just a wooden table with splintered legs that had been ripped away.

Theodora laughed and waved her hand, causing the table to slowly spin. On the first rotation, Charlee's mouth opened but no words came out. Chains held her dad to the opposite side of the table. His bloodied shirt hung from his shoulders in tatters. A large gash crossed his face. His head drooped against his chest.

"Dad!" Charlee charged the table only to be grabbed by Tribon's iron hands. The table spun faster, then stopped.

"Dad, it's Charlee. Dad!" She wrestled free of Tribon's grip, her magically enhanced strength nearly knocking him off his feet. He caught himself and grasped her arm one more time. "Get off me!" Sparks of energy spread between her fingers.

"It's all right. Let her go." Theodora nodded to Tribon. His hands shook and his lips quivered, but he did as his Empress commanded, releasing his grip.

Charlee ran to her dad's side. She grabbed the chains, and with her magical strength she tore them away. Her dad dropped into her arms. She held his head in her lap.

"Dad...Dad, can you hear me?" Tears streaked down her cheeks. She cupped his cheeks with her hands and gently nudged his head. His eyes remained closed, surrounded by dark shadows. "I'm here. I'll save you. I'm sorry I let this happen."

"You will not save him, Guardian, at least not in the way you think." Theodora placed Megan on the ground. Charlee's sister, eyes distant, slowly, unsteadily walked to a nearby chair and sat quietly. She never even looked at their dad. Instead, Megan happily hummed a tune Charlee had never heard. Droplets of blood slid from her ears.

"What did you do to him?" Charlee glared at Theodora.

"You're missing the point." Theodora sat on the edge of the desk. "I haven't killed him, so I believe I have shown great mercy."

Charlee laid her dad's head on the floor and climbed to her feet. Her eyes burned with fresh hot tears. Her hands vibrated as a new white glow emanated from her palms. "I'll kill you, witch."

Theodora's eyes flashed red. "Try. I'd like nothing more."

Charlee took a deep breath. She lowered to her dad. "Please, Dad, wake up." He coughed and his eyes shot open. Shallow breaths slipped from this mouth. His chest heaved.

"Dad, it's me...Charlee. I'm here. Try to be calm."

His eyes darted in every direction. "They're here!" he cried. "Megan, go hide."

"Dad, it's going to be okay." Charlee's voice quivered.

Her dad blinked and then focused on her. "Charlee?"

"Yes."

"Are you and Megan safe?"

Charlee glanced at her sister. Megan stared blankly without blinking. More blood dripped from her nose. Charlee sighed. It was better to lie to her dad. "Yes, Dad, we're fine."

He smiled weakly. "Good. Soon after you left, Theodora and Tribon surprised us. She came in a portal just like yours. I tried to keep them away from Megan. I really tried. I really—"

"Dad, it's all going to be okay. Rest now." Her dad released a long breath and his eyes closed again. His head fell limply against his chest. He breathed slowly but rhythmically.

Charlee wiped the tears away. "Let them go, Theodora. You have me. You don't need them."

"Perhaps, when you have given all you have to give." Theodora rose from the table. "The time has come for you to meet the Brotherhood. It is the reason you are here now. It is the reason you still live." The sorceress motioned to Tribon. "If you please," she directed.

Tribon bowed and slid around the table to a painting of George Washington on the wall directly behind Theodora. Like the other art throughout the White House, Washington's face had been replaced with hers. Tribon grabbed one end of the painting and pushed it aside, revealing a hidden enclosure in the wall. He reached in and grasped something with both hands. Carefully, as if holding a delicate antique, he removed the object and presented it to Theodora.

Charlee shrunk away. "The medallion," she whispered.

A wave of pain rose from her stomach, like she had just been slugged in the gut. Memories flashed through her mind of their battle in the castle throne room. She remembered the agony, the terror, and the loss. The feelings rippled through her body, just like they did when the medallion ripped away her powers, as if tearing away her flesh.

At the same time, her longing for the medallion compelled her forward. Her nerves fired all at once, like tiny electrical shocks. Her breath quickened as her arms extended toward the medallion. She had to touch it, to caress the smooth cold black metal that on one side had the image of a burning tree and on the other, a carving of her face. At least that's the way the medallion had appeared to her.

"You still crave its power, don't you, Guardian?" Theodora held the medallion close to her chest.

Charlee shook her head. Her eyes remained fixed on the dark object. "No."

"There's no need to lie, child." Theodora seemed to float toward Charlee. "In a way, the medallion still wants you, too."

Charlee's legs trembled. She forced them to be still. "If I'm here to meet this big, bad Brotherhood, then get on with it."

"You wouldn't speak so boldly if you knew your fate." Theodora raised the medallion over her head and chanted in her native Lengoron language. Charlee recognized the words.

Master, we await you. Come and bring your light into the world, so that others may know your glory.

The medallion rose from Theodora's hands and hovered above them all. A red flame rose from its center and engulfed the medallion in a ball of fire. Charlee shielded her dad. Her eyes shifted from the medallion to Megan. Theodora continued to chant, her arms and hands flowing as if thin branches blown by a wind. *Master, we await you. Come and bring your light into the world, so that others may know your glory.* She repeated the chant over and over. The medallion started to spin, crackling flames rising in every direction, soaring across the room, bouncing off the walls. Charlee tightened her muscles. How could she protect both Megan and her dad?

A brilliant flash exploded from the medallion, like an unexpected crash of lightning from a storm cloud.

Charlee winced and turned away. Slowly, she turned back. Gone was the medallion. In its place stood the burning tree, just like the real Theodora had described, only smaller. The trunk rose from the carpet, its fiery roots snaking along the floor. The trunk, bathed in orange flames, climbed to the ceiling where a network of branches ended in burning embers that fell, like glowing rain drops, back to the floor.

I can't believe it! Could it really be?

Theodora raised her palms to the flames, then gently caressed her face, as if warming by a campfire. Her body swayed like a dancing snake as her eyes bulged. Her lips curled back, revealing her yellow teeth. "Behold, the Brotherhood."

Chapter 23

The Master Rises

THE TRUNK'S CENTER burned with an orange glow, then red, then a blinding yellow. Crackling flames raged. Theodora stared into the blazing tree without blinking. Charlee took notice. *Now's my chance.* Shielding her eyes with one hand, she slid to Megan's side. Grabbing her sister, holding her tight against her chest, she scrambled back to her dad. Her only chance to protect them both from whatever beast rose from the fire was to keep them together.

Charlee lowered her head to her sister. "I'll keep you safe. I promise. Your big sister won't let anything happen to you. Megan, do you hear me?" Megan didn't answer. More blood seeped from her eyes.

A deep, throaty laugh spread through the chamber. It was not Theodora's, nor Tribon's, but someone else's. Shivering despite the fire's heat, Charlee peered through her fingers.

A figure stepped from the inferno as if passing through a portal. Flames engulfed the being who, once clear of the fire, stood in front of Charlee, head slightly tilted, arms outstretched. The flaming figure looked very much like the young Theodora had described from her experience in the cavern a lifetime ago. Could this be the same evil conjurer that imprisoned the real Theodora in ice? It had to be. Now the fiery being meant her and her family harm, and she had no one to help. She had to face this alone.

The being waved a hand and the fire tree vanished, leaving no sign that it had been there—not a trace of smoke, burnt odor, or any scorch mark.

"It is nice to meet you, Guardian." The figure spoke in the Lengoron language, his voice crusty but friendly. "Allow me to introduce myself. I am Serior."

"I know that name." Charlee stood with Megan in her arms. She spoke through gritted teeth, her words also in Lengoron. "Theodora, the real one, told me how she found the fire tree in a cavern, and you came to her."

The being, his features concealed beneath a layer of flames, crossed his arms and stepped closer to her "Ah, what else did she tell you?"

"Yes, what did that weak-willed beast tell you?" Theodora joined Serior. She crossed her arms and frowned, like an angry parent.

Charlee retreated from them. "She told me you were part of the Brotherhood, and that the Brotherhood was an ancient group of crazy-ass conjurers who figured

151

the best way to bring peace was to kill anyone who stood in their way. You said you'd teach her to use the medallion, but when she wouldn't turn on her sister, you attacked her…imprisoning her in ice and creating this clone." She pointed at the sorceress next to Serior.

"I hear so much contempt in your words." Serior shook his head, the flames swishing with his movement. "I am saddened that you hold an ill-will toward me, when neither I, nor any of my brethren, wish to be your enemy. The Brotherhood is not evil, as you seem to believe. We only want what is best not only for our realm but all realms where death and chaos rule because of failed leadership."

Charlee's thoughts turned toward opening a gateway to save her sister and dad, but how could she do it fast enough? Serior and Theodora would stop her. No, she needed to find the right time. Lowering Megan to the floor just behind her, she slowly inhaled a lungful of air. "All right, then, let's be friends. Start by taking this witch of yours and leaving this world. I'll even come with you, if that's what you want."

Serior rose above the floor, then floated toward her. Charlee raised her hands, igniting a magical glow. *Time to send this bastard back to whatever hell he came from.*

Serior stopped half the distance to her. "I'm afraid I cannot meet your request, Guardian, but you will join the Brotherhood as that is your destiny."

Charlee shook her head. "Never!" He spoke with such certainty. Instinctively, she reached out with her magic, sucking more energy from the soldiers gathered outside. She hated herself for it. She had no right to drain their energy again, but she had to. She needed as much strength as possible for the fight ahead. Her body tingled. She opened and closed her fists. Sparks danced from her fingertips.

"You cannot fight it. One way or the other, you will be a part of us. Do you think we would have allowed your grandfather to steal the medallion, which contains the souls of the Brotherhood, if we did not mean for you to one day join with us? Everything that has transpired has done so because we wished it."

Charlee gasped and her body froze momentarily. That couldn't be true. "I don't believe you."

"You must." Serior closed the distance between them as he reached a fiery hand out to her. Scooping up Megan, Charlee stepped back, shaking her head in denial.

He continued to speak, his voice calm and gentle. "We watched you grow into a fine young woman, and when the time was right, we initiated the chain of events that led you to the medallion. Why do you think you still live? We never intended your death. We had rather hoped you would one day grow to stand with our Theodora and lead our cause once you realized that our path was the only one and fighting us was futile."

"What are you talking about?" Charlee's voice cracked. "All Theodora has done is threaten to kill me and harm my friends and family." Charlee glared at the sorceress whose own eyes burned red again. "That's how you get me to join your side? That's peace to you?"

Serior turned toward Theodora. "Your point is well taken. Unfortunately, it seems our Theodora has a lust for power that has blinded her to our true intentions. We have sat by too long and allowed her to carry out our mission in her own way. For her mistakes, she will be punished."

Theodora's head tilted. Her eyebrows pinched together, and her mouth opened, but she did not speak.

"And what about me?" Charlee turned away from Serior to shield Megan.

"Guardian, you have but two choices." Serior hovered higher above her.

"What are they?" His words replayed in her mind. She didn't want to believe anything he was saying.

"You can choose to share in the power of the medallion, to tap into the full magic of the Brotherhood, and help bring our good will to all worlds that have lost their way." Serior paused again, extending a fiery hand toward Charlee. "Or you can continue this useless fight against us and never again know the glory of wielding the medallion."

Charlee's muscles involuntarily stiffened. Like addicts who can't control their base needs, her body longed for the medallion's power and to once again wield it. But that was wrong. She had to destroy it. That was the only way to end this nightmare, to end Theodora and the Brotherhood. She swallowed against a tightening throat. "And if I side with you, will you free my dad and sister?"

"Of course." Serior nodded.

"If I side against you, what will you do to me?"

Serior floated closer to her. "Then we will finish the extraction process we have already begun."

"I don't understand."

"Guardian, you are so young and naïve. You don't know the extent of the power you possess. You think when Empress Theodora used the medallion against you it took all your magic. The truth is you have so much more ability within you that you have not yet learned to access. It would be a shame for us to have to remove that magic from your very essence, but you would leave us no choice. We must have your power, whether you wield it in our name or we take it from you. Sadly, I do not think you would survive the extraction, but if that is how your life is to end, so be it. As I said, the choice is yours. But understand, not only would you forfeit your life, but the lives of everyone you love, starting with that dear sweet child in your arms."

Charlee kissed Megan on the forehead. Her sister, still in some zombie-like trance, slowly gazed into her eyes. "Ch…Charlee," she whimpered. Blood stopped dripping from her eyes, nose, ears—as if something deep inside Megan, perhaps the power of her magic, enabled her to break through Theodora's spell.

Smiling, Charlee kissed her little sister again. "Yes, it's me." Her sister was starting to come back to her. Warmth spread through her body, and her pulse quickened. She held Megan tighter.

Megan blinked her eyes. Her chin quivered. "Go home?"

A tear slid down Charlee's cheek. "Yeah, you're going home. I promise."

Her jaw stiffened. She planted her feet and stood solidly. She studied Serior, who floated in silent victory. He was lying. No matter what choice she made, he wouldn't free her dad and Megan, and he was not going to just hand her the medallion. What could she do to save them?

Her thoughts turned to Cryton, the old man who once served her grandfather as a great warrior on Janasara but sacrificed everything to care for her mom on Earth. In the short time she knew him, Cryton became her teacher, her mentor…her grandfather. He, more than anyone else, helped her become a guardian. She would never forgive herself for his death. She missed him so much, but he was still a part of her. Charlee could hear his voice urging her to stay strong no matter what.

He taught me to be a warrior. That's what I am.

Her path was clear. It had been clear from the first dreams she had about the world of Janasara and the Kingdom of Latara, from the visions of Theodora to her first meeting with the Changeling in bike form. She was a Guardian. That was her destiny.

"What is your answer, Guardian?" Serior's flames burned brighter.

Charlee released a long breath and dropped to her knees. She lowered her head to her chest.

"Good, my child." Serior folded his burning arms.

She slowly lifted her head. "I'm not your child!"

Spinning on her knees, she pushed her hands out in front of her. A blast of white energy shot from her fingertips, smashing into Tribon. The energy sliced through his stomach, ripping out threw his back. His flesh exploded behind him. He screamed out, falling backward.

Charlee didn't wait to see him fall. Leaping to her feet, she whipped around, then aimed her magic at Theodora. More white energy launched from her hands, crashing into the witch. The blast lifted Theodora off her feet, sending her crashing against a far wall, her arms and legs flailing like trash kicked up by wind.

With Tribon and Theodora momentarily out of the fight, Charlee willed a gateway open—not for herself, but for her sister and dad. It didn't matter where she sent them. Anywhere would be safer.

A gateway just large enough for two rose behind her. She grabbed her sister and reached for her dad. "I'm getting you—"

A burning rope wrapped around her legs, searing through her clothes, igniting her skin in white hot agony. She cried out until a jarring tug slammed her to the ground. Her head smacked against the marble floor, rattling her skull. Her vision tunneled in on itself. She lost her grip on Megan. *No, must save her…Dad!* She blinked away the blurriness. "Megan!" She stretched to her sister, ignoring the fiery rope scorching her legs. Another tug dragged her across the chamber and lifted her until she was suspended upside down.

"Oh, what fun!" Serior mocked her. He held her magically aloft. The burning rope vanished. His fiery body crackled. The flames engulfing him changed color from red, to orange, and finally yellow.

Charlee, gasping for a breath, peered at her sister. Megan clung to their dad. The gateway had vanished. It was too late now anyway. Tribon, somehow recovered from her energy strike, stood over them both despite a gaping, smoldering hole in his gut. He truly was a walking zombie as long Theodora possessed his blackened heart.

Theodora also recovered. Breathing heavy, she limped toward Serior, a grimace across her aged face. "Master, the child has crossed you. You must show her your threats are not idle. You must kill her family and end her miserable existence."

"No!" Charlee shook her body violently, but she couldn't break Serior's magical hold. She had to break free and keep fighting. But how?

"Yes, Theodora, I believe you are right." Serior nodded. "She may lack the vision to recognize the gift I have offered her. Guardian, you have left me no choice. I think we shall start with your father and see what impact that has on you. Then, I'll slowly burn your flesh away and watch you die slowly. But your sister…it would be a shame to kill her as she seems to show her own promise in magic."

"I said no!" Charlee closed her eyes, tapped the magic deep inside, and let it flow through her chest, arms, and hands. A pulse of blinding white energy shot from her palms. The energy burst collided with Serior. He turned away just for a moment, but in that second of distraction, he lost his grip on her.

Charlee dropped to the floor and rolled to her feet. She stood, ready to continue the fight. "This ends now."

The flames engulfing Serior crackled louder. A red glow rose from his chest. He aimed his hands toward Charlee.

An explosion outside the West Wing shook the Oval Office. Charlee fell to the floor. A second explosion shattered the windows, glass imploding into the office. What the hell was happening? She pounced on top of her sister and dad, ready to shield them with her own body. But from what or who?

"Theodora, what is this?" Serior retreated. With a wave of his hands, the fire tree reformed. He stayed close to it. Surprise, and perhaps fear, was etched in his voice.

"I don't know, Master." the sorceress remained in the middle of the chamber. She didn't budge.

A third explosion tore a hole through a side wall. A triumphant roar sounded overhead. Charlee gasped. She knew that roar—Kraannaannn's roar. A smile crossed her face. But how? She had sent him and the others through a portal back to Janasara.

A portal! *Do it now!* In the confusion, Charlee willed a new gateway open. The circular swirling blue vortex formed quickly. Grabbing both Megan and her father, she leaped through the opening.

As she did, laughter filled the office—the sorceress' cackle. She waved her arms wildly as if beckoning the dragon to cause more destruction.

Charlee, eyes wide, started to close the portal, but before it sealed she watched Serior crouch by the fire tree. "Theodora, we are under attack. Why do you laugh?"

"Because this is exactly what I was waiting for." She danced among the chaos. "Goodbye, Master. It is time for me to achieve my goals without the Brotherhood."

The sorceress threw herself upon Serior, reached into his chest, and ripped out the medallion. The leader of the Brotherhood slumped to the ground and didn't move. Then his body vanished. Charlee's mouth dropped open. *It should be mine!* She extended a hand as if to reach through the portal to grasp the medallion.

But the gateway closed.

CHAPTER 24

Reunited...Again

THE GATEWAY SURROUNDED Charlee, her sister, and her dad. She'd opened it so fast that she wasn't even sure where the portal would lead them. She closed her eyes. She had to forget the medallion for the moment. *Focus, Charlee. Get us to safety.*

"Open your eyes, Guardian."

The words bounced like a ricocheting bullet through Charlee's mind. The voice belonged to the sorceress but was distant.

Charlee slowly opened her eyes. The Gateway was gone. So were her sister and dad. Space surrounded her. Stars, other worlds, and brilliant nebulas all mixed together against an endless sea of pitch black. Charlee floated among all of it, like an astronaut untethered to any ship. Earth had slipped away. Beneath her, a blue marble hovered in space. Could that be Earth? Hadn't she just been on Earth? "Where am I, witch? Where's my family?"

"Oh, relax, Guardian. Isn't the universe a splendid place?" Theodora's voice drifted to her across space.

Charlee peered in every direction but saw no one. "More games, Theodora? Face me now. Let's end this."

"Soon, but first I wanted to thank you for freeing me from that painfully boring Serior and his Brotherhood." Theodora's disembodied voice was close now, as if Charlee could touch the witch. "I would have preferred your friends to arrive after every last ounce of your power was torn from your body, but that I can handle myself when the time comes."

"I sent them away." Charlee spun around, searching for the sorceress. "Did you bring them back? Is this all part of your plan?"

"There was no need for me to open a gateway for them. You never sent them away, Guardian."

"What are you talking about? I opened a portal. I saw them disappear."

"Oh, I know you thought you sent them away, but your friends deceived you, and I saw it all. And yes, it did fit into my plans. Their assault on Serior has weakened him. He will need time to recover, giving me just the time I need to soak up the energy of other worlds with magic and become more powerful than the Brotherhood. Then, I will rule alone—without theirs, yours, or anyone's interference."

"Where am I?" Charlee peered into the vastness of space. Shivering, she wrapped her arms around her chest.

"Do you not have eyes? You are in the realm where one universe links to another—where dimensions no longer matter. I summoned your mind, so you can see just how meaningless your life is. All of this is mine for the taking, and you lack the power to stop me."

"Why, Theodora...why do you want to rule the universe?"

"Oh, not just one. I wish to rule them all."

"Why?"

Silence filled the vacuum of space before Theodora spoke again. "Because I wish to be more than I am. More than a creation of the Brotherhood. I wish to be a Goddess—revered and feared by all beings."

"And if you achieve that, then what?" Charlee rubbed her arms.

"You would dare question me?" Rage filled the witch's voice. "I grow weary of you. Now watch as I use the Guardian abilities you so graciously gave me to open a portal to the first world whose magic I will bleed away."

"What will do with Earth?" Charlee swung around in all directions. "You've said it yourself. There's no magic here. There's nothing for you to gain here."

"Oh, but you are so wrong, Guardian." Theodora's voice grew more distant. "I will use every bit of Earth's resources to help me on my quest to conquer all, starting with these worthless human lives. They will serve as my army, just like the Horeng have. If there is one thing about these humans, they are good at waging war and have created wonderful weapons. Oh, yes, I will use everything Earth has to offer. When I am done, I will squash this planet just to hurt you, Guardian. And don't think I cannot control these weak-minded beings even as I spread out to the universe. The medallion is all-powerful, so I will maintain my hold on this world no matter where I go."

Charlee shook with rage. "Just like you did in Janasara? The people there rose against you. So will Earth."

"Stupid little girl, I am so much more powerful now. More powerful than Serior and the Brotherhood ever were." Theodora's voice was just a whisper. "I would say goodbye, but I am sure you will stand against me again. I've shared my plans with you so that you will understand that to stop me, you will have to kill these humans you care so much about. I look forward to seeing that."

Over Charlee's shoulder, the collage of space swirled together into a howling blue vortex, like a black hole forming in space. The world around her turned pitch black. A vast nothingness encircled her.

§ § §

"She's waking up."

Charlee recognized the voice, and it didn't belong to Theodora. *Sandra!* Charlee gasped and coughed. Her stomach churned violently, and her head throbbed. Darkness still engulfed her, but beams of light started to break through the void.

"Can you hear me?"

"Sandra?" Charlee blinked her eyes. More light blazed through the emptiness.

"Yes, it's me."

Charlee's eyes opened wide. She rolled over and the vomit came. When it passed, she wiped her mouth and sat up prone, as if in prayer. Daylight was giving way to the soft purples of dusk. The sweet smell of pine trees filled her nostrils. Snow peaked mountains stretched on either side of her. She ran her fingertips through the soft, lush grass beneath her. The beauty of her surroundings couldn't calm her panicked thoughts. "Theodora...she's going to attack another world... take its magic." Her words flowed out quickly, her voice hoarse.

"Slow down." This time her mom spoke. "We'll get to her. First, we must make sure you're all right."

"Mom...you're okay." Charlee raised her head. Both Sandra and her mom knelt beside her. Not far behind them stood the young Theodora and Mr. and Mrs. Flores, Sandra's parents. Even farther back, watching over them all were the young Dragon Lord—Kraannaannn—and the Changeling, back in the form of a 1960s Schwinn Stingray bike, with tall chrome handlebars, scratched white frame, and a huge banana-shaped seat—just like he appeared to her when they first met. Even Assara had returned, a rope still tied around her waist, the other end attached to the dragon.

A new thought raced through her mind. She leaped to her feet. "Megan? Dad? Where are they? I opened a portal, and then I didn't see them." Her head pounded, and her heart beat heavy in her chest. Her eyes shifted everywhere. "I lost them."

Her mom smiled. "No, you didn't. You saved them. You succeeded in opening a portal, and it brought you just beyond the gates of the White House. When it opened, you were unconscious. Your dad was, too. Megan was alert at first, but then sleep overtook her. She was so tired. When you were all safe, we brought you here to the mountains just above Maryland. Megan is still asleep, and I have your dad under a healing spell. He'll be all right. They're here. Look." Her mom pointed toward the young Dragon Lord. He had his tail wrapped gently around them for protection.

Her heart slowed and her shoulders rounded, and then her legs buckled. She dropped back to the ground.

Her mom embraced her. "You need rest, too. You've got some nasty burns around your legs."

Charlee lowered onto her back and grasped her head. "I don't understand. How did you come back? I sent you away through a portal. I saw the farmhouse disappear with you all inside. I saw Kraannaannn and the Changeling vanish."

Kraannaannn lowered his head to her. He grinned, his raised snout revealing his massive fangs. "Looks can be deceiving."

The young Theodora added to the explanation. "It seems the Dragon Lord and the Changeling combined their magic to generate a rather large cloak of invisibility and a barrier to your portal that together served as a force field. In a sense, your portal passed right over us without ever sending us away, but the invisibility cloak made it look like you had succeeded."

Charlee's stomach calmed. She raised herself into a sitting position, and for the first time noticed the charred hole in her pants and her blistered skin underneath. Rather than burning, it was more like an icy chill resonated from the wound. A tingling sensation spread through her body, probably the work of her mom's healing magic. She bowed to the dragon and the Changeling. "Thank you."

Sandra placed a hand on Charlee's shoulder. "Why would you try to send us away when we were just reunited?"

Charlee peered into her friend's warm eyes, so different from the cold stare the night before when Sandra told her to leave. "I had no choice. The witch told me I had to. She had Dad and Megan and would kill them if I hadn't." Charlee tasted the warmth of her own tears. "You all saved them. If you hadn't come, they would have died. Probably me, too."

"Please, don't leave us again, Charlee." Now it was Sandra's turn to give her a hug. Charlee lingered in the embrace.

Finally lifting away, she lowered her head. "But you told me to leave, Sandra, remember? I understood. Your family was way too mixed up in this, and it was all because of me."

"What are you talking about?" Sandra grabbed Charlee's arm. "I would never say that. I don't even believe it."

"But you did last night in the fields."

"I fear it was the sorceress." Young Theodora shook her head. "She used her magic to take over your friend's mind, just as she has the world under a spell."

"Charlee, you have to believe I would never say anything like that." Sandra teared up.

"I...I know." Charlee's thoughts returned to the night before when Sandra's face twitched uncontrollably. She should have realized that was a sign the sorceress had taken over her friend's mind, but Sandra's eyes hadn't bled. *She didn't even act like she wanted to kill me. It must not have been the same spell. Theodora only wanted to break my spirits.* Charlee hugged Sandra again. "I'm sorry I let her get into your head. I swore I'd keep you safe, and I'm still blowing it."

Sandra gently pushed her away. "Stop blaming yourself."

Charlee nodded. That was easier said than done. Again, she gazed at her surroundings. The sky was darkening as daylight slipped away. Pines and large rock formations extended as far as she could see. Cities stretched below toward the horizon. The air here was thin and crisp. She shivered against the cold. Mist flowed from her mouth with each breath.

Charlee turned her attention to the Changeling. She lumbered to her protector, nearly tripping over her own feet. Wooziness weighed her down, making it difficult to hold her head up. Charlee fought the urge to throw her arms around the bike. Instead, she gingerly wrapped her fingers around the handlebars. Her hands tingled. Sparks climbed her arms and spread over her body. Strength returned to her limbs. The remnants of any dizziness slid away, and clarity returned. She took a deep breath, filling her lungs. Her heart beat stronger. Releasing the bike, Charlee stretched her arms toward the sky and lifted her face to the setting sun.

Her thoughts shifted to the soldiers in the city below under Theodora's control. "How did you get us out of the city?" She gazed at her mom. "How did you get us out of the city? Did you hurt those soldiers to rescue me?"

Her mom smiled. "No, Charlee, I would never let anyone under Theodora's control come to harm. It was Theodora…this Theodora. She's powerful even without the magic of the Brotherhood."

"What did you do?" Charlee's attention shifted to the young Theodora.

"I simply cast a spell that put everyone to sleep in a mile radius of that castle you call the White House." Theodora folded her arms. Her golden hair, lighted by a youthful glow, was such a contrast to her clone's aged, bony form. "I didn't know I could do that, but it was either try that or let the dragon char everyone."

Kraannaannn huffed. "I would only have singed them a bit."

"And what about Serior?" Charlee continued. "Did you kill him? Did you destroy the fire tree?"

Theodora shook her head. "That was not the real fire tree—just Serior projecting an image of the Brotherhood. He would never allow the medallion to be so close to the fire tree when there are those who wish to fling the medallion back into the tree to douse the flames and the medallion's power. As for Serior, I can't say what became of him. Our magic collided in an explosion, and he simply disappeared. I doubt he is dead. He would not fall that easily. The Brotherhood is still powerful."

Assara, her hands bound together, laughed. "But now Mother is stronger, and she is growing stronger every day." This time she spoke in perfect English. "You won't defeat her. And when you are all on your knees begging for mercy, I hope she shows you none."

"Oh shut—" Charlee started to say.

"You're just scared, aren't you?" Sandra interrupted, stepping toward Assara. "I know a scared teen when I see one."

Sandra's clone tilted her head. Her eyes studied Sandra from head to toe. "Don't speak to me as if we are related."

Sandra took one step closer to Assara. "Kudos on learning English so fast. That will make this easier." Sandra inched even closer. "You're just a scared little girl. Just face it. You're scared your mother has left you alone. You think you're some bad-ass warrior, but down deep you're just like the rest of us. Right now, you just want your mom to hold you and tell you everything will be all right."

Assara tugged at the rope. "What do you know about anything?"

"I know what you're feeling because you and I are the same. Like it or not, we're sisters. Look at me. Look at yourself. You can't deny we have a connection. You know I'm right. I don't know how any of this will end, but I'm hoping that when it's finally over, you'll stand by my side as my sister, and I swear you won't have to be scared anymore. You can have a new home and a new family—a real family. You can be part of my family."

Charlee stepped in front of her friend. "Sandra, what are you—"

"I don't care about her past, Charlee. Whatever has happened wasn't her fault. How she feels right now isn't her fault. All that matters is what she does and what we do now. We can all start over."

Assara sneered but said nothing. Turning her back on Sandra, she walked as far away as the rope tied to her would allow.

Overhead the wind kicked up, rustling the trees and howling as it grazed the mountaintop. The sudden gust brought a blanket of gray clouds, racing toward the city below like stampeding horses. The purple sky quickly gave way. Explosions of thunder and the cracks of lightning soon followed.

"What's going on?" Mr. Flores held his wife and wrapped an arm around Sandra. More thunder boomed. Lightning slashed through a darkening sky.

"Oh no." Charlee ran toward the Changeling. *Damn it,* she cursed in silence. What is it?" Her mom had to shout over the wind's cry.

"I know what the witch plans to do." Charlee rubbed the back of her neck, digging her nails into her own flesh. "She wants to be a god, and she thinks no one—not me, the Brotherhood, no one—can stop her."

Charlee leaped on the bike. "I have to get back to Washington. She's going to sacrifice everyone to get what she wants. I must get the medallion from her. It's the only way to end any of this."

Sandra grabbed her arm and jumped on the back of the bike. Her dark eyes, as determined as ever, never blinked. "We go together."

Charlee peered at Sandra, then her mom. How could she endanger them again? "Mom—"

"Yes, together." Charlee's mom nodded her head, face tight and resolute, her lips parted in a knowing smile. Any sign of her wound slipped away. She lifted her chin and stood tall.

"Okay," Charlee mouthed. She bowed to her mom, placing one hand over her heart. She then climbed from the bike and ran to Kraannaannn. "Can you do this? Can you carry everyone? Can you do that and protect my dad and sister?"

The dragon lifted his head. "Like your mother said, together."

She turned back toward the bike. White feathered wings spread from the frame, like a proud eagle ready to take flight.

A slight smile crossed her face. "Okay...together."

CHAPTER 25

The Portal War Begins

THE BIKE STREAKED across the sky at breakneck speeds. Charlee clung to the handlebars, and Sandra interlocked her hands around Charlee's waist. Just to the right, Kraannaannn soared, his powerful wings more than a match against the gusting winds. Her mom and the young Theodora used their magic to create a translucent cockpit on the dragon's back that protected everyone—including Sandra's parents, who refused to be left behind. Charlee's sister and dad were protected inside the dragon's claws.

Swirling black clouds blocked the sun. The thunder rolled in like waves crashing against the shore, and the zigzagging lightning came dangerously close. The electrically charged air caused the little hairs on Charlee's neck to rise. She flinched at every rumble and ducked with each jarring flash of light.

"You're not scared of a little weather, are you, Guardian?" Sandra mocked from behind.

"Shut up."

"Touchy."

"Aren't you scared?" Charlee asked.

"Terrified." Sandra tightened her grip.

"It doesn't show."

"My dad's a cop. How do you think I learned to be so tough? Doesn't mean I'm not scared, but I believe in you, Charlee. You'll get us through this."

I hope she's right. She wanted to open a portal to hide everyone close to her inside where the sorceress couldn't find them, but the witch would always find her. Somehow a link, maybe one caused by the medallion, bound them together—maybe forever.

More lightning slashed across the sky, breaking Charlee from her thoughts.

"Oh my God!" Sandra pointed over Charlee's shoulder. "Look!"

Charlee's eyes widened as she bit her upper lip. Washington loomed ahead. A massive blue portal several blocks long rose from the streets, a towering tunnel, sucking everything in, like a black hole. "I see it." She leaned closer to the handlebars. "We have to get down there."

Theodora formed the portal just beyond the Capitol Building. Massive military convoys—hundreds of tanks, transports, and thousands of marching soldiers—

165

filed into the tunnel, disappearing into the gateway to another world. Jet fighters and helicopters joined them, flying into the dizzying blue light without hesitation.

Charlee tightened her grip on the Changeling's handlebars. Her insides ignited with a fiery rage. Theodora was sending these soldiers off to fight her war. They were going off to kill and die without having any idea what they were doing. *Damn her! I must stop this, but how? There must be a way!* Her muscles clenched. Theodora was going to pay for the lives she was putting at risk.

Energized by the bike, she scanned for signs of the witch with her enhanced vision. There! Above the White House! The sorceress hovered in the skies just above the West Wing, the medallion held high over her head. Her eyes glowed red, hair spinning wildly, and her white dress flapped behind her like a cape.

"Bike—" She didn't have to say more. The Changeling swung toward the sorceress.

"Theodora, stop this!" Charlee magically enhanced her voice to make sure Theodora heard.

The witch didn't answer. Instead, Theodora lifted a hand from the medallion and fired a crimson ball of energy at them. The Changeling dodged the blast with one mighty thrust of his wings, causing the glowing red ball to pass just underneath them. The bike's sudden shift in direction jolted Charlee's body, rattling her brain. She squeezed the handlebars to keep from being thrown. Her arms ached as if ripped from the sockets.

Sandra tightened her grip around Charlee's waist. "That was—"

Theodora hurled another at them. The bike swerved to the right, but this time her magic struck its right wing, igniting the Changeling's feathers. The bike spun away flapping wildly to extinguish the flames.

"Hold on to me!" Sandra shouted.

She whipped off the denim jacket she wore and threw herself onto the wing, smothering the fire. Charlee barely had time to grab Sandra's legs. The bike painfully struggled to stay airborne. The odor of burnt features hung heavy around them. Finally, the scorched wing proved too much for the bike. They plummeted toward the ground.

Charlee wrapped herself around Sandra. With her enhanced strength, maybe she could take the brunt of the collision with the concrete below.

"We're going to make it!" she told her friend.

"I know," Sandra answered.

Charlee tightened her body. She locked eyes with Sandra. Her friend squeezed her lips together. Fear widened her eyes, but she never screamed. For a moment, silence surrounded Charlee.

Heartbeats from striking land, a massive claw swooped them up, like a giant baseball glove.

Charlee gazed up at Kraannaannn. The dragon had made the most amazing catch ever. Kraannaannn stretched out his wings and landed softly on the steps of the Lincoln Memorial.

"You're safe for the moment," the dragon muttered.

Charlee and Sandra hugged. When they separated, Charlee turned to the dragon and patted his claws. "Thank you, my friend."

She swung to the Changeling, still in bike form. His burnt wing disappeared. The white frame vibrated, nearly liquefying as if her protector struggled to maintain his form. He was hurting.

Where was her mom? She could help. And where were Megan and her dad.

"Kraannaannn, where are—?"

"There." He pointed to the warped statue of President Lincoln. Sandra's mom stood there, holding Megan. Mr. Flores knelt beside Charlee's dad. "They've sworn to protect them with their lives."

Charlee nodded. Despite their own pain, their own suffering, the Flores' were still willing to stand by her to protect the members of her family. How could she ever repay them? If she survived, she'd spend the rest of her life trying to find a way.

Her mom and the young Theodora joined her on the stone steps. Charlee pointed to the Changeling. "He's hurt...can you help him?"

"I'll try," her mom answered.

"I'll help," young Theodora added, "but Guardian, I sense this is not the only portal my double has opened. I see portals across the planet and metal vehicles and armies just like this one streaming into the unknown."

"I must find a way to stop her...now. I must get the medallion from her!" Charlee jumped from the steps onto Kraannaannn's leg and crawled up onto this neck. "Let's get her." The dragon roared and took flight.

"What's your plan?' Kraannaannn asked, zooming skyward.

"Reason with her to hand over the medallion." Charlee allowed herself a momentary smile. It quickly faded.

"If she will not?'

"Then show her what dragon fire feels like."

Kraannaannn thrust his wings back and raced toward the sorceress. He circled her once, then hovered off to the right. Theodora didn't even bother to look at them, as if they were as insignificant to her as a fly. Her eyes still blazed red, hands locked on the medallion. Lightning crashed above. The wind screamed, as if in agony. The portal cast a blue glow over the city, swallowing up war machines and soldiers who marched into the swirling gateway to do battle with whatever they would find on the other side. They would die to serve their Empress—unless Charlee could break the spell.

What world was Theodora sending them to? Jeez, would they even be able to breathe there, or would they suffocate immediately? Maybe that was Theodora's plan—to kill tens of thousands of Earth's soldiers instantly. No, she could have done that with the medallion. She must have chosen a world like Earth but one controlled by magic. Would that world be peaceful or warlike? Charlee guessed peaceful.

The blood of two worlds would soon be shed.

"Theodora, you have to stop." Charlee's voice boomed over the wind.

"Never." Theodora's response thundered over the city.

"I'm warning you, witch." Charlee leaned closer to Kraannaannn's ear hole.

"You have no power to challenge me, Guardian."

"Kraannaannn, now!" Charlee commanded.

The dragon arched his neck, opened its snout, and an inferno spewed forth. Charlee turned her head away from the glare from the flames, and the heat that brushed her cheek. In seconds, the blaze engulfed Theodora. When Kraannaannn's fiery attack ended, black smoke filled the sky, consuming the sorceress, but the wind quickly brushed the charred air away, clearing the smoke.

Theodora laughed. Flames hadn't scorched her skin, burned her hair, or even touched her white dress.

"You cannot hurt me, child, but I can hurt you." Theodora lifted a hand away from the medallion and blasted a wave of energy, like a sonic boom, that smashed into the dragon. The magical wave threw Kraannaannn back, like a giant fist had slugged him across his mighty jaw. He tumbled over and over through the sky. Charlee struggled to maintain a grip, digging her hands into the dragon's scaly armor.

"Kraannaannn!"

The dragon didn't respond.

"Kraannaannn!" Charlee repeated.

This time the dragon groaned, but he continued to flip end over end. Charlee grunted, holding on with her enhanced strength. She cried out to the dragon, whose limp body plunged to the earth. Then her strength failed, and she lost her grip. Arms and legs thrashing, she plummeted alongside the dragon.

The ground rushed at her. *Can't give up. Can't die this way. My magic will have to save us. Open a portal!*

Free falling, Charlee squeezed her eyes closed, then slowed her breathing. She concentrated on each beat of her heart, focusing on the rhythmic pulses, using them to control each labored breath. Her muscles relaxed, her body became light, as if she were a feather floating in a breeze. Her mind focused.

Now! The blue gateway formed in her thoughts, a swirling doorway just a few feet above the ground—not yet large enough to save the dragon. Charlee forced her eyes open. The gateway was a distant target whose bullseye was much too small. The young Dragon Lord would be sliced in half by her magic.

Charlee gritted her teeth. *Have…to…make the gateway…larger!*

The ground raced at them. Charlee's body trembled. The portal expanded but much too slowly. *Come on…damn you!*

Charlee shrieked but the screaming wind silenced her. They were almost upon the portal. She flung her arms out wide as if to rip the portal open just wide enough.

"Kraannaa—!" The young Dragon Lord's name stuck in her throat. They both slipped into the portal moments before slamming into concrete.

Once inside the gateway, Charlee willed the portal to bend 180 degrees. Her own warm blood dripped from her nose, falling over her lips and sliding into her mouth. Her head ached as if squeezed by a vise, but she couldn't stop now. She had to guide them back to safety. Her skull felt as it might crack at any moment, but she willed the portal to bend 180 degrees, then opened the other end. The gateway spit them out as if the ground had just opened and the Earth spewed food it didn't like.

The dragon landed with a soft thud, his wings splayed on either side of his body.

Charlee curled herself in a ball, rolling several times along a hard rough pavement before she stopped. Pain radiated through her body, but she was alive. What about Kraannaannn? Had he made it?

"Kraannaannn!" Charlee screamed. She picked herself up and limped to his side. The young Dragon Lord didn't budge. Droplets of blood dripped from his nostrils. His eyes were closed, and his chest was still.

"Don't be dead!" Charlee placed her hands on his chest. "Come on, damn it. Breathe!"

The dragon remained silent. Charlee slumped to her knees.

Footsteps approached. She looked up as her mom crossed to her and the others followed. Standing, Charlee wiped away tears. "That's it. The witch goes down now! She's not going to hurt anyone else!"

"You're absolutely right." Sparks of green energy leaped from her mom's fingers. "We do this together. The only way we stop her is to combine our strength."

"I agree." The young Theodora stepped forward. "It's time this twisted version of me learns just how powerful I am."

The Changeling joined them, popping a wheely as if to say he was ready to join the fight as well.

"I'm…in, too." The words came groggily from Kraannaannn. The dragon painfully lifted his head.

Charlee gasped. Her mouth hung open. Her body lightened just for a heart-beat. She threw her arms around the dragon's neck. "You're alive."

The dragon parted his lips in a slight smile. "What, you think a fall is going to kill a dragon? We don't die that easily." He stood on wobbly hind legs, then shook his head rapidly like a dog. He slowly tucked his wings into his body. "Now, let's take this witch down."

Charlee shook her head. "You can barely move."

"I can fly, and the sorceress has not drenched my fire." The dragon stretched his wings to their full impressive length.

Wrinkling her eyebrows, Charlee gazed at everyone. They were all putting their lives in danger, but she needed each of them. She leaped onto the back of the Changeling, still in bike form. "Then we do this. We all strike her at once. If we hurt her, maybe I can swoop in and snatch the medallion. Game over."

Young Theodora nodded. "Yes, once you have it, I'll find a way to get us to the fire tree. This all ends once the medallion is destroyed in the flames that gave it birth."

Charlee's body tensed. Destroy the medallion? Did she have the strength? Deep inside, her gut still ached to possess it, to control its power. *No, stupid. She's right. It must be destroyed.* She shook away those thoughts. Right now, the time had come to take this battle to the witch.

Before they took flight, Charlee motioned to Sandra. "Stay with my dad and my sister and keep watch over Assara."

"I will," Sandra answered. "Just be careful."

"You to." Charlee grasped the handlebars. The Changeling took off into the air, rushing high over the Lincoln Memorial. The dragon followed without a rider. Instead of hitching a ride with Kraannaannn, her mom and young Theodora drew on their own powers of levitation to rise into the stormy sky.

The thunder still rumbled, and cracks of lightning spread out like a spider web glowing against the turbulent sky. Theodora hadn't budged. She wielded the medallion. Its power kept the towering portal open while soldiers poured in and vanished into the blue light.

Charlee and her Changeling soared up to Theodora, circling just above the sorceress. The dragon, her mom, and young Theodora all joined her. *I must get the medallion from her. It's the only way.*

The sorceress turned her eyes from the portal to Charlee with the disinterest of momentarily staring at a fly. Then, she turned back to the portal, her lips parted in a confident sneer.

"Enough!" Charlee took a deep breath and drew in as much of the Changeling's energy as she could. *Help me channel your power. Let me use it to stop her.* Her body vibrated. A white glow rose from her palms, surrounding her hands as if an electric current pulsated under her skin. She brought her hands close together, and an orange spark flowed between them. "This ends now!" Charlee shouted.

She extended her arms out toward the sorceress. Thunderbolts shot from both hands, slicing across the sky, striking Theodora in the chest. *When did I get the power of Zeus?* She formed another thunderbolt and prepared to lob it at the sorceress.

Across from her, the dragon roared. Flames flew from his mouth. Beyond the dragon, a sapphire ray flew from her mom's hands, and young Theodora fired an emerald beam. Each crashed into the sorceress with an explosion louder than any thunder—an explosion that shattered glass below and knocked the advancing soldiers off their feet.

The sorceress cried out and then was silent.

CHAPTER 26

No Time to Die

A WHITE MIST surrounded the evil Theodora, and when the wind blew it away, her limp body floated in the sky, arms and feet dangling beneath her. The medallion had vanished. Charlee was breathless. Her senses heightened with an adrenaline rush. Could it be true? Could they have defeated the cloned Theodora? Had their combined powers proved too much—even for the medallion? The emptiness in her gut told her something wasn't right.

Below, the portal remained open. The soldiers continued their zombie-like march into the vortex. If the evil Theodora was defeated, shouldn't her magical hold on the portal be broken? No, this wasn't right.

Charlee nudged the Changeling forward, urging her protector to fly closer to the twisted clone. Before she could reach her, the witch's lifeless body fell from the sky, slamming into the concrete below with a thud. Blood pooled around her.

Charlee's hands still glowed. Her palms burned, like she had just touched a metal spoon left in a boiling pot. She rubbed her hands together, eyes focused on the sorceress. She motioned for the Changeling to land but at a safe distance. The others followed.

Inching toward the body, Charlee could see bones ripped through the cloned Theodora's skin and her legs bent in an unnatural position. Her head twisted to the side. An eyeball hung loosely from its socket. Blood circled the body.

She scanned the street around the witch. Where was the medallion? How could it just vanish even if the witch was dead. She had to find it. She had to have it. *Damnit, where are you? Talk to me, like you once did?* The medallion, wherever it might be, was silent. Her mind spun out of control. The longing pierced her insides as if a knife sliced through her. Breathing heavy, Charlee hunched over.

"Are you all right?" Her mom's gentle voice was followed by her soft hand placed on Charlee's shoulder.

Charlee gazed at her mom. She couldn't tell her the truth—that she craved the medallion. She slowly lifted herself. "Mom, can she really be dead?"

Her mom shook her head. "She can't be. It was too easy, but look at her."

Young Theodora, glowing hands out in front of her, cautiously stepped toward her evil clone. "You are right. A creation of the medallion could not be defeated so easily. We must find the medallion." She knelt near the witch, gently touching her face, neck, and chest. "She's still warm. Her heart still—"

Young Theodora glanced back at Charlee. "Everyone, back away!"

A blood curdling laugh rose from the witch. The body creaked and bent, bones reconnecting with muscle and tissue. Blood along the street seeped back into the flesh as if being soaked up by a sponge. The crazed cackling grew louder.

Young Theodora lifted away from her clone, but the sorceress' hand shot up and grabbed her by the neck. A crimson glow spread from the sorceress' fingers wrapped around her prey's neck. Young Theodora cried out. Her clone stood, then lifted her into the air. With her other hand, she forced her loose eyeball back into its socket.

Charlee ran at them, but an energy pulse from the sorceress slammed against her, like a brick wall, knocking her to the ground.

"Sister, it is so nice to be reacquainted with you." The evil Theodora spoke for all to hear. "You should have stayed in your icy prison. Now everyone will see that the best part of you was ripped away by the medallion. Now I truly am the only Theodora."

The true Theodora gurgled and coughed, thrashing her feet and grasping at her clone's hand, which remained locked around her neck. Her skin sizzled and popped underneath the sorceress' grip.

Young Theodora's face blushed as blood dripped from her nose and mouth. "You. Will. Not. Win." Her words came out slow and phlegmy. She reached back toward the sorceress, igniting her own magic. An emerald beam slammed into her clone, loosening her grip. Young Theodora dropped to the pavement. Charlee's mom ran to her side, pulling her away to the protective cover of Kraannaannn's armored body.

Charlee's mom fired a sapphire beam at the evil Theodora, but the energy bounced off an invisible barrier. Charlee, her hands electrically charged, fired a bolt at her, but the translucent force field protected the sorceress.

Her hands outstretched, the witch tilted her head back and laughed once again. "Fools, you cannot destroy a God. You are nothing before me. Now, I grow weary of our time together and must bid you farewell. So many other worlds await my rule."

"Mother…mother, wait!" Assara, her hands still bound but free from the rope around her waist, ran into the street just below the sorceress. "Mother, it is your daughter, your general, your servant. Please take me with you. Let me fight at your side."

The evil Theodora glared at her. "You failed me. You think I do not know of your defeat at the Castle? And now you would dare seek to fight at my side. I have no daughter. You were clearly a mistake. Time for me to fix that mistake."

"Mother," Assara pleaded, falling to her knees. "I beg your forgiveness."

"Goodbye, child." The witch raised her hand over her head. Red energy formed into a spear within her palm.

"Mother, no!"

"Theodora, no!" Charlee bolted toward Assara.

The sorceress flung the glowing spear. It raced toward its target, Assara's chest, but it struck another. Young Theodora threw herself in front of Assara. The spear tore through her chest and ripped through her back. The true Theodora convulsed. Her head jerked back. Then, she fell to her knees and onto her side. Charlee slid next to her. Theodora coughed, blood spilling from her mouth.

The sorceress, still hovering high above, applauded. "Oh, sister, such heroics. And for what? To save a worthless being." She turned her attention to Charlee. A wide grin spread across her pale face. The medallion reappeared in her hands. "Farewell, Guardian. Your failure is complete. I am now more than you can ever hope to defeat. I leave you with this. Soon, everyone you love will die…painfully. When I have had my fun with them, and you have suffered enough, then death will come for you. Until then…"

The evil Theodora vanished—with the medallion.

Charlee's body trembled with rage, but she pushed it aside. "Theodora, hang on." She looked up at her mom. "Help her."

Young Theodora spit blood from her mouth. "Do not fear, Guardian. I'm not done yet." She placed shaky hands against her chest. Green energy flowed through her palms, resealing torn flesh, closing the wound both in her chest and her back until the only sign she'd been hurt was her charred robe. Her body trembled, and her lips quivered. She exhaled a long breath and smiled weakly. She gazed up at Charlee. "I can't die yet, Guardian. I'm certainly not going to let you have all the fun."

Assara crawled to her. Tears filled her eyes. "Why would you risk your life to save mine?"

Theodora coughed before she spoke. She spit blood one more time onto the street and extended a bloody hand to Assara's cheek. "Your life matters."

"Look, the portal closes!" Kraannaannn shot into the sky.

Charlee peered up. The last of the soldiers passed through the swirling vortex, and the gateway was closing in on itself. "We have to stop her!"

The dragon roared, blowing fire into the closing gateway. He was the first to enter. He quickly disappeared. Assara rose to her feet and backed away from Theodora. She then turned and ran to the portal.

"Assara, no." Sandra charged after her clone, but Assara disappeared into the misty blue doorway. Sandra stopped and looked back at her mom and dad. "I'm going after her."

"Don't do it!" Charlee motioned to the Changeling. Still in bike form, the magical being raced to her side. She started to swing her leg over the seat.

"You're not going anywhere, Guardian." Tribon grabbed her by the waist. Lifting Charlee over his head with his iron hands, he hurled her through the air. She landed hard against the street. The bones in her right arm crunched against the unforgiving asphalt. A yelp escaped her lips. She coughed to force air through her lungs.

Slowly, she stood. She pointed at the Changeling. "Stop Sandra!" The bike hesitated.

Tribon, with his tree-trunk-sized legs, lumbered toward her. Not even the hole in his chest slowed him down. "The Empress may have let you live, but I've waited too long to end your life."

Charlee peered over him at the Changeling. "I said go." The bike spread its white wings and took flight. She turned back to Tribon. She'd have to tear him in half to stop him or cut his head off. How else could she kill someone literally without a heart kept alive through the darkest magic? "Come and get me, traitor." Charlee took a painful breath.

A sapphire beam smacked Tribon from the side, knocking him to one knee. An arrow whooshed from the opposite side, striking him in the shoulder.

"You're done, Tribon."

§ § §

Charlee's dad stood off to the left with his quivering arms holding another arrow taut against the bowstring in his hands. A cut stretched from his forehead down his right cheek. A blackened eye remained sealed tight, dried blood crusted by the eyebrow. But he was well enough to join the fight. The words, *Tribon, you're done*, had come from him.

"Dad?" Charlee gasped.

He nodded to her, then nearly collapsed on wobbly legs, catching himself and holding his ground. Her mom stood to the right of him, her hands flared with blue energy.

"Get away from her." The words from Charlee's dad came whispery with a bit of a whine, like the time he broke cartilage in his nose on a hiking trip.

Tribon laughed hoarsely as if his throat had never healed from the dragons' fiery attack that engulfed him along the seashore in Janasara. Maybe he could never die as long as the evil Theodora possessed his beating heart, but his body could wither, like any rotting corpse. "Does the puny human man and his would-be queen think they can stop me? I am Empress Theodora's general, and I will destroy anyone who would stand against her."

He rose, plucked the arrow from his arm, and reached for the broadsword at his side. A sapphire beam slammed into his shoulder, and an arrow pierced his side. A second and third arrow struck his legs. The giant man faltered, lowering his sword. Wheezing breaths flowed from his mouth. "You cannot defeat me. I may fall, but you know I will rise again."

Charlee walked up to him. "Not when I stomp on your heart myself." Strengthened with the Changeling's energy, she delivered a kick to his jaw hard enough to smash through a brick wall.

Tribon's chin snapped. His bones shattered. He dropped to the ground and didn't move. Charlee, grasping her injured arm, bent down to rip away his iron hands, but the giant man began to fade. *No, I won't let you escape.* She tried to grab him, but her hand found no flesh to grip. Then she recalled why. Charlee had seen it before. He would be transported to wherever Theodora was as long as she possessed his heart.

In the time it took her to remember, Tribon completely faded away.

"We'll get him and Theodora." Her mom placed a healing hand on Charlee's injured arm. A tingling sensation warmed Charlee's flesh. Inside, her cracked bones reassembled and tendons tightened, reattaching to muscle.

She swung around to the portal. It had nearly closed. But where was Sandra? Her best friend had tried to stop Assara from entering the gateway. The Changeling swooped down beside her. The winged bike had no rider. No Sandra. That meant…

Sandra's mom rushed up to her. "My daughter, my husband, did they—"

Charlee didn't need to ask the Changeling what happened. For some reason, Sandra had decided not to give up on Assara even if it meant following her into the portal. Her dad, Mr. Flores, had obviously gone after his daughter. Even the young Theodora was missing.

"I'm sorry." Charlee lowered her head. "But I'm going to bring them both back to you. I promise."

She extended a hand toward the collapsing doorway to wherever the others had gone. Concentrating, her head pounding from the effort, she forced the portal to remain open—long enough for her to enter. "I must go through the portal and find a way to stop whatever war Theodora is about to start, and then bring Sandra, Mr. Flores, Kraannaannn, and all those soldiers home."

"We're going with you." Her dad leaned on his bow. Charlee, her body trembling from the effort to keep the portal open, shook her head. He could barely stand.

Don't argue with me, young lady." He offered a slight smile. She turned to her mom.

"You heard your father."

Charlee climbed onto the back of the Changeling, which shifted back to a unicorn form, and motioned for her parents to join her. When both climbed onto the Changeling's back, Sandra's mom approached. She still held Megan to her chest. "Please bring my daughter and my husband home."

"We will," Charlee's mom answered. "Please watch over my youngest daughter." Her words were choked between tears. "I leave her in your hands."

"I will guard her with my life." Sandra's mom reached a hand up. The two mothers interlocked their fingers for a moment, then shared a fearful glance that only mothers could understand before separating.

Charlee, lightheaded—her magic draining—nodded to Sandra's mom. With a final glance at her sister, she patted the unicorn's neck. The winged beast took the air.

Before them, the portal awaited.

CHAPTER 27

A World Under Siege

CHARLEE, HER MOM, and her dad soared on the back of the Changeling, charging into the dimension-linking tunnel. What would they face on the other side? Was the cloned Theodora right? Did she have the power of a God? These thoughts crashed through Charlee's mind. *No, I must believe she can be stopped.* With wings thrust back and his body stretched out like a racehorse bolting toward a finish line, the unicorn burst through the glowing blue gateway.

Charlee held her breath, leaning in closer to the unicorn. As the blue energy engulfed her, she stared in every direction and the events of her life since those first dreams of Theodora flashed around her, like a 360-degree movie screen.

Her dad gave her the ugliest bike she'd ever seen. She tried to ditch it in an alley only to have the bike returned by a strange old man who went by the name Mr. Levenstein. Tribon appeared to her at school and told her of her powers and pretended to be her mentor. She was manipulated to open a portal to this world, allowing in a dangerous sorceress — Theodora, her great aunt. She battled with Theodora on a skyscraper over San Francisco, and the bike swooped in with wings to save her. She tricked Theodora with a fake medallion back to her world. Charlee leaped across to that world with Mr. Levenstein, really Cryton, who had watched over her when she didn't even know it. He died at the hands of Theodora's cloned daughter, Assara.

Charlee saw it all painfully flash before her. Her chest ached and she struggled for each breath. The loss of Cryton left an emptiness in her gut that would never be filled. The excruciating torture of having her powers torn from her by the medallion was an agony that would haunt her forever. She shuddered reliving those moments. Still, the events of the past blazed around her.

The dragons saved the people of Latara. She fought Theodora in Castle Latara, wielding the medallion against her, only to lose it and most of her power. Theodora, after stealing Charlee's magic abilities, used them to open a gateway back to Earth to destroy all Charlee held dear.

The images vanished, forcing Charlee back into the moment. She emerged from the gateway, bleary eyed. Blinking her vision back to normal, she held her hands to her forehead as if trying to rub away a migraine. When her eyes cleared, she gasped. Her racing heart came to a jarring stop.

They'd arrived at a war zone on an alien world.

Theodora opened portals around Earth, and they all converged on this one battlefield on this new world. Massive blue gateways, like swirling whirlpools, meandered from crimson skies down to a blanket of ruby-tinted rolling hills covered by towering flowers that generated a phosphorescent orange glow. Columns of light reached toward the heavens. Beyond the hills, a city hovered on pedestals, like football field length cylinder staircases unevenly separated. Rounded skyscrapers rose from each pedestal, each joined by beams of golden light. The air was breathable but sweet, almost nauseating—like an overpowering odor of apple pie. She hated apple pie.

If this were another time, she'd bask in the glory of this strange world, but right now a war was at hand. Theodora's spellbound military, hundreds of thousands strong, poured from the portals and marched toward the city.

Military jets screamed overhead. Helicopters roared as the armored birds flew in "V" formations. The thunderous pounding of soldiers' boots striking the ground in unison echoed across the hills. With her enhanced hearing, the frightened cries of magical beings inside the city mixed in with the sounds of war.

"This is too big." Charlee leaned into her dad's chest. "I can't stop this."

"We have to find a way." Her dad held her shoulders.

"You're going to have to close the portals." Her mom pointed at the closest gateway. "Stop more soldiers from crossing."

Charlee shook her head. "But if I close them, how will the ones already here get back home?"

Her mom's face became rigid. "They may not, but at least you can keep the others away. Save the ones who haven't crossed over."

"Mom—"

"When this is over, you'll find a way to open a new portal and send these poor souls back." Her mother lowered her voice. "I know you can do it. But for now, close them."

"What if I don't have enough power?"

"Believe in yourself." Her mom smiled faintly.

"You'll do it, Guardian, because you don't have a choice," her dad added.

Charlee licked her dry lips. "I'll try, but where are Kraannaannn, Sandra, and her dad? I don't see any of them."

"Look!" Her mom gestured to a blood-red waterway—like an inland lake—at the base of a hillside away from the advancing soldiers. Kraannaannn lay on the shore, half submerged. Smoke rose from his back. The dragon didn't move. Mr. Flores lay motionless next to the dragon. So did the young Theodora. The witch stood over them. Sandra knelt before her, head bowed. Charlee's lips pulled back, revealing gritted teeth. Her vision tunneled on Theodora. Her insides ignited into a consuming fire, burning her from the inside out. The witch would pay.

"Dive!" she commanded the Changeling, who still held his unicorn form.

Drawing more of the Changeling's energy, Charlee summoned a thunderbolt, hurling it at Theodora like a javelin. Her attack slammed into a magical barrier, exploding into a dazzling display of fiery sparks long before it reached the witch.

The Changeling landed on the waterfront next to Kraannaannnn, whose head rested in a foaming blood red muck. Choking black smoke escaped the dragon's nostrils with each breath. He didn't open his eyes.

Close by, Mr. Flores lay face down, tangled in thick red brush. A painful half-conscious groan rose from this throat. "Sandra."

Young Theodora lay beside him on her side. A gash spread across her forehead. Blood seeped from the wound.

Sandra knelt on a grassy knoll overlooking the lake of blood water, which meandered between the rolling hills up to and underneath the pedestals upon which sat the city now under attack. She didn't move. Her arms hung loosely at her side, hands draped along the ground. Her chin rested against her chest, and her long brown hair covered her face.

Charlee leaped from the unicorn. She barreled from the shore up the hill toward her best friend. "Sandra, I'm coming!"

Before she could reach Sandra, she collided with Theodora's invisible barrier. The collision knocked the wind out of Charlee and sent her tumbling down the hill.

"No!" Charlee stood and charged forward, this time her hands out in front. When she reached the barrier, she pounded against it with closed fists. "Sandra, can you hear me? Sandra, look at me." Her friend didn't budge.

Theodora laughed. "Thank you for reuniting me with this feisty child, Guardian." Theodora placed an arm around Sandra's shoulders. "She'll make a wonderful servant whose very blood will create an army of warriors."

Charlee pounded again on the barrier. Her muscles and veins strained against her skin. She had to break through the force field. "Theodora, this is between me and you, no one else. Let her go."

"Actually, maybe I'll just kill her in front of you for the trouble you've caused." Theodora raised a glowing red hand over her head. "Yes, that would be best."

Charlee slammed a fist once more against the barrier. "If you hurt her, there will be nowhere you can go that I won't find you and make you suffer."

"Mother?" Assara appeared from the shadows behind Theodora. "Mother, please let me prove myself to you. Let me kill the girl. Allow me through the barrier, and I will make you proud of me again."

"Assara, don't do this!" Charlee slammed her body against the barrier. Over and over, she smashed her shoulder against the invisible force field. It would not break. The Changeling joined, ramming its hooves against the unseen wall. Her mom fired sapphire beams to no effect.

Her dad stood beside her. "Theodora, you don't have to do this. If you need to kill someone, kill me."

Theodora merely laughed. With a motion of her hand, she allowed Assara through the barrier. "Yes, my child. Here is your chance to redeem yourself and prove yourself worthy to me."

Assara bowed her head. "Thank you, Mother. I shall end her life with this blade I retrieved from one of your army." She pulled a dagger from the belt around her waist. "I shall use it to slice her throat."

Charlee's heart thrashed inside her chest. Tears rushed down her cheeks. "Sandra, wake up. You have to run." Her friend didn't move.

"Damn it, Assara, she came here to save you." Charlee raised a fist at Sandra's clone. "She cares about you."

Young Theodora, wiping blood from her forehead, joined Charlee. "Assara, you can be better than this."

Assara ignored them. The clone stepped behind Sandra, grabbed her hair, then placed the blade against her neck.

"Yes, my daughter." Theodora's eyes widened. "Do this for me."

Charlee screamed. Her hands ignited in a white glow.

"Yes, Mother. All for you." Assara released Sandra's hair. In one smooth motion, she twisted around and drove the blade into Theodora's chest.

Charlee dropped to her knees as her body froze. What had happened? Her eyes darted from Assara to Theodora. The twisted grin on the sorceress's face withered away. Her lips parted in a silent scream as her fingers fumbled for the hilt of the blade buried deep into her chest cavity. She faltered, lumbering backward away from Assara.

Sandra's clone approached her. "You tried to kill me, Mother. You said my life no longer mattered. But you were wrong, Mother. My life does matter. So does the life of this girl. I was a fool for ever believing yours was the right way. But no more."

Charlee slowly stood. Assara saved Sandra and struck down Theodora. Was any of this real? It was. It was all happening before her eyes. Thanks to Assara, Theodora was beaten. This nightmare might finally—

The expression on Theodora's face quickly shifted back to a grin. A terrifying laugh slid from her throat. She slashed razor-sharp nails across Assara's face. Sandra's clone cried out, grabbing her torn cheek.

"You would dare cross the one who gave you life." Theodora lifted into the air just over Assara. The blade remained lodged in her chest, but she seemed to no longer take notice of it. Her eyes glowed red. Her gray hair flowed wildly around her face. "Now, there is no one to save you."

Charlee steadied her legs. Her hands still aglow, she pounded one more time on the barrier. Maybe it was because of her own rage-fueled strength. Maybe it was because Theodora was weakened by the blade. The barrier shattered.

"Enough!" Charlee formed a thunderbolt in her hands and hurled it at the witch. It struck the blade, driving it deeper into the witch's chest. The evil Theodora cried out.

Young Theodora hurled her own emerald energy ray at her clone, striking her in her gut. The witch dropped to the ground and faltered to her knees.

"Does it hurt, you fake piece of filth." Young Theodora's hands glowed green, ready to deliver another blow.

Assara, face bloodied, placed her arms around Sandra, lifted her, and carried her away from the battle. Charlee heaved another thunderbolt, but the evil Theodora deflected it with her own magic. The effort caused her to breathe heavy. She grimaced as if in pain but quickly climbed to her feet.

Young Theodora heaved another energy ray, but her clone snatched it out of the air with her bare hands.

"You're done, Theodora." Charlee formed yet another thunderbolt. "You're no God. You're nothing at all."

Evil Theodora floated higher. "Do you want to see what a God can do? Watch now as I amuse myself and allow your people to forfeit their lives to serve me. The magic of this world will be mine. When I have absorbed it all, your death will come slow and painfully, I assure you." Rising back up into the air, hands stretched out like some benevolent ruler watching over her people, Theodora soared away to the front lines of her war.

She stopped for just a second and hovered over her army. In a commanding voice, she declared, "Destroy the Guardian and anyone who fights for her."

CHAPTER 28

The Front Lines

THE SOLDIERS CAME for them. Breaking off from those units converging on the magical city, a sizeable force marched toward the waterfront where Charlee gathered with her friends and family. The soldiers moved cautiously, as if approaching a dangerous enemy. Any moment, they could open fire in service of their Empress.

Charlee patted the unconscious dragon on the snout. "Kraannaannn, we need you. Come back to us."

Just behind her, Sandra stirred to life. "Dad! Oh my God. Dad!" Charlee peered at her. Sandra's voice, even if filled with terror, warmed Charlee. Hearing her friend break from Theodora's spell was like a beacon of hope.

Mr. Flores groaned, then turned over on his back. "I'm...okay. I think." Sandra embraced her dad.

Charlee longed to run to their side and join in the embrace, but now was not the time. "Uh, we have an entire army of soldiers about to attack us. Maybe the hugs could wait."

Sandra helped her dad rise. They lumbered to Charlee's side. Assara, blood dripping from the gash in her cheek, approached as well. Now, she clutched an assault rifle, studying the weapon, eyebrows furrowed in an expression of curiosity.

Mr. Flores pulled out a handgun from his pants and aimed it at Assara. "Drop it, little girl."

Sandra, her eyes on Assara, placed a hand on her dad's arm. "It's okay, Dad. She saved me from Theodora." She nodded to Assara. Her clone nodded back.

Charlee marveled at them. She would never forgive Assara for killing Cryton and the Dragon Lord, but she'd wrestle with those feelings later. For now, she needed to revive Kraannaannn. Without the dragon, they'd be lost.

Her mom, hands aglow, stood beside Charlee. Her dad, an arrow strung on his bow, knelt next to her. Young Theodora, her golden hair matted down by her own blood, stood next to Charlee's dad. The winged-unicorn—her Changeling protector—raised up on his hind legs and spread his wings.

"Kraannaannn," Charlee repeated. Still nothing.

She peered over her shoulder. They'd soon be surrounded by soldiers who, in their current state, had one thought on their collective minds. *Destroy the Guardian.*

Closing her eyes, Charlee ignited her hands in a white glow. "Kraannaannn, sorry about this, but I have to do something." She placed her hands on his scaly head. She then unleashed a pulse of energy against the dragon's skull.

The mighty beast's eyes shot open, and he roared in protest, raising his neck high above Charlee. She fell onto her backside. The others backed away. Kraannaannn shook his head violently and spit fire into the sky. Spreading his wings to their full length, the dragon glared down at Charlee. "Don't ever do that again."

Charlee shrugged her shoulders. "I had to do something. You were sleeping on the job. Look around. We're in trouble."

The dragon surveyed the approaching soldiers. "What? From these tiny human creatures? I'll feast on their bones."

"No!" Charlee shook her finger at the dragon. "You can't hurt them. Just keep them busy. Theodora is about to begin her attack on that floating city. I'm going to cut off her army by closing the portals. Then I need to find a way to break Theodora's mind control spell, but I need you to delay Theodora's assault until I can do that."

The dragon nodded. "Sure, sounds easy enough."

"We'll help." Sandra wiped away tears, climbed to her feet, and tied her hair in a ponytail.

Charlee's mom aimed her glowing hands at the soldiers. "Yes, we—"

Shots erupted, zipping along the waterfront, kicking up yellow sand and crimson water all around them. The first wave of gunfire missed them. Assara aimed her assault rifle at the soldiers. Charlee pushed the gun down and shook her head.

Before more rounds followed, Charlee's mom reached toward the sky and uttered an incantation in Lengoron. Young Theodora joined her, their voices becoming like one. An earthen wall rose from the sand before them. More rounds spit through the air toward them, striking the dirt barrier.

Kraannaannn bared his fangs.

"Don't kill them," Charlee reminded the dragon. "It's not their fault."

The dragon roared and took to the sky. He landed with a thump behind the soldiers and thrashed his tail around like a whip, striking them. The soldiers, thrown about like raggedy dolls, screamed. Their twisted bodies wreathed in pain, strewn along the waterfront. Some landed in the shallow water. Whimpering and moaning, they clutched injured limbs. Others lay silently.

Charlee placed her hands against her mouth. She prayed none were killed. At least her friends and family were safe for the moment. Kraannaannn didn't wait to gloat over the damage he'd caused. He took off toward the city.

Charlee turned away from the wounded soldiers. She couldn't linger in the moment. She bit her lip, then shot a glance at her mom. "I'm going to try to close the portal. I hope that's the right thing to do. I don't want anyone trapped here."

"They won't be." Her mom ran to her side. "You'll find a way to get them home when the time is right."

Charlee quickly embraced her mom and then leaped onto the unicorn's back. She and the Changeling took to the sky. Would she have enough strength to close the portals? She did feel stronger. Hard muscles in her usually rubbery arms served as proof magic still flowed through her veins. The Changeling's energy helped, but would her Guardian abilities be enough? The medallion had stripped her magic away. Though she got her powers back, maybe she'd never fully recover. Maybe, she'd never be the Guardian she was before the medallion ripped her very soul away.

Charlee and the Changeling flew to the closest portal. Soldiers still poured through the towering manhole between worlds.

Off in the distance, Theodora's voice boomed. Charlee glanced back toward the city. The sorceress brazenly levitated in front of her spellbound armies of Earth and spoke to the beings of this new world, like a conquering warlord. Charlee couldn't recognize the language, but that didn't matter. Theodora clearly gave these beings an ultimatum: give me your magic or die. But why hadn't she just cast a spell over these people, like she did on Earth. *Maybe mind spells don't work on these magical beings,* she thought.

Kraannaannn soared over Theodora and blew fire into the sky.

Fierce-looking military jets bore down on the dragon, unleashing a barrage of missiles. Charlee's eyes widened. Her face went cold. *No, Kraannaannn, get out of there!* The dragon thrust back his wings and shot higher into the sky, the missiles charging at him, leaving a trail of zigzagging white smoke.

The dragon spun and changed course, diving toward a hillside. Charlee's breath stuck in her throat. At that speed, how could he avoid a collision with the hill? The missiles outpaced the dragon. In seconds, they would slam into him.

"Kraannaannn!" Charlee cried.

He spread his wings an instant before striking ground, then showing incredible agility for such a large creature, angled toward the sky.

The missiles could not follow. They collided with the hillside in a brilliant explosion. A fireball bloomed skyward and shook the ground. A hurricane-like gust of air rolled over thousands of advancing soldiers, scattering them like trash in a windstorm. Kraannaannn flew high untouched from the attack, but more jets converged on him.

The mechanical roar of an approaching chopper shook Charlee back to her own battle. Astride the winged unicorn, she turned toward a massive gunship, an intimidating flying machine of rivets and steel with rotor blades bellowing, like an angry beast declaring its supremacy over a weaker prey. A cannon-sized gun affixed to the front of the chopper targeted her.

A second gunship flew toward her from the opposite side, and a third from behind, each as big as the first.

Charlee leaned closer to the unicorn's ear. "Get us out of—"

The guns erupted. Screaming rounds streaked toward her. Charlee ducked. She had been too slow; now, in a blaze of hot lead, she would die. She held her breath, but death never came. Not a single round struck her. Charlee peered up to see a cocoon of glowing yellow energy around her and the unicorn.

Once again, the Changeling's magic had saved them.

"Holy crap, thank you." Her tense muscles relaxed, but her head pounded. "Now get us out of here."

The Changeling had different plans. The winged-unicorn's body tightened beneath her and started to vibrate, gently at first but quickly with greater force. Her own teeth rattled. She grabbed the creature around the neck to keep from falling. "What are you doing?"

A pulsating flash of light flared from the unicorn's body, spread across the sky like the shock wave from an explosion, and smashed into the three heavily armored aircraft, throwing them around like they were toys. Sparks flew from the choppers. Their spinning rotors slowed. Damaged, they broke off the attack and dove toward land.

"That was amazing." She watched the helicopters limp toward a landing. *The Changeling's bought me some time. Must concentrate and close those portals.*

Charlee closed her eyes and extended her hands toward the closest gateway. The swirling blue cavern still raged out of control. About a dozen others across the landscape of this foreign world did the same. Their crushing size cast long shadows over the golden hills and the troops that marched toward the pedestal city.

"Come on, close." She squeezed the portal with her mind, like trying to deflate a beach ball. The portal before her didn't change.

She tried again. With fingers pressed against her temples as if to unlock some dormant portion of her mind, she concentrated on the gateway. A grunt leaked from her lips. Her head throbbed and her cheeks quivered. She maxed out her strength and slumped against the unicorn's back. All the portals remained open.

"I can't do it." She gasped for a breath.

"Yes, you can." Her mom's voice tugged at her thoughts. *"Remember your unique gift. Now is the time to use it."*

Charlee lifted herself and twisted in every direction, expecting to see her mom floating nearby, but she and the unicorn faced the portal alone. "Mom, where are you?"

"With your father, watching you from afar," her mom answered.

"I can't do it." Charlee's voice cracked. "I'm not strong enough. It's too big. There are too many portals."

"Charleya Smelton, you are a Guardian, like your grandfather, and you are a conjurer as powerful…no more powerful…than your grandmother. Quiet your mind and use your gift that separates you from all conjurers."

"Mom—"

"Believe in yourself," her mom interrupted.

Charlee inhaled slowly and exhaled. Her mom was right. It was time again to use her power to draw energy from other living beings, just like she did at the White House, even if it placed the soldiers in danger. Hell, they were already in danger. But it still wasn't right. How could she leech from the very people she wanted to protect? She'd have to reconcile that with herself later. There was no time, and she was out of choices. She'd just have to know when to stop herself and not bleed them dry of their life force.

Steadying herself on the unicorn's back, she held out her arms. Eyelids shut, her thoughts stretched out, like a network of invisible power lines, to the soldiers below. Unseen magical suction cups attached to every soldier. Charlee blew out a long breath then fed on their energy.

Her eyelids cracked and her eyes bulged. An electrical charge zapped through her body. She convulsed, her head jerking back and forth. Her forehead boiled as if a fever consumed her. Rivers of sweat covered her face. Smoke rose from her limbs, like she could spontaneously combust at any moment.

Charlee gritted her teeth. *It hurts. Too much energy. Must stop, but I can't. Have. To. Be. Strong.*

"Don't fight the energy, channel it." Her mom's voice echoed in her ears.

Body trembling, Charlee nodded. She extended her arms toward the closest portal, magically grasping onto its edges.

"Close!" Her hands slowly came together, crushing the portal. A warm salty liquid slipped between her lips—the taste of her own blood dripping from her nose. More blood oozed from her ears, tickling the sides of her face. Veins protruded through her skin, heart pounded against her chest, like a jackhammer slamming into concrete.

She screamed, then all went dark.

§ § §

Trumpets heralded the future queen.

Charlee stood in the arched entryway to the courtyard of Castle Latara. The citizens of the kingdom crowded together across the grounds to welcome the Princess and honor her for her service as Guardian. One day, she would assume the crown from her mom, the Queen and leader of the High Council.

Hand tensed on the handle of the sword at her side, Charlee began the long stroll, something akin to a red carpet walk during the Oscars, to the castle's footsteps where the Queen and High Council waited. The emerald skies sparkled, and the orange sun hung high overhead. Applause echoed through the courtyard as she waved to the people.

Is this really the life she wanted? What about her life back home on Earth? What about the life she could have had? Charlee pushed those thoughts away. She had a duty to fulfill as the first-born daughter. She would not let her mom or her people down.

She stopped at the stone steps leading to the castle's entrance. Her mom smiled widely, but her eyes reddened, and a tear slid down her cheek.

"Mom?" Charlee started to ask.

Her mom didn't acknowledge her; in fact, her eyes stared beyond Charlee, like...like she wasn't even there.

"Mom?"

"There you are, my little one. I'm so proud of you." Her mom walked down the steps toward another.

Charlee swung around. Her sister, Megan, strolled up to the steps. Older now, maybe thirteen, she wore a sword at her side, like Charlee. Long wavy blonde hair flowed behind her along with a white cape, wrapped around her neck with a golden tassel. Silver body armor covered her chest and thighs. Crimson knee-high boots adorned her feet. She walked with an air of confidence, her head raised high.

How did Megan get so old? What was happening? Charlee marveled at her sister even as a wave of panic washed over her.

"Our Guardian, my daughter, has returned," her mom declared. "All hail the future Queen."

"I'm here, Mom, can't you see me?" Charlee stood next to her sister.

Megan embraced their mother and whispered in her ear. "If only my sister could be here. She was the true Guardian before...the change."

Charlee's mom sighed. Another tear formed. "Your sister was once a great Guardian, like her grandfather, until the medallion consumed her. She is no longer your sister, and I have lost a daughter. My only hope is that one day she will overcome the darkness that rules her now and come back to me."

"What?" Charlee retreated from them both. "It can't be. I was just fighting Theodora. I was just fighting to save everyone. What happened?"

Her mom broke from the embrace with Megan. "But this is not a day for sadness. Today we rejoice at your safe return."

"Mom, please!" Charlee begged. "Mom! Mom!"

§ § §

"I'm here, Charlee."

Her mom's words burst through the coldness of her unconscious. Healing fingers stroked her hair. Charlee blinked away the haze. She lay on her mom's lap. Her dad stood over them both, bow in one hand, an arrow in the other. Overhead, the red sky blazed as if fireworks exploded just beyond her view. The sound of gunfire popped rhythmically. Cannons boomed and the ground shook.

Theodora had launched her attack.

Charlee tried to rise, but her mom held her down. "Wait a second. You need time to heal. You did it, Charlee. You closed the portals, but it took a toll on your body. I feared all that power coursing through your body had…" Her mom's voice trailed off.

"Whatever you did had another effect," young Theodora added. "You drained hundreds, maybe thousands of those soldiers of their strength. Many of them fell. Some still haven't gotten back up."

"I didn't mean to hurt them." Charlee slumped back into her mom's lap.

"You had no choice, Charlee." Her father knelt on one knee and kissed her on the forehead. "You just might have given us a fighting chance."

"Where are the others?" Charlee's head felt unbearably heavy.

"We're here." Sandra stepped up to her. She supported her dad, Mr. Flores, who leaned against his daughter.

"Kraannaannn is continuing to draw their fire. He's doing everything he can to protect the city." Her dad pointed toward the city atop pedestals. "The Changeling is helping. Assara rides with him."

"Charlee, you were saying something while you were unconscious." Her mom pushed away a strand of sweaty hair from Charlee's face. "You were probably just delirious, but you seemed to think I couldn't see you, that you were lost."

Charlee shook her head. "It was nothing, Mom. Like you said, I was probably delirious or something." *No reason to tell my mom the truth. No reason to tell anybody the truth that someday I will become evil, just like this version of Theodora. Maybe it won't happen. Maybe it was just a dream. Maybe.*

Placing her hands beneath her, Charlee stood with great effort. Her muscles screamed and bones creaked. Her stomach rumbled, and she fought off queasiness. "We have to help Kraannaannn and the Changeling."

"What do you suggest?" Young Theodora pulled her hair back in a ponytail.

"I don't know yet," she admitted.

Young Theodora lifted off the ground, her hands ablaze in green energy, her face rigid. "I will go and face that dark creature, and I will have my revenge."

Charlee shook her head. "No—"

"Wait, I have an idea," Sandra chimed in. "What if there was a way into the city? What if we could let these beings know we're here to help them and that we need to ban together. Maybe with their magic and yours, you can break the spell over those soldiers."

191

"How do we get past Theodora?" Charlee flexed her muscles. Most of her power had drained in closing the portals, but a bit of super strength remained. One good punch and she could stop the cloned Theodora.

"You and the dragon will keep them busy." Mr. Flores' eyes brightened. He spoke with authority as if issuing orders to his officers. "Use your powers to drain their strength again. Slow them down. With your mom's magic, we'll take a route under that blood sea. I bet there's a hidden doorway past whatever defenses that city has that Theodora hasn't even considered. Once we're inside, we'll find a way to communicate."

Charlee stood and shook her head. "I can't ask you to do that."

Mr. Flores placed his hands on Sandra's and Charlee's shoulders. "You didn't ask. But this is as much our fight as yours. I'm tired of this witch, and I just want to go home. Let's end this. Now!"

Charlee gazed up at the young Theodora, hovering just overhead. "I know you want revenge, but if we go with Sandra's plan, I need you to protect them."

Young Theodora clenched and unclenched her hands, then floated down next to Mr. Flores. She bowed to him. "I will join you, if you will allow it."

Mr. Flores sighed but nodded. "I suppose I have to trust you. Besides, we could use your magic."

She smiled back at him. "I will use my abilities to keep you all safe." She then glared at Charlee. "But I will have my vengeance on that beast before this ends."

"We all will." Charlee's mom placed a hand on young Theodora's shoulder. "I will join you as well. I think our magic combined will be needed."

"This sounds like a good plan, but I'm sticking by Charlee's side." Her dad leaned against Charlee, perhaps as much to keep himself from falling as to show support for his daughter. "Now get that dragon back. He's my ride."

Charlee bit her lip. She had to admit, Sandra's plan was a good one. Risky, but good. She ran her fingers through her dirty, oily hair. She gazed at her friend. Sandra stared back. Neither said a word. They didn't have to.

Stepping away from the others, she clasped her hands together. "Okay, we do this."

CHAPTER 29

A Test of Wills

CHARLEE FLEW ATOP the winged unicorn, gripping the creature's mane. Her skin burned at the touch of the person riding behind her, hands around Charlee's waist. Assara, Sandra's clone, asked to join in the battle to stop her mother. Charlee reluctantly agreed. The clone had saved Sandra, but did that one act make up for the deaths she caused? Assara was a cunning warrior. If she had truly turned against her mother, she could help. If they survived, Charlee would have to come to grips with the clone or kill her. For now, Assara clung to her as they both rode atop the Changeling.

Just off to the side, her dad rode atop Kraannaannn, two injured souls ready to fight till the end. Kraannaannn's heavily armored body and his magic had protected the young Dragon Lord from the worst of the blazing hot lead that had rained down on him from combat choppers and streaking jets, not to mention the endless rounds fired by the marching soldiers. Still, shrapnel riddled his arms and legs. Spots of blood marked his underbelly.

Her dad, though healed by his wife's magic, still belonged in a hospital bed, not a battlefield. His face swelled like a prizefighter who had taken a beating. He had one good eye; the other—blackened and half closed—had just started to open. Cuts and bruises marked his face, arms, and hands.

All of them charged toward Theodora to serve as decoys in Sandra's plan. Meanwhile, somewhere underneath the crimson waters of that inland lake, her mom, young Theodora, Sandra, and Mr. Flores, cocooned in a bubble of magic, swam toward the pedestal city.

Charlee shook her head. She shouldn't have allowed any of them to risk their lives. None of them should even be here. She never should have let it get this far. Theodora, the dark version created by the medallion, should already be dead. *They're risking their lives because of me…because I wasn't strong enough to stop her on my own.*

The sky exploded around her, nearly throwing her from the unicorn's back. A hail of gunfire whizzed by, some bouncing off the Changeling's force field.

Theodora's war had once again found her.

Kraannaannn circled her, spitting a ring of smoke as a fiery barrier between her and the choppers thundering toward her in all directions. Surrounded by a wall of flames, Charlee closed her eyes. One last time, she swore to herself, she reached out to the soldiers below to soak up some of their life force. She braced herself for the agonizing pain of absorbing so much energy at once. Sparks shot from her hands and climbed her arms. Her head tingled and limbs shook. Searing heat, like someone had injected hot magma into her veins, spread through her body. Charlee tore at her clothes.

She hissed through gritted teeth. *You can take it. You must take it for those soldiers who are unknowingly sharing their life force, for the creatures of this world, and for everyone the witch would try to hurt. Don't fight it. Use the power.* Charlee tilted her head back and shrieked violently. Her superhuman scream ripped across the sky, shattering the cockpit glass of the attacking choppers and jets.

Gasping for air, body aglow, she wrapped her arms around herself to stop her shaking limbs. *You must control it.* She breathed deeply. The fire inside cooled. Her racing heart slowed and her mind quieted.

Assara released her hold on Charlee. "Guardian, are you—"

"I'm fine." Charlee said through gritted teeth.

Kraannaannn's protective dragon fire vanished, the black smoke drifting away. Charlee surveyed the battlefield. Thousands of soldiers below had fallen, their bodies weakened by her magic. In the distance, two pilots parachuted to safety. Two separate columns of smoke rose from the wreckage of their aircrafts. Her ear-piercing scream must have damaged their navigational systems, causing the jets to crash.

"Charlee, look." Her dad's voice came from just over her shoulder. He pointed toward the city.

Theodora levitated in the sky before the city. A handful of winged beings, human-like but shorter with waifish bodies, blocked her path. In the time it took Charlee to focus her attention on them, Theodora raised the medallion over her head and fired on the magical creatures. A red beam cut them in half. Their lifeless bodies fell in pieces hundreds of feet to the rolling terrain below.

"No!" Charlee shouted.

The witch scowled at Charlee then struck the city. A blazing red cannonball exploded from the medallion, ripping a hole through the city's glowing force field, as if cutting through paper. The ball of energy slammed into a towering structure, one rivaling the largest skyscrapers on Earth. Upon contact, Theodora's magic tore a gaping hole in the structure. The building rocked back and forth. The pedestal upon which the building stood wobbled. Screams echoed throughout the city.

"No, Mom!" If her mom, Sandra, Mr. Flores, and young Theodora had gotten into the city…no, she couldn't think like that. With their combined magic, her mom and young Theodora could keep them all safe. For now, she had to focus on the fight she faced.

"Let's go!" she ordered the Changeling. With a thrust of his wings, the unicorn zoomed toward the chaos. Her dad and Kraannaannn charged after her.

A second discharge from the medallion assaulted the same building followed by a third blazing round. The structure couldn't withstand the bombardment. One of the towers cracked at its base and slid from the pedestal.

The falling skyscraper slammed into another tower, knocking it from its pedestal. Both buildings plunged into the crimson waters beneath the city in a bellowing dance of death and destruction. They landed with an earth-shattering explosion, fueling a blood red tsunami. Gigantic waves pounded the shoreline and careened into the soldiers whose screams pierced Charlee's ears.

She froze on the unicorn's back. "Mom...Sandra...please don't be hurt!"

"Charlee, we have to move," her dad called. "I'll get your mother and Sandra out of the city and get as many soldiers as possible from the water. Theodora is up to you. Charlee, are you with me? You must stop her."

She nodded. "Hurry, Dad."

"I'll get them," he pledged.

"Kraannaannn, protect my dad," Charlee implored the dragon.

"Trust us, Guardian." The dragon lifted a wing and dove toward the city. Her dad offered a wink before they slid away.

Her eyes followed them as they skimmed the water, dodging a mountain of rubble from the fallen skyscrapers. The dragon scooped up soldiers from the water with his hind claws and deposited them on the shore, then swung back toward the collapsed buildings. Together, her dad and Kraannaannn disappeared inside the shell of one of the fallen towers.

"Guardian, we must give them time," Assara shouted from behind.

"Bike," she uttered to the Changeling, using her affectionate name for her protector even as it held the shape of a winged unicorn. "Let's get Theodora."

The unicorn dove at the sorceress, who continued to assail the city with the medallion's magical cannon fire. Charlee, still glowing with energy, formed a thunderbolt and hurled it at Theodora. "Suck on this, lady."

The sorceress didn't bother to turn. She placed the medallion behind her head, like a shield, and the light-swallowing circle absorbed the thunderbolt.

"Is that your best, Guardian?" Theodora spun toward her, and the medallion spit out its own thunderbolt at Charlee. The sorceress' counterattack cleaved through the air, like a dagger bathed in fire.

Charlee swatted away the thunderbolt with a wave of her hand. "Put us between Theodora and the city," she commanded the Changeling.

"Wait!" Assara leaned in closer to Charlee. "Get me as close as you can to Mother."

Charlee peered over her shoulder. "What? Why?"

"Just do it." Assara smiled, not like her twisted grins before. There was kindness and determination in her eyes. "This is how I make amends for the pain I caused. I'll distract her long enough for you to end her."

"No, Assara!"

"Just do as I say!"

Charlee lowered her head. "Bike, you heard her. Get us close." The Changeling hesitated for just a heartbeat, then swung at Theodora.

Assara lifted herself into a standing position on the unicorn's back. "When, I give the word, fly away and attack when the time is right."

Charlee nodded. Assara was going to sacrifice herself. Charlee's grip on the unicorn's mane tightened. If this was the plan, she had to make it work. She couldn't let Assara's sacrifice go in vain.

Theodora fired on them. A red beam sliced through the sky. The Changeling outmaneuvered the sorceress's attack, swerving to the left, then to the right. The air around them sizzled and burned from Theodora's magic.

They were close now, a stone's throw away. Theodora's eyes blazed with rage. From this distance, she'd easily cut them in half. The witch raised the medallion one more time.

"Now!" Assara leaped off the unicorn, and like an arrow, launched herself at Theodora. The Changeling raised his wings, skidding across the sky until managing to turn away from the sorceress.

Charlee peered back. Assara slammed into Theodora in midair. The witch howled in protest. The two toppled over and over. Assara fought wildly, wrapping her legs around Theodora's waist, then pounding her fists into Theodora's chest.

Charlee patted the unicorn. "Now's our chance. Let's get the medallion away from Theodora."

The unicorn thrusts his wings back. They streaked through the sky, charging Theodora, who was still locked in combat with her daughter. Charlee reached her hand out to grasp the medallion. "Just a little farther."

They weren't fast enough.

A red beam shot from Theodora's eye, slicing through Assara's shoulder. The clone's right arm tore away from her body. She cried out and lost her grip, plunging toward the lake below.

"We have to save her." Charlee pulled on the unicorn's mane, steering the magical beast toward Assara. Another beam, fired just beneath the unicorn, nearly struck the magical beast. The Changeling came to a jarring stop. Charlee was nearly thrown off but tightened her legs against the unicorn's body to keep her in place.

Far below, Assara's body struck the lake and disappeared.

The witch tilted her head. "How many more will have to die because you will not bow to me."

Charlee's body shook. Every muscle screamed with hate. "None!" She leaned into the unicorn. "We have to save what's left of the city." The unicorn heeded her command, soaring around the witch until they hovered in front of her half a football field away.

Flames and choking black smoke rose from the wrecked city behind her. Charlee gazed over her shoulder. The angelic beings of this world flew around frantically, scouring their damaged and fallen buildings, probably searching for their injured…and their dead. An army of them gathered behind her, like a swarm of bees protecting their hive. They joined their voices in a hauntingly high-pitched chant Charlee couldn't understand.

Their song started softly, but quickly became a deafening mantra. Charlee covered her ears, but the shrill tone bore into her brain. The unicorn shook his head in obvious pain and dropped from the sky, spreading his wings just before they struck ground, but not in time to prevent a rough landing.

Charlee fell from the Changeling and rolled in the golden grass, hands still cuffed around her ears. She glanced up at Theodora, who seemed unfazed by their ear-piercing chant.

Her focus shifted to the soldiers. The magical hymn pulsated through their endless ranks across the rolling hills, like a massive shock wave. They squirmed, dropping their weapons and crying out for mercy. The magical beings' penetrating chant cracked the metal in tanks, bent cannons, and knocked aircraft from the sky.

Finally, the beings silenced their ear-splitting voices. Charlee lifted her hands away from her ears. Fresh blood covered her fingertips. She shook her throbbing head to clear the excruciating ringing stabbing at her brain. *What the heck was that? Are those creatures trying to kill everyone?*

All but deaf, her balance shaky, Charlee climbed to her feet. All around her, the soldiers threw off their helmets. They waved their heads side by side, crawling and lumbering around, like lost children.

One soldier, his own blood dripping from his ears, crawled to Charlee on his hands and knees. He had hazel eyes, red hair, and couldn't be that much older than her—maybe nineteen or twenty tops. He blinked and gazed around as if seeing this strange, crimson-skied world for the first time.

He tried to speak, but either he couldn't form actual words or Charlee couldn't hear them. She reached a hand to him, and he extended his own hand. Their fingers interlocked, and the soldier smiled.

He spoke again, and this time his words—though muffled—broke through the harsh ringing. "Are you okay, Guardian?" the soldier asked.

Charlee grabbed the soldier, embracing him like a lost family member. Tears flowed down her cheeks. Was it possible? Was he free of Theodora's spell? Was there finally reason to have hope?

"I'm all right." She pushed away from the soldier. "What about you?"

The soldier rubbed his head. "I feel like someone took a sledgehammer to my head. Some woman put ideas in my head. She did it to all of us. Told us of an evil Guardian. Made us want to kill you. I couldn't stop myself. I'm sorry, but I can't believe any of this is real. It's all so crazy. I mean, look where we are. But I remember everything. I can't shake it."

"I'm sorry," Charlee answered. Her voice still sounded far away.

"What is this place?" the soldier asked.

"Somewhere far from home." She grabbed the soldier and with her super strength still intact, lifted him to his feet.

"Is it over?" he asked.

She shook her head. "Not yet."

"It's time for you to die, Guardian." The declaration of death came from behind Charlee. She whipped around. Tribon charged at her, his broadsword bathed in red energy held over his head ready to slice her in half.

With only seconds to react, Charlee forged a thunderbolt and clumsily flung it at Theodora's giant lackey. The bolt whizzed by Tribon who leaped into the air, like a pouncing lion, and brought his sword crashing down on her.

Something shoved Charlee out of the way—she flew back, landing hard on her side, rolled several times, and launched to her feet.

The unicorn, her Changeling protector, stood in her place, Tribon's radiating blade—infected with Theodora's dark arts—buried deep in the beast's thick, muscular neck.

Tribon cursed. "I've had enough of this creature." He ripped out his blade and plunged it into the unicorn's side. Tribon's eyes swelled with rage, and he raised the sword once more to slice through the unicorn.

"No!" Charlee screamed. She ran forward, a new thunderbolt in her hand. Before she reached Tribon, gunfire erupted. Rounds pounded the giant man, shredding his chest. Tribon dropped his sword and fell to his knees. He laughed as black liquid spilled from the holes that covered his body. With one last breath, he fell face-forward into the golden grass, now covered with his own oozing fluids.

Charlee glanced over her shoulder. The soldier with hazel eyes and red hair stood with a rifle in hand. White smoke rose from the barrel. Two other soldiers stood behind him, also with smoldering guns in hand.

"Why?" Charlee asked.

The soldier smiled and lowered his weapon. "I have a feeling you're the reason I can hear my own thoughts, not some crazy witch telling me what to think, and that crusty giant dude probably had something to do with why we're in this freaking strange place and why my brain feels so scattered."

"Thank you." Charlee nodded, turned from the soldier, and ran to the unicorn.

The great beast had fallen onto its side. Glowing yellow ooze seeped from a gaping neck wound and from its side. The unicorn's head lay in the golden grass. Shallow breaths slipped from his snout. His big black eyes started to close.

She wrapped her arms around her Changeling protector. She then whispered into his ear—a private moment between the Guardian and her protector. When finished, she patted the unicorn's snout and buried her head in his mane. Tears came. "You're going to be okay. Please, stay with me. You can't die. You're a Changeling, the most powerful magical being in all of Janasara. You hear me. I won't let you go."

The unicorn painfully lifted his head, nudging her in the shoulder as if pushing her away.

"No, I'm staying with you," she cried. "I love you."

More glowing ooze fell from the unicorn's snout. He lowered his head back into the grass. Charlee's hot tears dripped onto the beast's hide. A spasm shook the Changeling's unicorn body.

Charlee shook her head. "No, I said stay—"

The Changeling's unicorn body morphed into a bike, a white dove, and back into a unicorn. Then, his body lost all shape as he returned to his true amorphous form—a shapeless glowing blob. His amoeba form oozed along the ground, his glow dimming.

Charlee reached for him, but her hand passed through his transparent form. "Bike...please."

Her Changeling protector extended a faint tentacle toward her, but before they made contact, the magical being who had saved her so many times simply vanished out of existence, like he had never existed at all.

Charlee screamed and crumbled into the grass.

"You don't know how much it moves me to witness such a heart-warming moment of death." Theodora's voice stung, like salt on an open wound. Charlee punched the ground then lifted herself to face the sorceress who landed gently in the grass just a few feet away.

"You'll pay for what you've done today." Sparks circled Charlee's fists. Her veins still bulged with the life force of thousands of soldiers coursing through her blood.

"Oh, I think not child, for you've forgotten one very important object that I possess." Theodora reached into her white dress and removed a pulsating glob of dead flesh—Tribon's dead heart. Black and crusty, his heart still beat in her hands, which meant...

Charlee swiveled around. Tribon stood over her, his sword already hefted in the air to crush her skull. His eyes, veiny and red, bulged. "Die, Guardian." His iron arms cleaved the sword down on her.

Something else swished through the air, whizzing by Charlee's ear. Then another, and a third. Three arrows smacked into Tribon's chest. A fourth arrow lodged in the giant man's throat.

"Not today, traitor." Her dad fired a fifth arrow.

Tribon, blackened blood spilling from his mouth, cut the arrow in half with his blade, then turned his attention back to Charlee. The arrows had slowed him down but not stopped him. "Die, girl."

"I've had enough of you." Charlee formed a thunderbolt and hurled it at Theodora. Her magic found its target, impaling Tribon's heart in Theodora's hands.

The witch shrieked, dropping Tribon's heart.

When the blackened glob touched the earth, Charlee leaped into the air and brought her foot down upon the pulsating flesh, squashing it into slimy goo.

"What have you done?" Theodora screamed.

Charlee turned toward the sorceress. "Put the damn zombie out of his misery."

Tribon dropped his sword. He gasped and clutched his chest. The giant man dropped to his knees as his eyes found Theodora. He reached for her. "My…Empress…save…me…"

He rolled onto his back, hands extended to the sky as if asking forgiveness for his treachery against those he was supposed to fight for and those he was supposed to protect. He gasped once more.

"My Empress," the giant man bellowed. Flesh began to fall from his body, turning to ash and floating away. With one final scream, Tribon's cheeks melted, his eyes slid back into his head, and his forehead cracked open. In another heartbeat, nothing remained but a withered skeleton and a pair of iron arms and hands.

Charlee allowed herself a momentary smile. *One down, one to go!*

Some distance away, Kraannaannn roared. Charlee shifted her attention from the grizzly corpse toward the ravaged city. The dragon stood atop one of the fallen towers, which rose from the lake, like a twisted man-made island forged from shattered stone and warped steel. Her dad balanced on the dragon's back, bow in hand, as if he had just launched an arrow.

"Dad," Charlee mouthed. He lowered the bow and nodded.

Her mom, Sandra, Mr. Flores, and the true Theodora walked into view. More of the winged beings joined them, hovering just above Kraannaannn.

Charlee sighed. Her family and everyone she cared about had survived Theodora's vicious assault on the city. They were all okay, for the moment, but what would the sorceress do next?

Theodora still possessed the medallion.

If the sorceress had been shaken by Tribon's death, the moment didn't last. Her evil laughter chilled the air. "Do you think you've won, Guardian?" Theodora now gripped the medallion in both hands.

CHAPTER 30

Drink It In

CHARLEE AND THEODORA circled each other. The witch walked hunched over, her shoulders rounded. Deep lines spread across her cheeks, like cracks in her skin. Strands of gray hair hung loosely around her face. She nestled the medallion close to her chest. Bony fingers caressed the round object.

Charlee focused on the medallion. She had to rip it from Theodora and get it to the fire tree to end this, but her heart beat fast so close to the medallion. A cold sweat spread across her forehead. Her muscles ached...as if her body needed the medallion and being so close was a reminder. She licked dry lips and rubbed her fingers together. If she took it from Theodora, could she destroy it and overcome her own desire for it?

Theodora noticed. "I see, child, how much you want what I possess. You've touched the power, and you like it."

Charlee pretended the witch's words meant nothing. "You're alone now, Theodora." Charlee kicked one of Tribon's iron arms. "This is where it ends. This is where you pay for everyone you've hurt and killed."

Theodora raised the medallion with both hands. Her lips parted in a sneer, her eyes glowing red. "You are right. This is where it ends for you, but first I think I will wipe these weak-minded humans from existence."

The sorceress aimed the face of the medallion at the closest soldiers, many of whom still hunched over on their hands and knees in a dazed state. Those who could hold their weapons—and understood the danger—opened fire on Theodora, but their rounds struck an invisible barrier and fell uselessly to the ground.

Laughing, Theodora returned fire. A red beam exploded from the medallion and swept across a line of soldiers. They vanished in a glare of crimson light before they had a chance to cry out—before they could even beg for mercy. Of course, the sorceress wouldn't have cared if they did plead for their lives. She wanted revenge.

"No more," Charlee shouted through clenched teeth. Before Theodora could sweep her killing ray over any more soldiers, Charlee leaped with super strength over the sorceress' head and landed in front of the soldiers just in time to shield them with her body.

The medallion's beam slammed into her chest. Charlee turned her head away, wincing from the searing energy that poured into her body. Theodora was right. This was the end. The beam would erase her, just like it had the soldiers.

In the distance, her mother screamed, "No, Charlee!"

Kraannaannn roared and spit fire at the sorceress.

Young Theodora fired her own emerald ray at the witch.

"Get out of there!" her dad shouted.

Charlee's body vibrated with bone crushing violence, like an earthquake with an epicenter deep inside her chest. Blinding light, brighter than the sun, engulfed her. She shielded her face with her arms and squeezed her eyelids tight, but the brilliance still scorched her face and burned the whites of her eyes.

She screamed. The scarlet beam drilled into her chest, ripping away skin and flesh. A flood of memories suddenly danced across her mind of the last time Theodora attacked her with the medallion. The beam had torn into her, sucking out her soul, leaving her powerless and empty…so empty. Almost nothing had remained of her then but a shell. Somehow, she had survived and found a way to remain alive. Somehow, her powers had returned.

Charlee turned her head toward the beam. She hadn't vanished…hadn't melted…hadn't fallen like before. She opened her eyes and gazed beyond the brilliant light toward Theodora. The sorceress no longer laughed. Her face contorted into an expression of bewilderment. She wrestled against the medallion as if trying to break off the attack, but she couldn't budge the object nor stop the beam.

"What's happening?" Theodora bellowed.

The beam still pummeled Charlee, but it no longer seemed to want to harm her—or steal her power. This time the medallion fed her power. Energy, the kind she had never felt before even from the Changeling, absorbed deep within her body, bonding with her bones, her heart, her lungs, and every single tissue within her skin. She drank it all in, like a thirsty dog lapping up water from its bowl.

Nightmarish images filled her mind.

A tree made of fire blazed and crackled. Men in cloaks danced around it, chanting in an ancient language. It was the Brotherhood! Each wielded a knife with a golden handle. One by one, they plunged the blades into their hearts then jumped into the flames, joining their spirits with the tree. As their bodies vanished in the blaze, a round object formed in the heart of the fire.

The medallion emerged from the inferno, spinning like a quarter flicked by a finger. When it stopped, two etchings had formed. One side of the medallion bore the mark of the burning tree. The opposite side possessed a face…her face.

Charlee lowered her arms, stuck out her chest, and stepped into the beam. A blood-red crystalline glow surrounded her as if she were encased in a gemstone.

A crimson hue covered her pale skin. She took another step and a third, inching closer to Theodora and the medallion. One thought eclipsed all others. *The medallion belongs to me. I will be the vessel who spreads the word of the Brotherhood.*

"Stay away from me." Panic etched into Theodora's gaunt face. She tugged at the medallion, straining to move it, but the medallion hovered in place, held by some unseen force. "It belongs to me. I am Empress...I am a Goddess!"

"You are a mistake." Charlee's voice deepened, like she had suddenly aged years. She lumbered forward, leaning toward the beam, energy coursing through every molecule of her body. Dark magic had embraced her.

Somewhere deep within her mind, the girl Charlee had always been struggled against the evil voice flooding her very being. What was she doing? What was she allowing herself to become? *What you were always meant to be*, a scratchy voice not her own told her. *You were meant to wield the medallion in our name. Accept that fate and welcome our power.*

Yes, Charlee responded.

"No, girl, you will not take what is mine," Theodora raged. Another step and Charlee stood before the medallion. The beam stopped, but the red glow emanated from her chest.

Theodora still held the medallion. She could only manage short shallow breaths from her struggle to maintain a hold on the object. "You. Will. Not. Take. It." The sorceress released one hand from the medallion and folded her fingers into a fist. Though Theodora gripped nothing but air, the motion magically crushed Charlee's throat.

Charlee gasped and coughed, grabbing at her neck. She dropped to one knee, lowering her head, raising her hands as if to beg for mercy.

"Does it hurt, girl?" Theodora squeezed her fist tighter.

An unearthly laugh greeted the sorceress. "Not really, witch." Charlee raised her head and wiped a bit of black gook from the side of her mouth. "The power of the medallion flows through me now. Do you still think you can defeat me?"

She stood and grabbed Theodora by the neck with both hands. It would be so easy to choke the life out of her. The sorceress deserved it for all she had done... for everyone she had killed. Charlee's fingers tensed. Her face burned red hot, like her cheeks would melt to the bone. *I want to kill her so much. I want her to understand the pain she's caused. But, no, the Brotherhood will deal with her.*

Charlee released her grip on Theodora's throat and, harnessing the medallion's power now embedded in her limbs, drove a punch into her stomach. As the sorceress hunched over, spitting up blood, Charlee slammed a fist into her face. A jawbone cracked and teeth shattered against Charlee's knuckles. Mucous and bile spilled from Theodora's nose. She fell, her body sprawled along the ground.

A gurgled moan rose from the sorceress.

"The medallion is mine." Charlee clutched it with both hands, pulling it from the air and tucking it against her chest. This time, the medallion bent to her will. She embraced it, just like she had the sword Cryton had once gifted to her. *That old fool. He deserved to die for wanting to destroy the medallion.* Wait, what was that thought? Cryton deserved to die? That wasn't her thought, was it? *Everyone who would challenge the Brotherhood deserves to die, even my mom, dad, sister…everyone.*

What was she saying? Her parents deserved to die? No, that's not right. What were these thoughts crashing like waves through her head? Her heart pounded heavy in her chest with hate. So much hate! *This is the way. Hate all who defy us. Let the hate make you strong. Let it guide you to act swiftly to crush your enemies.*

"Yes, it's so clear to me now." Charlee reached down to a bloodied Theodora.

"Guardian, you are not the medallion. You are not the Brotherhood. You can choose right now your own path just as I would not join them." Young Theodora approached Charlee from behind and placed a hand on her shoulder. "Do not give in to the darkness. I have seen into your soul, and you are a being of light, just like your grandfather and grandmother, just like your mother. Fight this, Guardian, and realize your destiny to be the greatest Guardian that ever lived."

Charlee struggled to breathe through gritted teeth. She shrugged young Theodora's hand away. "But I can do so much good with this power. I can make worlds bend to my will and force peace on them."

"Charleya," her mom called from close by, using Charlee's actual name rather than the nickname she preferred. Charlee glanced over her back. Her parents stood close. Sandra and her dad lingered behind them, and Kraannaannn towered over them all.

"Charleya, I see the medallion's sickness all around you. A black aura has infected your being." Her mom walked up to her with slow cautious steps. "What you did was very brave. You saved these soldiers, but in doing so you allowed the medallion to possess you. But you can fight it. You are a Guardian. You carry the blood of your grandfather. You have his strength. You do not need the medallion's power to be strong. Most of all, you're my daughter. I love you. Remember that."

A twisted grin split Charlee's lips. "Sorry, Mother, but I kind of like the way this feels. For the first time in my life, I'm not scared. No one's going to bully me or push me around now. Everyone will bow to me and the Brotherhood. If they don't, they'll fall under the wrath of the Brotherhood."

Her mom drew closer. "Baby, listen to yourself. That's not you. You are talking like this cloned version of Theodora. You fought so hard to stop her. Do not allow yourself to become just like her."

Charlee scowled at the fallen sorceress. "Just like her? She's nothing but a failed experiment, and I'm going to return her to the Brotherhood. Then I will take her place in spreading their good word."

"Guardian, listen to your mother." Young Theodora extended her hand to Charlee again, but Charlee slapped it away.

"Charlee." Her mom got to within an arm's distance and stopped.

"Get away from me, Mom."

"I can't. You're my daughter, and I'm going to do whatever I have to—even sacrifice myself—to save you."

"Save yourself." Without touching her mom, Charlee lifted her into the air, squeezing her chest, making it impossible for her mom to breathe. Like twisting a vise grip closed, she slowly started to crush her mom.

"Stop it, Charlee." Her dad ran toward her. With a wave of her hand, she threw a pulse of invisible energy at him, knocking him off his feet.

"Charlee, please," her mom gasped.

"Pathetic...look how quickly you beg for your life. I can't believe I'm your daughter." Charlee loosened her magical grip and hurled her mom across the sky. Charlee's mom would have slammed into the ground, but Kraannaannn caught her.

"Guardian, stop this." Young Theodora grabbed Charlee's arm. Charlee shoved her backward, knocking her off her feet as easy as if she'd pushed over an empty trash can. "Guardian, we must stick to the plan. Destroy the medallion in the fire tree. You must do it to end this and save yourself. We'll do it together."

"Never." Charlee gripped the medallion to her chest. Hate burned her insides. "You will not destroy what is mine."

A phlegmy laugh rose from beneath her. "You have become just like me, haven't you?" Theodora wiped blood from her mouth and spit out a tooth. "We are sisters now, connected by the medallion. Stand by my side and we shall rule. Not even the Brotherhood can stop us." Theodora started to climb to her feet.

Charlee shoved her down. "Quiet. You will answer to the Brotherhood for your crimes."

Footsteps approached. Sandra ran up, her dad trailing her. "Charlee, remember me...your pal...your *besty*. Please, stay with me. Whatever's happening to you, fight it. You're a hero. You've always been. Now let's go home. Let's go back to M's Diner and have some burgers and play some video games. Come on, Charlee."

"Sandra, get back here!" Mr. Flores ordered.

"Listen to him," Charlee faced her friend. "Don't come near me again. Don't address me again. If you do, I'll kill you. I'll give you this one chance to go home because we were once friends, but if I see you again after this day, you will suffer."

Tears slid down Sandra's cheeks. Her dad grabbed her by the shoulders and pulled her away.

Charlee, her hands wrapped around the medallion, watched as her friend was dragged away back to the protective cover of Kraannaannn's wings. Her mom and dad clung to each other beneath the dragon. Young Theodora lowered her head. The winged beings of this world hovered behind them all. Charlee glared beyond them at the thousands of soldiers. They studied her in silence. Many had their weapons trained on her, this time not because they were under Theodora's control, but because they feared her.

Good, they should fear me, for when I return, I will bring suffering and pain worse than anything cooked up by Theodora.

Charlee grabbed the sorceress by the hair and lifted her. "Time for us to go."

"Where?" Theodora seemed like a frail elderly woman now.

"Back to the place you were born." Charlee no longer needed young Theodora to get her to the fire tree. She no longer needed anyone. The medallion had shown her the way. The medallion would be her new teacher.

One hand on Theodora's neck, one hand on the medallion, Charlee closed her eyes and willed a gateway into existence. Thoughts of the Brotherhood guided her to the fire tree. They welcomed her. The swirling blue portal glowed bright, beckoning her to enter with her prisoner.

Charlee pushed Theodora through, then stepped in herself.

From behind, a voice called out. "Charlee, no!"

Chapter 31

The Birthplace

INSIDE THE PORTAL, surrounded by a swirling blue mist, Charlee held the medallion in front of her with one hand. The other held onto Theodora's dress. The sorceress's head drooped, and she drew shallow wheezing breaths, as if Charlee's punch damaged her lungs. Theodora still managed pained laughter, even as she spit blood.

This portal acted differently than others. A vaulted corridor stretched before her, like sewer tunnels under a city. The swirling mist danced wildly all around her, hiding a clear view of the passageway. Lightning bursts slashed through the maelstrom. Each flash brought ghostly images—faces that haunted her. Cryton appeared beside her, shaking his head as if in disappointment. Her dad and mom held each other. Assara, back in her dark armor, pointed a blade at Charlee. The real Theodora lay encased in ice. The Dragon Lord roared at her.

She shook the visions away. Those images no longer mattered. Now she wielded the medallion and served the Brotherhood.

Now she would be an Empress.

Some unseen force latched onto the medallion and pulled her deeper into the passage. A gusting wind rustled her hair and made her eyes water. The lightning strikes came faster, and the mist thickened into a murky blue wall of glowing energy.

A voice barely audible over the storming portal called to her "Charlee, come back with me."

Charlee swung around. Her one-time friend had somehow entered the portal with her. The sight of Sandra should have warmed her heart, but not this time. Ice ran through her veins. The only emotion was hate. "Go back, Sandra. You shouldn't have come."

"Don't say that." Sandra's words bounced off the portal's walls.

"You'll die," Charlee warned.

"How do you know?"

"Because I'm the one who'll kill you."

"I don't believe that."

"Then you're not as smart as I thought."

Theodora laughed harder. "Kill her now."

"Quiet, Mother." Another voice echoed inside the portal—Assara's.

Charlee eyed the cloned version of Sandra. She wasn't alone. Young Theodora held Assara. They both stood inside the portal, Assara grasping the wound where her arm had once been. She was pale, stood hunched, water dripping from her drenched clothes and hair. Charlee grinned ear to ear. Good thing the clone survived the fall. Now, she'd have the joy of making the clone suffer.

Assara and young Theodora moved closer to Charlee. Blood dripped down a side of Assara's mouth. She swayed on weak legs. "Guardian, you are not evil, not like me or my mother. Look inside yourself. The real you is in there somewhere."

In the deepest regions of Charlee's mind, there was a faint voice, her own, calling to her, but it faded into silence. The only voice that mattered belonged to the Brotherhood. Theirs was the way of peace through blood. With their medallion she'd rise to power, and all would come to bow to the might of the Brotherhood—and Empress Charlee.

She turned away from Sandra, Assara, and young Theodora. Her grin faded. A single tear slid down her cheek, but it quickly dried. Her smile returned. "You will all serve the Brotherhood or die this day."

The portal reached its destination. The passageway collapsed around them, revealing they had arrived in the dead of night at a desert ringed by towering mountains. A scorched, barren landscape marked by cracks and jagged rocky outgrowths hundreds of feet high extended in each direction to the foot of the mountain ranges. An emerald afterglow hung over the land under the radiance of three moons overhead in a triangle formation.

That meant they had returned to Janasara, the world of her bloodline, where the Three Queens of the Night—the three moons—rule over all. Charlee slid her fingers over the medallion. *Fitting that my conquests in the name of the Brotherhood should begin here.* The cloned Theodora knelt at Charlee's feet.

Sandra approached but kept her distance. "Where are we, Charlee?"

"Home," Charlee answered. "My home."

"Your home is back in San Francisco." Sandra inched closer. "You're a student at Myron Applebee Middle School. We eat lunch together every day with our friends. You like comic books and video game, remember?"

"That person is gone." Charlee smirked at Sandra. "Your words no longer have meaning to me."

"I don't believe that." Sandra circled Charlee. "If that's true, kill me now."

"Do it," Theodora urged.

"Enough, Mother." Assara knelt to Theodora. "Your reign is over. Release the Guardian from whatever spell you have her under."

Theodora cackled, then spit more blood. "You think this is my doing? She is under no spell of mine. She has willingly given herself over to the medallion, like all of you will."

Young Theodora stood off to the side. "You're wrong, foul creation, and I've come to ensure the mistakes of my past end on this day. I intend for you and me to reach our end together, as one, the way we started...when there was just me."

Charlee ignored them all. She hugged the medallion to her chest. Its energy flowed through her. The power was delicious, better than when sucking energy from the soldiers. Every fiber of her body tingled. Yes, this was home—where she belonged. "Brotherhood, your servant has returned."

The ground rumbled beneath Charlee's feet, softly at first, but soon with jarring force. Cracks formed in every direction, cutting the landscape into slices of pie. The desert moaned in protest. Charlee tumbled backward, landing on her back, medallion still tucked tight against her chest.

"Is this an earthquake?" Sandra struggled to remain on her feet.

"Foolish girl," evil Theodora mocked. She stood, her arms folded in defiance. "This is nothing your little mind could ever fathom."

The land roared and steam rose from fissures. The sides of mountains toppled, sending boulders tumbling to the desert floor in a thunderous song.

Charlee braced her feet. She twisted toward Theodora. "I didn't give you permission to rise." With a wave of her hand, she threw an invisible blast of energy at Theodora. It struck the sorceress in the back, knocking her to the ground. She landed on her stomach, arms splayed out in front of her.

Theodora slowly lifted herself, coughing and laughing at the same time. "Good. The more you use the power, the more it will control you." The evil Theodora wiped dirt from her face.

"Quiet," Charlee ordered. The ground gave way, collapsing into a dark abyss, not far from where Assara stood. In her weakened state, she crumbled to the ground. Lava gurgled up through the pit, oozing toward her. She slid away just in time to avoid the burning liquid. The crater widened, then the tremors stopped. Silence spread over the land, save for the gurgling of the flowing lava.

"Is it over?" Sandra asked.

"No, it's only begun." Charlee raised the medallion over her head.

An explosion shook the earth, like a dormant volcano suddenly came to life with mountain-crushing force. Fire spewed from the hole, extending toward the sky. The flames seemed to reach higher than the mountain peaks before blossoming into an umbrella of fiery branches that blocked out the night sky, casting the desert in an unnatural orange glow. Burning embers fell all around, like the remnants of a fading firework.

"Behold the Brotherhood," Charlee declared.

Assara stood, hand still clutching the hole where her limb had sliced off. "Can this truly be the birthplace of evil?"

"Yes." Young Theodora joined her. "This is where I allowed the Brotherhood to take everything from me. Now, I intend to take my life back." She raised her voice. "Do you hear me, Serior? I've returned, you snake."

Sandra ran to Charlee's side, her eyes open wide. "This is the actual fire tree you told me about. It's here, Charlee. All you have to do is throw the medallion into the flames, and this can all end. That's what your mentor Cryton wanted you to do. You can do it, Charlee. Get rid of it. Do it now. It's the only way."

Charlee struck her friend across the cheek. "You dare suggest I destroy the very object that I have longed for—the object that will herald a new beginning for the Brotherhood and bring true justice across the dimensional plane."

Wiping blood from her cheek, Sandra backed away. "Charlee, don't give in. Fight the medallion. I know the real you is somewhere still inside you."

Assara joined Sandra. "Guardian, do as your friend says. It's the only way to save yourself, to save everyone."

Young Theodora ignited her hands in an emerald glow. "Guardian, don't make me fight you for the medallion. Do what must be done."

A gnarled hand grabbed Charlee's leg. "They do not understand, child, but I do." The witch reached for Charlee with her other hand. "The medallion has chosen you now. Please, let me serve at your side."

Charlee kicked the sorceress's hands away. "Your time comes to an end, now. You never should have crossed the Brotherhood."

"Theodora," a solemn voice called from the towering inferno.

The sorceress stood on shaky legs. "Please, give me another chance. I beg you. I will bow to the Brotherhood and serve you well."

The real Theodora stepped beside her clone. Her hands still glowed with green energy. "Remember me, Serior? You can take back this dark creature you created, but you'll have to leave the safety of the fire tree if you want to end me."

Serior laughed from within the fire tree. "I see the silly child who defied me and gave up the greatest gift anyone could ever see has returned. Yes, I will deal with you in short order, my child."

He emerged from the fire tree, his body encased in orange flames. He pointed a fiery finger at the fake Theodora. "First, it is time for our Theodora to return home." He spoke in Lengoron, his voice serious, like a judge issuing a sentence. "Do not fear us. Your energy will join with our own, making us stronger. That is how you can best serve us now."

"But I want to live," the sorceress pleaded. She grasped Charlee by the arm. "Don't let them do this to me. I'm your great aunt. We're family."

Charlee wriggled free. "No, we're not."

A flame leaped from the base of the fire tree, crackling and sizzling as it extended like a tentacle from a squid to wrap around the fake Theodora and welcome the sorceress home.

"Please, no!" she cried. "No!"

"Return...return...return," a mix of ghostly voices chanted.

The cloned Theodora turned to run, but the tentacle ensnared her, engulfing her, dragging her into the inferno.

"Guardian, help me," she cried. "Help..." Her voice faded away as the flames returned the witch *home*. A scarlet hue raced up the fire tree. The flames turned blood red, casting the desert in a crimson glow.

The witch was gone—finally.

Charlee grinned. "I am the new Empress."

"Welcome, Guardian, we have been waiting a long time for you to be ready to assume your place as our agent of peace." The same solemn voice that had just spoken to the fake Theodora addressed Charlee. The fiery being—tall and thin—marched toward her.

"You will know me as Serior, your teacher, and I will guide you in the ways of the Brotherhood." The being spoke without a mouth.

The true Theodora stepped in his path. She held up her glowing hands, ready to fight. "You will not take—"

With a wave of a burning hand, Serior magically lifted her and sent her flying across the rocky terrain. Her body smashed into a boulder. The young Theodora slumped into the dirt, motionless and silent.

Charlee bowed to him, the medallion tucked under her arms. "I know, master. You appeared at the White House from a much smaller tree of fire."

Serior chuckled. "That was merely an image, a projection if you will. This before you...this is the true burning monument to those who sacrificed all for a righteous belief. Within the dancing flames are the spirits of the Brotherhood, all encompassed in me. We have watched you your entire life, waiting for the time when you would be ready to join our cause, share our light, and strike down all those who stand against us."

"Master, forgive me, but if you've watched me my entire life, why have you not shown yourself to me until now?" Charlee took a step closer to Serior.

"We needed to prepare you, child." Serior spoke like a father talking to his daughter. "Everything that has transpired in your life—even the creation of our misguided Theodora—was meant to build you into a young woman with unrivaled magic ability and a thirst for the kind of power only the medallion can provide."

"All of this was a test then?"

"We like to consider it...an education...and you have done exceedingly well. You are truly ready to become an Empress in the name of the Brotherhood. You will rule with merciless certainty. We are proud of what you have become, child. We now extend to you the full might of the Brotherhood."

He paused and looked toward Sandra. "We have but one task for you to prove yourself worthy. Kill the human girl."

CHAPTER 32

The Choice – Of Life or Death

ERIOR'S WORDS SPREAD through Charlee's mind like a fog rolling up the bay, shrouding every bit of light from a morning sun. Darkness filled her thoughts. *Cleanse worlds. Kill the non-believers. Consume all their magic. Bring order to the chaos that spans dimensions. Kill the human girl.* Yes, what did some human girl matter to her now that she possessed the medallion. Now that she would be the steward of the Brotherhood's righteousness. Sacrificing one life so that she may achieve her destiny was the only choice.

Charlee gazed at the fire tree. The blazing trunk rose toward the sky, cresting in an umbrella that set the clouds ablaze in a display that cast the desert in an orange glow for miles in every direction. This was the birthplace of the medallion, the sacred vessel from which her power as Empress would flow. How magnificent it was.

She peered at Serior, who crossed his burning arms over his fiery chest. "Are you prepared to do all that is necessary, Empress Charleya?"

Empress Charleya! Coldness swept through her body. Yes, she would be Empress. "Yes, master."

Serior nodded. His head burned brighter. "Good." With a wave of his hand, a dagger slid from the fire tree and floated to her. At first, flames engulfed it, but by the time it reached Charlee's outstretched hand, the blade had turned to gold with a handle encrusted by gems. She grasped it, pulling it close to her chest, next to the medallion. "Now, kill the child, prove yourself, and accept your destiny."

"Yes!" Charlee turned to Sandra. Like she told her one-time friend, she shouldn't have come. Now she had to pay the price.

Sandra didn't budge. She lifted her head, but her eyes widened as her cheeks quivered. "Charlee, you don't have to do this."

Charlee closed the distance, the knife raised over her head. "Oh, you're wrong about that. Just like you were wrong to follow me here."

Assara stepped in front of Sandra. "Guardian, wake up. You're stronger than this. I know. I've seen it."

"Stupid, girl." Serior uttered. A stream of fire smashed into Assara's chest, hurtling her backwards. She landed with a thud on her back and didn't move. Smoke rose from the wound. The stench of burning flesh tickled Charlee's nose.

She grinned. Sandra's clone was nothing more than an annoying gnat hovering around. Serior was right to strike her down. Hopefully, she was dead.

Charlee continued toward Sandra.

The human girl stood there unmoving. Why? The tears sliding down her cheeks showed her fear. "Why don't you run, human?" Charlee spoke the words, but the voice was not hers. Instead, the words were throaty and raspy, like Theodora's voice.

Sandra shook her head. She wiped away the tears. "I'm not going to leave you, Charlee. You need me, just like I need you. You won't kill me. You can't. I know you won't. You're still there inside somewhere, trying to escape."

"You would be wise to try to run, though it wouldn't do you any good." Charlee tightened her grip on the blade. "I would still find you and cut your throat to prove myself to the Brotherhood."

"Can you hear yourself, Charlee?" Sandra retreated a step. "This isn't the Charlee I know. That Charlee stood up to bullies. She'd found the confidence not to take crap from anyone. Remember that person?"

Charlee stopped and laughed. "That person was a fool. That person didn't know how powerful she could be."

"Yes, she did." Sandra stopped back stepping, and instead closed the gap between her and Charlee. Her eyes no longer shed tears. Her cheeks no longer quivered. "But, if that person is gone, I mean really gone, then do what you must do. Kill me. I know it's not your fault. I know they're controlling your mind now."

Charlee lowered the knife. She bowed her head. "I'm sorry, Sandra."

Her friend placed a hand on her shoulder. "I knew—"

Charlee drove the blade into Sandra's stomach and twisted the blade. "I'm sorry, but you're wrong. I'm thinking clearer than ever before."

Sandra gasped. Her body trembled. She stared at the blade, then with large eyes looked back up at Charlee. "I…forgive…you. Still…my…friend." Sandra grasped Charlee's arm with both hands, then slumped backward. Falling to her knees, her eyes rolled back up into her head, and she crumbled to the desert floor. A final breath slid from her throat, and she was silent. Her eyes shuttered. Her blood seeped onto the sand, pooling around her.

Serior clapped his burning hands together. "Empress Charleya, you have proven yourself worthy." His voice lightened as if experiencing joy.

Staring at her dead former friend, Charlee sneered. "Thank you, master."

Serior floated closer to her. "Now, Empress, come to my side and swear your allegiance to the Brotherhood, and we shall begin anew our mission of spreading our good word from world to world."

Bowing her head, Charlee approached him. The medallion, pressed against her chest, began to hum. She lifted the round object to her face. The darkness that engulfed it gave way to a sizzling orange glow. An image formed on the side facing her. It was a face, her face, scratched and warped. She smiled. The medallion truly belonged to her now. The time had come to let everyone know.

"Serior, I have but one request before we begin." Charlee bent on one knee before him.

"What would the Empress request of me?" He floated down to her, his hands outstretched, motioning her to stand.

"May I share the good word with my family." She lifted her head to him but did not stand. "May I bring them here and give them a chance to serve me…to serve the Brotherhood?"

Serior's head tilted to the side. "And if they refuse?"

Charlee stood. "Then they die."

"By all means, summon them to your side." Serior once again rose above her. "Bring them here so they may understand there is no other way but ours."

"Yes, master." Charlee closed her eyes and focused her thoughts on the world where she'd left her parents with Kraannaannn. Her mind fully locked on that world, she created a doorway for them to enter—a doorway that would lead them to the fire tree and the birthplace of true and lasting peace. She beckoned them all to enter. *It is safe. We have won. Come and see.*

She felt, more than saw, her parents and the young Dragon Lord enter the portal. Their presence added tension to her mind's lock on that world, like a limp string pulled tight from both ends. The only one missing was Mr. Flores. What did he matter? His daughter was dead. He'd never accept the way of the Brotherhood, and she'd have to kill him. He'd die soon enough anyway.

With one hand still clutching the medallion, Charlee extended her free hand out as if to grasp an invisible line. She then began to tug on it, drawing her parents and Kraannaannn back to the Janasaran desert…and the fire tree. They emerged from the swirling blue tunnel, stepping onto the rough landscape, and Charlee sealed the doorway behind them.

"Charlee!" Her mom scrambled toward her.

"Stop!" Charlee ordered. She pointed her palm, bathed in a reddish glow, at her mother. "Move closer, and I'll tear you in half."

Her mother slid to a stop. Her eyes drifted from Charlee to Serior to the fire tree. "I don't understand."

Charlee held up the medallion. "Understand this. I have brought you here to accept the ways of the Brotherhood, to accept me as your Empress, or to die."

Her dad rushed to her mom's side. "Charlee Smelton—"

"Empress Charleya." Charlee fired a red beam from the medallion that struck the ground in front of her parents. "You will refer to me as Empress."

Kraannaannn roared and thrashed his tail. "What evil is this?"

Serior laughed, a mix of a chicken's cackle and a guttural wheeze. His body burned bright orange. His laughter soon faded. He hovered closer to them. "Your Guardian has come to accept her destiny. You can either join her or die. It is your choice."

Her mom shook her head. She tried to run to her daughter, but her husband held her back. "Charlee, my love, don't give in. You've fought so hard and so bravely. Don't give up now." She fell to her knees. "This is my doing. I never should have let it get this far. This should have been my fight, not yours."

Charlee crossed to her mom. She stopped an arm's length away. "Woman, I will ask you this only once. Will you become a follower of the Brotherhood and help me deliver their word nation to nation, world to world, dimension to dimension?" She extended a hand to her mom. "Will you kiss my hand and accept me as your Empress."

Her mom reached out, grasping Charlee's hands. Terms formed in her eyes. Her chin quivered. "Never, but Charlee, my daughter, will always have my heart. I will always embrace her in my mind."

Charlee ripped her hand free. She grimaced at her mom. "I could care less for your heart or your mind. What good will they serve me when you are dead?" She raised the medallion over her head. The object hummed to life. "Now, you will know just how powerful I have become."

"Charlee, don't do this!" Her dad grabbed her mom by the shoulder, dragging her away. Kraannaannn roared again. His snout opened wide. An orange glow rose from deep in his throat.

Serior floated down beside Charlee. "Strike the non-believer down, Emp—"

Charlee spun around and fired a red beam from the medallion through Serior's chest. The fiery being's mouth fell agape as a scream escaped his burning lips. He dropped to his knees, and then onto his back.

"What...have...you...done?" The words from his mouth were a whisper.

"What I was always meant to do." Charlee stood over him. Her heart raced. "Bring an end to the madness you created."

Charlee's mom held shaky hands to her mouth. "You're still with me?"

Her dad smiled. His chin quivered. "This was an act?"

Nodding to her parents, Charlee took a deep breath. "I had to." She peered at Sandra's body. "It's okay now." Sandra climbed to her feet.

Serior coughed. "I...don't...understand."

A crackling noise rose from Sandra's body. Her body began to tremble, then a yellow glow flashed from her palms, chest, and legs. Sandra began to morph, her limbs fading away, her head disappearing. When the transformation was complete, all that remained was a floating yellow blob—the Changeling in its natural form.

Assara also slowly climbed to her feet, clutching her burned chest. "What is this magic, Guardian?"

Charlee knelt to Serior. She brushed hair from her eyes. She should run with the medallion to the fire tree, but possessing it, even if only for a few more moments, made her heart beat stronger. Her body tingled with excitement. Yes, she'd destroy it, but first Serior should know how a fourteen-year-old girl bested the almighty Brotherhood. "You fell for my plan, slime ball."

"But...I saw...the Changeling...killed," Serior uttered.

She leaned in closer. "You don't know anything about Changelings, do you? I learned long ago you cannot kill a creature of pure energy with a blade. When the Changeling survived being run through with a sword the first time in San Francisco by Tribon, I discovered just how powerful he is, and so I used that knowledge. When Tribon stabbed the Changeling this time, I whispered a plan into his ear. I had to deceive you, to make you believe I'd joined you."

Charlee stood and back stepped toward the fire tree. She hugged the medallion. The thought of parting with it made her insides ache and slowed her movements. She continued to gloat. "Once here, I figured you'd try to stop me if I tried to throw the medallion into the fire. And you might have beat me. I had to make sure you and Theodora were out of the way."

She stopped. Her gaze shifted to the fire tree, her family, then back to Serior. "You were stupid to think I'd ever kill my friends and family."

Serior blinked his eyes. "But...I saw...into your mind. Your thoughts...gave way...to my thoughts. You heart...was dark."

Charlee continued toward the fire tree, the medallion tucked against her side. She shivered a bit. He wasn't wrong. His thoughts had filled her mind. The darkness was nearly all consuming. But she was stronger now despite her craving for the medallion. "You saw what I allowed you to see. But you didn't probe deep enough. I hid away my true self. I locked away my real thoughts."

She neared the fire tree. Its heat engulfed her, like massive hands outstretched to smother her. Sweat dripped from her forehead. Searing steam burned her skin. Her clothes seemingly melted against her body. Each breath scorched her throat. She backed away. It hurt too much. But was it the pain of the fire or the desire not to let go of the dark object? No, she had to finish this and send the medallion back where it came from. She pressed on, one hand held up to shield her eyes. Each step became tougher and tougher, like her feet were sticking to the desert floor.

She was almost there. Fire embers slapped her face, stinging her over and over. The roar of the blaze deafened her. *Almost there!* The heat intensified. Her skin sizzled and popped. Fear made her want to turn back, but she couldn't. Even if this killed her, she had to end it here and now to save everyone and herself.

The Changeling joined her, wrapping his gelatinous glowing body around hers, protecting her as always.

She breathed just a little easier. "Thank you, my—"

A familiar laugh flowed from the fire tree.

Charlee froze. *No, it couldn't be!*

CHAPTER 33

The Dead Rise

THE FIRE TREE'S color shifted from orange to blood red. Its crackling flames danced wildly with new burning branches expanding from the trunk. Charlee inched closer. She knew the laugh. It belonged to the fake Theodora. *I can't let her escape from the flames. Must throw the medallion into the tree.* Charlee pulled her arm back as if preparing to throw a baseball. Theodora's laughter grew louder. *Now!* She flung the medallion toward the flames. Heart pounding, she watched the dark object soar toward the blazing tree.

Then it stopped and just hung there suspended by…

"Silly Guardian. Do you honestly think the Brotherhood would fall so easily?" She heard Serior's words deep inside her thoughts.

Charlee, still inside the Changeling's protective shell, swung around. Serior stood and took to the air, floating toward her as if he'd never been wounded. *No, it couldn't be.* She'd blasted him with the medallion. She'd won. It was over. Charlee lowered her head to her chest. She struggled to force out a breath.

Crossing the distance to her, Serior hovered just above Charlee. "You thought you could trick the Brotherhood, you, a stupid little girl. We have thrived for thousands of generations. No, we will not be done in by a child."

"Go to hell!" Fueled by rage, Charlee reached for the medallion.

Another hand, withered and bony, thrust out from the fire tree and snatched the medallion away from her. The rest of the fake Theodora's aged body stepped free from the flames. The sorceress, her face more bone than skin, tucked the medallion against her chest. "You dare call yourself Empress? You have always been a sad, confused little girl. And now you must be punished." Theodora floated up to Serior. She bowed to him. "Please forgive me, master, for my transgressions, and allow me to serve you once again."

Serior nodded to her. He then pointed at Charlee. "Now Guardian, you and everyone you love will suffer at the hands of the Brotherhood."

Charlee peered at those she loved. Her plan failed. Serior and Theodora were too strong. *No, think of something. There still must be a way.*

Stepping free of the Changeling's protective cover, she ignited her hands in a white glow. "Serior—"

"The time to talk has ended." Serior raised his arms. "Brothers, join me."

Charlee retreated to her parents and the young Dragon Lord. The Changeling and Assara stood by them. Her parents wrapped their arms around her.

"Whatever happens, at least we are together," her mother said loud enough for all of them to hear.

"Together," her dad repeated.

Kraannaannn nodded his massive head. "Together."

Assara held up her one arm and formed a fist. She locked eyes with Charlee. "It would be an honor to fight alongside you."

From the fire tree came a stream of ghostly figures. Men and women, more apparition than physical beings, slid from the flames. They were dressed in raven-black robes. Their faces were thin and sullen, their eyes glowing red. Charlee's body tensed. A faint gasp cut through her parted lips. The dark figures marched out from the flames in the hundreds, armed with glowing staffs, spears, swords, and daggers. They surrounded Charlee and the others.

Serior and Theodora floated down toward Charlee. Serior placed a hand over his chest. "Behold, the Brotherhood! Their souls live on in me, but tonight I have summoned their ancient forms to bring about your end."

A dark, mournful chant rose from the undead creatures in the Lengoron language. Charlee recognized the words. *Life to those who are cleansed. Death to the non-believers. Life to those who choose our path. Death to the non-believers. Un-ending life to those who succumb to our way. Death to the non-believers.*

The last phrase repeated over and over. *Death to the non-believers.*

Charlee's dad leaned into her ear. "Uh, I believe in a good fight, but perhaps it would be wise to open a portal and get us the hell out of here."

Kraannaannn lifted his long neck, rearing his head back. Unleashing a rage-filled roar, he spewed a fiery inferno at the undead Brotherhood. When his flaming spew ended and the black smoke cleared, the robed figures remained un-scathed by the blaze. Their chant grew louder, and they began to close the circle, inching closer to Charlee and the others.

The Dragon Lord shook his head, then lowered to Charlee. "I believe your father to be right. Open a portal, Guardian so that we might regroup and find reinforcements. I promise to unleash the wrath of the Dragon's Realm."

Charlee nodded. She'd open a portal for her friends and family, but she'd stay behind to make sure the others were safe. She closed her eyes and envisioned the world Theodora had attacked where the real Sandra and her dad remained, kept safe by the magical creatures there. But something was wrong, as if her powers were short circuiting. She couldn't form a mental lock. She pressed her hands against her temples, gritted her teeth, and tensed every muscle until she shook, but she couldn't generate a portal.

She gazed at her dad. "Something's wrong. Something's blocking—"

"No, Guardian, there will be no escape for you this good day." Serior held his fiery arms outstretched to her. "Your powers pale to mine, child. You cannot form a portal in my presence unless I allow it. Now, accept your fate, Guardian. You have chosen dea—"

"I'm not looking to escape." Charlee ignited her hands in a white glow. "I'm here to finish this."

Serior's flames crackled louder. His color shifted from orange to red. "I suppose you are. What a shame. You could have done so much with the gift I offered to you, but you are as shortsighted as those in your family who have come before. You will pay dearly for your choices today."

Charlee turned her back to Serior. She gazed at her mom and dad. A calmness came over her. "I love you guys."

"We love you, too, baby girl," her mom uttered, offering a comforting wink.

"Now, let's kick this guy's ass and get home. I'm a little hungry." Her dad grinned. He still held his bow in one hand. He placed his other over his heart.

Charlee swung back around to the fiery leader of the Brotherhood. "You want to know the truth, Serior?"

"Enlighten me, child." He crossed his arms.

"I'm over you and all of this bull—"

Serior launched a red flame at Charlee. She ducked, the fire passing inches over her head, igniting strands of her hair. Charlee swatted away the flames.

"Is that the best you got?" Charlee stood tall, shoulders straight.

Serior shook his flaming head. "I think not. On this night of blood, the Brotherhood will have its revenge for the evil done to it so long ago. Brothers, kill the Guardian." Serior pointed a finger at Charlee.

The shadowy members of The Brotherhood marched forward, like a wave of fog rolling onto the coast. They again chanted over and over, *Life to those who are cleansed. Death to the non-believers. Life to those who choose our path. Death to the non-believers. Un-ending life to those who succumb to our way. Death to the non-believers.*

Charlee peered back at the others. "Everyone, stay behind me."

Kraannaannn roared. "I think not." He spread his wings wide. The Changeling, back in the form of a unicorn, leaped beside Charlee. The dead lumbered slowly toward them. Their eyes blazed red. Their terrible chant continued.

Charlee raised her glowing hands. She searched her own thoughts. How could they fight the dead? *Come on, Guardian, think!* There was only one answer. *Get to the medallion. Get it back—somehow.* She grabbed hold of the Changeling's neck and swung onto her protector's back. "Bike, we have to—"

A wild scream came from above.

Charlee arched her neck just in time to see young Theodora dive from the sky and tackle her clone to the ground. They rolled over and over, wrestling along the ground. The real Theodora then stood, dragging her clone to her feet.

"Did you think I was dead, sister?" The real Theodora gripped her clone by the arms. "Did you think you could wipe me from existence and replace me. No, sister, the time has come for our reckoning."

The cloned Theodora tried to shake herself free. She still clutched the medallion. "Why won't you just die?"

"Because that is a journey I wish to take with you, sister." Young Theodora gripped the medallion with both hands. "But first, this no longer belongs to you."

"No, it's mine." The cloned Theodora's eyes bulged. Her body shook. "You will not take it from me."

"Do I hear fear in your voice, sister?" The true Theodora tugged on the medallion, wrenching it free from her clone.

The fake Theodora shrieked in rage.

"Guardian, now!" Young Theodora held the medallion out to Charlee with one hand. Her other held the clone by the neck.

"Bike!" Charlee shouted to the Changeling despite her protector holding his unicorn form. The Changeling took flight, and with one mighty flap of his wings raced toward the medallion, soaring just above the approaching dark misty forms of the Brotherhood.

Serior blasted the two Theodora's with a wall of fire. "You will not stop the Brotherhood."

Engulfed in flames, the cloned Theodora cried out, "Mercy, Serior."

The true Theodora said nothing. Though burning alive, she kept her hand outstretched, the flames that covered her licking at the medallion.

Charlee and the unicorn reached the dark object. She leaned over, snatching the medallion away from the real Theodora. Charlee gripped the medallion tightly as the Changeling changed direction, swerving toward the sky.

Looking back, she saw the real Theodora grab her clone in a fiery death embrace and throw herself and the dark being that for far too long went by the name Theodora into the heart of the fire tree.

The cloned Theodora cried out, "I. Was. To. Be. A. Goddess." She shrieked one last time, and then her voice faded away. Both vanished. The real Theodora, in a final act, had given Charlee the chance to fulfill her destiny…destroy the medallion.

Now the question was—how to get past Serior?

"Get us skyward." Charlee tugged on the unicorn's main. With a thrust of his wings, the Changeling soared into the night sky. Serior gave chase. Flames shot from his palms at Charlee. The unicorn swerved left to avoid the fiery assault.

Serior fired again. The unicorn slid to the right just in time. The fire passed just over Charlee's head, charring the air around her.

Charlee peered at the earth below for just an instant. The young Dragon Lord stood over her parents and Assara, defending them from the advancing Brotherhood. But there was no way to kill those who were already dead. Kraannaannn and her parents would not last long.

"Keep going!" She leaned her body against the unicorn, squeezing his mane between her fingers. "Get us a little distance, then turn around and stop."

Serior fired again on her. The Changeling one more time outmaneuvered him. The great beast then swung around and came to a jarring stop. Charlee held the medallion out in front of her. Giving over to its power, becoming one with the dark object, she willed it to fire on Serior.

The medallion refused.

Serior laughed. "You cannot use the gift against me, child, not after defying me. The Brotherhood created it, gave it life. We are one with it the way you could have been. No, you have no way to defeat the Brotherhood, young fool. I will give you one last chance, child. Return the medallion to me and give your life over to the Brotherhood. It really is the only way."

Damn! Charlee's thoughts focused on her parents, her sister, all those who had sacrificed themselves, the Dragon Lord, and Cryton. She thought of Sandra and her parents, and all the soldiers lost in that other world. They all deserved a chance at living their lives.

They needed her to truly be a Guardian. And that meant...

"Attack speed," she uttered.

The Changeling hesitated, rearing his unicorn head back.

"Do it now." She patted her protector on the neck. "I must do this. It will be all right. I promise."

The unicorn lowered his head. Charlee tucked the medallion into her side, like a football player racing to the end zone. Together they dove at Serior.

"Serior, you want the medallion, then take it—and me!" When the unicorn was close to the leader of the Brotherhood, Charlee leaped from the beast's back, launching herself at Serior.

"What are you doing?" Serior held out his fiery hands.

With every bit of her magical strength, Charlee slammed into Serior, grabbing him by the waste, driving him into the fire tree. His flames surrounded her, scorching her skin, but in that moment, the pain didn't matter. Nothing else mattered but ending this.

"Stupid child, you'll die!" Serior cried. Terror struck his red eyes. He pummeled Charlee with his fists, but Charlee ignored every strike.

The fire tree was in reach.

"We. Both. Will!" She held in her own fearful scream. She didn't want to die, but she had to save everyone. She had to save Earth and every other world that would suffer if the medallion and the Brotherhood were not destroyed. She had to be the Guardian she was born to be.

"No, Guardian!" Serior begged.

Together, they crossed into the fire tree, the medallion still tucked against her side.

CHAPTER 34

Tearing Down the Tree

CHARLEE SHOULD HAVE been instantly incinerated, but a shell of yellow energy cocooned her, protecting her from the inferno all around her. She hovered inside the heart of the tree, as if afloat within an endless sea of flames. There was no beginning, no end—just a fiery plain of existence that stretched forever.

Somehow, she could see through the firestorm as if she were a creature of fire herself—as if she belonged in this burning world, this hell.

She should have been panicked. She should have cried out, but a wave of calm washed over her. Death by fire was a horrible way to go, but at least everyone she loved would be safe now.

The energy field around her was holding, enabling her to breathe, but for how long? How long until the fire consumed her? Her body already began to feel numb as if she'd soon vanish into nothingness.

First, she had to see the medallion destroyed.

She stared down at her hands, expecting to see the medallion still in her grasp, but she no longer held the dark object. Her heart thudded nearly as loud as the crackling fire. Had she lost the medallion before crossing over? Could Serior have snatched it from her?

Charlee spun around. Her body untensed. Just ahead of her, the medallion spun wildly suspended within the blaze. The image of her face flashed on one side and then melted away. The dark object began to warp into a misshaped ball.

"What have you done?" Serior, his body twisted and contorted, crossed to her. His limbs wilted away as the medallion shrank. "This will not be the end. The Brotherhood shall rise again. This I swear to you…"

His words trailed off. He bowed his head, watching his own body vanish in the flames of the fire tree.

Charlee's hands tightened into fists. "You've cooked long enough, Serior. You're done."

Then he was gone.

For a heartbeat, the shrinking medallion sizzled and popped before turning to black liquid. Charlee reached for it. Even in her final moments, she longed for it and felt the pain of loss in her gut.

A skeletal hand grabbed her shoulder from behind. "Guardian, there is still a chance." The hand swung her around, and Charlee found herself face to face with Theodora, half of her flesh burnt away, revealing a blackened skull. Charlee's eyes widened. Was it the good Theodora or the evil clone? "Guardian, hear my words. You can save us both. You just need to remove the medallion from the fire."

Charlee shook her head. The face belonged to the evil Theodora. "Go to hell, witch." With as much strength as she could muster, Charlee gripped Theodora's neck. "Let's watch our precious medallion die together."

"No!" Theodora screamed. Before their eyes, the liquefied medallion spun faster and faster, and with a pop it turned to ash and vanished as if it had never existed at all.

Theodora convulsed. "You hateful little—"

"Time to die, Theodora." Charlee smiled. In that moment, the evil Theodora slid from existence.

She would not be back. Hopefully.

Charlee wrapped her arms around herself. The energy field was fading. She gasped for air. Her lungs burned. Heat engulfed her. Her flesh began to bake. She cried out. *Please let death come quickly!* She took a painful breath, ready to join Cryton and the Dragon Lord in whatever awaited her in death. She'd done what she had set out to do.

The flaming tree began to shift colors around her from blood red to orange to a dimming shade of white. She closed her eyes. She was so tired, and darkness beckoned to her.

A pair of hands latched onto her. Then, a second pair. They hauled her from the blazing tree. Emerging from the diminishing inferno, fighting to keep her eyes open, she coughed violently, her chest spasming, trying to force her lungs to work. Black smoke and spittle flew from her mouth.

Her mom held her with hands awash in blue energy, surrounding Charlee in a pocket of sweet air. "Breathe easy, baby. You're going to live. I'll not lose my oldest daughter today. I swear it."

Charlee coughed more, her body shuddering as she lay on the ground in her mom's lap. But with each shallow breath, she sucked in cool oxygen from her mom's healing magic. The burning in her lungs eased. The coughing stopped and her skin cooled. Maybe she wasn't going to die today. Maybe, she would have another chance at life.

Her dad placed a hand on Charlee's forehead. "Charlee, thank God. I thought we were going to lose you to that damn tree or whatever the hell it is. But thanks to your mom's mental lock on you, we were able to reach—"

Bellowing screams erupted from the remaining shadows of the Brotherhood.

They cried out in agony as the branches of the fire tree crumbled away. Cracks appeared in the burning trunk. Flaming pieces of the tree chipped away, falling to the ground only to vanish.

One by one, the Brotherhood was swept back into the dying fire tree. Finally, the tree itself extinguished. All that was left was a giant burnt wood, which quickly toppled to the ground.

"Guardian." The voice belonged to the cloned version of Sandra. Assara had found a way to rise above the darkness and fight on the side of Charlee and her family. The clone dropped to her knees. Her cheeks sunk in, and her chin quivered. "I'm…dying."

Charlee reached out to her, but she couldn't stand. "No…why?" Her words came as a scratchy whisper.

Assara grinned…differently…kindly. "I am a creation of the medallion. My time comes to an end." Her hands began to fade.

"No, there has to be a way."

The clone shook her head. "This is better. I caused too much pain. Time for me to pay. Please remember my final acts."

Charlee nodded. "I promise."

"Thank you." Assara tilted her head back. Gazing up at the night sky, she slipped from existence.

Charlee cried for her.

§§§

A quiet settled over the Janasaran desert. The stench of fire quickly gave way as a breeze blew in from the west, pushing away the last remnants of smoke. The Queens of the Night, the three moons that circled Janasara, shown brightly in the sky.

All that was evil had been swept away. Serior. His Brotherhood. Theodora. The medallion. For the first time in what felt like forever, Charlee's body seemed lighter. Then again, maybe she was just growing numb from the injuries she sustained. She lay on the desert floor, cradled in her mom's arms.

"It was your magic… saved me…inside…tree?" Charlee could hardly speak the words. She gazed into her mom's dirt smudged face. Her mom's hair hung loosely around her face.

Her mom smiled and nodded. "I wasn't going to lose my oldest. But it wasn't my magic alone. The Changeling threw his life force around you as well."

The unicorn swept in from the sky, landing near them. He lowered his head to Charlee, softly nudging her.

"Thank…you." She reached up with a shaky hand and touched his snout.

Her dad knelt beside them. His face was starting to heal, but blood dripped from new wounds in his side. He placed his hand on her head. "You are truly a hero, Charlee. You've earned a rest."

"She most certainly has."

Charlee blinked her eyes. She recognized the voice, but that shouldn't be possible. She looked all around, expecting to see her mentor, Cryton, but there were only his words.

"You did well, Guardian."

With unexpected strength, Charlee painfully climbed to her feet and stood on shaky legs. Her mother helped her stand. "Cryton, is it you?"

"Yes, Guardian." A transparent, glowing version of the old man appeared where the fire tree had fallen.

He was not alone. On either side of him were two glowing beings—one a tall, muscular man with a short beard dressed in shiny armor, a long sword at his side. On the other side of Cryton was a slender woman with long dark hair flowing down her back. She wore a purple robe, but what stood out the most to Charlee was the woman's kind eyes. They were just like her mom's eyes.

Cryton offered a wide smile. His gaze first fell on Charlee's mom. "I'd like to introduce you to Queen Assara and the Guardian Michala." He nodded at Charlee's mom. "Your parents." He next nodded at Charlee. "Your grandparents."

Michala and Assara, aglow in a white light, approached them. They were so regal and such powerful beings. They first addressed Charlee's mom.

Assara reached out and touched her face with a transparent hand. "My daughter, the woman you have become. I wish I could have been there to raise you. But know I was always there. I never really left you. And I am so proud of the woman and the mother you have become."

Charlee's mom gasped. "I...I love you," she muttered.

Michala reached for her hand. "Daughter, I think you are stronger than you realize. Remember that, because our people are going to need you now. They are going to need their Queen to show them the way."

Charlee's grandfather tuned his attention to her dad. "And I am pleased you found yourself a good man and a true warrior, even if he is bit meek of build."

Her dad cleared his throat. "Thank you, sir."

They then focused on Charlee.

Charlee spoke first. She couldn't hold back the tears. "How is...this...possible? Is this...just a dream?"

Michala was the first to speak. "Granddaughter, the strength of your magic in destroying the fire tree allowed us to cross through a portal no other Guardian has ever opened—a portal to the afterworld. I fear it is only temporary, and our time is short, but we had to meet you and our daughter if only for this moment."

He bowed to Charlee. "You truly are the greatest Guardian to ever stand against evil." Her grandfather lowered to one knee. "You have become the Guardian that not only Janasara will need to rebuild, but that countless other worlds will need, too. I have a feeling you are bound for even more greatness."

Charlee's heart beat heavy in her chest. The words started to come easier. "I have...so much...to learn...from you."

Michala shook his head. "There is nothing you need to learn from me."

Assara placed her glowing hands on Charlee's shoulder. "You and your sister are the last Princesses of Latara. Be there for each other. Love each other, as I loved Theodora, the real Theodora."

Charlee blinked away tears. "I will."

Assara backed away. "I believe Cryton would like to have a few words with you, as well."

With his staff in hand, Cryton approached. His eyes shifted from Charlee to her mom and back to Charlee. He rubbed his mustache between his forefinger and his thumb. "Well, kiddos, you did it. You saved the universe. I couldn't be prouder of the both of you. Not even if I was truly family."

Charlee sobbed. So did her mom.

"You are family." Her mom choked over her words. "You are every bit a father to me."

"And...a grandfather...to me," Charlee echoed. "Please, Cryton, I need you...to stay with me."

The old man smiled. "I wish there was a way. But that's just me being a selfish old man. You don't need me any longer. Neither of you do. You are ready for the challenges ahead. Just be there for each other." He began to step away.

"Cryton!" Charlee cried. She couldn't lose him, not again.

"I will always be there for you—in your heart, your soul, and your mind. Look for me there when you need me. Goodbye, for now."

He joined Michala and Assara. They retreated to the charred ground where the fire tree had stood.

High above another voice boomed over the desert, Sheorrriaaaan's, the Dragon Lord who had sacrificed himself to save Charlee. His glowing body flew alongside his son, Kraannaannn. "Guardian, the dragons will always be there for you. Call on them whenever you need. I have to say, I am so glad I didn't eat you." Sheorrriaaaan nodded to her. He then gently bumped heads with his son and vanished in the night.

Michala, Assara, and Cryton also faded away until their glow was no more, until nothing but darkness filled the desert night.

Charlee embraced her parents and didn't let go.

CHAPTER 35

Rise of the Kingdom of Latara

THE BATTLE AGAINST evil had ended weeks ago. Charlee had healed from her wounds. The soldiers had returned to Earth. Lives had returned to normal as much as they could. But in the wake, three worlds had forever been altered—Earth, Janasara, and the alien world Theodora had attacked, Ut-illa-rey, as the creatures that inhabited that world called it.

Charlee, dressed in a fine purple tunic, tied with a golden belt—a sword at her side—walked with Sandra along a hillside just beyond the gates of Latara. The Changeling, in unicorn form, strolled behind them. The sun had started to set. The sky's emerald hue had started a shift to the darker greens of dusk. Blue grass had started to re-grow along the hillside, a sign life was quickly returning to Janasara after being sick for so long under the cloned Theodora's rule.

Sandra, dressed in a similar blue tunic, tied her hair into a braid. "So, I guess my dad and I will be returning to Earth tomorrow after your mom is sworn in as Queen. I'll be glad to see my mom and sister again, but…" Sandra's voice cracked.

Charlee bit her own lip to keep calm. She brushed her clean, sweet-smelling hair out of her face. It felt good to not stink after all they'd been through.

"I wish I could stay on Earth, but I have to help my mom." Charlee stared down at the grass. Anything to avoid eye contact with her best friend. "But, you know, Earth is my real home. When I can, I want to return there for good, but I'm just not sure when. I can visit you all the time. I mean, I am a Guardian after all."

They both laughed, but it didn't last.

Sandra changed the subject. "It's going to be weird back home. Everyone remembers what happened. The world won't be the same. We know we're not alone anymore. There's some scary stuff out there. I mean, dimensions and all. It's crazy."

Charlee sighed. "There just aren't enough conjurers to place a large enough *forgetting* spell over the world. I'm not strong enough to do it. Besides, Mom said it's best not to mess with their minds any more than has already been done. I guess I agree, but that's another reason I can't really go back, not yet anyway. Everybody on Earth knows who and what I am. It would be strange—and dangerous."

"I know, but it still sucks." Sandra wiped her eyes. "What am I going to do without my best friend."

Charlee placed her hands on Sandra's shoulder. "I'll still be your best friend.

231

When you need me, just call out. I'll know, and I'll be there. I guess I see myself as a daughter of two worlds, you know. I won't abandon Earth. And I'll never abandon you." Charlee smiled wide. "Besides, I don't think there's too many malls here. I'm going to need my mall fix, so I have to visit…often."

The two girls chuckled. Again, it didn't last.

§ § §

In the early morning hours of a new day, the day her mom would be crowned Queen, Charlee rode through the Gates of Latara to the site where Sheorrriaaaan had died. His son, Kraannaannn was already there, his head bowed as if in silent prayer. The first rays of light poured from the sky over the mountains beyond the kingdom by the time she reached him.

Kraannaannn took no notice of her at first. His eyes downcast, he didn't move a muscle. He seemed more like a statue than a living creature.

Without uttering a word, Charlee knelt and brushed her fingers over the dirt still stained green with Sheorrriaaaan's blood. She tried to be strong and to hold back the tears, but it was impossible. Finally, Kraannaannn lifted his head, spewed fire into the early morning sky, and unleashed a terrible roar.

Charlee backed away. "I shouldn't be here. I shouldn't disturb you."

His chest heaving, the young Dragon Lord again lowered his head. "No, it helps to have you here, Guardian."

She patted his leg. "I am so sorry you lost your father. I never meant—"

"It's not your fault." Kraannaannn inched his massive head closer to her. "If anything, you gave him a renewed chance at life in the end. You returned him to his glory, just like he had long before Theodora used me to force my father into the shadows. He will be remembered for his finest hour, and that is because of you, Guardian."

Charlee wiped away tears. "Still, I wish he was here."

Kraannaannn nodded. "At least I got to see him once again and to know he believes in me. I must be honest, I'm not sure I am ready to be Dragon Lord."

Charlee circled directly in front of his snout. His hot breath pushed her back, but she held her ground. "You are. You are a true leader. You'll do an awesome job. I know it."

"As will you, Guardian." The dragon gently nudged her. "You will make a fine Queen someday."

Charlee shook her head. "I'm not so sure I'm cut out to be the future Queen. I might leave that for my sister, who'll probably be a much stronger Guardian, a much stronger person, than I could ever be."

"Either way, I know you'll be there for your people." Kraannaannn fluttered his wings. "And I vow to be there for you and your people, to be there for all of Janasara, if I am ever needed. If you are in danger, I will know, and I will be there. I will always fight at your side. That is my promise."

Charlee leaned in close to the Dragon Lord's snout. "Same here. You and me, we're in this thing together."

Kraannaannn smiled, bearing his fangs. "Agreed."

§ § §

The trumpets echoed across the Kingdom of Latara. Charlee rocked back and forth on her feet in the castle's courtyard, refurbished through magic to its glory before the battle that ravaged the castle. To her left stood Sandra and Sandra's dad. To her right, the warrior Aryean, healed from his injuries. His missing eye was covered by a black patch. A scar spread from underneath the patch up his forehead to his hairline. Charlee glanced at him and blushed. If anything, the patch made him hotter. She still got a bubbly stomach and found it hard to breathe whenever she was around the warrior. Sure, he was probably too old for her, but with the war over, what was wrong with a little harmless crush. Unless this was more than just a crush.

Aryean gazed back at her with his one dark eye. Charlee quickly glanced down at her black boots.

Sandra elbowed her in the ribs and laughed. "He's cute," she uttered.

"Shut up," Charlee whispered.

"Shhh," Aryean nudged Charlee. "Guardian, your mother is being crowned Queen. Now is not the time to talk."

"Sorry." Charlee giggled slightly. Sandra, too. It was good to joke with her friend—like they once did. It was good to just be normal girls again, if only for a while.

But Aryean was right. This was a solemn occasion, and a Guardian should act like it. She gazed around the courtyard at the Latarans gathered in a circle. They had all suffered so much, but now they smiled wide. Their eyes were bright. They had their home back, and their Queen to lead them.

They had reason to hope again.

In the afternoon skies, touched by the sun's golden rays, Kraannaannn circled above with four other dragons, all there to honor the new Queen who would rebuild the Ten Unified Kingdoms. With her gaze cast skyward, she glimpsed a white dove flying just overhead—the Changeling. She pointed to her shoulder, and the bird fluttered down to her, landing softly on her.

"Glad you could make it." She softly rubbed the dove's feathered head.

The trumpeters ceased their playing.

In the center of the circle, her mom and dad stood side by side with Megan in her mom's arms. Her mom wore a long purple dress tied at the waist with a yellow sash. Her hair was tied tightly back. Her face was resolute but still warm. She was still Charlee's mom, but suddenly she seemed older. Even a touch of gray lined the sides of her hair. Charlee's dad was dressed as a knight with a golden chest plate, long black gloves, and black boots up to his knees. A sword hung at his side. He still wore his familiar round wire-framed glasses.

Penaiya, who had led the ragtag leftovers of Latara for so long, gathered with them. A white cape fell from her shoulders, down her back, and to her feet. She held a crown in her hand.

Aryean leaned close to Charlee. "Shouldn't you be standing there with them, Guardian?"

Charlee shook her head. "Not today."

He tilted his head. "But why?"

She placed a finger to her lips. "Shhhhh."

Penaiya held the crown over her head for everyone in the courtyard to see. She slowly turned in every direction. "My countrymen, today I bid you good tidings." Her words, spoken in Lengoron, bounced off the courtyard walls. "For today we begin anew. Today we take a stand and say we will rebuild what once was and make it better. Today, my friends, after long suffering, we crown our Queen."

The courtyard erupted in deafening cheers.

Penaiya stepped forward and placed the crown atop the head of Charlee's mom. "May your reign usher in a new time of peace and prosperity not only for the Kingdom of Latara, but all of Janasara."

Penaiya produced a second tiny crown. "And, my brothers and sisters, lest we forget, Princess Megan, who will grow up wise and strong and one day have the chance herself to serve as Queen."

More cheers arose from the crowd. Aryean peered at Charlee in confusion.

So did Sandra, who had taken to studying the Lengoron language and was learning at a fast pace. No surprise there, given she was the smartest girl in school back home.

"What the hell?" Sandra raised her arms.

Charlee shrugged. In English, she said, "I told my mom I will be a Guardian. I will help rebuild this world. I will protect it with my life, but I have no wish to be Princess, and certainly not Queen. I must be able to move freely between worlds. I have a feeling Earth may need a Guardian as much as Janasara now that so much has changed."

Sandra brushed hair from her face. "What do you mean?"

Charlee scratched her chin. "I don't know. I'm having weird dreams again about other worlds where there are freakish creatures out to do harm who have now seen Earth thanks to the portals Theodora opened."

"Oh my God, Charlee." Sandra put a hand to her mouth.

She shook her head. "They could just be dreams, you know. Who knows how bad my head is messed up?" Charlee bit the inside of her cheek. She didn't really believe that. Truth be told, she didn't know what to think.

She just knew the best she could offer her mom was to be a Guardian...nothing more. She turned her attention back to her mom.

The Queen stepped forward, Megan still in her arms. She grinned in the same comforting way she always smiled at Charlee. "My friends, long ago my parents, Queen Assara and the Guardian Michala, sent me to another world to save my life. I cannot say whether their actions were right or wrong, but I always knew my destiny was to return to Janasara. I am sorry it took me so long to find my way back and that I didn't do more to prevent your long suffering. What I can tell you is I will devote the rest of my life...my heart, my soul, my very essence...to make sure you never suffer again."

More cheers sounded throughout the courtyard.

Her mom continued. "We will rebuild. Conjurer and non-magic alike...every creature on Janasara...will live in peace. And we will do so in a way where everyone has a voice. The High Council will rise again, and every woman and man, no matter their wealth, land, or family name, will have a chance to serve."

She extended a hand to Penaiya. "I appoint Penaiya, the true hero of our people, to lead the rebuilding of the High Council. She more than anyone is the reason we can celebrate today. She deserves your praise more than anyone."

More cheers erupted. Penaiya bowed.

Charlee lifted her head and stood tall. She couldn't hold back a smile. Together, her mom and Penaiya would be great leaders.

Her mom wasn't finished speaking. "That we have this chance to rise from the ashes is due to your combined strength, and I thank you all for what you have done to make this day possible. But we also must give thanks to one other." Her mom pointed to Charlee. "Charleya, the Guardian!"

The loudest cheers yet sounded from the crowd. They all turned to her, then began chanting, "Guardian!"

Charlee bit her lip. She had asked her mom to leave her out of today's celebration, but moms will be moms. She cursed under her breath. The Changeling launched from her shoulder into the skies. "Hey, where are you—"

Sandra grabbed her shoulder and pushed her forward. "Go. Your fans want to see you."

Maneuvering past the Latarans, she smiled and nodded, but inside her stomach churned. What was she supposed to say? Hands reached for her, grabbing her arms and shoulders. She allowed it, but each touch made her want to shrink away. These people needed a Guardian, and that was her destiny.

It reminded her she'd never live a normal teenage life.

She reached her mom, who mouthed, *I'm sorry.*

Charlee touched her mom's arm, then leaned in to give Megan a kiss on her forehead. Megan squirmed in her mom's arms. A wide grin crossed her face. Someday, Megan could be Queen, maybe even Guardian. Maybe she'd be stronger than Charlee. She looked forward to teaching her sister to user her powers.

She turned to the Latarans. *Okay, dummy, say something.* "I, uh, I mean we…we've come a long way together to reach this point. Uhm, I know you have lost so much, and I can't promise you times ahead will be easy, but I will be your Guardian to the best of my ability. I will stand with you no matter what comes our way. I will always fight by your side, as I know you will fight by my side. I've seen it. We are strong together. And like the Queen said, we will rebuild our lives together. But we cannot forget those who sacrificed everything to make today possible." She looked to the skies. An image of a smiling Cryton filled her head. "We will never forget."

In a whisper, she said, "I will never forget."

Chapter 36

A Cloudy Future

DRENCHED IN SWEAT, Charlee awoke in her chambers. Flickering candles shrouded the room in a dancing orange glow. She blinked her eyes and then slowly lifted from her bed into a sitting position. Her heavy sleeping garments clung to her body, like a thick wet towel. Stretching her limbs, she stood and walked over to the open window. The three Queens of the Night hung low in the northern sky. Morning was still hours away.

It had been hours since the coronation. Kraannaannn had led his dragons back to their realm, vowing to join with the Guardian to protect Janasara from any threat that might come its way. Sandra and her dad had also left. Charlee had opened a portal for them, and with one final tearful goodbye, delivered them back to Earth.

Now, her chest ached. Her mom, dad, and Megan were sleeping in a nearby room, but she felt very much alone. Even with the Changeling in dove form asleep on her windowsill, she couldn't escape the emptiness in the pit of her stomach. It was almost to the point where breathing became difficult. Each breath lodged in her throat.

What good was it to think about how much she missed Sandra? Destiny had set her down a path, and for now they couldn't be together.

She should just go back to sleep and try to forget the sadness. But when she closed her eyes, the damned visions returned of scaly one-eyed beasts that walked on two legs and stood at least twice the size of humans. They seemed to stare through some device at a blue and green dot in space.

Earth.

For some reason, the vision filled her with an icy dread. So, she'd rather not sleep or think about the evil out there.

"Well, Guardian, it's good to see you again." Theodora appeared as a glowing apparition, leaning against a side wall. A young version of Theodora, with long flowing blond hair and porcelain skin, smiled wide—too wide.

But which Theodora was it? The real Theodora who sacrificed herself for Charlee or the evil one who screwed with Charlee's life for far too long.

Charlee sighed. She feared she knew the answer to her next question. "Which Theodora has come to me?"

"Oh, Guardian, you cannot tell me from that dull original after all we went through together." The cloned Theodora floated closer to Charlee.

Charlee's hands formed into fists. This couldn't be happening. "Theodora, how? This can't be real."

Theodora folded her arms. "Relax, this isn't real. I'm not really here. Or am I? I don't really know. I'm not here out of choice. You summoned me from the dead as you sleep. Look upon yourself."

Charlee glanced at her bed, at herself in a fitful sleep, grimacing and turning over, body shivering. Then, she peered at her own body where she stood across the room from her sleeping self. Her body was more ghost than solid. She glowed bright yellow. *Is this real? Have I brought the evil Theodora here, or is this just a dream? Am I actually going crazy and having a conversation with myself in a dream state?*

Theodora glided beside her. "Dream or not, Guardian, I find it fascinating that you would choose to have a conversation with me rather than the good Theodora or your mentor, Cryton. I must really have left my imprint on your brain."

"You're nothing to me, witch." Charlee crossed the room away from the sorceress. But that was a lie. The evil version of Theodora was still locked in her brain somewhere as if always scratching to get out. The witch would always be with her. They'd shared the medallion. Too much darkness had bled into Charlee's minds. She'd always have to fight to block it out.

"Say what you like, but I'm the one who is here." Theodora circled Charlee. "And I think I know why we are having this little reunion."

"Yeah, why?" Charlee crossed her arms.

"Because of your visions." Theodora grinned ear to ear. "You want to know if they're real. You fear there are alien beings at this very moment targeting Earth thanks to me and the doorways I opened across space and dimensions."

"Well, tell me before I send you back to whatever dark place you're rotting in!" Charlee grabbed Theodora's arm.

The sorceress laughed. "Oh, touchy, aren't we? The truth is, Guardian, if I'm just you talking to yourself in a dream, how could I know if the visions are real? Then again, maybe I'm not you and—"

Charlee held out her hand. A sword handle formed in her palm, and then a blade extended from the hilt. "Enough, witch. This will be the last time we ever talk."

Theodora bowed her head. "We'll see."

Charlee swung the blade, slicing Theodora in half. Her ghostly form vanished. Charlee glided to her bed. Whatever awaited her when she awoke, she'd face it. If evil was on its way, she'd find a way to defeat it.

After all, she was a Guardian.

Also by Darren Simon

Guardian's Nightmare
Book One of "The Last Princess of Latara"

Charlee Smelton is an average thirteen-year-old girl struggling to adapt after her family moves to San Francisco. She thinks her biggest obstacle is facing the bullies who brand her a nerd. She's wrong. Can Charlee find the hero inside her, the hero she must become, to save her friends, family, city, and world from an evil only she can defeat, an evil she allowed into this world?

Guardian's Return
Book Two of "The Last Princess of Latara"

Theodora lives, and if Charlee's dreams of death and fields of spilled blood are true, her great aunt has avenged herself on that world across the dimensional divide. Charlee knows what she must do. Can Charlee defeat Theodora—for good—or will evil consume her? Can she even survive so far from home? Her only hope may rest in the Dragon Lord, but that beast turned his back on her grandfather long ago…

My Summer Job in Hell
Gail Kellner

Fynn Hardin is an average, everyday high school slacker, voted most likely to be overlooked. He needs a summer job, a car, and a girlfriend, not necessarily in that order. After sleeping through the high school job fair, he stumbles upon an elevator to Hell— and Hell is hiring! Fynn get a job and even meets the girl of his dreams. Unfortunately, Lily is also demon that Fynn accidentally helps to escape Hell. Now, Lucifer wants his demon back…

The Altered Manuscript
Ellen Taylor

The accidental discovery of the narration device completely changed entertainment and proved too dangerous to use without strict laws in place. Junior understood the reason behind these laws, which is why Bree does not know she's a character in a story. When a rogue narrator hacks into the system and begins creating chaos in Junior's story, does Junior continue to follow the laws to keep herself safe, or does she risk it all to protect the characters she loves?